Becoming Fenimore

Rebecca Bryan

Heathcliff Publishing

Cover photo © Meg Cowell

Cover design Jerry Skinner

ISBN: 10:0692581359
ISBN-13: 978-0692581353

DEDICATION

To Stephanie, for encouraging me to keep writing. And to my daughter Ellie, thanks for letting me use your name. I love you

ACKNOWLEDGMENTS

Thanks to all my early readers, Val, Dan, Amy, Susan, Stephanie, Melinda, Byrle, Jake, Lindsey. Reading drafts isn't fun, so thank you. Thanks to Val Serdy for your great insight and expertise, again. Thanks to Jake Alvord for your mad editing skills, if there are mistakes it's because I went back in and made additional changes. Special shout out to Stephanie for reading it more than once and to Byrle for your great suggestions. And thanks to Meg Cowell for granting me permission to use her gorgeous photograph on the cover. Excerpt from poem by Eliza Acton, *I love thee.*

Big thanks to Dan for supporting me in this endeavor and making my trip to Mackinac Island possible so I could do research, wink, wink. I cannot do this without your blessing. And thanks to my children for being so sweet about my writing. Last, but not least, thanks to Constance and Henry for lending your beautiful words. May they live on through my voice and the voices of future writers who long to tell their tale.

Like the ghost of a dear friend dead is time long past.
~Shelley

Henry

May 1894, Venice, Italy

The gondolier's oar sliced through the soft black water, parting the thick night fog with the bow of his boat. His passenger, a stout, smartly dressed American, sat near the front as if he were a dog sniffing for a scent. Beside him lay a heap of women's dresses. "There will be no return of the dead," he muttered as he plunged each dress deep into the water with an oar, only to have them rise to the surface, their busts and sleeves swelling like balloons.

The dresses had belonged to his friend, another American writer who had fallen from her third story apartment window to her death only a few months before. She'd been sick, recently suffering from influenza and a bout of depression passed on from her father. Or was there another reason?

One that involved our American, a close confidant and friend of many years.

Months passed and eventually our well dressed American left Italy, but the speculation as to the cause of her death rose on every corner in Venice.

"Some say she was desperately in love with him," a huddle of friends speculated in the San Marco plaza months later.

"And he refused her?" a short, stout woman asked.

"Maybe she refused him," said a tall skinny English woman with a nose resembling a crooked tree branch. "Miss Woolson had left him in England only a few months before."

"I heard she hadn't answered any of his letters," said another.

The stocky woman whispered, "I heard he burned all their letters." Someone gasped. All eyes turned to Marie Holas, a dark-haired woman with kind eyes who had been hired on as a caregiver a few weeks before the author's death and was the last to see Miss Woolson alive.

Finally she spoke. "He was here for four months going through her belongings with her niece. It was cold and there was often a fire, but I never saw him burn letters. It is hard to say what their feelings for each other were beyond that of a friend."

The first woman, with shark-like eyes and a small puckered mouth, spoke as if she had known them intimately. "I saw them take many walks at midday. I never saw two people better satisfied together."

"You said she talked of death as something not to fear. Did you worry that she might be suicidal?" the crooked nosed woman asked.

Mrs. Holas pondered this for a moment and then reluctantly answered. "Looking back now I can see that she was preparing me, but when I asked why she should talk thus, she stated that Americans had a habit of making jokes, even on their deathbeds. She'd only had a mild case of influenza."

The shark-eyed woman wasn't satisfied. "If she didn't commit suicide, could someone have tried to kill her? Perhaps the American author with the dresses?"

Maria frowned and shook her head. "I don't think so. He was living in England at the time and held nothing over her."

The round woman asked, "Perhaps he needed money or maybe she learned of some great secret of his?"

Tito, the gondolier who had gone that night to bury the dresses spoke up.

"Mr. James was as distraught as a friend could be at the

news. He was too upset to even come to the funeral. I saw how he suffered."

"But why was he trying to drown her clothes in the river? What was he hoping to hide?" Marie Holas asked.

"He said he was only fulfilling her wishes," the Gondolier remembered.

"By drowning her dresses?" the women wondered aloud.

"But they refused to sink," Marie Holas whispered.

And thus the rumors graduated into legend. And still the mystery remains.

Life is eternal, and love is immortal, and death is only a horizon; and a horizon is nothing save the limit of our sight.
~Rossiter Worthington Raymond

♛

Elle

Present day, St. Augustine, Florida

It never occurred to Elle Curtis that the sound of a doorbell would one day be as foreign as a fog horn in July. When it happened, instead of jumping up to answer, Elle continued to lay in bed and stare at the ceiling wondering if it had been a figment of her imagination, or a false ringing in her ear. It hadn't been rung since the last condolences had been made, which had been nearly two months ago. Sweat gathered around her temples. It was late. The swimsuit hanging on her bedpost reminded her of her once early morning dips at the Y, and the linen suits lined up in the closet, the job she used to have.

She wondered how much longer could she avoid the world. It had been two months since her mom had passed, two months since she'd gone to work, swam at the pool. Talked to anyone. The bell rang again, bouncing throughout the otherwise silent house like a rubber pinball. Whoever it was wasn't going away.

"Alright," she mumbled, climbing out of bed, and dressing in white cotton shorts and a navy blue shirt. She pulled her blondish/brown hair into a messy bun.

She paused as she approached her mom's closed bedroom

door. It was always closed. Even before she died. As long as Elle could remember, Linda had kept Elle close, discouraging outside relationships the minute a best friend or a boyfriend came into play. After Elle graduated from nearby Flagler College, Linda became more reclusive, spending large amounts of time in her room and Elle took over the household. There was no father. He had died before she was born.

To be truthful, Elle didn't know why she couldn't bring herself to open it. It was time, she knew that, but the idea of going into the dead woman's bedroom, changing the last sheets her mom ever slept on, moving things she had touched or getting rid of anything felt so final. She told herself she'd do it tomorrow. She would always do it tomorrow, and then tomorrow turned into next week, and then next month.

The doorbell rang again, breaking her thoughts up into tiny pieces. She turned and walked down the stairs. Through the window she could see an outline of a short and roundish person. Could it be someone from work wondering if she was coming back? An old friend of her mom's? The city inspector saying she needed to cut her grass? Running the house was nothing new to her. It wasn't that her mom had been incapable, just unable. Depression can do that to people. So when Linda suffered a stroke, it took her quickly. And then Elle was alone, and there was no one to care for. It was frightening and ashamedly freeing all at once. And in her freedom she chose to do nothing.

She opened the door to a mail carrier in her mid-fifties wearing a blue polo and official grey shorts, a bundle of letters in her arms.

"Linda hasn't collected from her mailbox in several months so I thought I'd drop it by and see if she was okay. Are you her daughter?"

Hearing her mother's name in such a causal way surprised her, as if any minute Linda might step from the kitchen wearing her famous silky blue robe and holding her favorite mug of coffee. The image was so real it made her dizzy. She gripped the doorknob to steady herself.

"My mother died two months ago." She was careful not to look too sad. It always made people uncomfortable when she got teary-eyed which in turn made her uncomfortable for making them uncomfortable.

The woman gasped. "I'm so sorry."

Not wanting to dwell on it, Elle scooped the mail up from the carrier's outstretched arms and said, "I don't understand. I check the mail every day."

The woman nodded. "This here's her post office box stuff. There's a lot of letters from the same place. They seemed kinda important."

Elle frowned. "A post office box?" *What would she have needed a PO box for?* Elle's face grew hot. Why did it upset her so much?

The woman shifted nervously. "So sorry to hear about Linda. You can close out the box. Or just not pay the next bill and we'll change the lock and take it over."

She thanked the woman and promised to do something soon. *Along with all the other things she still had to do*, she thought to herself as she shut the door with her foot and headed to the kitchen where she dumped the mail onto the small breakfast table covered in other financial and government docs.

She picked up the top letter. The return address was from a law firm from Mackinac Island, Michigan. Mackinac Island. She recognized that name from something. Then she remembered that Mackinac Island was the name of the ice cream her mom always got when they went to their favorite shop on St. George Street.

She turned over the large manila envelope and removed a letter dated the fifth of January.

Dear Ms. Curtis,

This is the third attempt to reach you. From the previous letters I will restate that in order for probate to be completed we must hear from you and get some necessary information. We encourage you to sign the papers so we can move forward.

What were they talking about? Her mom's estate was already in probate and she was the intended beneficiary.

She read on.

We are sending the paperwork again along with a copy of the will. Please send us a phone number at which to reach you. Thank you for your attention in this matter.

It was signed, *Jace Stokes, Attorney at Law at Littenby and Stokes.*

She turned the page and read aloud, "I Lois Curtis, Being of sound mind and body on this 7th day of September, do bequeath my estate to my sister Linda Curtis." She paused. "Sister?" Her mom had a twin sister named Lois, but she had died years ago. At least that was what she had believed.

She read the note again just in case she had missed something. Could this really be her long-thought-dead sister? She picked up the yellow phone still hanging on the wall from a hundred years ago, with its long twisted cord and dialed the number immediately.

The man answered on the second ring and seemed to brighten at the mention of Linda's name.

"There's been a mistake." Elle went on to explain that her Aunt Lois died many years ago. Before she was born.

"She actually died two months ago. November 26th to be exact."

"That can't—." She stopped as the date sunk in. Her mom had suffered a stroke five days later. Had she known about this?

He went on. "We've been trying to reach your mom for months. Is she available?"

He was silent for a moment after she explained about her own mother's death. His voice softened. "I'm so sorry to hear this." She could hear papers shuffling in the background. "I've...never had this situation before. I guess the estate would become yours as you are Linda's beneficiary. Lois had no children so yeah, It should be pretty simple, but I would highly recommend you travel up here in the spring to wrap everything up."

Travel to Michigan? She wrapped the cord nervously around her fingers. "Are you sure she was my mom's sister?"

She paced the kitchen floor, stretching and twisting the ancient telephone wire tethered to the wall.

"This is the information we were given from Lois when she made the will two years ago." He paused and then added, "Of course, we would do our own due diligence when you get here, but I'm sure everything will be in order."

"Did you know her?"

Though she doubted she was the same Lois, she secretly hoped to hear something that might confirm her identity.

"Lois?" He seemed genuinely surprised by the question. "Not really. Kept to herself mostly. She did most everything through the mail. People thought she was...different."

Sounded like her own mother. "And she had no family?"

"Never married. But all that information would be in the house. Like I said, it would be easier if you came here. The city really hates to leave houses abandoned. I'll be in Grand Rapids until May and then I'll be in Mackinac for the summer. If ownership isn't taken on the house by next year the city will take it back by default. The land is too valuable to leave a piece of property unaccounted for."

Though she knew nothing about Michigan or this island except that her mom loved the Mackinac Island Fudge revel at the ice cream shop, she was curious about this long lost aunt and promised to see what she could do.

The metal receiver clanked noisily as she hung up, her thoughts like scattering fish escaping their prey. She sat at the table and stared at the mess of letters. In the middle of the pile set a small box from the bank. She took scissors from the kitchen drawer, sliced the top open, and removed wadded tissue paper to reveal a silver box, elaborately ornamented with scrolls, crests, and detailed stenciling along the bottom edges. By the intricate detail and weight it seemed old and valuable. She outlined the etched date of 1886 across the lid with her forefinger surprised at how soft the patina felt. And how heavy it was.

She set it down and tried to open it, but the lid wouldn't budge. There appeared to be a keyhole on the front. She rechecked the box, but found no key. Had the bank forgotten to send it? She tucked the silver case under her arm and slowly climbed the stairs. When she reached her mom's closed bedroom door again she stopped. An estranged aunt she thought was dead. Years of silence, of wishes gone unfulfilled, of birthday parties she never had, and sleepovers she never attended. Why had her life been like this? It was time to face the truth, whatever that was.

She gripped the cold metal handle and pushed the door open. The room smelled stale like a peanut shell and old perfume. Linda's lotions sat on the nightstand. Her bedspread, rumpled, as if she'd just sat down to put her shoes on. The closet, full.

Her fingers perused the collection of gold frames—photos of her when she was eighteen, and one of her mom and her twin sister, Lois around five—and wondered why she'd been told she was dead.

She set the silver box on the desk and opened and closed the drawers looking for anything resembling a key. There was no key, but she did find something else tucked in the back. An identical looking envelope from Michigan, the side split open as her mom was prone to do. It was a very similar letter from the same Jace Stokes stating Lois Curtis had died of Pneumonia, and was dated a week before Linda's death. So she had known about Lois. Why hadn't she told Elle? Had that letter caused the stroke? Next to the envelope she found a receipt from the bank for a safe deposit box, and a small note attached saying they would send the item in the mail as she requested asap.

Could this silver box be what was kept in a safe deposit box? And what would have caused her mom to fetch for it now?

When music sounds, all that I was I am ere to this haunt of brooding dust I came. ~ *Walter de la Mare*

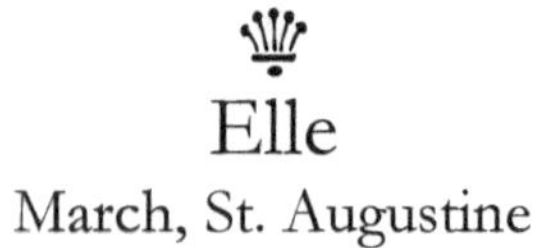

Elle

March, St. Augustine

Elizabeth." She sat up in bed, darkness all around her. The digital clock on her nightstand read two in the morning. She strained to listen, but could only hear the howl of the wind from outside. It must have been the storm brewing, she told herself as she readjusted her pillow and tried to go back to sleep.

But there would be no sleep, because creeping like a silky web into the inky spaces around her rose the sound again. This time she recognized it as music. And it was coming from her mother's room. She slipped out of bed, her feet silent as they crossed the cold wood floor to the shadowy hall where her eyes were forced to adjust to an even deeper blackness. The floorboards creaked loudly. She shivered. *It's just an old house that creaks in the night*, she tried to assure herself.

The sound grew louder behind her mom's closed door. She opened it a crack and Chopin's familiar "Nocturne" escaped, giving her the courage she needed to fling the door wide and flip the switch.

The blaring light silenced her fear, but not the sound coming from an old music box by the bed. *I must have bumped it when I was in here earlier*, she thought.

The room had a very different appearance than it did two

months ago. Piles lay in heaps all over the floor. Things to go, things to throw away, etc, etc. She walked around all the stacks of giveaways to where the small jewelry box sat open, it's song winding down. She picked it up.

The stiff ballerina twirled and spun, her plastic arms high above her head, her leg bent effortlessly as the sharp, tin can-like music played in her ears.

The painted lips, drawn-on brows, red and white striped costume, tight bun and serious, beautiful face were a big part of her childhood. She used to sneak in and listen, closing her eyes and humming along. This ballerina symbolized another world. The idea that somewhere, there was something greater than what she knew or had. A family, a lover. A doting mother.

Inside were several necklaces her mom used to wear. She held a long silver chain up and gasped when she saw what was hanging on the end. A key. Silver and small as a thumbnail with a tiny fin at one end. She had seen this before, but had forgotten it.

She hurried to her room where the silver box had remained on her nightstand since January, inserted the key, and gave it a small twist. It clicked, releasing the lid. She peered in. The box itself was lined in red velvet and smelled like old paper. An old leather-bound book with the outline of a sparrow lay beside a bundle of letters and a decorative pin made of a green beetle stone. She lifted the book from its resting place and carefully turned the crisp pages covered with old fashioned writing in the margins.

As she turned the next page a photograph dropped onto her lap, stiff, parchment-like, and definitely old. The young woman in the photograph had her hair pulled back in a low bun. Her smile was straight, yet tipped up in the corners, held up by her secrets. Her deep-set eyes curious. She turned it over to find an inscription written across the back in fancy cursive. *To HJ from longtime friend CFW*.

She tucked it back into its hidden spot so she could examine the pin. It was a small green brooch, beetle-like with gold wings, something you'd see in ancient Egypt. Strange, but also interesting. She returned them both to the box and held up the single pearl necklace. Pretty, but nothing extraordinary. Next was the stack of letters. She returned everything except the letters, which she was careful not to rip as she unfolded the thick paper and read.

Dear Henry,

I am here to tell you that it is time to marry. Father and I suggest Miss Woolson. Haven't you said she is intelligent, and your equal? Or perhaps Mrs. Van Rensselaer. I hear she has moved close to you in London. Do the two women often cross paths? Please respond quickly as Father is pacing the floor.

Lizzy

Elle quickly opened the next letter which seemed to be a response.

Lizzy,

Tell your father that I will not even have The Constanza. As far as your other suggestion, The Rensellina, she is more than close. She is practically breathing down my neck like a crazed dragon just beside me on Bolton Street (as if Half Moon Street hadn't been close enough.)

As far as the two women crossing paths, I am relieved to say they have kept to their separate spheres—The Rensellina with the titled, The Litteratrice alone with her pen— and I remain undevoured.

Henry

As she returned everything to the box her head spun with questions. Who were Lizzy and Henry and why had her mom kept the box hidden all these years? And did it have something to do with her long lost sister Lois?

Rich smile of fading day, which lingereth, like the look we cast, on rapture pass'd away. ~ *Eliza Acton*

♛

Constance

Florence, March 1879

"Tell me again where you came from, Miss Woolson," Henry James inquired as he took a wine glass from the server and handed it to her.

"I'm sorry, what was that?" Constance held her hand up to her ear. "With all the commotion I'm having a hard time hearing you." She didn't want to admit that lately she'd had trouble hearing in crowds such as this.

"Then move closer. I don't bite." His eyes twinkled.

She set the drink down on a sideboard behind the burgundy velvet sofa where they sat and scooted closer to the man she had met only a few hours earlier. She'd never been one for dinner parties, but it was the only way to mingle here in Florence. The only way to become acquainted with *the* Henry James. They were much closer now. She could see the shadow of a beard across his jaw, which made him more real, and more handsome. To think she was finally here in the presence of such talent. She only hoped she wouldn't appear as eager as she felt.

She cleared her throat and said, "I've spent the last several years amongst the marshes of Florida."

"Have you ever been there?"

"No." His answer was short, but not rude.

Constance Woolson felt unusually warm under his stare. Her face was red, she was sure, which only made her more self-conscious. She wasn't bashful, she was just hot. Constance had done her best to nod and curtsy like the other ladies and pretend to enjoy all the pomp and circumstance that accompanied lavish dinner parties, but she was suffocating for want of air. With all the people and the blazing fire in the center and the rich food now digesting in her stomach, she wished for a fraction of the breeze coming from the woman cooling herself with an elaborate Spanish fan across the room.

One would hardly know they were in Italy. The people, mostly Americans mixed with a few English expatriates living a grander life in Italy than they could afford in their own countries, were dressed in all the finery they could afford.

Even some of the servants were English, hired by those who wished to bring their culture and food with them.

"I spent most of my youth in Cleveland. You have heard of Cleveland, have you not?" She blinked innocently. She'd heard Henry had sworn off his homeland and she planned to rib him about it.

"Cleveland, Ohio?" His manner seemed condescending, but his eyes appeared engaged. Something about him made her eager to play a part. To get to the core of Henry, so she continued on.

"How long have you been in Europe, sir, for it appears you have forgotten even the very continent on which you once lived." She did not bat an eye or apologize for her frankness, but continued on, having a splendid time with it. "Or are there only maps of Europe in these far superior libraries?"

He eyed her carefully. *Yes,* she thought to herself. *I did hear you speak of such in a previous conversation with the good doctor before coming to chat with me.*

Finally he responded. "I suppose it was in Cooperstown that you met my cousin, Henrietta?"

Henrietta had written the letter of introduction for Constance.

She nodded. "She had nothing but praise for you. It seems her whole family adores you as a very kind and attentive cousin."

There was a flash of recognition, perhaps even a tinge of sadness that crossed his countenance when she mentioned Henrietta's family, but he quickly recovered himself and changed the subject by saying, "I should very much like to see Florida. My brothers spent some time down there after the war. Marshes, alligators, swamps. You didn't see any of that I'm sure." He took a drink of his brandy.

"On the contrary, I spent much time on the water. It was an amazingly jolly time."

His glass came down, his eyes wide with disbelief as he swallowed hard. "Not by yourself?"

She shrugged. "No one would go with me." A faint smile crossed her lips at the memory. "I would pack myself a lunch and take the canoe out through the everglades searching for snakes, alligators, and whatever else I could find. I have journals full of the sights. The headlands are simply beyond description if you haven't seen it."

"Do you wish to go back?"

"Perhaps someday. But for now I'm thrilled to be in Florence for it is such a lovely place. The gardens are spectacular, and I have heard the museums are as well."

Her eyes brightened. "You see I am a student of life and I have come to embrace and absorb all that Florence has to offer. After all, I am like you—an observer first."

He took another drink and added, "That has long been my motto."

"Henry!" A high-browed American woman in a silky red dress touched Henry's shoulder like they were well acquainted and sighed dramatically. "Henry, you must settle a score for me."

Henry stood and helped Constance from her seat.

"Miss Spedding, have you met our new arrival from the

mainland...Miss Woolson? She is a novelist as well."

"I have been acquainted," the tall woman said, eyeing Constance's simple black dress with disinterest. "Come, Henry. We really must have your opinion." She slid her arm under his and led him towards her group of matching high brows near the fireplace.

Henry turned back to Constance, "I do hope to have another word with you before the evening ends."

"Yes. That would be nice." She nodded excitedly. Henry had been a much friendlier person than he had first appeared. The night had been a success already.

Miss Spedding spoke loud enough for Constance to hear. "Henry we really must know. Would you say that Michelangelo's statue of Lorenzo has a true to life reference of day and night? Or not?" Some in the group began to giggle.

"I find it a compelling work of art. Miss Woolson, what do you say?" Henry asked, looking back at Constance. The group all turned in her direction.

Constance fumbled for words. She hadn't even heard of this night and day statue. And she wasn't ready to be the center of attention. "I...I haven't seen it so I can't say." There were muffled chuckles. Miss Spedding smirked. Even Henry suppressed a smile. Her face grew warm with embarrassment. She hated being ignorant of something or rather the subject of a joke.

"What a shame you should have missed it. It is quite divine." Miss Spedding snarked, as she took Henry by the arm and attempted to close Constance out of the conversation, but Henry refused and turned back to Constance.

"If you'd like, I should be pleased to escort you myself,"

Miss Spedding frowned but Henry went on. "Did you all know that Miss Woolson is niece to James Fenimore Cooper of *Last of the Mohicans* fame?" There were gasps and sighs of approval. The circle widened. The men and women smiled at her now, as if she were now worth something.

"Well, Miss Woolson, what's it to be?" Henry asked.

They waited, staring at her. Henry lit a pipe. She tapped

her forehead feeling one of her headaches coming on. The attention was unsettling. "I think something could be arranged," she stammered. The crowd sighed in agreement and then dispersed. Henry took Constance by the arm and introduced her to the group, names flying in one ear and out the other. She politely shook hands and greeted each one, hoping to match each face to a name. But how could she remember Mrs. Cartwright from Mrs… there, she'd forgotten it already. She rubbed her temples with her thumb and forefinger. Henry took notice and in a quiet voice inquired, "Are you feeling well?"

"Just a small headache."

"My driver would be happy to take you home if you'd like."

"Thank you, but no. I can send for a carriage just as well."

Henry frowned. "Oh dear, a modern woman in our midst."

"I'm afraid so. Dreadfully modern," she returned, still rubbing her temples.

"With no need of a man or his carriage."

"I never said I was without needs." She couldn't suppress a small grin. "Don't put me in a category I do not deserve."

"You don't profess to be Joan of Arc?"

"I am sure that even Joan had needs."

Henry eyed her with keen interest and a slight smile on his lips. Constance's face flushed at the idea of what he must be thinking. She wished to change the subject. If that meant accepting his carriage she would. "I suppose if it isn't too much trouble."

"Excellent." A smile of achievement crossed his face. "Then, you will be familiar with it when it comes to pick you up at nine tomorrow morning."

"That is if you are feeling well enough."

"Thank you. But I think it would be more fun to walk. That is, if my head and the weather should cooperate."

His frown was exaggerated. It almost made her giggle. "I almost forgot. The modern woman. Very well. I'll be there with my best walking shoes. Where are you staying?"

"The Barbensi Pension... near the Carraia Bridge."

"Yes, I know it." He stopped a server who held a tray of crackers and cheese and took some as he spoke. "Good man, please inform my driver that he will be giving Miss Woolson a ride home." The servant nodded and disappeared behind a door.

He handed her a piece of cheese and said, "He'll pick you up in the front. Will you be okay getting home?"

"I will, thank you." She took a bite of the mild white cheese, not because she wanted it, but because Henry had offered it to her.

A servant returned with her long wool coat and Henry helped her put it on. He grinned. "If there is nothing more I can do for you I shall bid you goodnight." He kissed her gloved hand. His attention left her stunned. This was a very different Henry from the man she had heard about.

"Good night sir." She offered a small bow of her head.

Henry nodded, turned. "Until tomorrow," he said.

"Until tomorrow," she repeated under her breath.

Oh heart, if one should say to you that the soul perishes like the body, answer that the flower withers, but the seed remains.
~Khalil Gibran

Elle

Mackinac Island—June

Due to work issues, a swollen tendon from swimming too hard after months of doing nothing at all, Elle's trip to Mackinac didn't happen until June.

After nearly missing her flight in Detroit and having to run—bags and all—the length of the airport and narrowly making it just before the doors were closed, landing at Pellston Airport was a welcomed sight. It seemed straight out of an episode of *Wings* with its open, single ticketing desk and smiling gate attendant.

She walked to the shuttle counter where two old men sat shuffling cards and offered her name.

"We thought that might be you," the bald gentleman with a silver mustache whose nametag read Charlie said, pointing at the whiteboard displaying her name in capital letters.

Elle could feel her face warming.

"It's a game we play. Match the name to the face.

She was sure her face was red. "I'm not sure what that would look like." She wasn't used to so much attention. Had she really been away from people so long that she couldn't even make small talk anymore?

"It looks like you," they said with a laugh.

They finally set their cards down. The other man named Bill, weathered like a shirt put away wet, took her bag and led the way outside. He appeared to be much older, seventies, but he didn't seem fatigued at all as he stored her luggage in the back and helped her into the white van.

She looked out the window, hoping they would forget about her and just drive. But their chatty, easygoing banter continued and she realized they were not going to leave her alone. Since there was nowhere to go and only two other passengers in the back, she realized she might as well try to enjoy herself.

The rolling hills and towering pine trees reminded her a lot of Florida. In fact, she'd never traveled so far away, yet felt so at home as she did along the double lane highway towards the ferry that would take her to the island.

When they asked what brought her to Mackinac, Elle explained about her aunt passing and her need to take care of the estate.

They offered condolences in echo of the other. They reminded her of Tweedledee and Tweedledum. The thought made her smile. And relax a little.

"Who was your aunt? Maybe we knew her," Tweedledee asked

"Lois Curtis." It felt funny to even say the name aloud after thinking she'd been dead for so many years.

Charlie frowned. "Don't think I know that name. What about you, Bill?" He looked over at the older gentleman in the passenger seat. "You grew up on the island."

Bill, Tweedledum, nodded thoughtful. "I think I remember her. Recluse out on the east side? Lived in a dilapidated house? If I remember right she had a twin sister."

"That's my mom, Linda."

He nodded excitedly. "Yeah, they were real cute girls in school. Never saw Linda after we graduated. Come to think of it, I never saw Lois, either, but again, I don't live there anymore."

"Strangely enough I didn't even know Lois was still alive. I thought she died years ago," Elle admitted.

They both looked back at her in surprise. Elle went on to explain, unsure of why she felt comfortable enough to share.

"What happened?" Charlie asked, rubbing his chin. The car grew quiet as they each contemplated that question.

They parked the van at the ferry, left her bags at the docked boat, and then walked her over to the ticket booth to make sure she had everything she needed. She'd never seen such service or people more happy to help. They either wanted a big tip or they were just genuinely nice people. She watched the only other couple on the shuttle slip some bills into Charlie's hand. She hadn't traveled in so long, the tipping thing confused her, so she gave them each a handful of bills, unsure of how much was customary to tip a driver, and then waved them off. By their smiles she figured she'd done okay.

While it felt similar to St. Augustine with the tall pine trees and the pristine waterways, the temperature was much cooler, low seventies. The man taking tickets suggested she sit below if she was worried about the weather. But Elle was not about to miss the scene from the top. Perhaps she should have taken his advice as the wind whistled through her hair when the boat started across the water. She zipped up her jacket and pulled her hoodie tight around her face, trying to save her hair from an unsavory knot. Could it really be June? She'd never felt more cold in her life.

As the turtleback island came into view, the bay sparkled with sailboats, similar to St. Augustine, yet very different, and of course, much colder. A large, white hotel, surrounded by several other quaint, colorful houses and hotels set on the hill like something out of a magazine *It should have it's own puzzle,* she thought, deciding she would look for one while she was here.

Puzzles. She and her mom would sit for hours in the living room with the window open, the ocean breeze filtering contently between them, as they quietly solved puzzle after puzzle. It had been their happy place.

She reminded herself that this island had once meant something to her mom, yet had been kept a secret from Elle. Sadness dug in her chest, as it disappointed her to think of it like that.

After twenty minutes the horn announced their arrival. While the dock workers tugged ropes, working to tie them in, she joined the other travelers below and stepped off the boat.

Looking around at the throng of tourists., Elle wondered how she would recognize Jace, the lawyer handling Lois' estate. He had promised to be at the dock to pick her up and take her to her hotel as he had made all the arrangements for her stay. She hated to admit it, but she had begun to think the man on the other end of the phone sounded handsome, not that it mattered. He was probably married with children and she shouldn't be looking anyway.

When she saw a man a few feet away holding the second sign of the day with her name on it, she was secretly pleased to see sandy brown hair, dark blue eyes, and soft lips. His charming and somewhat familiar voice was a welcomed relief.

"You must be Elle," he said when she had made her way through the crowd to him. He had an air of confidence that was rather intimidating yet pleasant all at once. "Jace Stokes. How was your trip?"

She rubbed her lips together, wishing she'd combed her hair and put on some lip-gloss before she'd gotten off the ferry, but it was too late now. "It was interesting. I haven't traveled in a long time." *Would this justify her looking rather weathered?* she wondered.

"Are you cold?" he asked, acknowledging her parka- like hoodie. That's when she noticed he was wearing khaki shorts and a button down, short sleeve Hawaiian shirt. She pulled the hoodie back and ran her fingers through her tangled tresses. "It was a bit breezy on the boat."

"Florida blood." He smiled like it was an inside joke. She unzipped her jacket and worked her fingers through the knots as she followed him out of the gate and into the street.

Mackinac Island (sounded out 'Mackinaw' as Jace had

explained) was filled with people, carriages, bicyclists, and ringing bells. There was not, however, one single car on the street. It was like she'd traveled back in time.

Jace seemed to sense her shock when he said, "No motorized vehicles are allowed on the island."

"None?" She stared at the row of whinnying horses. A maroon carriage with *The Grand*, stenciled in gold paint sat near the entrance. Jace handed the driver Elle's suitcase.

"It'll be waiting for you in your room. In the meantime I thought we'd get something to eat and then I'd show you the house. Is that alright?"

She nodded. She hadn't eaten since Detroit and since she'd pretty much ran a 5k to catch her flight she was starving. She followed Jace down the boardwalk, glad to see a man who thought like she did – through her stomach first.

Main Street looked and felt like a movie or a beautiful coastal getaway or Disneyland or home. The clapboard building fronts were crisp and white, the trims painted in blues, reds, or yellows. Colorful purple petunias, orange gingersnaps, and white alyssum hung from baskets along the boardwalk, filling the air with a sweet honey fragrance. While bees buzzed hungrily from container to container, shop owners swept the sidewalk and waved to the tourists as they passed on their way to the beach or the ice cream shop. Again, similar to St. Augustine. The two cities could have been related.

Horse drawn carriages clopped along in a syncopated rhythm. It felt like a simpler time, one people craved as evidenced by the large crowds enjoying the thousands of blooming lilac trees dotting the hillsides, their sweet fragrance permeating the air and making everything look and smell like a picture book.

"It's beautiful here!" she exclaimed.

"Our winters are long, which is why I live in Grand Rapids. I'm thinking about moving here full time though. Right now I'm just staying with my Dad." Jace stood overlooking the town, his hands proudly on his hips.

"It feels like heaven," she whispered, instantly in love with the picturesque island. She couldn't imagine having an aunt that could be a recluse in such a beautiful place. Yet, what about her own mom in St. Augustine? Perhaps it is more than just where you live that makes you happy.

Jace stopped in front of a café with the menu listed by the door. The smell of fried meat danced between them. The smell made her stomach gnaw with want. "Is this okay?" he asked. She nodded eagerly. He held the door for her to pass. "This is a great little hole in the wall."

"My favorite type," Elle admitted, already in love with the brightly lit and packed with tourists, cafe. Jace led her to the back booth where he ordered a Monte Cristo ham fried sandwich and Elle ordered a Cobb salad and an iced tea. As soon as they ordered Elle started in on the questions about her long lost aunt.

"Did you meet her? Did she have any other family? Did she ever talk about Linda or me?"

Jace laughed as he tried to answer them one at a time. She noticed there was no ring on his finger, not that she cared if she ever got married. At least that is what she always told herself.

"I met her once last year. She wanted me to make sure nothing was taken from the house when she died. She was certain someone was going to break in and steal her things the minute she kicked the bucket. And she was really worried about her sister, Linda. She was adamant that we make contact."

"You said she was different?"

"People said she was crazy. Wouldn't go near her. But to me, she was just sad. She had a profound sadness in her eyes. The kind that can't lie through a smile."

Elle was impressed with his description. "What do you think she was sad about?"

He opened his napkin with crisp precision and set it across his lap. "That I don't know. She was extremely private. There was no funeral. I really don't know much else about her. But if you want to know more, we could ask the bookshop owner down the street. He was the only one that asked about a funeral. He offered to hold her remains until family came, but we felt it was more appropriate to keep them."

Elle tried not to appear surprised. "Remains?" She took a drink.

"She was cremated. That was what she wished. We tried to get ahold of Linda, but as you know, that wasn't possible."

Their food came and the conversation grew more casual. She learned that Jace had grown up on the island with his dad, mom and brother. His brother and mom had died in a car accident five years ago and his dad had recently remarried.

Throughout the conversation Jace went from distant to warm and curious. She couldn't decide if he was bored or not. It was a bit unsettling. Especially since she couldn't keep her eyes off him.

He stirred with his plastic straw. "Ironic that they would die in a car accident even though they spent most of their life on the island." Warm again. Puppy dog warm. She wanted to take his hand and offer her condolences. She settled on stirring her own iced tea and asking how it happened.

"We lived in Grand Rapids during the winter. My dad fell asleep at the wheel on their way back to the island. He still hasn't forgiven himself."

"I'm so sorry." She could tell this upset him.

Jace sat back. "Did you ever see the film *Somewhere in Time*? It was a time travel movie in the Eighties."

"Yes, of course. With Christopher Reeve. I watched that movie a dozen times. It never got old."

A grin crossed his face. "Then you'll be happy to know that I have you booked in the very hotel they filmed it in."

"That big white hotel? I saw it from the ferry." She smiled broadly. She couldn't help it. It had looked so beautiful and romantic and grand up on the hill. She never dreamed she'd be staying there. No one had ever been so thoughtful.

He nodded proudly. "Only car ever allowed on the island

was the one that Christopher Reeve drove. And even then they had to get special permission. There's a museum about it in the hotel. You'll have to check it out."

"Darn, I should have brought my 1979 penny!" she teased, referring to the penny that eventually brought Christopher Reeve's character back to the present.

"Anyway, my dad has since remarried, but he is obsessed with the idea of time travel. He's bought every book and seen every movie on the subject. He wishes he could go back to make sure they never went on that car ride that day."

"How is his new wife with this?"

Jace set his sandwich down and played with a piece of lettuce. "She's kind of into it too. I don't know. They're interesting." He dropped the lettuce on the plate, straightened his shoulders. "But enough about me. What about you?" His smile didn't quite reach his eyes and Elle wondered if this was a very sensitive subject for him.

She stabbed her salad with her fork as she spoke. "There's not much to tell. I lived with my mom in Florida. She was kind of sickly and needed me near her. I worked at a book publishing company."

"Worked? What do you do now?"

"I still work there. Technically. But after my mom died, I had a hard time…moving on. She was all I had. I was all she had. I guess I lost my purpose for a while. But I've gone back to work. I lost my position, but they've found a place for me. It's not glamorous and it doesn't pay nearly as well, but it's enough." She looked up. His eyes showed no judgment. She wasn't sure why this surprised her, but it did. And it relieved her.

"What about you?" she asked. "Are you married? Have children?" He hadn't offered the information and she liked him well enough that she wanted to know the facts before she got any more invested in his handsome smile.

"No. I was engaged once, but it didn't work out."

"Oh, sorry."

"It's okay. It was a blessing in disguise. She wasn't my

type. Living on the island makes it hard to date. There's not a lot of choices unless you like one night stands with tourists."

Elle nearly choked on her salad. She coughed and reached for her napkin.

His face suddenly turned an eggplant color. He backpedaled. "Because most people are just passing through. It's hard to start something long term."

He looked down at his food and said with an embarrassed laugh, "I didn't mean it like that. How did we get on this subject?" The wall was down again. She liked this guy better than the wall-up guy.

She laughed. "I guess I asked. I'm curious like that."

"Then you're going to love your aunt's place." He wadded up his napkin and dropped it on his plate signaling he was finished and desperate to change the subject.

"I'm ready when you are," she admitted, pushing aside her empty plate.

"I'll call a cab." Jace signaled for the check.

As they drove in the carriage, Jace pointed out local landmarks: the gazebo from the movie, the old fort up on top of the hill from pre-Civil War days. Arch rock, a place she should see before she left, and the Round Island lighthouse out in the middle of the Lake, which she recognized from *Somewhere in Time.*

His pride of the island shone through, and it made her smile.

"It's not too much farther," he stated as they passed large picturesque homes atop a bluff overlooking the pebbly beach where sailboats drifted in the otherwise calm Lake Huron to her right.

"This place is so much like St. Augustine. I think it's strange that we never came here," she whispered.

But if she were in a movie, the music abruptly ended when they turned into what remained of a dirt-packed driveway overrun with weeds. A meadow, once probably filled with wildflowers, sat besieged with weeds and noxious thistles. The house itself was rundown, a neglected, wood-sided, Cape Cod-style with a wraparound porch that looked long abandoned. Perfect for a ghost story.

"It was built in 1917 by the Mathers, a rather wealthy, well-regarded family that used the home primarily as a vacation property," Jace explained, helping her down from the carriage. "My dad remembers them coming to visit during the summer. They stopped visiting all together around 1975 or 1976. About 1980 Lois was living in the house again. Nobody knows when she came back or if she'd ever left."

"What was wrong with her?"

"I can't remember. I'd have to ask my dad. People said all kinds of stuff, but I never buy into gossip. She spent some time in a mental institution in another town."

"My mom said Lois died before I was born. I wonder what happened to make her say that."

"Too bad that your mom can't tell you what happened. It sounds like an interesting story." Jace paid their driver and then helped Elle up the path.

The concrete sidewalk was split and pulled out in large chunks. Weeds and dandelions littered the spaces where the cement had once been.

"Careful of these stairs," Jace warned as she climbed the wood-rotted steps. The wide patio creaked. Something skittered underneath the porch. Elle jumped and grabbed Jace by the arm.

"Probably just a skunk," he said with a grin.

"Oh...just?" She let go of his arm, embarrassed by her typical girly behavior.

He pulled out a set of keys and unlocked the door. "This is the biggest surprise of all." He pushed the door open. "Check this out."

Elle caught her breath. The rooms were spacious; the windows wide open to a breathtaking view of the lake. The red velvet sofa sitting in the middle was sun rotted, but the tufting and fancy wood trim still held strong across the back. French Provincial side tables and coffee tables completed the grouping, while fancy bone china remained unscathed in the hutch against the wall. Though worn, the wood plank floors seemed solid underfoot, and the handful of scattered oriental rugs, though faded and covered with dust, at one time had been very opulent and expensive as shown by the tight weave and the rich patterns.

"This is beautiful." She wondered how her mother had never told her about this place.

"The inside is sealed up tight. As far as I can tell there is no water damage. I don't even think there are rodents. And the house is full of antiques, all period to the Twenties and Thirties. Some even older."

He ushered her past the living room to a corridor kitchen the size of a shoebox. The dishwasher was non-existent. A porcelain farm sink looked like it was original to the house. The green stove and classic rounded top fridge; a flashback to the early Seventies

Elle opened the fridge and gagged. She threw her hand over her nose. The smell was horrendous. She couldn't close it fast enough.

"I should have warned you. The power was shut off a few months ago so the fridge…"

The residual smell lingered. "Put it on the list." Elle's voice choked and her eyes watered as she held her nose and left the kitchen. They quickly went through the rest of the first floor. A bathroom, a laundry on the back porch, a small bedroom.

Up the wooden staircase to the second floor, Jace showed the first of two bedrooms. It was decorated in Fifties pinks. Pillows—ruffled, some embroidered—lay on a once-silky, pink bedspread. Above the bed hung a painting of three women at a river, each with a basket to fill with water. Across from the bed stood a dressing table covered in perfumes and doilies. A silver brush and comb set and facial powders lay on a mirror.

Elle touched the handle. Her mom would have done the same. There were two photos on the dresser. One of Linda, at around eighteen, one of, a baby, probably Lois. Both much too serious for their own good. Elle had been told multiple times in her life that she needed to lighten up, have more fun. She had never been one of "those girls". Maybe it was because she lived alone with her mom. No dad to speak of, no siblings. Unfortunately, she had no pictures of her father and knew very little about him other than she had been told she had his mouth. That was the one way she was different from the two sisters. Their lips were full and beautiful. Elle's was thin and straight.

She opened and closed the drawers and found them still filled with clothes. Clothes that had belonged to a complete stranger. A dead complete stranger. It had been hard enough to go through her mom's things. She moved to a bookshelf filled with photo albums and journals. While it was unsettling to be in a stranger's house, particularly one that was deceased, she also felt oddly comfortable. There was a familiarity in the way things were placed. The pictures and paintings on the wall, even the pink rug at the side of her bed, all set her at ease.

She peeked in the other bedroom. No knickknacks. No pictures. The drawers were empty, the closet filled with empty hangers. A child's rocking chair sat in the corner. The room felt like it had been waiting for a guest to arrive or someone had just left. The rocking chair looked brand new. Elle's chest tightened. She felt strangely emotional and had no idea where it was coming from. She'd never even met the woman, yet she felt a familial connection she couldn't ignore.

"The attic's full of stuff too. Do you want to see it?"

She peered out the small window that gave way to a clump of the forest and sliver of the lake. "It's so beautiful," she barely could whisper. It almost made her cry.

She shook off the emotion and climbed the steep staircase to a dust-covered attic filled with furniture, rugs, and other odds and ends. The roof came down low, the walls short on the edges in true Cape Cod-style and bookended by two small, water-stained windows on both sides. Old furniture sat clustered together in the corner while the opposite wall held a large hope chest, long forgotten. There were old rugs, a rocking chair, and an oversized, gold mirror against one wall. The strong scent of mothballs and dust lingered in her nose.

Elle breathed it in and smiled. She loved old things: houses, furniture, books. This place was a gold mine. She couldn't wait to go through everything. Especially the trunk. But she didn't want to do it now with Jace watching. She wanted to take her time, examine each piece, feel the purpose they once served. She was sure he was eager to be on his way. They returned to the kitchen where Elle signed papers and Jace called for a cab. "Ready to see the hotel?" he asked.

"I'd like to see that man at the bookstore first. Ask him about Lois." Jace gave the cab driver the new directions when he arrived.

"I'll stop by tomorrow and bring you your aunt's remains. And afterwards I could take you on some of the great trails here."

"I'd love that," she agreed,. holding his gaze a minute longer than she should have, her cheeks blushing red as a berry.

A human life is a story told by God. ~Hans Christian Andersen

♛

Constance

April 1880 Florence

"Look at the Apennines, all snow-capped and majestic." Constance smiled brightly and continued. "Such a contrast to the valley with its leaves of the prettiest green. Everything is so fresh and alive. It is more beautiful than…"

"Florida?" Henry interrupted, a sparkle in his eye.

"Never Florida," she teased back.

"Then perhaps Cleveland." Henry always had witty comebacks. Constance admired that most about him. She looked around at the beautiful Arno River and the park to her right and sighed. "I'm quite content right here. Though I am determined to make you a George Washington, yet."

"I would never be suited for the job."

"Nonsense. You are still a patriot at heart. And one day the tune of Yankee Doodle Dandy will have you crawling back to your homeland."

Henry grunted. But Constance didn't acknowledge it. They crossed the cobbled street, pausing for a carriage to pass before continuing on. "I wasn't even in the war," Henry admitted. "My brothers were, as were several cousins. I can't say I regret not being a soldier, as I hated everything about the war and what it did to the men on the fields and the people at home. I don't think I'm a Benedict Arnold, but I can't regard myself as highly as General Washington."

They entered the park, nodding at a similar looking couple who smiled as they passed on the dirt path. Henry quietly said, "That is the duke of Edinburgh. He summers here, though rarely does he bring his wife."

"Then, who was the woman on his arm?" Constance asked, straining to see the couple who had disappeared around the bend.

"Ah. His cousin. I believe."

Constance snickered. "Everyone is a cousin these days." Henry laughed as well and patted her on the hand which pleased Constance. Henry knew everybody and every piece of gossip in Florence and Constance adored being by his side on their long walks together even if the bottom of Constance's peach dress had turned a soft grey from the dust.

Eventually Constance returned to their previous conversation.. "I agree about war." Her voice grew quiet and reflective. "Something happened to all of us during that time. I can pick out a face that was affected almost immediately, can't you?"

"That's because you're a writer. Writers have a way of knowing the expressions someone wears like a tailor knows a man's suit size."

Constance pulled at her gloves as she spoke. "Instead of a suit of arms he wears a face of loss."

"And pain," Henry added.

Two small boys wearing short pants and suspenders

ran past yelling back to their mother in crude Italian. All Constance could understand was something about black licorice.

"I think we're going the wrong way," Constance said as a young mother with a mock look of disgust passed by.

"She pretends to be discouraged, but she loves every minute with her two hooligans," Henry observed and then added, "Up ahead is something better than black licorice. And perfect for this time of year."

Constance clapped her gloved hands. "My interest is piqued. Pray tell."

"Hot cross buns."

She sniffed the air expectantly. "I'd dare say you're right."

"Good, because that's where we're going." Henry offered his arm and Constance took it. Nothing had ever felt so natural as being arm in arm with Henry. He was like her other half. They continued walking before she returned to their previous subject.

"Do you think that is why so many come here to Europe? Hiding so we don't have to face that which destroyed so many of our loved ones? To see good strong men become subject to all manner of hardness." She was thinking of her brother Charles, whom she'd heard had gone west to California and had fallen to drink.

"Perhaps. I've never been a patriot in the way you seem to be, though you don't seem homesick." He gave her an inquisitive look, "Are you?"

"Oh no! I find this to be a great adventure."

"I am curious, what did you think of Bacchus? You seemed quite absorbed."

"The statue by Michelangelo? I found him to be

unique, so sleepy serious, as if it exposed his great capacity for profound dreaming."

"Hmm. Very interesting indeed." Henry rubbed his chin with his free hand.

"Well, it's just my opinion. Not that it means much."

"I like hearing your opinion. Speaking of, have you had a chance to read about my dear Isabel yet?"

"Oh!" She turned to him and grabbed his forearms. Isabel was the main character of his latest novel Portrait of a Lady. "Have I not told you of the dear kinship I feel with your darling girl? I loved her, of course!" She couldn't believe she hadn't told him how much she had enjoyed reading Portrait of a Lady and how much she had related to the heroine, Isabel Archer. It was because of the book that she had wanted to meet Henry in the first place.

She let go of him, realizing how excited she must look. She regained her composure and said.

"I must say that you know more of women than they sometimes do of themselves. Many men profess this gift, this ability to understand the fairer sex, but you, my friend, actually have it."

They continued down the dirt path, immersed in the subject of dear Isabel Archer. "Truly, Henry, from the moment I first met Isabel, I found myself thinking of her with perfect...comprehension, and a complete acquaintance: everything she did and said I judged from a personal standpoint.

"It was as if you knew my thoughts and way of thinking before you ever knew me."

"So you approve of my Isabel?"

Her excitement grew. She couldn't hold it back and had to touch his arm yet again. "Strangely enough, I feel as if she is my Isabel as well." They stopped in front of the bakery.

Henry released her hand and held the door of the bakery open for her. "Here we are."

A few minutes later they were back on their path, going in the direction they had come, warm pastries in their hands. Constance lifted her face towards the warm sunshine as a few pigeons waddled around her feet looking for abandoned crumbs of bread.

"I find birds to be some of the most amazing creatures. So unassuming, yet, given a second look there is nothing unassuming about them. They follow protocol, but still manage to soar freely above the highest trees in order to scavenge and peck for the tiniest morsel of food. And to watch them in flight, their patterns, their order, it's most intriguing."

She turned to Henry, anxious to know his thoughts. "I should love to take an afternoon and go bird watching."

"My favorite bird is the dove. Their plump grey breasts and smooth heads are among the most beautiful."

"Florida has birds with legs and beaks as long as a man's cane. And such colorful ones as well. Bright blue, orange, yellow. Such stunning creatures."

"Miss Spedding has a pair of eyeglasses called binoculars, made by a man here in Italy. I could ask to borrow them."

Constance gave a faint look of disapproval at the mention of his friend Miss Spedding.

"I don't think she'd like knowing you were using them with me."

"Nonsense. Writers struggle to be happy for other writers. Especially successful ones, but she will come around."

"I have opera glasses. They might work as well."

"Bring them. Shall we go day after tomorrow?"

Her heart skipped a beat. He too was a man of action. It thrilled her to find a true comrade. "I'd love that."

"Now, what were we talking about before the bakery?"

"We were discussing our dear Isabel Archer."

"Ah, yes." He took a bite of his pastry and when he had swallowed asked, "Was there anything you disagreed with?"

"I do have one minor discrepancy."

"Discrepancy?" His eyebrow went up. Constance grew anxious, worried that she might offend him.

"It's probably not important enough to bother over." She fiddled with her black gloves. She had grown so comfortable in their conversation that she had burst onto a subject she wasn't sure she should have broached. But it was too late to go back on it. He would dig and dig until she was out with it.

"On the contrary, I'm deeply curious. Is it Lord Warburton?" Henry's smile seemed a bit strained.

"Well," she sighed, looking into the blue sky. "I have issues with your Lord Warburton as well, but what I was going to tell you about was, when Isabel says to Mr. Warburton, 'Poor Lord Warburton!' It isn't right. A woman of Isabel's age and her delicate feeling would never say that to a man; perhaps behind his back, but never to a man directly, unless she intended to yield to him sometime."

Henry was quiet as they walked along the trail. "It is something to consider," was all he said. Constance worried that she had offended him. Characters were precious to a writer, like a family member, or a child.

It was easy to become offended even by well-intended comments.

"I assure you I loved the book. It was just something that I didn't think she would do. Not a woman of her standing."

"Of course." Then he asked, "Have you visited the Duomo?" He seemed ready to move on to another subject.

"I have."

"What did you think of it?"

"I found it too cold for my taste."

"What?" He gave her one of his deep over the shoulder stares, but kept walking. Her comment seemed to trouble him as he said a minute later. "How can you go away from there with only, 'vast and cold' as your opinion? Certainly there was something worthy of your admiration."

"It was a cold and rainy day and I believe I was the only person in that great gloomy space. I went right home and made myself a hot cup of tea."

"Well then... Miss Woolson, we must do our best to change your opinion right now." He offered the crook of his arm again and she took it. He was built like a well-made statue, strong and solid and she found it intensely satisfying.

At the Duomo Henry spent an exuberant amount of energy pointing out the magnificence of the building. The fine details, the colors of the tiles. "It took over two centuries to complete. And look here," he said pointing to the frescoes in the ceiling called The Last Judgement. "It was begun in 1572 by Vincenzio Borghini, executed by Giorgio Vasari, and was finally completed by Federico Zuccaro in 1579."

"That's a lot of names."

He smiled, pleased that she appreciated his knowledge. Then he pointed to an enormous clock "It was made in the fifteenth century and runs on the 'ora italica."

"What is that?" she asked.

"It's when the 24th hour of the day ends at sunset. Most impressive...it still works!" His eyes sparkled. He was like a little boy pointing out all the parts of a new toy. It made her happy, not to mention, honored, to think that her opinion was so important to him.

He pointed to the floor and added, "And here, such a beautiful mosaic tile."

She admired his passion, his ability to see the beauty in the architecture and his desire to share it with her. "What do you think?" His eyes were eager.

She gave a short laugh. "It is very impressive."

She wondered why he should care so much.

"And has your opinion improved any, Miss Woolson?"

"Very much so, though I still think it is a cold and vast building."

His shoulders rounded in defeat. "You are a stubborn woman," he said with a hint of sarcasm.

***

Two days later they sat in a field at the top of a hill and struggled with the binoculars Henry had borrowed from Miss Spedding. Constance preferred the opera glasses with which she was much more familiar.

"And what is your payment to be for use of the glasses?"

"Payment? What payment?" He looked shocked.

"Come now, Henry. I know the Miss Speddings of the world. What did you offer her?"

"I am taking her to the opera on Friday night," he admitted sheepishly as he pulled out a small bag of nuts and popped a handful into his mouth.

Constance laughed. "I do hope it's a good one, for those binoculars or whatever you call them are impossible to use."

Henry turned them over in his hand. "It just needs some tweaking."

He held out the bag to Constance and poured a few nuts into her outstretched hand.

"As do most of my stories," she said under her breath. "Oh look! See there." She pointed to a flock of birds in a tree and then flipped through the small pages of the book open on her lap. "Black redstarts, I believe." She popped a few nuts in her mouth and chewed happily.

"Mark them off." Henry's eyes grew wide with excitement. They had agreed that they would mark off as many birds as they could find while they were in Florence. They also checked off a golden eagle and a heron, though they couldn't agree to which type. When the clouds gathered and the wind picked up, Henry helped Constance up and then led her down the grassy knoll, their shoulders bumping to Michelangelo's house where he pointed out the statue of Lorenzo.

"Now, what is your opinion of it? I know you have one."

She laughed. "How quickly you have read me."

"I am a writer, too, Miss Woolson. Now, what is your opinion?"

"It's supremely beautiful." She paused, studying the grand marble statue. "He conveys to me the sadness of the strongest kind of human mind—almost the sadness of a God, remembering all the past; conscious of all the future; and waiting."

"Interesting." Henry said looking at her carefully. "Of course you admired those grand reclining figures?" he asked, pointing to the figures at the base of the statue representing Day and Night.

She blushed, "They are beyond me. I cannot admire them because they look so distracted."

"Ah yes," he said with a short laugh, "They are 'distracted' as you call it." Words seemed to fail him as he walked over to a fresco. She turned her face away so he wouldn't see how red it had become. The statues had been naked. He must think her so simple. She felt she must explain herself. She went to Henry.

"I must admit that I am not so readily acquainted with naked torsos, flanks, and the lines of anatomy to know when they are supremely beautiful."

Henry chuckled at her answer. He turned to her and stated simply, brushing her loose hair from her face as he spoke. "You needn't be well acquainted to know supreme beauty when you see it." She opened and closed her mouth. He had left her speechless. And blushing all the way to her toes.

As they walked towards home, sharing their bag of candied chestnuts, Constance told Henry of the book she had discovered at the library the day before.

"It was called Excursions in Italy. Written by my great uncle Cooper." Besides Last of the Mohicans, he also wrote a small travel guide about Italy. "To think that fifty years ago my family was here, seeing what I see, living in old palaces, walking amongst the beautiful gardens. I've pretty well been swept off my feet by the place and I think they were too."

Henry nodded in agreement. "Florence is the most feminine of cities. It speaks to you with that same soft low voice which is such an excellent thing in women. Other cities beside it are great, swearing, shuffling rowdies...Florence has an immortal soul." He stopped walking and looked straight into her eyes. "You look into her deep grey eyes...so studious, so sensitive, so human."

She stared back, her face growing warm. "You speak as a poet." She began walking.

When Henry caught up to her he took her arm and said, "There is a dinner tonight at the Klein residence. Would you do me the pleasure of accompanying me?"

"If it were any other dinner party I'd have to decline as I am not interested in such social events. If you haven't noticed, I don't hear well, and I don't care to listen to idle wives rant about the social society in which they mingle."

"Is there anything in which you don't hold an opinion, Miss Woolson?"

She blushed and offered an apologetic smile. "I suppose I am quick with my thoughts. I don't mean to be. I mean to be cordial and endearing, but my feelings are often quite intense. I feel obligated to share my opinion."

"Don't apologize, I like that about you."

"Believe it or not, I hate the social scene myself, but find it necessary in this day of maintaining professional ties."

"Is it?" She couldn't resist as she continued with, "Or could it be that you love the idle gossip that comes from these 'ties' too much to break them?"

"I do like to know what is going on. Don't you?"

"I suppose I am mostly interested in the people I know and care about, which is why I would be happy to accompany you tonight." She turned to Henry. They had reached her villa.

He began, “It has indeed been a pleasure.”

“As it has been for me, Mr. James.” She handed back what was left of the small sack of nuts.

Their hands touched as they both held onto the sack. “I thought you were bound to finish it yourself.”

“I share on occasion.” Constance was feeling quite bold today, perhaps it had been the statues representing Day and Night. Finally she let go of the bag.

He held on to her outstretched hand and kissed it. “Until tonight.”

“Tonight.” She bowed her head and then disappeared behind the large oak door. No. There was no danger in falling in love. Not at all.

Oh heart, if one should say to you that the soul perishes like the body, answer that the flower withers, but the seed remains.
~Khalil Gibran

Elle
The Bookshop

It was closing time and the store was nearly empty, so it was easy to spot the bookshop owner behind the cash register wearing a rather snug, green corduroy jacket and tan slacks. He was heavy set with large jowls and drooping sad eyes. She stood in the doorway trying to decide how to introduce herself when, seeming to sense her presence, he looked up from the cash register and stared at her as if he had seen a ghost. Finally he called to his assistant, busy replacing books on the shelves, to take his place at the checkout. Elle met him in the center aisle. She held out her hand and introduced herself.

"I didn't know she had a daughter. Is she with you?"

She explained about the stroke. He swallowed hard. His eyes grew moist.

"You look so much like your mother. When I saw you standing by the door I thought you were her."

His attention made her blush, but instead of being aggravated by it, she felt endeared by his honesty. He finally introduced himself. "Joseph Gordon. I own the bookstore. I went to school with Lois and Linda."

"Mr. Gordon, I actually came here to ask you about that. You see, my mother told me Lois died years ago."

"Your mother…" his voice trailed off again. He rubbed his hands together. The old fellow was a bit odd, but his admiration for her mother and aunt was sweet. He found his voice, though his eyes seemed far off. "Yes, Lois always loved Linda and hoped she'd come back, but they were two very proud women. Neither willing to admit fault."

"Another infamous Curtis trait," Elle admitted with a smirk. It was not her finest quality, but one she admitted to possessing as well.

"I was hoping to learn more about my Aunt Lois. I have so many questions." She unzipped her bag and pulled out the silver box and held it out to him. "I found this after my mom died, but I don't know what any of the things inside mean. I was hoping you might look at the items and see if anything jogs a memory."

"It's the stamp box!" He looked around the store, nervously rubbing his double chin, and then eagerly back at the box.

"I can't believe it. It was very dear to Lois. And to me. She lost it years ago." He reached out to take it and then pulled back. "You said you found it? Where? Where was it?"

Elle explained how she got it and then said, "If it belonged to Lois, why did Linda take it?"

"Linda thought it was responsible for what happened to Lois. She wanted to destroy it. Lois looked and looked for that box. Losing it did nearly make her crazy." His hands hovered over it as if afraid to touch it, but wanting nothing more. "Could I look inside?"

"Sure. I was hoping you could tell me what it means." She unlocked it and opened it to Mr. Gordon. He was sweating, his face, red as beet juice. He picked up the stone beetle and turned it over in his shaking hand.

"It's called a scarab pin.." He held it out to Elle, who slipped it back in the box and returned it to her bag. He started walking down an aisle. Looking for something.

"Could we meet later? I'd really like to know more about my aunt."

Scanning the shelf he said, "Tomorrow…I could in the afternoon."

"Great." she said. "So I'll just call the store?" He didn't seem to be listening. She turned to leave.

"Wait!" He removed a book from the shelf and handed it to her. "It's my gift…to you." He smiled anxiously.

His generous gift seemed a little unusual, but judging by how interested he was to know that she was Linda's daughter, she took it. "Thank you." She turned to leave.

"You'll need my number," he remembered, bumbling over to the counter and knocking a stapler onto the floor. He picked it up and set it upright, then reached beneath and pulled out his card.

"Do you have a pen?" she asked. He fumbled through his pant pockets, and then found one in his shirt pocket and handed it to her. Elle jotted her number on the back of a piece of paper and then waved him off as she walked out the door with her new book. "See you tomorrow."

"Tomorrow," he repeated staring after her.

***

The hotel overlooking Lake Huron was more beautiful than she remembered from the movie. Maybe Jace always booked The Grand for his clients, but to her it felt like he'd done it especially for her. She climbed the carpeted stairs to a sprawling porch lined with American flags being removed by two well-dressed gentleman as the last light of day tucked itself behind a distant hill. Guests, full from dinner, milled about drinking wine and eating hors d'oeuvres in fancy dresses and suits and ties. Elle felt completely out of place in her jeans and jacket.

Inside there were green carpets with large pink and red flower motifs and matching velvet sofas clustered together from previous conversations now abandoned for the restaurant or the ballroom. An orchestra played in the distant dining room while the remaining patrons enjoyed the sounds of a harpist a few feet away. A waiter passed by with a tray of cheese and meats without acknowledging her. Apparently she didn't look like a guest of the hotel. She'd never felt more under dressed. Up ahead a woman sat at the concierge desk.

She gave her name and said, "Sorry I'm so underdressed. I just got here, and I didn't know it would be a formal affair."

The woman smiled politely. "We do require dress and suit coat after six, but if you are going directly to your room it's no problem. Within reason of course." She winked and handed her an old fashioned key. "Breakfast begins at eight and goes to ten. There is a museum and a gift shop downstairs and a bar on the top floor that you must check out just for the view if nothing else."

Elle thanked her and took the metal key. She couldn't remember the last time a hotel had used real keys. Her room was on the first floor in the back corner and was decorated wall to wall in large yellow and red poppy flowers. The bed was enormous. She noticed it had only a single thin blanket. Her Florida blood was not used to the cooler temperatures of the island. And she would freeze under that. She'd have to call and ask for something warmer. Next to the window was a small sitting area, which reminded her of the book Mr. Gordon had given her. She pulled it out of her bag and proceeded to scan the cover of a photograph of a young woman from the nineteenth century. There was something familiar in her eye, but she couldn't figure out what. She sat in her chair, pulled off her shoes and began reading, but after a short period her eyes grew heavy and she couldn't remember what she'd just read. It had been an exhausting and very long travel day. She put the book down, changed for bed, and then climbed under the thin blanket, too exhausted to call for a warmer one and fell fast asleep.

***

With the first sign of light Elle was up and headed to the pool. After her mom's death she'd fallen off the wagon, but in the past few months she had gotten up every morning at five to swim at the local Y. The early hour guaranteed her a lane so she didn't have to share with anyone else and also allowed her enough time to ride her bike to work.

The pool was cold. And since she had it to herself it appeared everyone else already knew that. When she left an hour later she saw a sign advertising bikes for rent. It would be a perfect way to get around the island. She made a mental note to get one reserved when they opened.

After a hot shower and a large buffet breakfast, she called down for a bike and then went to pick it up. Remembering there was no way she'd get that awful fridge out on her own, she texted Jace to inform him she was going to the house and if he had time he was welcome to join her. Then she hoped on the bike and headed down the path, map tucked in the front basket so she could find her way through town and towards the house.

It was easier to find than she had remembered. She parked in back, not wanting to draw any attention to herself, and made her way to the door, careful to avoid broken boards and loose skunks that might be beneath.

She was glad Jace had shown her where the extra key was hidden under a rock so she didn't have to wait for him. Being alone gave her the freedom to wander around, open drawers, and sift through cupboards and closets without any watchful eye. Inside was cool and dark. The kitchen was tidy and organized. It didn't seem like a crazy recluse had lived there at all. What had she expected? Strange writings on the wall? Bizarre clothing? Hoarding? Something that yelled that this woman had needed to be locked up in a mental hospital. But there was nothing except a ridiculously large collection of books in the office downstairs by the back bedroom. Many of them were old hardbacks dating back to the Twenties. Just the book collection alone would bring a hefty sum. Not that she was sure she would sell, but it was something to consider.

There was a single bookshelf with a handful of albums in the corner. She pulled one out and made herself comfortable on a chaise lounge. The first was filled with black and white photos of Linda and Lois at the cabin on the lake. They both sported blond, Shirley Temple ringlets and big smiles in their little swimsuits. The mother behind them, Grandma Curtis, a woman she had never met, wore large sunglasses and a Marilyn Monroe-type bathing suit. The pictures showed a well-to-do family, playing bocce ball, tennis, hiking along narrow wooded trails, and dancing at fancy balls.

She looked through the entire book and then moved on to the second. They were teenagers now. Still pictured together, big smiles, beautiful. The parents looked proudly on at their two darling girls as they went to school dances, posed in front of waterfalls and sat along fallen logs in the forest. Soon the black and white photos were filled with other teenage friends, boys and girls alike. On the sailboat. Taking hikes. Sunbathing on the beach. In rowboats and on bicycles. One carefree activity after another. It felt like she was looking at an album of the Kennedy Family. So different from life in Florida, where Linda had mostly stayed inside. Only occasionally would she go out on the boat with Elle or join her at the beach.

As she turned the pages the crowd thinned. The large group of boys turned into one. A handsome young man stood between the two beautiful twins. And then it was just the handsome young man and one of the girls. She wasn't sure, but she believed that the woman was her mom, though with their similar haircuts it was hard to say. She finished the album and moved back to the bookshelf where she found a small brown leather book, a diary of some kind. She opened to the first page.

September 1975

J has been coming around more often. Linda has been in Grand Rapids all week so I guess he was stuck with just me. He is so kind though. We like to discuss poetry and books we've both read. Yesterday we went on a hike to friendship rock. We talked about all sorts of interesting things. Like his favorite flowers and what type of birds are on the island. He knows so much

The next entry was even shorter.

J and I hiked Arch rock this morning. He brought a basket of biscuits and jam, but I got a terrible headache and had to go home early. Linda is back from her trip, but he still asked me to come with him. I told her I was going with Ginger. Will she be mad when I tell her the truth?

October 14, 1975

Still haven't told L about J. The headaches continue to grow and now there is something else. Voices. Rather one voice. Sometimes I don't feel in control of myself. I find myself saying things to J that I'm not sure I even mean. Am I falling in love with him? I'm so confused. I like him, but what about Linda?

We went bird watching today. We were both amazed at how much I knew.

"Where did you learn about birds?" he asked. I had no idea. Perhaps I picked up a few things in school after all.

Just then there was a knock at the front door. It was probably Jace. She returned the diary to the shelf and made her way to the front door, but stopped when she realized the shadow in the window did not fit Jace's outline, but appeared to be someone much shorter and much curvier.

She opened the door with a fair amount of caution.

"Miss Curtis?" The woman in the doorway appeared to be in her late sixties, round in the middle, wearing an ill-fitted, pink pencil skirt and white blouse that needed straightening.

"Yes?" How did she know her name? Or did she think she was Lois?

She smiled wide and shook Elle's hand. It was soft and plump. She looked like she'd be more comfortable knitting afghans for her grandchildren. "I'm Nedra from Worthington Realtors. I hear you may be selling your aunt's place."

Elle's eyes grew wide. She knew it was a small town, but this was a record. "Wow. I didn't even know I had an aunt a few months ago. So I'm not sure what I'm going to do with it."

"Of course." The woman named Nedra batted her fake eyelashes and nodded in agreement. "Personally, I think it's too soon for you to make a big decision if you have any doubts, so I'm with you in that regard. Being well informed is imperative in a situation like this. And with you living in Florida and all. Which is a lovely state I might add." She sighed longingly.

"How nice to have good weather all year long."

Elle nodded as the woman continued. "It's almost impossible to build anything new here so I'm going to get a lot of inquiries and I want to be as clear with them as you are with me. Having said that, I want you to consider the large sum of money this house will bring to you. As the sole beneficiary you would *benefit* handsomely." She smiled wide, proud of her pun, as if this information would make Elle's day. She was wrong. It irritated her.

"I'm not interested in making a fortune."

The woman's smile faded. "Of course. Like I said before, it's not good to discuss money matters so soon after the death of a loved one. But since you live in Florida and your aunt owed so much in back taxes we felt this discussion…"

Elle interrupted. "Wait. Back taxes?"

"Didn't Jace tell you?"

"No he didn't." Her face went hot. She hated being unaware of things. And something as big as back taxes frightened her. "What do you mean?"

Nedra's hands flitted around her head like she was swatting a gnat. "I'll leave that up to Jace. He knows all that stuff. But do you mind if I look around for a minute. I won't stay long. It will just give me an idea of what the house might go for and I'll be able to describe it to anyone that might inquire."

While Elle had no intention of selling, she was aware that she might not have a choice if there were back taxes due. And if that were true, why didn't Jace tell her, and how did this woman know all that?

Elle's silence was taken as permission to enter. Nedra was

already at the kitchen by the time Elle shut the door.

Nedra poked her head in the closets, and peaked in the drawers and plotted how much the square footage was worth, making Elle very uncomfortable. "This way, we can help you see what the house will bring and you can better know what your options are."

"Um...okay. Thank you." Elle didn't know what else to say.

When they'd looked at all the bedrooms Nedra seemed unsatisfied. She glanced up at the ceiling. "Doesn't this house have an attic?"

Elle went to speak, but Nedra was already out of the room and heading to the end of the hall. "Is that it?" she asked, pointing to the last remaining door.

Elle hesitated answering, for she didn't really want her up there, but didn't know how to stop her without being rude. Nedra took it as a yes and opened the door.

"Yes, I thought so," Nedra said half way up the stairs.

"Now the family that built this house was very wealthy at one time. Descendants of a famous early American. I'm sure this furniture would bring you a pretty penny. Oh look, what is this?" she stopped in front of the chest and admired the well- warn shine on the wooden trunk with the palm of her hand. "The lock hasn't even been broken. It's so exciting. Shall we do it now?" She smiled at Elle like they were best friends.

"I'd rather not. I'll just wait to do that when the house is actually mine."

Shaking her head in complete agreement, she said, "Sure, of course. It's just so interesting isn't it? So many things to see in here," as she examined each piece of furniture before offering a generous high-to low-pitched sigh.

"Hello!" A male's voice called from downstairs. It was Jace. While she was relieved to hear his voice, she was also upset that he hadn't told her about any back taxes and she was anxious to have a discussion about it, though without Miss Realtor in the room.

Elle led the way downstairs to the kitchen where Jace stood waiting, a brown grocery sack in one arm and a small urn in the crook of the other.

Jace's smile faded when he recognized Nedra hobbling down the stairs. "Nedra. I didn't realize you'd be here so soon."

"Might as well get it done early, I always say." She turned to Elle and said in a more authoritative voice, "I'll have someone come get the square footage by tomorrow." She handed Elle her card.

"I don't know. I guess," Elle agreed. As much as she didn't want to be pushed, knowing the square footage couldn't hurt anything.

Nedra rubbed her palms together like she was trying to make fire. "all right then. I'll leave you two now. Don't open any old things without me!" She stopped, stared at the urn briefly, and then was out the door.

As soon as she was gone Elle confronted Jace about the taxes. "What is this? Nedra says my aunt was way behind."

Jace set the sack down and pulled out an envelope from his inside jacket pocket. "I was going to mention this yesterday, but decided to wait until today. I don't think she'd paid for several years. Michigan State can't take the inherited house for back taxes, but once you take ownership they will put a lien on the house and they'll go after your money."

"And you didn't think it might be important enough to tell me?" As nice as Jace had been to her, this seemed like a big blow.

"I didn't find out myself until a week ago. I was going to tell you yesterday, but I wanted you to enjoy the evening. Today we deal with the hard things. Selling the house, going through her accounts, taking that fridge out."

"There's no money right? I saw the bank statements."

He took a deep breath. "To be honest, I'm amazed that she made it this long. I don't know how she survived. The good news is there are enough antiques you'd probably only need to sell a few to pay the bills. And if you do sell you will do quite well. The property is amazing."

Elle nodded in agreement. Then she noticed the bag. "Hope you didn't bring anything that needs refrigeration."

Her snarky comment caught him off guard, but he laughed anyway. "It's just a few things for the house. A bottle of wine, some bread, and salt. Something I saw on *It's a Wonderful Life*. And donuts. My idea. And these are the good kind."

She was touched by his thoughtfulness.

He looked down at the urn, "And this. Your aunt. Not sure if that was the best way to introduce it. I mean her. I hope that's not disrespectful."

His sudden insecurity made him even more likable. "I don't think she minds."

"Where would you like it, er her?"

She looked around. "Um. Maybe on the hearth?" Jace set it down and Elle repositioned it a few times to give it the attention it deserved and then turned back to Jace. "Should I say something?"

He nodded.

"I really don't know what to say. Sorry I never knew you." She gently caressed the clay vase.

"Amen," said Jace. Elle suppressed a laugh. "Would it be disrespectful to say I'd like to eat a donut now?" she asked. He opened the box and handed her one. "I think it would only be right to celebrate."

"Celebrate?"

He jangled a set of keys. "The house is yours. Earlier than expected." Elle felt a pulse of excitement as she took the keys from his outstretched hand.

Relationship is an art. The dream that two people create is more difficult to master than one. ~Don Miguel Ruiz

Constance
June 1880

"What are you writing today?" Henry asked. Constance only looked at him. Afraid to ask again what he had said. It had happened at least three times on this one occasion. The noise from the Italian children whooping like little cowboys was affecting Constance's hearing very ill. Finally, she had to ask,

"What?" Although Henry was forced to repeat himself yet again, the day was bright and lovely, and the company was pleasant enough to make up for the small grievances that came with Constance's hearing loss. Eventually the children moved on and Henry and Constance were able to resume their conversation.

Constance gingerly rubbed her forearms. "It was mostly copying. I have such a cramp all the way to my shoulder."

"Copy? I never copy."

She stared at him in disbelief and continued to rub her sleeved arm. "How can you never copy?"

He spoke assuredly. "I just don't."

The idea was too unbelievable. "I am amazed that perfection in a first draft should come so easily."

"Do you think that my work has the air of having been

copied and perhaps more than once?"

"I do not acquaint copying or not copying with good writing, rather an appendage to being human." She offered a weak smile, willing her annoyance away so she could explain. "Some of us find writing a difficult task. I struggle, waking at the crack of dawn to make a sentence presentable." She stopped rubbing her arm and turned to him, hoping to break down his proud walls.

"Do you ever have that moment when your characters aren't doing anything you'd like them to and you could just snuff them out with the flick of a wrist and be done with it?"

She spoke animatedly with her hands as she went on.

"I don't think you appreciated, over there among the chimney-pots, the laudation your books received in America as they came out one-by-one. We little fish did!"

"We little fish became worn to skeletons owing to the constant admonitions we received to regard 'the beauty, the grace, the incomparable perfections' of all sorts of kinds of the proud salmon of the pond: we ended by hating that salmon."

Henry's upturned lip told her he enjoyed her attempt to compliment him. "We mustn't let our scales be ruffled by others who have meager fits of success. I have had many failures as well. My plays haven't gotten much attention...though I have one in the wings that I hope will change all that."

"No doubt it will be a rave success. I only ask that you be as determinedly good, as though you were a failure, because failures often fall back on their goodness; let us see a man of genius who is good as well."

He turned to her on the bench and steadied his eyes on hers. "Do you not think I am good?"

She shook her head, "Of course you are good. I just ask that you stay that way, for the smaller fish who wish to be in your company."

"Dear Miss Woolson, you will be a good writer, too. But you must come to more dinner parties. I get some of my best ideas sitting around a table with ten or twelve other guests or while smoking cigars and listening to the men boast of their incredible hunting success or business ventures."

"I haven't much appetite for cigars. Maybe you could just tell me about them."

"I'd like it more if you came with me. You're much more tolerable than most of the women who show up to these things."

"You'll have to whisper everything in my ear. After listening to those children scream I am certain my hearing is worse, if that is possible." Determined to talk no more of herself, she lightly tapped his leg and said with enthusiasm, "Now, tell me about what you are writing. I'm always eager to hear about the works you never have to copy."

And soon all hints of self-deprecation and hearing loss were forgotten as Henry wove his latest tale in her tender ears.

***

"Henry. What a surprise," Constance said walking into her parlor to find Henry, in a black tuxedo and white bowtie, sitting in a chair and lighting a cigar. He'd been let in by her sister, Clara, a new widow who had lost her husband in a train crash and had traveled with her daughter Claire to visit Constance. Cigar smoke curled from his fingertips. She sat in the opposite chair wearing a blue and white, striped night dress, her hair long.

"I am sorry I missed dinner tonight," she said.

"You promised you'd be there." He took a puff on the cigar.

"And I meant to, but I had one of my infamous headaches."

Another pause and then she continued. "You don't think I would make it up?"

"Of course you did. I had a feeling you wouldn't come. I saw you nearly roll your eyes when Ruskin spoke about his paintings at dinner at Mrs. Popes the other night."

"Mr. Ruskin can see nothing without a ladder and a magnifying glass. The little details are all he sees. To say I don't enjoy his company would be an understatement."

He chuckled and blew the smoke out. "See, that was what I was longing for. Some base comment from our sweet Miss Woolson. Without you one can bank on a dull evening."

"Well, there you have it." Curious, she had to ask. "So was it?"

"What?"

"Dull?"

"Of course. And Mr. Ruskin wasn't even there." He took another puff of his cigar and then said without meeting her eye, "I have been invited to dinner tomorrow evening with Mrs. Greenough. Do you remember her? I introduced you a few weeks ago."

"Yes, she was quite friendly. I should like to be acquainted with her very much."

"Good. You must join me at her home for supper tomorrow night. I told her you would be there."

"Henry."

"I will be around to pick you up myself. I can't risk you getting lost or your carriage losing a wheel or you having another fit of a headache again."

"I never lie about these things."

"Just as I never copy."

She met his eye with a raised brow. He took another puff of his cigar, his eyes twinkling. Was he admitting to something? He chuckled and said, "Wear that new dress your sister brought from Paris. It's very becoming on you."

"What do you care about fashion?" she questioned smugly, though secretly her heart raced.

"It's good for your career, my dear Constance. You must look the part if you are to be a successful writer." He snuffed his cigar out on the silver plate resting on the end table. "And your frame is too lovely to hide under an atrocity like that thing you are wearing now."

She looked down at her robe. "This 'thing' is my housecoat and it is very comfortable. You did arrive very late. I'm sure my sister is beside herself with worry in the other room."

He returned the hat to his head and grabbed his cane. "Please tell your sister she has nothing to worry about. Your God awful housecoat is a secret I shall never share...with anyone." He sniffed and stood. "Now good night. Don't forget about tomorrow. And no, we won't be walking. I'll pick you up in my carriage." Henry tipped his hat to her and disappeared behind the door.

After Constance's unexpected visitor had gone, her sister, Clara, appeared, a concerned look on her face. Constance ignored it. "Dear sister, that look is not becoming on you."

"Connie, I worry about you. I don't think you understand men like Mr. James."

Constance shot her a warning look, her voice quiet, but intense as she spoke. "Because I do not know men in the way a married woman knows them, you think I do not understand them? I understand our friend Mr. James better than he may understand himself."

"Connie, I've known men like him and women like you who fall for his... divination. I don't want to see you... grieved."

Constance let out a short laugh. "I wrote all about Miss Grief, so I can assure you that I understand the trappings of which you speak." She crossed to the door and locked it as her voice grew low and dark. "I know men like our dear Henry are dangerous. They have a habit to divine and then forget."

She returned to Henry's chair and picked up the silver tray filled with his cigar ashes and stood before the fireplace.

"He is like his characters who offer women an awareness that charms them, but at the very moment of mutual rapport remove themselves." She dumped the ashes into the fireplace before continuing. "Such men are not cold or cads." She turned to meet her sister's eye and smiled. "On the contrary, they appear benign, with a genuine liking for women and an easy delicacy in their treatment of them."

"Yes, but Connie…"

Constance interrupted her. "I, in turn, am willing to forgive him for the sake of his Hawthorne." She set the tray down, walked to her sister, and kissed her gently on the cheek. "And you must forgive me for the sake of my Grief. Now I will bid you goodnight."

"A good writer does not, a gentleman make," Clara snapped. Constance only stared back at her. Clara relented. "I'm sorry. Goodnight, Connie."

Sitting at her dressing table in a white, ruffled nightgown, her rippling hair loose around her shoulders, a small candle flickering beside her, Constance absently slid a silver-plated brush through her wavy locks as she thought about what Clara had said about being wary of Henry.

It was true. Henry was dangerous to a woman like herself. She enjoyed being with him, but it was more than just admiration. She gathered information from him as much as he did from her. They had a preferred connection and connections were essential in this business as were insightful discussions. Just two days before she had shared her current storyline with Henry and he had given her two or three insights that proved valuable to her work. At the same time, as much as he helped her understand men, she helped him to understand a woman's mind. A tit for tat. But it ran deeper than mutual understanding. It seemed a deeper admiration grew with each meeting, each jovial conversation. An appreciation of his wit, his chuckle, his deep voice. His lips. His eyes.

Still, she wondered if there was anything in the mirror that Henry James found admirable. He had called her deep-colored cheeks and fair, almost-transparent skin beautiful once.

She set her brush down. Entertaining such thoughts would only lead to grief. She was older than him. And he was in no way looking for a wife. Nor was she looking for a husband. But truth be told she liked the look of Henry James. His keen eyes, hair cut close to his head, revealing a fine profile— and she was partial to profiles. But mostly it was the way he looked at her, as if he appraised her every word, thought, and cared about her like none other. He was unlike other men in the way he was readily aware of her dress, her speech, her feelings. And though she was perfectly satisfied with their friendship as it lay, the womanly side of her echoed the question that had her sister Clara concerned: did Henry feel anything towards Constance?

Sadness flies on the wings of the morning and out of the heart of darkness comes the light. ~Jean Giraudoux

Elle

The Curtis Estate

"Can I show you something?" Elle asked Jace. They were sitting on the broken steps watching the boats go by. She unzipped her backpack and removed the silver stamp box and told him how she had received it and how peculiar Mr. Gordon had acted when she showed it to him.

She held the beetle up in the sunlight, its gold edges shimmering back at them. "He said Lois lost it years ago. He called it a scarab pin."

"Can I?" Jace asked, reaching for the pin and turning it over in his hand.

"He gave me a book about a local author as a gift. It seemed a bit peculiar."

"Oh that's not unusual. That's what he does. He gives books as gifts. Last year he gave my dad a book called *Fly Fishing for Seniors*." He laughed at the memory.

"But why me? I had only met him."

"She was a local author, you say?"

"Yes. Her name was Constance Woolson. Have you ever heard of her?"

"Oh yeah. I remember learning about her in school.

There's a monument dedicated to her. I could take you there now if you'd like."

She brightened. "Do you have time? I could use a walk."

"I have a guy coming to pick up your fridge later, so, yeah. We have time." He returned the pin to Elle who shut it back in the box and returned it to the backpack. They walked around to the backyard and joined a well-worn path through the tall aspens.

"I've never gone this way, but it shouldn't be hard to figure out. It's a small island, but I still get confused."

"You must know a lot of its history," Elle said. As they walked deeper into the forest, the tall pine trees grew like giants, darkening the path that was littered with fallen needles, which cushioned their every step.

"I should know more, but I didn't pay attention in school. If you keep going on this path you'll run into Fort Mackinac. Have you seen it?"

She nodded, "I haven't been inside yet, though."

"They do reenactments. Wear the old uniforms. It's kinda fun."

Jace proceeded to tell her about Fort Mackinac, which was once occupied by eighteenth-century British Redcoats and later nineteenth-century American soldiers. The faint trail eventually joined a clearly marked path thick with people who had the same idea. He took her to Arch Rock first, a thousand year old formation carved out by wind and water overlooking the lake. Below them several picnickers enjoyed the summer weather on the pebbled beach. Farther away a young couple—probably honeymooners— snuggled affectionately on a rock facing the lighthouse. It made her uncomfortable to watch them, but Jace seemed unfazed by their affection and went on speaking as if he hadn't noticed it at all.

"There's an old Indian legend that says a beautiful, young Indian woman met the son of a sky spirit, while gathering wild rice. They fell in love, but she was forbidden to marry the non-mortal, so her cruel father beat her and tied her on a rock high on the bluff. She wept so long that the tears washed away the stone and formed the arch. In time the young man returned, untied her and carried her back to the people in the sky."

"I wish someone would carry those two away." Her comment was directed to the couple now kissing on the rock. Jace turned and looked at her with curious eyes.

"You disapprove of public affection?" he asked.

"When I am not the recipient, yes. It makes everyone else so aware of how alone they are. It's not nice."

"I don't think they are doing it to be mean. I think they do it because they are madly in love."

"I sound like an old prude, don't I?" she admitted with a laugh. It made her think of Linda and Lois. "I wish I knew what happened to my aunt and mom. Do you think it was over a man?"

"It usually is," he admitted, staring down at the couple.

"Maybe that's what's dangerous," Elle said, walking away from the cliff.

"Kissing?" There was a slight upturn to his lip. A dimple in his cheek. Again, she found him difficult to read. Was he offended? Amused?

"No. I mean, yes, maybe. But I was thinking of love. It makes people do crazy things."

He pulled a weed and stripped it of its leaves. "What about the box Linda took from Lois? Seems like you can blame their split on that."

He was right. But it still didn't make sense. What was in the box that would cause such a riff? "So where is this monument you wanted to show me?"

"It's just down the path a ways. If you're not looking you'd walk right past it and end up at Skull Cave or Sugar Loaf Rock."

She laughed. "Arch Rock, Skull Cave, Sugar Loaf Rock. This place is like Neverland: I expect to see the Lost Boys come around the corner any minute."

He nodded. "In some ways it is a kind of Neverland. Nothing changes around here." His smile faded. She was sure he was thinking of his mom and brother.

She wanted to reach out and touch him, but instead just said, "Everything changes. Even the island changes. Otherwise the arch wouldn't exist."

"True," Jace agreed as he swept a large branch aside, showing off a large dell canopied by shade trees. "Here we are." Elle passed and was struck by the remarkable view of the Straits and Haldimand Bay. There was a faint smell of cedar and the floor was dotted with limestone rills covered in myrtle. Ironwood trees and cedar pine circled the opening, while down below a ferry deposited another crowd of tourists. Off to one side stood a large memorial with a bronze plaque, titled "Anne" embossed with a picture of a woman looking over her shoulder. Elle read the words aloud:

"She loved the island and the island trees; she loved the wild larches the tall spires of the spruces bosses with lighter green…"

Elle paused. The words clung to her chest like magnets. Her heart began to thunder. She swallowed and continued.

"The gray pines and the rings of the juniper. Hear the rustling and the laughing of the forest and the waves of the waters on the pebbly shores."

The words on her tongue made her head buzz. Her heart stormed through her chest. She glanced over at Jace to see if he felt the same way, but he seemed unscathed. She touched the embossed figure. It stung her fingers. She pulled back in surprise.

"Are you okay?" Jace asked.

She stared back at him, grappling for words. "It shocked me...or something." Her fingers buzzed. The grove was beginning to feel more like a cave. Even the trees seemed to be closing in on her.

"I need to go," she whispered, pushing her iron clad feet towards the exit, or what she thought was the exit.

She pushed branches aside to escape. She couldn't breathe. She wanted to run into an open field, but there wasn't anything but trees and a skinny path. The weight on her ankles loosened with each step away from the grove until finally she felt like herself again. She didn't know why she'd felt so charged up back there, but the minute she touched the plaque a single bolt had shot through her fingers.

"Are you okay?" Jace asked after a few minutes.

She wanted to explain it, but she didn't think he would believe her. "Yeah, sorry. I just got sick for a minute. Maybe I am claustrophobic." She had no other explanation. "I'm fine though." She offered him a weak smile as proof.

They sat for a moment in silence. Finally, Jace checked his watch and asked, "What time are you meeting Mr. Gordon?"

She pulled a loose lock of hair behind her ear. "This afternoon I believe." She was glad he didn't ask any more about what happened back in the grove. "He promised to call."

Then she remembered her wardrobe issue. "Oh I have a problem. You have to dress up after five at The Grand. I didn't bring anything."

"That's right. Maybe Lois has a dress you can borrow." Elle crinkled her face at the idea. One thing she knew about Lois, her wardrobe lacked fashion sense. Everything the poor woman owned had been grey and at least twenty years old. Jace laughed. "Just kidding. There are a few dress shops around. And I've got a friend that could loan you something."

"Oh no. I can buy a dress, I'm just not sure where to look."

Jace looked at his watch and remembered, "We've still got to see that trunk in the attic and get your fridge out."

Elle laughed, "My fridge. Lucky me. But I am excited to check out that chest. I've been thinking about it all day."

Just then his phone rang. It was his friend Patricia. Perfect timing. He asked her about finding a dress, and then pulled the phone away to tell Elle that his friend could meet her right now. "She says there's a couple nice shops around the corner from the bookstore."

Elle forced a smile. While she appreciated her kindness, she was not anxious to go shopping with some girlfriend of his. She'd never had many girlfriends and the idea of going shopping with a stranger was not very appealing, but what else could she do? She really did need to get a dress. "Okay." The chest would have to wait a little while longer. Then she realized it might work out in her favor after all.

"Maybe afterwards I could meet Mr. Gordon."

An hour later Elle found herself meandering through neatly converted dress shops with little interest in the merchandise. She had never enjoyed shopping much and this was no different. As she shopped, she kept her eyes out for the redhead that you "can't miss" as Jace had described his friend Patricia. As she rounded a dress rack she nearly bumped into a pretty redhead with hazel eyes. The woman stared at Elle for a moment. Elle stared back, waiting for the moment of recognition or introduction, while realizing neither one really knew who they were looking for.

She spoke up first. "Are you Patricia?"

"Yes." The pretty woman looked surprised, but quickly covered it with a smile. "You must be Elle. I was expecting someone much older. But that's okay." She took Elle's arm and said, "These are more for… *older women*," she emphasized in a hushed voice. She only let go of Elle's arm once they reached a cute boutique with designer dresses a few shops down. Elle looked at a price tag and tried to keep from yelling out from shock.

"So you're staying at The Grand?" Patricia asked, sizing her up while pulling out several dresses in Elle's size.

Elle pretended to be interested in the overpriced dresses. Is this what girlfriends did? Why did she feel so awkward?

"Yes. Jace got me a room there."

The dress in Patricia's hand hung in mid-air. She said, "How nice of him." She cleared her throat. The metal hanger clanked as it returned to the rack.

"It is nice, but he failed to tell me about their dress code and I didn't bring the right clothes." Elle ran her hand over her hair, wishing she had done more with it.

"Men!" Patricia bemoaned, holding a green and blue

diagonal striped dress up against Elle. The dress made Elle feel like a candy wrapper. "Nope. Too bold," Patricia said to Elle's relief.

"Tomorrow night is a big, dress up ball. I hope you'll still be around to enjoy it."

Elle frowned. She planned to fly out tomorrow night and told Patricia as much.

"I work there. I could probably get you a special rate for another night."

"Thanks. I didn't realize this would be so complicated. I thought it would be an open and shut deal, but now that I'm here I can see I should have planned for a longer trip."

"Plus, it's a beautiful island. You can't possibly see everything in a day."

"True." Elle admitted stopping to admire a cream, lace, fitted dress, but upon seeing the hefty price tag quickly moved on. "So how do you know Jace?" she asked nonchalantly.

"Through his stepmom."

"You know his stepmom?"

"Oh everybody knows Nedra."

Elle's head shot up. "Nedra? The realtor?"

"Yeah, in fact you should get her to list that house if you're going to sell. She's fabulous."

Elle felt her face flush hot. Why hadn't he mentioned that Nedra was his stepmom? Or had she just missed it? And why did it feel as if Jace had purposefully kept it from her? Was he trying to get some kind of kickback from her? Sure, she didn't get out much, and she was probably naïve in a lot of ways, but she didn't like being taken advantage of, and this smelled very much like an under-the-table deal. She felt sick and no longer cared to shop for a dress or even pretend to be having fun.

"I've got to call Mr. Gordon. I was supposed to meet with him and I haven't heard from him yet."

"You know Mr. Gordon already? You get around fast." The woman grinned. But Elle didn't appreciate the innuendo.

"He was a close friend to my aunt. He was going to tell me about her."

Patricia didn't seem to sense Elle's rising voice as she calmly went on pulling out dresses. "I've only lived here a few years. But I hear she was a recluse."

Elle glanced at her phone. "Something happened to her. I'm hoping Mr. Gordon will know."

"Didn't he have a thing for her?" Patricia looked up for the first time and met Elle's eye.

"I don't know." Elle was surprised by the comment, but then again, she wasn't surprised. She remained still, unsure what to say.

"It's all a rumor, but he was the only person to go in that house."

"Sure," Elle said. Patricia stared at her. Maybe she needed to act more interested. "I mean, that's interesting." She'd never been good at girly talk.

She checked her watch. "Speaking of Mr. Gordon. I better get going."

"What about a dress?" Patricia asked holding up a white shift dress with a price tag that would pay for a month's worth of groceries. Elle took it from her. "That's the one," she said, buying it without even trying it on. As soon as she left the building she immediately called Mr. Gordon. He answered on the first ring. Since neither had had lunch he offered to meet her at the local bar where he said they made the best Reuben sandwich in town.

Elle had only just arrived when Mr. Gordon walked in. She noticed a small limp, and his forehead was sweating. "Hurt my ankle in an accident years ago," he explained as if he read her mind. She wondered if she was always so obvious since both Jace and Mr. Gordon seemed to read her mind. Maybe it was something with the island. Maybe she needed to work on containing her true feelings better.

"So nice to see you my dear," Mr. Gordon said, kissing her on the forehead like he'd known her for years. "I always sit in the same spot. It's the one with an imprint of my derrière." He gave a small wink and led her to his favorite booth where a young waitress brought them both waters and then took their orders. As soon as she left he asked about the silver box. "Did you bring it?" he asked anxiously.

She nodded and unzipped her backpack. As she set the box on the table his eyes grew moist. She waited for him to open it, thinking he would go right for the scarab, but he didn't. Instead he picked up the single pearl on a gold chain and said, "That was Lois' necklace." He set it back down and moved to the book, then the scarab. Elle had removed the letters, feeling that they were an entirely unrelated mystery. He wiped at his face with his napkin, but she wasn't sure if it was because of a tear or something else.

"Thank you for this. For letting me see it again." He blew his nose into his napkin. Elle waited patiently for him to expound, but every time he went to speak he was only able to clear his throat.

"You have a real treasure here. Linda thought it was dangerous. Said it ruined Lois." Mr. Gordon swiped another napkin from the table behind them as he spoke in a low tone. "People call things dangerous when they don't understand them. Religions are dangerous. The internet is dangerous. Microwaves are dangerous. Is there the potential for danger? Yes. Is there a greater potential for happiness? Yes."

"Is it the box or what's inside?" Elle hated to admit that she didn't know what he was referring too. But he didn't answer as the waiter arrived and set their plates of food in front of them.

In a hushed voice Mr. Gordon admonished her to quickly put the box away. "And don't let anyone else know you have it. We'll have to meet again. But not here. Not in public. Would you bring the box to me tonight?"

She nodded, anxious to understand what was so special. She stuffed the box back in her backpack. Then, as if guilty of something he said loudly, "So how do you like the book? Have you started to read it?"

She unfolded her napkin and set it across her lap. "Yes. I started last night."

He nodded his approval. "Are you enjoying it?"

"So far, yes."

"Had you heard of her before?"

She took a drink of her water and then set it down. "The woman in the book? No."

He cut his sandwich with a fork and knife. "Most people haven't. But in her day she was very famous."

As nice as this sounded, she was more interested in learning about her aunt and mother. She thought of how to get him back on course. "Did you go to school with Lois and Linda?" She picked up her fork and knife and cut a small piece of the sandwich and began chewing.

He nodded, and took a bite of his sandwich, wiping his mouth and chin nervously. Elle felt impatient to get answers so she went on hoping to land on something he would talk about. "My mom told me Lois died years ago. Why would she tell me that?"

He dropped his napkin into his lap. She waited for him to answer, either with a no, that he didn't know, or with a yes.

"I don't know why your mom would tell you that Lois was dead. I didn't know Linda even had a daughter. So they both kept things from each other."

"But you and Lois – remained friends?"

"There were some things…"

"Well, hello there," a voice called from behind. Elle turned to see Nedra standing with her large, bright, pink handbag over her shoulder.

Elle frowned. Not excluding the fact she had just learned she was Jace's stepmom, she was also swimming in the sad story that was her mom and Aunt Lois' life. Was this what living on a small island was like? Always running into people you didn't want to see?

"How fitting that the two of you would have met already." Nedra cocked her head and looked at Mr. Gordon, but he only nursed his beer.

"Nedra," Mr. Gordon said without standing or meeting her eye. Nedra didn't take her gaze off Mr. Gordon.

"I suspect you're hoping to get a few mementos of your old friend?"

"I'm not interested in the house."

"Of course not. I remember." Nedra said. Elle pushed her food aside. Now she'd really lost her appetite.

Mr. Gordon stood and laid down two bills. "I hate to cut it short, but I've got to get back to the shop." Elle felt like the child in the middle of a custody battle. Should she leave with Mr. Gordon? Should she stay and finish her sandwich? Did she have to invite Nedra to join her?

"You don't have to pay for me." Elle went for her wallet in her backpack, but he grabbed her hand and held it in his.

"Nonsense." He continued, "This is my treat." He looked down, realizing that their hands were touching, and slowly pulled back.

Nedra spoke up. "Don't leave on my account. I didn't mean to intrude on your lunch. I was only passing through." She turned to Elle.

"We'll be in touch shortly." And then she walked past them and into the ladies room.

"Sorry about her," Mr. Gordon said, unable to meet Elle's eye. "Ya know what they say, Hell hath no fury like a woman scorned." He patted her lightly on the shoulder. "Can we talk again tonight? Where are you staying?"

"The Grand."

"I'll call you." Mr. Gordon walked to the door with a toothpick jammed between his teeth. As if having a second thought he glanced back at Elle. She smiled and gave a little wave, feeling emotional even though she had nothing to feel emotional about. He nodded, and hobbled out the door.

But I like not these great successes of yours; for I know how jealous are the gods. ~ *Herodotus*

Constance
June 1880 Florence

Constance glanced past the polished silver candlesticks and trays of roasted duck, chyne of mutton, pork slices, bread pudding, buttered French beans, and baskets of hard rolls, to watch Henry cut his duck with proficient strokes. While he cut, he talked absently with a woman to his left. She knew he was unhappy with his company by the way he refused to meet the woman's eye, and yet he continued on in a most disgusting fashion. It was all Constance could do to keep from rolling her eyes.

How he played these women, pulling the truth of how a woman thinks between, 'pass the mutton,' and 'more mashed potatoes, please.' It was like watching a surgeon at work. Or a magician. And how they swooned, eager to please, as they stuffed themselves with bread pudding.

The murmur of voices and the clanking utensils made it impossible to hear what he, let alone anyone else in the room was saying. Two candelabras down the center of the table blocked her view leaving her to visit with only the two people on her sides, both, of whom were chatting ceaselessly to the persons on their left and their right. She cut her mutton in small pieces and chewed deliberately, wishing she could disappear from this ridiculously dull dinner party Henry had insisted she attend, though he hadn't spoken a word to her since they arrived.

He was upset with her. That was obvious. What wasn't obvious was what had vexed him so. She'd been running the events through her mind trying to figure it out and had decided it must have been during the carriage ride, but really it was so ridiculous as to make her laugh. But Henry was far too sensitive for mockery. Sensitive. That was an understatement. She thought back to when he arrived to pick her up. He had seemed happy enough then. He had complimented her hair which Clara had done up in the latest fashion, a less-than-pleasant experience, as Clara had pouted the whole time that they should leave Florence and go somewhere else.

"The lease will soon be up," Clara had complained while she folded and pinned Constance's long hair. "And I hoped we would see Venice before we moved on to Switzerland. Did you see the advertisement? It looks to be a most beautiful country." Constance had seen the paper, but she wasn't ready to make any final plans yet. She tapped her sister's hand resting on her shoulder and looked at her through the mirror.

"We will see every part of Italy that you desire. But I am not quite ready to leave." When that didn't seem to satisfy her sister she added with a tad more excitement, "Perhaps we shall go to Venice in the fall and then on to Switzerland in the spring."

She shifted in her small dressing chair and smiled up at Clara, patting her new updo with satisfaction. "I hardly recognize myself, I look so fashionable." Mrs. Beard, her stout English traveling maid, had then announced Mr. James's arrival. Constance rose quickly. A welcome escape from talk of leaving Florence, Constance had thought.

Henry noticed the dress and commented on how ravishing she looked with her hair up in that silver comb. "Is it new?" he had asked as he helped her into the carriage.

She touched it lightly with her gloved hand and stated excitedly, "My agent sent it as a gift for the grand success that my book, *Anne*, is having, so I had Clara put it up." *Anne* was her most recently published novel, and according to Harpers, was fast becoming the most popular serial in their history. She said as much to Henry, adding that they had surprised her by doubling the sum already paid for the book.

"I was in disbelief when I received the telegram. I thought it must be a joke, but then I read on, and…" She hesitated, not wanting to boast, though she was ready to burst with excitement.

"And what?" he asked waiting.

"They have offered me royalties on *Anne*. I think I had mentioned that they had refused that in our contract, but have since decided to renegotiate. I am just astounded! All because of my little book." She sighed in delight. "I suppose some little fish can make a small ripple in the current once in a while." She kicked at Henry's black dress boot, feeling giddy enough to tease him. She readjusted her skirt and went on talking.

"It made working on my next story quite impossible today, so Clara and I walked along the River Arno and fed the ducks, and then we visited the Palazzo Pitti, which is enormous! Did you know," she began, not noticing how quiet he'd gone. "That it was once owned by the Italian King? Well of course you did. You know everything and have been everywhere. But one day I am going to shock you with something that you don't already know."

"You already have," he said, softly rubbing his cane with the edge of his thumb.

She sat back and gave him a raised brow. "I have?"

"You know how to win the admiration of the fickle American public, and that is something I seem to fail at with each procurement I secure with my little 'Atlantic monthly.'" His mouth fell in a deep frown.

This was not what she had intended with her good news, "That is simply not so." She paused in confusion to his change in mood. She hadn't meant to sound boastful. What had she said to make him feel like a failure?

At that moment the carriage stopped and they had arrived at the Greenough residence. He had helped her from the carriage, and then since that time Henry had done everything in his power to avoid her, even to the point of sitting next to Mrs. Sanderson, whom Constance knew he very much disliked.

She would have to battle to win back his good humor. At any rate, she must stop his moping; for that was the task she bore as his friend.

However, Constance didn't have another chance to do anything to improve Henry's foul mood until the next afternoon when Henry made a surprise visit to the Barbensi Pension.

As if the previous night's stonewalling had never happened, he removed his hat and asked if she'd like to go for a walk along the river. She was more than happy to get out of the stuffy hotel on such a hot Sunday so she took her parasol, said goodbye to Clara, who gave her a stern look, a look Constance ignored completely, and followed Henry out into the glorious, warm, Italian sun.

Constance slipped her arm through his as they strolled along the River Arno and lost no time getting to the business of self-deprecation.

"I'm sorry that I told you of my small success with *Anne*, yesterday," she began. "It might have seemed boasting, but I didn't think like that. Even if a story of mine should have a popular sale, it could not alter the fact that the utmost best of my work cannot touch the hem of your first or poorest."

"There is no need to set off on an illusion of failure when you haven't any. You have your audience of the fairer sex, and I have mine. There is no need to belittle your success."

"To be sure, my work is coarse beside yours. Of another grade entirely.

"The two should not be mentioned on the same day."

Henry chuckled. Out of the corner of her eye she sensed a lightening of his step. This pleased her very much. But she also sincerely believed her next comment when she turned to him and said, looking straight into his eyes, "Do believe how acutely I know this. The public will recognize you eventually as the supreme novelist of the age."

"And I shall be long dead and never live to see a penny of it."

"Your nephews and nieces shall love you all the more for it." She worked to remove her gloves and commenced with her groveling. "And while you may be remembered famously, I shall be long forgotten, my little success, a tiny fish in your big ocean."

They sat down at their regular bench and watched the pigeons flutter about in silence for several minutes, but Constance couldn't stop until she knew she had righted her wrongs. "If I, by chance, talked of myself, it was merely because I live so alone and, out it came before I had time to think what it might sound like."

Henry patted her gently on the leg and said, "My dear, you are a gifted authoress and have every reason to boast of your success. It is a great thing to double your income. I shall expect more parties and dresses in your future."

Constance shook her head. "It's just that with you—well, you see, I like so few people! Though I pass for a constantly smiling, ever-pleased person, my smile is the basest hypocrisy. You know that and yet you still tolerate me. I can't bear to lose your friendship."

"It isn't because of you that I shall be running off."

"Running off?" Her eyes grew wide, and he looked away as he spoke.

"I already have meetings set up. One with a sweet, old authoress, at a remote region of Paddington." He sighed in disgust.

"London?"

He nodded. No afternoon walks, talks of impending deadlines or characters. No more advice. No more closeness. She was surprised how disappointed this made her feel. She would be alone again. Even with Clara visiting she often felt so alone. What was there to look forward to?

"And will you be in London long?" She offered a weak smile. She did not want him to know how deeply upsetting this news was.

"Through the winter at least. My sister Alice is keen on visiting, though I'm not sure if she is up to it. Her health is very fragile. Luckily, she has a good friend in Ms. Loring who has chosen to be a companion for her. I am grateful for that."

"You love your sister very much. I can see that. I had a close friendship with my brother Charles until all the trouble a few years ago. He should never have gone to California. I think it has ruined him." They sat in silence for several minutes as Constance allowed the news of Henry's departure to sink in. The last few months had been beautiful and exciting. Never had she had a friend, especially that of the opposite sex that had touched her like Henry had. And now he was leaving. And he didn't seem the least bit upset by it. Why did she feel like her heart was bleeding?

Henry pulled out his pocket watch and exclaimed, "Four o'clock. Just in time. Now my dear Fenimore, would you join me for some gelato?" He stood and extended a hand to help her up. She took his weakly. The groveling had come too late.

When she returned home she called for Clara to join her in the parlor. "I thought you and Claire would enjoy this." She handed her the leftover gelato. While Clara and her adolescent niece Claire fought over the remaining flavored ice Constance announced her plan. "I've been thinking of what you said, and you're right. We have been in Florence long enough. I shall call Venice tomorrow to procure a place for the summer, and then it will be on to Switzerland in the early fall. Does that sound agreeable?"

Clara raised her spoon in celebration "Wonderful! When shall I pack?"

"We shall leave within the week." She walked to her door. "I'll be working tonight so I'll have my dinner brought to my room tonight." Careful to keep a smile on her face until she was safely behind closed doors.

Sorrow is the mere rust of the soul. Activity will cleanse and brighten it. ~Samuel Johnson

Elle

The Grand

Elle tossed and turned and fluffed the pillow, trying to fall asleep, but she couldn't get Jace or his stepmom, Nedra out of her mind. She felt betrayed that he would have kept their relationship from her. And on top of that she was upset about Mr. Gordon. They were supposed to have met, but he never returned her messages. And when she went to the bookstore, his assistant Jared stated that Mr. Gordon had taken the rest of the day off for personal matters. Maybe he had changed his mind, or something else had come up, but she had hoped to hear the story behind the silver box before she left. Now she may never know what everything meant.

She flung the ice thin sheet aside and crawled out of bed. Even if it was two in the morning, she wouldn't get to sleep for a while. She dressed in sweats and a hoodie and walked out of her room, down the hall, and out a side door to the large porch. She looked around. The porch was empty. Lights shined from the lobby through the windows. A lone woman sat at a desk. Everyone else was smartly asleep. Where she should be. It was breezy, and cool, but she didn't mind as she plopped down into one of the rockers and. pulled out her phone. Jace had left her four messages. She hadn't responded to any of them. She wasn't mad at him. Or was she? And did she have any right to be upset?

She read Jace's last message about meeting the guy to take out the fridge. *Was she planning on being there?* She should have met him. She should have responded. Why was she so bothered about Nedra? Did she feel used? Gullible? Had she really thought Jace might be interested in her? A nearly forty-year-old woman, never married?

She was an old maid. She didn't feel old, but sometimes when she looked in the mirror she was shocked to see the woman looking back at her. Guys didn't notice her anymore. She'd never been unattractive, but she'd long passed the desirable stage. Would she end up like Lois and Linda, alone in the house, waiting for something to happen?

Thinking about the house reminded her of the trunk in the attic. She'd always been fascinated with attics and old relics from a previous generation. She'd been on a first name basis with the curator at the museum in St. Augustine. Whenever they'd gotten something new they'd give her a call. For a time she'd even worked there until they made budget cuts and had to let her go. But she'd never done it for the money anyway, so she still found time on weekends to ride her bike down to the museum and help catalogue, dust, answer questions, whatever they wanted. She'd loved it. And now, not even a few miles away, was a whole attic full of treasures. Her treasures. She glanced down the hill towards the pool house where her bike was chained up to a rack. There was no one around. Would it be totally crazy to go there now? Of course it was.

There was a chill in the air as she pulled her hoody over her head and hurried down the stairs to the bike rack. Once she started peddling though, she forgot all about the wind as she zipped down the hill and then through Main Street.

When she reached the eastern shore, the wind seemed to switch directions, pushing her backwards even as she inched forward across the black pavement. Clouds covered the sky and moon leaving her in total darkness. She turned on her phone light and held it out in front of her, but within seconds raindrops began to fall and she had to put it away. The wind rocked the trees and the waves rushed across the rocky beach sending a chill across her wet face. Just as the storm began to rage she reached the dark house. She carried her bike up the broken stairs and left it by the front door, her hands shaking from cold as she struggled to insert the key into the doorknob.

Inside, the house was dark and warm. A welcome relief from the storm. She was soaked. She removed her hoody and went to the kitchen to find a towel to dry off. That was when she noticed a hole where the fridge had once stood and a note from Jace. She held it in her guilty hands and read that he had gone ahead and taken care of it when he couldn't get a hold of her. She slowly dropped the note on the counter, trying to ignore the huge shame pushing down her wet shoulders. She tried to justify her actions. He would probably charge her for doing it. Or had he done it as a friend? Either way, it was a nice thing to do. Maybe he wasn't a jerk after all.

Using her phone as a flashlight, she climbed the stairs and stopped in front of the door leading to the attic. While she hadn't been scared thinking about coming here when she was surrounded with lights from the hotel, she was now having huge second thoughts. It was dark and silent and she was very alone. But the storm was going to prevent her from going home anytime soon and she was dying to look in the trunk., so why not just check it out. She was fine. The door was locked, the house was dry. Better here than in the storm.

Plus, something urged her on. A feeling of longing that propelled her forward, up the rickety old stairs to the dusty cold attic even as the wind howled its sorrowful song outside. Damp air slithered through the old-fashioned clapboard walls and rain pitter–pattered against the roof. She shivered. A mixed pot of cold and nerves. That was when she spotted the old trunk. She ran her fingers across the cold metal trim, outlining the rusty lock, the hinges, the wood panels. She tugged the lock. Despite it's worn appearance it was still holding strong. Outside the wind shuttered through the tall trees like a distant maraca. A metal chain clanked against a flagpole up the hill. Lightning flashed. Elle jumped. In surprise, her heart rate skyrocketing. It struck again, its brilliant light exploding in the room and illuminating an old iron hammer hanging on the wall. She walked over and pulled it down. It was heavier than she expected, she realized as she carried it back to the chest.

This is ridiculous, she told herself. *It's storming outside, and I'm traipsing around a dark attic in the middle of the night.* But that didn't stop her from holding the heavy hammer above her head and coming down hard against the lock. The lock snapped in half and dropped with a thud to the floor. She set the hammer down and slowly lifted the lid.

As if exhaling, stale old air that smelled of mothballs and dust filtered through the room. Shining her light over the contents there appeared to be several dark dresses folded prostrate in prayer. She pulled one out after another, some with front bustles and puffy sleeves, others more tailored, skirts straighter, some with pin stripes and V-necks, one purple, one grey- and yellow-striped.

Once the dresses were all out she could see there were several other items on the bottom. A set of silver spoons and a coffee cup made of glass with solid silver holders, old fashioned opera glasses, and a bundle of letters.

The letters were what she was most excited about. She untied the very old string, pulled off the top note—careful not to rip the crisp yellowed paper—and began reading.

"Dear Clara, *January 1884*

These are a few of my precious things that I wish for you to hold for me. If I do not get it sent off in time, quietly send it by boat yourself.

I am always your devoted sister,

Connie

She counted the remaining letters. There were three. One from a Doctor Baldwin explaining the treatment for an ear infection. The second and third written in a hurried hand. Had she seen it before? She carefully opened them and began reading.

Fenimore,

What you saw was nothing more than friends buoying each other up in a time of stress. Your silence scares me and I know not of your next move. Dearest Fenimore, answer my letters for I am sick to think that you are angry with me. Haven't we been the closest of friends these ten years? Answer me at once that you are fine, that you are not getting any unwarranted notions in your mind? I am worried about you. More worried than I ever have been. You know that if I could, I would be on the first train to see you. I would take you for long walks along the River Arno, I would buy you a hot cross bun. We would finish our bird book. But that is not possible. My work forces me to be away. I have obligations. So do you. Finish your book. I promise I will visit as soon as it is done. Most possibly in the late fall.

Henry

Hadn't the previous letters been addressed to Henry, but from another woman? Could these things belong to the same Henry? She anxiously unfolded the last letter. It was written on hotel paper in short hurried sentences. There was a date of November 30th.

Fenimore,

Unfortunately my schedule has made it impossible for me to travel until after the new year. Congratulations on finishing your book. It is sure to be another raging success amongst your fans. I am busy at work on the play and cannot say I am having as much success. Deadlines are coming and I am falling behind. Furthermore, I cannot stop my work to check in on you like I have in the past. All I ever said to you was true. Do not be angry with me. My work is my passion. As is yours. We are the same. In the end.

One last theing. I ask that you be rid of our letters, particularly the ones that relate to our friend Mr. Harris. Will you do this for me?

Henry.

Elle frowned. Where had she heard the name Fenimore?

It had been just recently. She thought for a minute and then remembered the book Mr. Gordon had given her. She grabbed her backpack, found the book, and flipped it open to the first page. She read aloud. "Constance Fenimore Woolson spent her childhood years between Ohio and Mackinac Island in upper Michigan off Lake Huron."

She turned the page and stopped abruptly when she saw a familiar face staring back at her. The picture from the bird book. The one of the pretty young woman. The caption read, "A well-established author in her time, she lived overseas for many years. In January of 1894 Constance fell from a window to her death while living in Italy."

Her hands fumbled nervously as she turned the pages and continued reading, scanning the pages until she found exactly what she was looking for.

"After Constance arrived in Italy she became acquainted with fellow writer Henry James. The two had a very close friendship for fourteen years." She pulled up Henry James on her phone and read a few paragraphs about the American writer who spent most of his career living overseas.

Elle leaned against the trunk and surveyed the items. How did all of these things end up here? Did they belong to Constance? And if they did, how did her aunt get them? And what about the silver stamp box? Had that belonged to Constance as well or had it been Henry James'? How did it fit into this story? She skimmed the pages of Mr. Gordon's book until she landed on a paragraph that stopped her cold. "Woolson believed in posthumous telepathy. She believed the dead, 'whose acute feelings had pervaded their rooms, could make themselves felt there.' She once told a friend that she believed one's soul remained in their belongings, particularly their clothing, to return again and live through another."

These things: spoons, coffee cups, dresses. Could a piece of one's soul remain in them? She held up a dress to her face and breathed in the dust, the past, the stories untold. The fabric became intertwined in her fingers. Her heart wanted to burst. She was a child who's toy or silver spoon had been unearthed in a garden, the feeling was an intense physical longing that nearly choked her. Light from her phone created shadows that danced across the ceiling. Before she could think about it, she pulled the t-shirt over her head and slipped from her jeans and quickly stepped into the salmon colored satin dress with Ostrich feathers that exposed her porcelain shoulders. It was tight at the waist and wide at the bottom and fit like a glove. The lace sleeves caressed her bare skin like lover's arms.

She closed her eyes. A song filled her ears. She hummed along, the unfamiliar melody. Chimes accompanied her raspy tone as a scene danced through her mind. Water boats, dinners, flickering candles. Eyes that pierced her soul. Eyes she loved and knew and missed and admired. Eyes that watched her as she glided across the room and glowed with hidden desire, matched only by her own. A strong hand led her along a dimly lit hallway, the voice, deep and rich. She swooned to the sounds of rippling laughter, glasses chiming, china tinkling. He led her to the dance floor. His lips, soft, prominent as he spoke. His voice, hypnotizing.

"Fenimore," he whispered. "My dove,"

"Yes?" Elle said aloud. Then silence. Elle's eyes flung opened. She stumbled forward in the darkness and called again. "Hello?" But the voice was gone, as was the music, the laughter. Only the hum of the wind whirling through the leafy trees and the nearby chimes filled her ears.

Light bled from beneath the heap of dresses on the ground. Nervously, she pulled them back to find her phone light shining up towards the ceiling. She sighed in relief and swiped her phone. She looked down to find she was still wearing the dress. Had she been dancing? Sleepwalking? Had she really heard voices and music? *What is happening to me?* She glanced at the time on her phone. It was past three in the morning. Was she going crazy?

She couldn't get the feathery costume off fast enough, telling herself that she didn't believe in ghosts and that she was just tired and had probably fallen asleep. But the fact she'd put the dress on? There was no explanation for that. She changed back into her wet clothes and hurried to the doorway, anxious to leave. She caught sight of the silky material sprawled across the floor. It reminded her of the poor woman who had fallen to her death. She couldn't leave it like that so she gathered the dress into her arms and ran down the stairs. As she opened the front door she was met by wind and rain. She'd have to stay put a little longer. At least until the storm blew over. She shut the door, laid down on the couch, and eventually fell asleep.

The sun was just peaking through the windows when she awoke. Anxious to get back to the hotel before anyone saw her, she drew the partially dried hoodie over her head and stuffed the dress into her backpack. There was so much dress that the extra ruffles spilled from the opening, and she couldn't zip it up. She climbed on her bike, careful to maneuver around the loose sticks and debris littered across the road.

Just as she entered town she spotted two people walking towards her on the boardwalk. To her surprise it was Jace and Patricia. It was early, too early for them to have met by chance. *They must be more than friends* she thought.

Embarrassed to catch them together at such an early hour, especially when she looked like this, and secretly ashamed for thinking Jace liked her in any way other than just a client, she made a sudden, miscalculated and unfortunate turn up a hill to avoid them only to find a horse and buggy coming straight at her. She swerved to get out of the way, but her tires got caught up in some storm debris, flinging her over the handlebars and landing her on the pavement.

"Whoa!" the man steering the buggy called out. Footsteps ran to her side.

"Elle, are you okay?" It was Jace. Next to him stood a man with a thick mustache, the carriage driver.

She got on her hands and knees, her red face down as she attempted to stand. "I just caught some stuff in my wheels. It was completely my fault."

"You have to look where you are going. Especially when the roads are covered in branches," the man barked at her. He turned to Jace. "These tourists don't pay a bit of attention. Think horses can stop on a dime just cause they aren't cars."

"It's okay Mr. Pritchard. She's a friend of mine. It was just an accident."

The man, huffed and then returned to his carriage while saying quickly, "Glad it wasn't worse," before snapping the reins and continuing down the hill.

"It really was my fault," she insisted as Jace helped her up.

"Don't worry about it. Are you hurt anywhere?"

She looked down and dusted herself off. Her hands were the only things scraped. "Just my pride."

Jace noticed the silky dress tossed on the road and picked it up, it's sleeves dripping from the puddle it had landed in. "Is that the dress you bought with Patricia?" Elle limped over to the dress, the humiliation rising like froth.

"It's just some of my aunt's things." She did her best to avoid eye contact as she took it from him. *Could this be more embarrassing?* she wondered as she stuffed it back in the bag.

"Wow!" Patricia had finally caught up to them. She was wearing yoga pants and a thin exercise jacket. Her auburn hair in a high pony tail. She examined the fabric with her slender hands. "Nice dress."

"It was my aunt's." Elle attempted to zip the bag. She didn't want them to know that she'd been at the house, let alone that she'd gotten into the trunk. And she really wished she weren't wearing such baggy sweats. She felt like an oversized sofa next to Patricia.

"You should wear it to the costume ball tonight," Patricia said.

She didn't want to bother explaining again that she was leaving today so she just nodded in agreement. "Well, I gotta get going. Thanks for your help." She hopped back on her bike, ignoring her stinging road rash and offering them a carefree smile.

"Are you sure you're okay?" Jace called again as she

attempted to turn the pedals with shaking legs.

He apparently wasn't falling for her fake smile.

"Fine," she called with the wave of her hand still not looking them in the eye. She did not slow down until she safely turned the corner.

Letters are among the most significant memorial a person can leave behind them.~ Johann Wolfgang von Goethe

Constance

January 1882 Rome

Henry has written me four letters in as many weeks, Constance wrote to her sister back in the States. *I think it is solely because he is homesick as he has been away to Massachusetts since October and he only wishes to see envelopes with foreign stamps on them. I refuse to be drawn in.*

Her letters to Henry were frequent and filled with false scorn.

If you didn't say any very horrible things in Florence and Rome, you are mentioning a few from Washington – when you tell me my letter was full of amiable elements. I don't think a letter could be described in a more depressing way.

Henry wrote back soon after, but his letter took a serious turn. His mother had just died.

It is with heaviness that I bring you such news. I was hoping to get back to Europe soon, especially to Rome, but one cannot always plan these things out. I must go where the wind of need blows.

Constance's voice was tender when she wrote him next:

I know about the desolation one feels at losing a parent. But death to me is not frightening. I do not fear death or even dread it. To me it is only a release; and if, at any time, you should hear that I have died, always be sure that I was quite willing, and even glad to go.

Henry returned with a shorter letter soon after:

Do not be so morbid as to speak of death. I hope to see my father and sister settled in Boston soon before returning in the spring to England, as soon as May. I have another piece of news to share with you, but I pray you keep it a secret. I have dramatized Daisy Miller and have three theater managers currently looking at it.

Constance returned with her promise:

It is under lock and key, and no one has seen it or heard of it; or shall ever see it or hear of it. I am a very faithful sort of person in such respects. I can't wait to read it!

In the spring he sent her a copy of the play. Henry's next letter was less sure of himself:

No one wants to put on the play. I am frustrated with it all. Have you had a chance to read it? Whatever happened to your novel? Have your furious little fingers finished in record time to please your publishers?

Dear Henry,

I have been in Baden-Baden trying to meet a most unrealistic delivery date for my novel. I feel that I am always obliging editors who have no idea the pains it takes to write a novel. Thirteen hour days for eight consecutive weeks. Truly, from five in the morning until six in the evening. I do hope to get to 'Daisy' soon. Please forgive me that I have not had the strength up until now. I promise a full and honest report.

She sent him that honest and personal report by post in late summer.

You know I have found fault with you for not making it more evident that your heroes were in love with the heroines; really in love. There is no trouble about that here! Winterbourne is more in love with Mme de Katkoff—or has been—than any of your other men have been in love before. It has the true ring.

Though Constance kept her personal feelings on Winterbournes similarities to Noel, a character in her latest novel, she did add that, *Winterbourne will be a good husband.* What she did not say was that he was also like her Noel. He would treat Daisy with deadly kindness and nothing more.

She went on to confess that she had been ill with the

American lung-fever. *I am now in Dresden where I hope to recuperate through August.*

Henry answered with a pleading: *Pray do me the favor not to recommence. I too know what it is to be alone and ill while abroad.*

She sat at her small writing desk in her close quarters, still holding his letter as she stared out the window. "Not to recommence," she echoed with a far-off look in her eye. She was surrounded by her spoils from her travels: a picture of yellow jasmine, a weighing machine, etchings of Bellosguardo and the Arno, her favorite glass cups with the pewter handles. And yet they brought her little comfort. She was exhausted and homesick. And she was tired of being alone. So very alone.

There never was a woman so ill fitted to do without a home as I am. I am constantly trying to make temporary homes out of impossible rooms at hotels and pensions. I never give up, though I know it cannot be done; I keep on trying. Like...the beaver I saw in the Zoological Gardens here in Dresden, who had constructed a most pathetic little dam out of a few poor fragments of old boughs. I stood and looked at that beaver a long time. He is an American – as I am! But I suppose you know nothing of beaver hats. You don't know beavers, or prairies; you only know – Mme de Katkoff.

It might have seemed she was jealous, and maybe she was. After all he had trailed a Mrs. Van Rensselaer in Venice and everyone knew she was a worldly-wise woman. 'Research' he had called it. They spent much time together, and it seemed to have paid off as he had, for once, really written a character that seemed to know love. "Research, pfhh," she said in disgust as she sealed the envelope and sent off her last letter, feeling frustrated with Mr. James.

"I wish to pack up and leave," she said to her dear friend the doctor as they visited over tea the next day. Doctor Baldwin sympathized and even shared in her bouts of depression and they had become close friends.

"But there is something that keeps you here in Europe."

He eyed her carefully. "What is it? Or should I say, who is

it?"

Constance stared out the window. Yes she wished to go home, but she knew she wouldn't leave anytime soon. Her desire for seclusion, possible in the European lifestyle, outweighed her homesickness. "I can't say it is only one person. I do wish to know all the best people in the world, and only those.

"You need to meet new people. Come with me to Paris. I have a friend, a Mr. King I'd like to introduce to you."

So Constance joined the good doctor and his wife in October as they traveled to Paris to meet Mr. King. Dr. Baldwin had said only wonderful things about the man, but when she actually met him at the Grand Hotel she was less than impressed. He was old and frumpy and the dullest man she'd met so far in Europe. They were to meet for an early super. As she descended the stairs for dinner wearing a dark purple dress cinched at the waist with puffy sleeves and an ivory brooch on her lapel, none other than Henry James appeared at the bottom of the stairs.

A large smile broke across her face and she nearly stumbled in surprise. Henry took a drink of his brandy, watching her. Once she reached the bottom other guests surrounded her making it impossible to speak with Henry. The doctor was suddenly at her side, and with him an older unattractive man, the dull Mr. King. She knew in an instant she wouldn't be interested, especially with Henry just a few feet away. When she could get away from her 'intended,' she walked over to where Henry had been standing, but he was gone and all that remained was his brandy cup, empty on a side table.

The next chance she had to see Henry he offered but two words of compliment to Constance and spent most of the evening conversing with other guests. Constance clung to Mr. King, though personally she had no interest in him of any sort. This had a two-fold purpose: to keep the dear doctor happy, and to keep Henry from thinking that she was torn with grief because of his lack of affection. If he wasn't interested in her company, she wasn't interested in his.

When Henry announced that he would be leaving in the morning, Constance put on airs and talked excitedly of the wonderful time she had had with Dr. Baldwin and Mr. King, "And wasn't it a shame poor Henry couldn't join them, but that is the way for the big fish of the world." Then she bade him a quick ado, as easily as if he were just a man and walked off, careful not to look back. It wasn't until she was alone in her small hotel room hours later that she yanked the brooch from her lapel and threw it onto the dressing table, cracking the ivory face in half.

A few weeks later she received a letter from Henry. She read and reread it as she sat at her dressing table combing her long hair with her favorite silver brush given to her by Clara on their last trip to Switzerland.

My father passed in December and I was forced to cross the Atlantic once again. As executor of his estate I have a mess to untangle in reference to my father's less than favorable will towards his son in whom he is determined to shun for fear that he has 'too much'. It is a punishment of ill-will that I'm afraid can never be righted, but I will do what I can.

Constance wrote back immediately, her earlier frustration in Paris already forgotten:

I am sorry to hear of your father. I know your brother William always wished to please him. Has the wrong been righted? How is your sister Alice? You have been gone nearly nine months. Perhaps you have rediscovered your paternal roots and wish to stay on? I, on the other hand, have returned to Florence and have been welcomed back by dear friends, who have helped me feel less displaced. Please tell me of the news of the great United States. Send me a description of all the places you visit.

Henry quickly returned a letter:

Do not think that Washington has ties on me. I wish to return as soon as possible, once my sister Alice is taken care of. She is worse than before and needs a constant companion in her sorry state. I almost feel married to her, but I have no intention to remain with my sister. As for me, please send a visual picture of the Bellosguardo so that I may keep going in Boston. I want full descriptions, including the smells, and the company.

Constance wrote back on the seventh of May:

Your letter was forwarded to Venice as I moved on the twentieth of April and am only now able to sit and rest. I offer, in place of the Bellosguardo, a picture of my two large, low-ceilinged rooms on the top floor of the Palazzo Gritti-Swift. A thrillingly dilapidated yellow palace, in which I live directly above the English aesthete Arthur Symonds. So you can picture it, I shall describe my little palace. There are two arched windows with small balconies overlooking the Grand Canal. They are so small they serve as sofas with freshly covered red cushions next to a red ledge. Out one window there is a commanding view of the Riva with its masts. The other window looks out on one of the darkest of emerald-green canals, so narrow the gondolas can only pass by hugging the walls.

I often imagine your future arrival at the winding staircase that leads to the top floor, like one in a lighthouse. A maid would inspect you before I would let you in. And when at last you were in, you wouldn't imagine where to go, so involuted is the hall, with all sorts of inscrutable doors and curtains, and even steps. I wonder sometimes if I should live and die here. It is a delectable sort of place.

Constance tucked the letter under her arm, placed a straw hat on her head and headed out the door. She nodded hello to perfect strangers as she walked, not a common thing for someone as shy as Constance. The weather in Venice was perfect and the smells of blooming roses and vines creeping up the aging buildings floated through the air. She would have to remember that in her next letter

It didn't take long for Henry to reply:

I have held out the prospect of talking over your impulse to return to America. I imagine an Italian church wall as the background to our future talk.

Your letters, she retorted around the first of June, *are better than you are. You are never in Italy. I don't complain; for there is no reason why I should expect to see you, only, don't put in those decorative sentences about 'Italian church-walls.'*

Henry was quick to reply, his tone concerned. *I have written a piece I think you will like, and hopefully feel comfort from. I shall recite it here. 'She has high spirits or low, she is...cold or warm, fresh or wan, according to the weather or the hour. She's always interesting and almost always sad.'*

She wrote back immediately. *Thank you for sharing that piece. I know it by heart, as though it were my very self. The lagoons and still canals send their love to you. They wish you were here. And so do I.*

Wanting to lighten the mood and take attention off her last sentence she added, *I picture passing by Mrs. Bronson's balcony in a gondola to see you eating her sweets or smoking a cigar. That would be something.*

Mrs. Bronson, a kind but busy woman, loved to hobnob with the rich and famous. She even came to Constance to offer praise about her book, *Anne*, and had informed her that she was 'dearest of friends with Mr. James,' and then went on to paint a picture of Henry smoking cigars and eating peppermint chocolates while watching the gondolas go by on Mrs. Bronson's balcony every evening. Mrs. Bronson had insisted Constance join her some evening. In a succeeding letter Constance complained to Henry of the matter:

I do not want to make calls there. There is a woman who often visits Mrs. Bronson and is given to feminine malice and petty jealousy. She is a discontented bore propped by a doting husband.

I don't want to be appropriated, even by such respectable admirers as Mrs. Bronson, or Mrs. Greenough who offered me an apartment on Bellosguardo in Florence. I refused her offer knowing that she would have insisted on excursions and drives. I can't be locked in an engagement for four o'clock. How would I be able to write? Can you understand me?

Henry returned, *I understand you perfectly.*

Perplexity is the beginning of knowledge.
~Khalil Gibran

Elle
The Grand

Back in her hotel room, Elle showered and dressed, tended to her scrapes, and then attempted to remove the mud from the dress before hanging it over the shower curtain to dry. Dressed in shorts and a t-shirt she went to the stamp box and opened it. If it had belonged to Constance or Henry, how had it ended up in Lois' attic? And why had her mom taken it? Hadn't Mr. Gordon said that Lois had been looking for it for years? What was the significance?

Her phone rang. It was Jace. She didn't want to answer. It wasn't just because she saw him with Patricia, well maybe it was. Finally she answered.

"When are you leaving?" Jace asked. He sounded out of breath.

"Tonight, on the five o'clock ferry."

"I think you better change it. Something's happened."

"What's wrong?"

"It's your friend Mr. Gordon. He never came into work this morning. His employee went over and found him dead at the bottom of his stairs.

"Apparently he fell and hit his head."

She gasped and then went on to explain that they had

never met because Mr. Gordon never returned her calls.

"How long can you stay?"

"I don't know." She pace and clicked on her calendar. Her next big meeting was Wednesday. Today was Saturday. She'd have to be back by then. "Probably three days at the most."

"I'll try to get you on a Tuesday flight. Will that be okay?"

"Sure." Her head was spinning. She sat down on the bed. "I just can't believe it."

"When you talked with him did he tell you what you needed to hear?"

Elle frowned. Had she? "No. Not really. Nedra came and there was this funky vibe between the two of them and he got up and left abruptly. And then he never answered his phone after that."

Jace seemed confused. "Nedra? I didn't even know they knew each other. What was it about?"

"I have no idea. But it was obvious they didn't like each other. I can't believe he died! This is terrible. He was the only one that could tell me about the box. Now I don't think I'll ever find out."

"That's the other thing I wanted to talk to you about." It sounded like Jace was walking as he talked. "I did some research about Constance Woolson. You remember the scarab?"

"The green brooch?"

"She believed it had special telepathic powers. That it could bring people back to life again."

Elle remembered what she had read the night before about telepathy. "I read something about that too, but I didn't know she believed the scarab was responsible." She glanced down at the silver box.

"Can you meet me at Mr. Gordon's? I'm helping with the investigation. Then we could talk." There were voices in the background. He pulled away from the phone to speak and then returned and asked again if she could come.

She was already pulling on her shoes. "I'll be right there."

After he gave her the directions she set out on the bike. But getting to Mr. Gordon's house proved difficult as the Lilac Parade was in full swing downtown. Beautiful horse-drawn lilac floats meandered down the crowd-lined streets. Music soared over the crowd as dancers performed, while not too far behind a band blared their folk tunes. In the distance, fort re-enactors in full uniform, some with muskets on their shoulders marched. No matter which way she went roads were blocked on every side. She meandered up side roads and alleyways until she reached the yellow two story surrounded by yellow tape.

"With the parade and all, they're trying to keep this quiet," Jace explained when she finally arrived at the house. He was wearing a camera around his neck.

"You work for the police department, too?"

"It's a little town," he chided. "Just a side job. I do some photography and they hire me to take pictures at crime scenes."

"Was foul-play involved?" Elle asked.

"They don't think so. But they asked me to take photos just in case."

"So how did it happen?" she asked.

"He was older and slow. Probably got tripped up," said Chief Doug Phillips, a fifty something year old man with curly dark hair and a thick greying mustache. Jace introduced them and then Elle told the chief about her last encounter with Mr. Gordon while he took notes.

A young police officer walked out of the house and stopped cold and stared at Elle like he'd seen a ghost. Elle ignored it, or at least tried.

"Sir. Could I speak to you?" the young police officer called to the Chief.

"Excuse me," Chief Phillips said to Jace and Elle as he turned and met with his deputy, who once or twice turned back to look at Elle, who was twisting her hands nervously. What could they possibly be talking about and why did she feel so guilty? When Chief Doug, as he'd been called by the locals for years, returned to her he asked,

"How well did you know Mr. Gordon?"

"I just met him. But he was a friend of my aunt."

"Any reason he would have had a photo of you in his house?"

"What?" She frowned at the idea. Where would he have gotten a photo of her? He said he didn't know Linda had a child. "No. None whatsoever."

The police chief sent the officer back inside. A few minutes later he returned with a small photo in his hands. Chief Doug examined it and then handed it to Elle. "Looks an awful lot like you wouldn't you say?"

Elle recognized the photograph from the book Mr. Gordon gave her. It was Constance. Now she knew why they thought it was her. Even she had seen the resemblance in the attic mirror while trying on the dress. Though she was embarrassed by her behavior, hadn't she even believed she was Constance for an instant?

She handed the photo back to the officer. "This is from a book Mr. Gordon gave me about a nineteenth century writer who lived on the island. Mr. Gordon asked me to read it. I think he was a big fan of hers."

Jace peered over the officer's shoulder to see for himself. "She does look like you," he admitted.

Elle told the officer about how she was supposed to have met him last night but he never returned her call. "Do you think he was already dead?"

"Coroner hasn't set the time of death, but we think it happened sometime last night.

She frowned. Maybe it had just been an unfortunate accident. But if so, it was really bad luck. She had so many things she had hoped to ask him. He was the only one that knew Lois very well. And with them went their secrets.

Jace seemed to sense her frustration. He led her away from the house and said, "I'm sorry about Mr. Gordon. I know how much you were looking forward to meeting with him."

"I just can't believe it!"

"I was thinking, there's a great trail not too far from here. We can pick up some breakfast on the way. Get away from all this."

She stiffened. "It's okay. I'll be fine." The fact that Jace wanted to spend some alone time with her after she saw him with Patricia upset her.

"It's no problem. Really."

"I think I'd be better on my own. Besides, I don't think Patricia would approve." She turned and walked off, though she had no idea what direction she was going. It didn't take long for Jace to catch up with her. He touched her arm and turned her around.

"What does Patricia have to do with this?"

"Jace." She took a deep breath, not wanting to get angry about nothing. And it was nothing. Wasn't it? Had he really done anything wrong? Led her on? Held her hand, kissed her? No. He'd only been nice. And somehow she had misconstrued it to mean something more.

"I appreciate your kindness, but I think we've passed the point of tour guide and tourist. At least for me."

"I'm not trying to be a tour guide. I mean, not really. I want to go...with you."

Elle stared at him. Finally she asked, "What about Patricia?"

"Patricia is just a friend. Truly." He looked confused, so Elle enlightened him.

"Remember this morning? It was like seven in the morning. Did you just happen to meet and decide to take a stroll?"

"I was on my way to work. So was she. It's a small town and you run into people."

A grin crept across his face. "Wait, did you think we'd been together? Like all night?"

Elle remained silent. Jace ran his fingers through his hair, "Oh man, I'm sorry. It's not like that at all between us."

His soft eyes were already weakening her sloppy resolve.

"It's none of my business." She turned to leave.

"Elle. Come on. Let's go for a hike. You need a break and so do I. And it is your business. If you want it to be."

"Are you sure?" She was such a pushover.

"Come on." He walked her to her bike and then hopped on his. After a quick stop at the local café where they ordered Danishes and egg and bacon sandwiches, they rode to the trailhead, locked up their bikes and started up the path.

"So this morning when you saw Patricia and I, had you come from the house?" Jace asked.

Elle bit her lip. She was afraid he was going to ask and she was still dealing with what had happened herself. "I couldn't sleep last night so I rode over there. Then it started raining so I ended up staying the night. Thanks for taking out the fridge. I guess I missed your calls."

"I was worried you were mad about my stepmom and the back taxes thing."

"I was. I am a little. But I suppose you were just trying to help her out."

"Her company has a contract with my company. My partner set it up. I guess I didn't tell you at first because I thought you would think that I was trying to pull some insider job. I should have told you from the start. I'm not close to her. She loves money and talks all day long about ways they could make more of it. My dad was never like that before. He's changed a lot since my mom died."

"That must be hard." Feeling satisfied with his answer she was suddenly anxious to tell him about what she'd learned about Constance. "I did some reading about Constance, too. She had a stamp box just like the one I found."

Jace held an overgrown branch away for Elle to pass and asked, "What is a stamp box?"

"It was used for stamps and envelopes and paper. Anything to do with letters. This is a bigger one than normal. It's almost the size of a jewelry box, but from the mark on the bottom it appears to have been made in Italy in the late eighteen hundreds."

"Does that mean the brooch also belonged to her?"

"Probably. Get this. The book said that Constance received a scarab pin on a trip to Egypt in 1891 by her physician friend, Doctor Baldwin. She held it close to her all her life." She looked up at Jace and asked, "Do you think Lois thought it was important. Too?"

"You said Mr. Gordon was excited to see it," Jace reminded her.

"He was. At least I think so. What else did you learn?"

"That the Egyptians believed the scarab symbolized transformation and immortality and it was often buried with the deceased to help them start a new life."

Jace stopped on the trail and turned back to Elle. "Do you think Mr. Gordon believed that, too?"

"When he first saw me he stared at me like he'd seen a ghost." Then she thought about the scarab and its so-called powers and added, "Do you think Lois was as superstitious as Constance, believing it actually had real power?"

"Maybe. I have to admit, that photo of Constance at Mr. Gordon's place does look like you." Jace picked up a big rock and chucked it off the trail.

"You mean like reincarnation?" Elle gave a false laugh. Even saying it sounded ridiculous.

"Maybe," was all Jace said. They were silent for a few minutes, then Jace asked about Constance. Elle told him about her lifelong friendship with Henry James and how he had been the one to gift her the silver stamp box.

"Were they secret lovers?" Jace asked.

She shrugged. "If they were they kept it very hidden. There's not even a rumor of scandal." She then added, "I don't understand why Lois and Mr. Gordon never got together. If they liked each other, why didn't they get married? And why didn't Linda forgive Lois? All because of a guy?" Elle pulled her hair back to air out her sweating neck.

Then Jace asked, "You don't think they could have just been friends?"

"Sure, why not. I've had lots of friends who were of the

male persuasion. What about you?"

"Yeah, but if they were just friends it was because I wasn't interested in anything else," Jace admitted.

"What about Patricia?"

"Who?"

"Patricia."

"We're friends."

"I know. Tell me about her."

"She teaches yoga at The Grand and we really are just friends," he insisted.

Yoga. "How nice," she stated shortly. She didn't know why this bothered her. She shoved any semblance of jealousy aside and continued with her theory. "Anyway, last night I read that after Constance died Henry came and acted as executor over her things and burned all their letters."

"How do they know he burned their letters?"

She shrugged. "They don't, but the pair kept up a constant correspondence for 14 years and only a handful of letters survived her death. I read that when Henry came to take care of her things, he kept a fire going all the time. Think how easy it would have been to just toss the letters in the fire when no one was looking. Of course, the weather was cold and rainy, so a fire wasn't unusual, but that only made it more convenient."

"So there are no letters?"

"There weren't. Until now."

"What do you mean?"

She told him about the trunk and finding the extra letters and dresses, but kept the way she felt in the dress to herself. They rounded a bend and came upon a small pond, surrounded by wildflowers of every shape and size. Jace and Elle sat down by the bank and pulled out their breakfast. By now Elle was famished and sweat was dripping down her back.

"This place reminds me of a story my mom used to tell me," Elle said taking a bite of her Danish.

"About a little boy who dies and an angel comes to take

him to heaven, but along the way they stop to gather flowers to take to the garden in heaven."

She pointed to a few of the wildflowers growing around the pond. "I always imagined they stopped at a place like this to gather a few buttercups or forget-me-nots or some of those lady-slipper flowers. My mom loved forget-me-nots. They were her favorite flower." It made her think about the journal she'd read and how Mr. Gordon loved them as well.

Jace unwrapped his sandwich. "How does it end?"

"What?"

"Your story with the crippled boy," Jace said taking a big bite.

"The angel takes the boy to a very poor area where there is a dead lily in a pile of garbage and explains that the lily comforted a dying crippled boy. And at the end the boy realizes that the angel was that crippled boy."

"Did your mom always tell you such sad stories?" Jace asked.

Elle sighed. "Come to think of it, yeah. She loved a tragedy. Macbeth, Romeo and Juliet, that airplane movie."

"Airplane movie?"

"You remember, what was it called? Always."

"Oh yeah, that's a killer. What was your mom like?"

"Overprotective. Kind, suspicious, sad. Sure that someone would steal me. But deep down I knew she loved me very much."

"And your dad?"

She shook her head and took a bite of her own sandwich. When she swallowed she answered. "Died in a car accident right before I was born. He had no family and she said that was why we had no relatives. But I always felt like there was somebody out there. And all that time Aunt Lois was here on Mackinac Island." She couldn't keep the disappointment from infiltrating her voice.

A butterfly landed on a cluster of spring beauty wildflowers. Its vibrant yellow and purple polka dot wings sparkled in the sun. When the wind stirred the butterfly flew across the pond.

Jace waded up his wrapper and said, "I read once that when Hans Christian Anderson got discouraged about the hard and disappointing things in life he reverted to his childlike faith and turned it all over to God. I think that's why he wrote so many children's stories. The simple faith of a child could explain everything."

"How did you know he wrote that story?" Elle smiled. He hadn't said a thing when she was telling it.

He couldn't conceal his own smile. "My mom told the same story. They must have learned it at the island school." A bright blue jay landed nearby and pecked at the pebbly ground for food.

"Maybe that's how we'll solve this mystery about Lois and Mr. Gordon and Constance Woolson. Revert to childlike faith," Elle said.

Jace studied a flower at his foot. "And turn it over to God." He stood and then helped Elle up.

Easier said than done, Elle thought for she wasn't sure she had faith in anything, let alone an all knowing God, but she kept quiet about it as Jace took her hand to help her over a fallen tree. A few minutes later they entered a clearing where an enormous rock, with ferns growing out of the top like a potted plant, sat in the middle of a field. The late morning sun shone down like gold at the end of the rainbow.

"It's called Friendship Altar," he announced. "It's tradition to come here and pledge your friendship." He hesitated. "I've never brought anyone here."

Elle blushed and tried to deflect by letting out a short laugh. "I'm your first friend?"

"Sounds kind of pathetic doesn't it?"

"It sounds hard to believe. Are you sure you want me to be your first friend?"

"No," he hesitated. "I mean yes. We are friends. I think we've been through a lot in just two days. But you're also a client. It's kinda confusing." He took her hand. Gone was the confident Jace. This one seemed nervous and unsure. It made her almost believe he'd never brought anyone else here.

"I've got an idea. Why don't you join me for dinner tonight."

She gave him a cautious glance. "A business meeting?"

"Dinner. As friends. I want to take you to the ball.

"The ball at the hotel? You don't have to do that."

"I want to. And since Patricia works at the hotel you could ask her about Mr. Gordon. She used to work for him."

Her smile faded slightly, but he didn't seem to notice. "You could wear that dress you found in the attic. Have you tried it on yet?"

"Yeah." She thought about telling him about her experience, but decided to wait. "Did you get my flight changed?"

"Sal is on it. When we get back I'll have her text you the info."

"Well then, I guess I'd be happy to go to the ball with you," Elle said, displaying the first real smile of the day.

Life is made up of sobs, sniffles, and smiles, with sniffles predominating. ~O. Henry

Constance

October 1883 London

"I dare say, Mr. James, your calling me 'worthy' is subject to revenge. I pray you not try to tame me or scale me down." Constance held on to Henry's arm while they walked the edges of Hyde Park one unusually warm and sunny October day. She'd brought with her their shared book of birds hoping to cross a few off the list.

"Then what would you have me call you? Amiable woman? Perfect lady?"

"I am nobody. Who are you?" she teased, borrowing a phrase from Emily Dickinson.

Henry nodded to a couple strolling by. Finally he turned to her and answered. "You are somebody." He paused and touched her chin with his hand. They exchanged a look. A look that Constance could hardly dream to be true.

Then he dropped his hand and began speaking again. "Now, shall we walk to the lake? We might find some interesting fowls."

Constance nodded, feeling undone by his touch. "This is what heaven will be like. You, me, rowing on the lake."

"You might want to reconsider. I'm not much for

rowing."

"That's not what I hear from all your lady friends." She couldn't hold back a grin with the stories she'd recently heard of Henry and a rowboat full of oversized, well-to-do ladies.

"I haven't any lady friends besides you."

She grunted. "Oh Henry! You only have every lady in England worshiping you. In fact, Mrs. Van Rensselaer has moved to Half Moon Street and shall be soon swooning just as she did in Italy."

"You mean the Rensellina?" He scrunched his brow in worry.

Constance rolled her eyes. "Don't try to fool me with that false sense of depravity. You enjoy every moment of it."

Henry chuckled. They walked to Serpentine Lake, where Henry commandeered a rowboat and helped Constance climb in. When they were out a ways Constance asked about his sister.

"Alice is well enough. She plans to stay in London for a time."

"Your life will change dramatically with a sister nearby."

"My life will stay as it is," he said assuredly.

"She will need your assistance."

"The last thing Alice needs is me hovering over her."

"Oh, Henry! You only say that because you hope it. The truth is, you are selfish and do not wish to be bothered."

Henry remained silent. Constance began to regret her harsh speech.

"If I am so truly selfish, why do you enjoy my company so much? You say it all the time," he finally returned.

"Perhaps I am as selfish as you. Perhaps that is why marriage is not an option for either of us. But be that as it may, I don't mind so long as you write as you do, for it is in your writing that I find my true country, my real home. And nothing else ever is—fully—try as I may."

She opened her book of fowls and pulled out her opera glasses from her carrying bag. "Now tell me about what you have been working on these many months."

"Besides devoting nine months to the care of my sister and brothers?"

"Oh Henry. That's right. I judged you too harshly. Though you know that there was a smidge of truth to it."

"I know," he admitted. "Anyway, you ask what I'm writing so I will tell you that I have just turned in an outline of The Bostonians to my publisher.

She spotted a bird with yellow feathers resting in the trees off the bank. "I am very pleased to hear it. Just think! Now that George Eliot and Turgenev are dead you are the foremost living novelist."

"Fenimore, how you puff me up."

She set her opera glass down on her lap to look him square in the eye, "I mean it Henry." A look of surprise and appreciation crossed his bearded face. Henry turned his attention to the book on her lap. "What did you find there?"

"I'm still looking. A small bird with yellow feathers."

"Let me have a look." She handed him the eyeglass. "Ah, yes, I see it. It looks to be a Goldcrest. See it here. Tubby, and round, and no neck." He pointed down to the page. "One of the smallest songbirds in Britain. Listen and you'll hear his song." They were quiet for a moment. "There it is. It sounds like tree, tree, tree."

"The high pitched trill?"

"That's it."

"I hardly hear it, though that's no surprise." She marked off the bird in the book with her pen.

"Did you get the books I sent over?" Henry asked.

"Thank you, yes." She nodded. "Shelley's poems are remarkable."

"Share one with me," Henry insisted.

"I am unprepared, but I do like this one. 'A man, to be greatly good, must imagine intensely and comprehensively; he must put himself in the place of another and of many others; the pains and pleasures of his species must become his own.' I think that is true of any great writer as well."

He rested the oars in his hands. "Tell me another."

"I can't think of another," she answered though it wasn't true. She had spent that very morning pouring over some of his most romantic verses, but she couldn't quote them to Henry. Not yet. Not here. They returned to the boat dock and Henry threw the rope to the dockworker who tied them off and helped Constance out of the boat.

Afterwards, they ate a lunch of vegetable soup and thick, crusty bread at the small restaurant near the park, and then Henry walked Constance home to 116 Sloan Street.

"Will I see you soon?" Constance asked, feeling wild and free from their perfect day.

"I hope. But for now I will be bogged down by my latest project. Try not to mark off all the birds without me."

She frowned. "Of course I shall wait. But for how long?"

"How will I find time to write if I guarantee carriage rides or walks at four o'clock every day?" There was that unmistakable twinkle in his eye. Hadn't she said the same once?

"How you use my words against me. I should call you a tease."

"You may call me your closest friend," Henry kissed her hand and bade her farewell. Constance glided up the steps and into her house with a small smile upon her lips.

***

Henry came to visit Constance late one evening. She had offered to meet him to go bird watching, or take a walk through Kensington gardens, but he had insisted on coming to her place. Constance had noticed that he was more nervous when they were out in public; as if he were about to get caught doing something wrong.

She decided to ask him about it.

"Must we remain so discreet in our friendship? Have we not been writing and conversing for over three years?"

"Fenimore, we have talked at length before and we both agreed that if we are together in public too often rumors will begin."

"And, in reality, it will make even our discreet meetings

impossible. Tongues wag."

"Why do we care about rumors? We are friends and also professionals. Is it because I am a woman?"

"Of course it is because you are a woman. A lovely, perfect woman. And rumors of wedding bells would fly. Connie, I will not marry. I can't. You know that."

"I wasn't asking for marriage." She began rubbing her temples.

"Come," he said softly, patting the seat next to him on the sofa. She sat, but couldn't look him in the eye. The argument was mute. Henry had been quite insistent on this point, but still it frustrated Constance. Could they not find a way to coexist without being man and wife? His fingers gently caressed her temples, softly, as if they recognized they had a fragile bird's egg between them. His warm skin was comforting. She closed her eyes. Henry had always liked her no-nonsense, 'I'll never get married and settle down' attitude that had matched his own. But tonight she was struggling with loneliness. The need for companionship was like a physical ache. The rain didn't help her depression either. It had rained constantly for nearly a month. It didn't make sense for her to be in London in winter, and yet in London she remained, hoping for more time with Henry.

The next time they met was in January at a gala for the Children's Orphanage hospital. The last few months had taken their toll on her as she had experienced tragedy and a severe depression that would have knocked another to their knees. And Henry had been too busy to meet with her. They met in the hall. Almost ran into each other actually. Constance's eyes were glassy as she stared at him with no feeling or emotion.

"You look unwell," he stated.

"I have been unwell." There was coldness to her voicc that scared Henry.

"You should never have come to London. I warned you of the weather and how it would affect your spirits."

She shook her head, "That isn't it. Or all of it. My brother

Charles died in December. They aren't sure why, though I have told you of his certain habits." She had indeed confided in Henry about Charles drinking and his taking to morphine.

This news startled Henry, for he had only received positive notes from Miss Woolson stating she was busy writing. He'd been busy too and hadn't checked in on her. "I had no inkling." He wrapped his arms around her, something he rarely did in private and never in public. "You sweet angel of quiet virtue." His warmth and sincere compassion lightened her burden instantly.

His kindness unloaded a flood of emotion. She dabbed her tear-filled eyes with a hanky. "I have mourned greatly for a brother who was misguided, and lost, and was as lonely and sad as I have ever been."

He kissed her head. "And I have not been here for you."

"You have been busy."

"You suffered with me over Wilky's death in November. And I have left you quite alone." He shook his head.

"I would like to have you near me always. But I do understand that you must write and have your freedom. I feel the same. Yet I feel something missing, too."

"When you started questioning our arrangement, I fled. I am sorry." Henry looked around to see who was watching them. The women were still at dinner and the men had moved to the drawing room to smoke cigars. When it appeared that no one was watching, he whispered for her to follow him, which she did in perfect obedience. They ended up in a coat closet, surrounded by all shapes and colors of furs, the smell of damp animal thick between them.

Henry wiped her tears away and whispered. "My dear Constance. You are lonely and grieving a brother, and as your protector I have failed you. From now on I promise I will come immediately when you are ill. I'll pull you up by your hairpins to make sure you get out and walk, breathe fresh air, whatever it takes to keep you well and writing."

She couldn't help but smile. Henry cared for her. He wished to protect her. "Thank you, Henry."

Later that night she wrote in her journal of her struggles: Though I am alone in a strange country through a long northern winter and unable to work, I rest my soul in England's soft still light. And as the stars glitter above, I think of Charles and I am reminded that all is not lost.

The boundaries which divide life from death are at best shadowy and vague. Who shall say where the one ends, and where the other begins? ~Edgar Allen Poe

Elle

The Grand

"Constance."

Elle sat up. She rubbed her eyes. It was that voice again. She was back in the hotel room. The drapes were closed, the room, stuffy and warm. She'd fallen asleep on the bed. The clock read 4:45 P.M. It was late and she was supposed to meet Jace for dinner at six. She stood up and slowly moved to the bathroom to check on the dress. The water spots had disappeared and the strong mothball scent had lessened. She hurried and dressed, glad to see the gown fit almost to perfection, and then put her hair up in a double French knot. It was 5:45 when she realized she didn't have shoes and had to settle on wearing her leather slip-ons.

As she sat on the bed, her arm bumped against the stamp box and gave her a strong jolt. She jumped back in surprise. Had the box shocked her? She slowly touched it again. It was hot against her fingers. She opened the lid to find the scarab on top of the book, its jeweled eyes staring back at her. She picked it up.

What happened next would be impossible for her to describe to anyone and expect them to believe her. Her fingers clamped around the green brooch like a powerful magnet. She went twisting like she'd been sucked through a straw into a blinding cosmos of white rays. She tried to cry out, but the white light flashed and the rush of wind whisked her into a tunnel of darkness and then silence. Just like that, it was over.

She sat at an unfamiliar hearth lit by the flame of the fireplace with several letters in her lap. There was a great conflict in her heart, like she was about to do something she didn't want to do. Elle didn't know where the letters had come from or who had written them. Suddenly a voice spoke.

"I hate doing this." Her mouth moved, but didn't sound like her voice. It was as if she were looking through someone else's eyes. She caressed the letter on top. *Just one more time*, she thought, as she opened it and reread the last paragraph, her favorite part.

I have imagined what it would be like to hold you in my arms. To caress your neck and touch your cheek. My lonesome dove.

A blush kissed her cheek. "Oh Henry," she whispered sadly. She flicked the letter into the fire and watched it curl and blacken and then ignite into flames and just like that turn to dust. As much as she didn't want to do it she knew it was necessary. She picked up the second letter and reread the middle paragraph.

What is intimacy? What is the touch of a hand? Can you not have as much ecstasy in writing of angst and intrigue? Try it my dear. Touch me sometime and see if it is not less than one of your forbidden love stories. What we do for each other is stretch the other to experience a greater thing than real life. Say no more to me. Am I not a man, after all?

"Are you?" she murmured to herself as she tossed it into the fire. She didn't bother rereading the third letter and flicked it in as well. Elle sensed great frustration and some anger might have been directed to that letter or had it been something even deeper? That of desire, hot as the coals burning black and orange before her?

Suddenly her body went numb and she felt herself being sucked from this unknown place, soaring over the clouds, then darkness, then bright light again.

Elle's eyes shot open, the sounds and feelings—the otherworldliness—were gone in an instant. The room was silent. Too silent. Had she really sat at the hearth and burned letters with the familiar strong writing much like the ones she'd found in the trunk? A phone buzzed in her pocket. She tried to move, but felt dizzy and lightheaded. She glanced down at her hand. It was hot where the scarab had been. It was now laying on the bed.

The phone continued to ring. She felt disjointed, like she'd been dreaming, only it had been more real than any dream she'd ever had. Whatever it was, it was over now, and her phone was unrelenting. She finally got her arms to move and she was able to answer. It was Jace waiting for her in the dining room.

"I'll be right there." She sat up. Her reflection stared back at her. What had happened? Had she passed out? Should she tell Jace? Something about the experience felt so intense and personal that she decided to keep it to herself. At least for now. She said goodbye, smoothed out the loose parts of her hair ,and put some lotion on her red mark to lessen the stinging. Feeling more like herself, she made her way to the lobby.

She was quite conscious of the stares that met her when she entered the lobby wearing the peach Victorian dress. Feeling slightly off after her bizarre dream, she stood in the lobby surrounded by beautiful people in all kinds of dresses and suits and questioned the reality of the moment. Women promenaded in full-length ball gowns while men sported tuxes and fancy canes with extravagantly carved handles. The theme from *Somewhere in Time* sang from the harp, as waiters delivered wine glasses to their guests. Maybe this was a dream as well.

A woman wearing a white and gray pigeon breasted dress and feathered hat and a man in a black evening coat and top hat smiled approvingly. She nodded back, still scanning the room for Jace.

"Can I help you madam?" a smiling dark skinned woman with a Jamaican accent asked.

"I'm meeting someone."

"What is the name? Maybe they have left a message?"

"Jace Stokes."

"I'll be right back ma'am." She turned and walked to the restaurant entrance where the maitre' de stood welcoming a line of guests.

"Elle!" Elle turned to see Patricia walking toward her in a green fitted gown down to her ankles.

Patricia grabbed her hands, a troubled look on her face. "Jace told me about Mr. Gordon. It is such a shock."

"Yes. It is." Patricia had grabbed her hands awkwardly. Elle suppressed a desire to adjust the grip or let go altogether.

"Hey there." The two women turned to see Jace, his hair slicked back, his brow glistening with sweat. Elle dropped her hands. He wore a tan suit that looked very much like the suit that Christopher Reeves wore in *Somewhere in Time*. He held a bowler hat, identical to the one in the movie. "Beautiful dress, Elle."

He turned to Patricia. "Looking great as always. I assume you'll be leading the dancing."

"Yes, of course." Patricia offered a thin smile and then looked at Elle. "I'd be a liar if I didn't say I'm a little jealous that you will have the best dancer on the floor tonight. But I'll be happy to help answer any questions about Mr. Gordon."

"I don't really know what to ask. Did you know him well?"

"I worked for him for a few months when I first moved here. He was very friendly. Very." Her eyes widened.

"Maybe we should find a table first," Jace suggested.

Patricia pointed towards the dining room "I have the perfect one." She led them to a table that offered a view of the lake from the long white porch lined with American flags. "I'll be over in a bit to talk." Then she turned and disappeared.

"It's beautiful here, isn't it?" Jace said, adjusting in his seat. "My mom loved this hotel. Before I came along she worked here. She did all kinds of odd jobs. When I was sixteen I worked in the ice cream shop downstairs. I met the most interesting people from all over the world."

Just then an older woman wearing an old-fashioned, cobalt blue ball gown and dangling, diamond earrings approached their table. "That dress is exquisite. Where did you find it?" she asked Elle.

"It belonged to my aunt. I have no idea where she got it."

"It's so authentic looking."

Elle smiled tiredly. The dream had really taken it out of her. "I'm pretty sure it's the real deal."

The woman gasped. The man, presumably her husband said, "That must be over a hundred years old."

"I'd say it's Victorian," the woman countered. Elle was uneasy with the attention. What would they say if she told them it had belonged to Constance Woolson? She kept her lips tightly closed.

"I hope to see you later. I want to have a closer look at that dress!" The woman patted her shoulder and the gentleman winked and said, "You two lovebirds enjoy your dinner."

"Oh, we're not—" Elle started to explain, but they had already gone.

Jace leaned forward. "In all the craziness I failed to state how stunning you look. For some reason I don't see Lois dressing like that." He reached for the menu. "I hope you don't mind Patricia joining us. I mentioned your concern about Mr. Gordon and she offered to tell you what she knew."

"Oh that's fine." Elle's head throbbed. It felt like she'd taken a really long afternoon nap. She might as well go to bed for as much fun as she'd be. Finally, their waiter arrived and they moved on to the menu. Elle ordered the herb crusted beef medallion buffalo bolognese with porcini sauce and Jace ordered the baked Mackinac whitefish with roasted marble potatoes and kafir lime sauce. While they waited for their food they chit chatted about life on the island. She was curious about his suit choice and said as much.

"Did you borrow it from your dad?" she teased.

"I told you he is obsessed. He thought the suit was magical. I won't tell you how many 1979 pennies he owns."

What would he say if she told him of her experience? Should she tell him about what happened in the attic and then again today when she put the dress on? As much as she wanted to tell him, she didn't dare. What if he didn't believe her? He might think she's crazy and walk away for good. The thought about her being crazy gave her pause. Lois had spent time in a mental hospital. Had she had the same experience? Her forehead began to perspire.

Just then Patricia showed up. She took the chair closest to Jace and rested her thin arms on the table. "So what can I tell you about Mr. Gordon?"

"What was he like? Did he have any odd beliefs or habits or anything he seemed obsessed with?" asked Elle.

"Wow, that's a lot. I just thought you wanted something for a eulogy." Patricia rearranged the silverware next to her empty plate and said, "He was a nice guy. Kind of private, but when you got to know him he was very thoughtful. He asked me out once. I couldn't believe it. The man could have been my father. That was when I quit. But as far as weird habits? He had a few weird ideas."

"What kind of ideas?" Jace probed.

"He was big into reincarnation. I swear he ordered every book on the subject. Once he even asked me what I thought about it. And he was serious." She looked from Jace to Elle and asked, "Is that what you want to know?" Her eyes shifted suspiciously between them as if she was being set up for something. "That's all I know about him. Just an old bachelor with no friends and few acquaintances."

She looked nervously over her shoulder and stood. "Miss Holly is looking at me. I better get back to work." Patricia walked off without looking back at them.

Elle was about to ask him what he thought of Mr.

Gordon being interested in reincarnation when they were interrupted by the arrival of their rich smelling food. The waiter set the hot plates of steaming food in front of them and then walked off. Elle took a deep breath. "Wow, that smells so good."

"You ordered my favorite meal," Jace admitted.

"Why didn't you order it?"

"I thought this way we could share. You said you liked seafood."

"I'm glad you said something or I would have eaten the whole thing without offering you one bite."

Jace looked on both sides of him. "If you haven't noticed yet, people can't take their eyes off you."

She laughed it off, "I think it's the feathers. There are probably rules about this many feathers on a dress. I may have PETA after me soon."

"Mackinac Island isn't famous for its extreme groups, unless you call the National Quilters of America an extreme group. They hold their convention here every summer."

"Maybe it's my bare shoulders. I do feel a bit naked."

"The men are staring at your shoulders, the women are staring at the dress."

When they finally sat back in their chairs, practically as stuffed as the feathered creature on her dress once was. Elle asked where he'd met Patricia.

"Yoga class." When Elle gave him a funny look he explained. "Nedra wanted to try it out, but she didn't want to go alone so Dad insisted I come with her. I later figured out she was trying to set me up with Patricia."

"Are either of you interested in dessert?" the smiling Jamaican waiter interrupted, presenting them with the menu.

"I may have to unbutton this dress in order to dance." Elle admitted as she perused the menu. They decided on a roasted pineapple and cherry brioche bread pudding to share, and then opted for a walk through the museum in the basement before returning to the ballroom.

The museum held mementos and photographs from the

movie production, including the suit, bowler hat, and lots of pictures on set. They stopped in front of the hotel replica that played the movie soundtrack. It seemed like a good time to broach the subject of Mr. Gordon.

"So what do you think about Mr. Gordon being obsessed with reincarnation?"

"Might explain his obsession with Constance. My buddy told me there was a whole shelf dedicated to her in the house. Books, magazine articles."

"But it doesn't explain why he was so obsessed with her."

"Maybe it was just her picture. The guy that wrote *Somewhere in Time* was obsessed with an early actress named Maude Adams. That's how he got the idea for the book."

"Maybe." She took a deep breath and then asked her next question, "Do you believe everyone has a soul that can go on existing after death? Maybe even in another person?"

He admitted, "I've never thought about it."

She glanced down at her palm that still glowed red. Would he think she was crazy? "I hadn't either until now," she agreed.

But it was Jace that asked her the next question. "If you could be reincarnated, who would you be?"

She was surprised that he was making a game out of it. "Do you think it is so much of a choice?"

"I don't think it is really possible, so we can say anything we want, but if it were a choice, what would yours be?"

"Well, it would have to be a future character, right? We can't travel back in time to be reincarnated, can we?" she asked.

He thought about this for a minute. "I think I'd want to know what I was getting into if I was going to do this whole living thing again. So let's say that, yes, you can travel in the past. Who would you pick?"

"Joan of Arc," she said quickly.

He laughed out loud. "Really? Burned at the stake sounds interesting to you?"

"Sounds excruciating. But honorable. What about you?

Who would you pick?"

"I'd keep it closer to current times. Running water, even toilets would be nice. Maybe John F. Kennedy."

"Assassination? You're as morbid as I am."

"I guess it's not as much about their death as it is their life."

"Exactly."

"Reincarnation," he said quietly. The word hung heavy around them like a rain cloud. How could she tell him that she thought—though she wasn't sure— that she had been Constance for a few minutes? Would he say that she was getting caught up in the *Somewhere in Time* idea except it was the Henry and Constance saga?

She shrugged. "It's an interesting theory." And left it at that.

As iron is eaten away by rust, so the envious are consumed by their own passion. ~Antisthenes

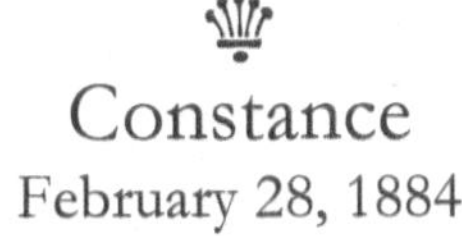

Constance
February 28, 1884

Surrounded by London elite, Constance stood in her new, crepe, black dress with V-shaped waistline scanning the crowd for Henry's familiar top hat. The theater was awash in the newest electric lamps, creating an unnaturally bright atmosphere in the lobby filled with dignitaries and royals mingling together, but alas, no Henry. She had worked extra long to get her hair just right and had even worn the new dangling earrings that matched her brooch. She tried not to look out of place, as she fiddled nervously with her new silk fringe handbag embroidered with a dragonfly she had brought from Venice.

Finally, the crowd parted, and Henry James, looking dashing in his long tails and bow tie, stood in the center of a group of women. Constance couldn't help but grin. He was telling some fabricated story no doubt. It was time for her to rescue him from his entourage. She started towards him but just then the new lights flickered and went out. There was a collective gasp throughout the crowd, mingled with a few high pitched screams. She froze in place.

Within a few seconds the lights flashed on, and then off, and finally on for good. There was a collective sigh. "All's well," the curator called to calm the frightened patrons. Constance spied Henry and almost laughed out loud. The women who had all been listening to his amazing story were now hugging him on all sides.

"Oh, Henry, you poor creature," she whispered under her breath. She saw him place an arm around a much older woman, probably very beautiful in her youth, but now well into old age, her beauty, that fickle friend, had deserted her.

"Henry," Constance called to get his attention.

"Miss Fenimore Woolson. You are a fan of Othello, also?" Henry said.

"And of Salvini," she admitted with a smile. Salvini was a famous Italian actor.

"No doubt fine on the eyes I hear."

She laughed. She was feeling particularly confident tonight. Maybe even pretty. She smiled at Henry like one of her heroines might smile in one of her stories.

"Do you have a seat?" he asked.

"I was just about to get one from the ticket window when the lights went out." It was partially true. She would have bought a ticket if she hadn't found Henry first.

"No need. You will take mine," Henry said. The old woman frowned; her deep lines around her mouth revealing her great displeasure.

He took the older woman by the arm. "May I introduce you to a fellow American writer, and a very good one at that: Miss Constance Fenimore Woolson, grandniece of the famous James Fenimore Cooper."

"Pleased to meet you," Constance said, holding out her hand. The older woman nodded grimly, but refused Constance's extended hand. Henry didn't seem to notice as he took each woman by the arm and announced, "Come ladies," and led them through the curtain to Henry's private booth. He showed them their seats and then disappeared to find an extra chair for himself.

The elderly actress turned to her and with comic rudeness said, "I am sorry Mr. James has introduced you to me. I shall be obliged to tell you, now, that I will not speak to you or look at you, or be conscious of your existence even, during the entire evening." She then turned back to the stage with a huff.

Constance's mouth fell open in disbelief at the woman's boldness. While she did her best not to let the woman's rudeness affect her, it felt no worse than Henry's blindness to it. For, true to her word, the woman did not look at her the entire performance. If it hadn't been discouraging enough to go to the opera alone, and then have to share Henry's attention, the woman had been very harsh. She was now more depressed than ever. Perhaps she would quit London and go back to Italy. But Italy held nothing for her if Henry were not there to enjoy it. What she really needed was to quit Henry altogether and go back to America. Back to the everglades of Florida. But she knew she wouldn't. She was long past that now.

As soon as the play was over, Constance bid Henry a tense goodbye, said nothing to 'Mrs. Old-body', and stormed out of the theater. Her face was flushed; her eyes glowed like red coals. Whatever research he was doing was not worth the cost of spending one more second with that weathered old carpet bag.

"Fenimore!" It was Henry's voice that called her, but she refused to acknowledge him as she was too angry and didn't want him to see. After all, it wasn't his fault exactly that he chose to mingle with rude people.

She called for her driver, and a man went to fetch him.

"Connie," Henry took her elbow in his firm hand and turned her to face him. "I only told you I would be coming to the theater, not that we would go together. Mrs. Kemble is old and feeble. Do you expect me to leave her to fend for herself?"

"And rich." The words burned off her tongue. Her anger was only muffled by the carriages passing by. "I must congratulate you on keeping me from all of your London acquaintances."

"What do you mean? I introduced you." He stepped in closer and whispered, "Do not make a scene."

That's right. It's all about appearances, she thought, but did not say. Instead she said, "You are the one holding me back from my carriage." Her voice was calm, but underneath was a river of currents and Henry knew it.

"Will you tell me what happened?"

She looked beyond Henry's shoulder where the opera crowd was beginning to spill from the building. "Apparently, I ruined Mrs. Kemble's night by taking your seat. She told me so herself."

"No!"

"Yes. Now I must go. Heaven forbid the socialites of London know that we are intimate friends." Her mocking tone was biting.

"Fenimore." He seemed shocked. But his moment of compassion was quickly lost as the patrons filled the spaces around them. He let go of her arm and took a step backwards. "Go home, get some rest and think on this a little. I will call on you." She held her head stiff, unwilling to let him see how hurt she felt as she climbed in and shut the door before the driver could do it.

She refused to look out the window as they drove away, so she didn't know if he watched her leave or if he had already turned back to find his dear old actress friend, Mrs. Kemble. "Oh, yes, I will 'think on this'," she muttered, raking off her gloves and slumping into the soft velvet seat of the carriage. She felt no better than she did before she spoke to Henry. If anything, she felt worse. She was used to people not respecting her as a writer merely because she was a woman, but this had fired her up more than usual. Perhaps it had been the woman's total disregard for her as a human being. Perhaps it was all the rain. Perhaps it was how oblivious Henry was in regards to her affections. He was always with a woman. What had she expected?

Something romantic. That's what. Silly, stupid, romantic Constance. She needed to stick to her stories.

When she had heard that the Italian actor, Salvini was performing in Othello, she had told Henry she planned to attend. She knew he would be there as well and secretly hoped he would invite her to join him. She hadn't many friends with whom to sit and had daydreamed of being publicly seen on Henry's arm at last. She was convinced that if the lady had known she was a 'dear friend' of Henry's and not just an obscure writer from America, she would have never spoken to her the way she did.

Once home, she removed her wet, wool coat and hung it on the rack near the fireplace. Everyone had gone to bed, but she was too upset to sleep so she threw two logs on the fire to warm her cold hands. Soon after there was a short knock at the door and was surprised to find Henry standing in the rain, with only his coat and hat to protect him.

"May I come in?" he asked.

She opened the way for him to pass. He pulled off his soaked coat and hat and hung them on the rack next to hers and then walked to the fire. Rubbing his hands over the flame he asked, "Did she really tell you that she was sorry I introduced you?"

"And that she would not even look at me the entire night." Constance quoted. "She was so disappointed to not have your company all to herself. What she had planned that I ruined is certainly a mystery."

He turned to her, his face earnest as he spoke. "But you do understand that I didn't have anything to do with her awful behavior or her whimsical daydreams."

"That is why I didn't want to talk to you about it. It isn't all your fault that you mingle with despicable creatures."

He laughed out loud. "She was a green-eyed monster towards your beauty," he said, stealing a line from Shakespeare.

"Harry, do not patronize me. She did not know me from Othello's Desdemona. If we are dear friends, as you are constantly reminding me, then why must we tiptoe around with such great discretion?

"What is wrong with being more public? Are you ashamed of me?"

"Of course not. At every chance I talk up your good name."

"Then take *me* to the opera." She added slowly, "As your guest."

"But don't you see? There is no fear in Mrs. Kemble. She is old and no one would ever talk of scandal while I help her to her seat. But you and I out on the town even a few times would disrupt our close friendship. I find solace in you and you find solace in me and we have much more freedom, comme c'est." He brushed his fingertips along her brow. Constance closed her eyes. The feel of his touch was heavenly. He held the tip of his finger over the bridge of her nose for several seconds. The intimacy was as real as anything they'd ever shared.

Finally he slowly dropped his hand, but did not move away, "And because we are discrete, the time will come when we will be rewarded."

"I'm sorry, Harry. I let my vanity get the better of me tonight. I shall be patient. I shall be... discreet."

Their hands hung close, their fingers touching. "Our freedom rests in our words. Words meant only for us."

"Yes...in our words," she repeated, less sure of them than he was.

•••

"Have you ever seen such a wind?" Henry called to Constance who gripped his wool coat in an effort to keep from blowing away. It was the fiercest wind either had ever seen.

"It's deafening," she said.

"It's cataclysmic," he topped.

"What? I can't hear a thing!" she yelled, laughing.

"It's all the more amazing that the whole thing hasn't fallen down because of it!" he yelled over the howling winds that tugged at Constance's bun and whipped at their overcoats. It was September, and the sky was as blue as a topaz ring, yet it was colder than a Northeastern storm in February.

They were visiting the charming historic town of Salisbury, England for a few weeks and had agreed they should see one of the Seven Wonders of the World: Stonehenge. And a wonder it was, though more for the fact that it was still standing after the vicious wind than for its impressive rock formations. Instead of picnicking on the plains, they returned to the carriage under the protection of an overhanging cliff and dined on Michaelmas goose and bread pudding. Afterwards they attended a play in a hall that Henry described as being 'not much better than a barn.' It might have been true, but Constance had enjoyed herself enough that she didn't wish to disparage the small village.

"I find it charming in a country sort of way." Constance insisted with a pleasant smile as they made their way out of the theater. She slipped her arm through his. "It was well done."

"In a cow and chicken sort of way," he said, once again using her words against her. She lightly squeezed his arm and laughed. He always made her laugh.

Henry's carriage slowly made its way back to Constance's hotel. The streets were desolate, allowing them to take advantage of their seclusion on their journey home.

"How are your hands? Have they thawed from earlier?" Henry asked, taking her hands gently in his and rubbing them together though they had been many hours since their coldest state.

"I must admit the weather was not what I had hoped for a picnic."

"Welcome to England!" he mocked. "You did get to see the great Stonehenge. That is something."

"Yes, it is." She glanced down at her hands cradled in his and wished they would remain there a few minutes more.

As if he heard her, Henry released her hands and changed the subject. "I am told we will be sharing a space in the latest publication of *Stories by American Authors*," he said reminding

Constance of their shared success as authors, as if he were trying to build up that wall that was so quickly crumbling between them.

She nodded. Her story, *Miss Grief*, was to be published. "I am thrilled to be alongside you and feel totally unworthy of the recognition."

"Nonsense. It is a great blessing to have such a worthy friend as yourself."

She stared back at him in surprise. It was rare for Henry to be so generous. It worried her that he had bad news coming. He went on. "Before I take my leave, I wanted to give you this." He held out a wax envelope holding a photograph of himself. "To inspire you in your writing."

"Oh, Henry!" she exclaimed, taking his gift and studying its likeness. She tucked it deep into her wool coat pockets.

"Alice has written to inform me that she is on her way to London."

Constance clapped her hands together. "How wonderful! I'm sure you will love to have your sister near you. When does she arrive?"

"Next month. I'm working to find her lodgings right away. I encouraged her to bring only those things she can't live without." He gave Constance a look that only she would have understood.

"If you mean to tease me of my things, be reminded that my things are all I have." She stared out at the outlying city crested by a cool autumn sunset and added under her breath, "They show me no affection, but they do bring me some joy."

"Some?" His look was earnest. It took her breath away.

"Enough," escaped her lips. She looked into his eyes. "Enough that I hope to have them with me wherever I go."

"Where will you go next?" he whispered.

"To meet my sister in Vienna."

"London shall miss you."

"And I, it." There was a pause, an exchange of looks.

Henry, his face half in shadow asked, "When will you return to England?"

"In the spring." The space between them disappeared. All that existed was Constance and Henry together.

The carriage came to an abrupt stop, knocking her into Henry. "Are you alright?" he asked, holding her close.

"Yes," she whispered, their lips nearly touching. Then the door swung open. She quickly moved away as the driver held out a hand to help her disembark.

"Good night, Henry." She stepped from the carriage. The horses slowly began their journey home, their hoofs echoing against the pavement. Constance stood alone, encircled only by the small light of the new streetlamp, until the carriage had turned a corner and disappeared from view.

Love is the joy of the good, the wonder of the wise, the amazement of the Gods.~ Plato

Elle

The Grand

As the handsome couple entered the dimly-lit room, the sound of an old-fashioned fox trot played from the band. Those close by stopped and turned, looking in their direction. Elle had never felt more beautiful, nor more on display.

The music changed to something more modern, a waltz. The crowd parted and Patricia appeared in a beautiful cream colored organza gown reminiscent of Elise McKenna's dress in *Somewhere in Time*, taking some of the attention from Elle. She glanced over at Jace with his tan suit. A coincidence?

Patricia moved towards them with a dancer's grace and with a sad smile said, "You missed the lesson."

"That's okay, I'm pretty good already," Jace boasted, missing the meaning behind her words.

Patricia turned to Elle. "What about you, Elle? Do you need help with the waltz?"

Elle hadn't waltzed since junior high, but she wasn't about to admit that to Patricia. "I've got Jace so I think I'm okay." Her face turned red. That had sounded meaner than she meant. Patricia frowned. Silence grew like canyon walls between them.

Finally, Patricia patted him on the arm. "I've got Douglas as a partner tonight and about a dozen other men old enough to be my father." Jace laughed. She batted her eyes. "Save me a dance? I'm sure Elle wouldn't mind." She looked over at Elle with a kind smile. Elle had no choice but to nod supportively.

"Sure," Jace agreed. Patricia returned to a balding gentleman wearing a plaid suit and red suspenders underneath. Jace led Elle to the dance floor. "When I push step back, and when I pull come forward. We'll do one big step and then two side steps closer together. That's about it."

"Got it." She was more nervous than she realized. But her worries were unwarranted as he led her around the floor as if they were on ice skates. She only stepped on his toes a couple of times.

"I thought you said you didn't dance," Jace said halfway through the song.

"I don't. I guess you're right, all I have to do is follow." Over Jace's shoulder Patricia watched them as she danced with an older man who seemed to be having the time of his life. His wife was dancing with the plaid-suited gentleman. Patricia kept a pleasantly professional look on her face.

They danced two more songs and then Patricia, not able to contain herself any longer brought her partner over and introduced him to Elle. Before Elle knew it she was dancing the samba with Mr. Suspenders, and Patricia and Jace were dancing together.

"Are you having a good vacation?" Doug, the suspenders man, shouted over the noise of the music.

"I'm not really on vacation."

"What?" he shouted.

"I'm not really on vacation. My aunt died," she yelled.

"You're here with your aunt?"

"No, I came to take care of her estate."

"What?"

She began to explain it again, but then changed her mind. It was too much trouble so she nodded and said, "Yes, I'm having a wonderful time." This seemed to satisfy him and they danced in silence for the rest of the song. When the song was finally over, she walked over to Jace and asked if he'd like to take a walk or go get ice cream or something. Getting away from Patricia's watchful eyes sounded good.

He agreed.

The ice cream shop was closed so they walked outside and down the long stairway to a sizeable lawn containing the remnants of an earlier croquet game. They made their way to a water fountain and sat down on the cement edge. Elle dipped her hands into the water to cool herself off.

"So? How does it feel to be wearing her dress?"

She pursed her lips, weighing the consequences of telling him about her experience. "Do you really want to know?"

"Sure." His eyes seemed to lose some of their sparkle, but she was so anxious to tell him she went on anyway.

"The first time I touched it, was like the dress had a life of its own."

He nodded. "What?"

She bit her lip. Maybe she had just read into it more than was really there. Maybe she'd been daydreaming. It was hard to say what it had been exactly. "It was as if I entered another sphere. I could see what life was like. I could see this person dancing in the dress. And then it happened again tonight. Before I met you. But this time it lasted longer and was more concrete. I was Constance. I could hear her thoughts. When I woke up I felt like I'd been in another life. And now I have a headache."

"You don't feel well?"

"I'm fine. And I have had a great time tonight. It was a rough morning and you helped take my mind off everything, so thank you."

They walked a little ways farther before he asked, "Did it really feel like you were in another world?"

She wanted to tell him everything. "It was like an out of body experience. I don't know how else to describe it. I was suddenly sitting beside a fire reading letters written in Henry's handwriting, and after I read them I threw them in the fire. But when I spoke it was another's voice. Even some of my thoughts weren't my own. It was like sleeping with my eyes open."

"Sleeping with your eyes open," he repeated.

"I don't expect you to believe me. But you asked." She rubbed her temples with her forefingers. The pain was getting stronger.

"Are you okay?"

"It's just my head."

"Would you like to go back to your room?"

"No. It's okay. I was just thinking. My aunt spent some time in a mental institution. People thought she was crazy. But ever since…ever since I discovered that stamp box and the scarab and this dress of Constance's, I haven't felt like myself. It makes me wonder if she had a similar experience. I just wish I could ask her."

He stood up. She was afraid he thought she was making excuses and didn't want to be with him. "I really did have a great time," she reassured him.

He helped her stand. "But you don't feel well." She nodded. They walked across the grass to the stairs. Jace took her hand to cross the street as he spoke. "I forgot to tell you that I called the city and the power should be on in the house by tomorrow."

"Maybe I could even stay there."

"When are you leaving?" He held the door open for her. The foyer had cleared. Music sounded from the ballroom, but they turned in the opposite direction towards her room. Elle was glad he was taking her back to her room because even though she had said she was okay, she felt strange and distracted and she worried she wasn't a good date.

"Tuesday. Your assistant was able to get me on a 2:00 flight out of Pelston Airport."

"That gives us two days. I can pick you up in the morning and help you clean out the house or whatever you need." A couple passed by arm in arm. Jace waited until they were farther down the hall before he continued. "Strictly as Jace the friend, not Jace the lawyer." They stood outside her door.

"So, it's official. We're friends?" She smiled at him. Was she teasing him? She hadn't flirted in years. She'd forgotten how fun it could be.

He smiled back. "I hope so."

Elle was unsure of protocol. Should she invite him in? To a hotel room? They were just friends. It felt so awkward.

"I would like to get an early start on the house. Like you said, I've only got two days." More awkward silence. Finally Jace spoke.

"Sounds good. I'll pick you up. You name the time."

"Five." She came back quickly.

His eyes bulged. "Seriously?"

She laughed and nodded.

"Jace!" It was Patricia waving her hands as she hurried down the hall, her white dress floating like dust clouds towards them. "The bass player just got sick. We need a backup."

Elle looked at Jace. Her eyes going wide. "You play bass?"

He shrugged. A small upturn of the lip. A bit embarrassed, perhaps. "A little."

"Don't be ridiculous. He's amazing," Patricia grabbed him by the arm and yanked him in the opposite direction. "Hurry."

"I'll see you in the morning, bright and early," Jace said with a small wave. Elle watched Jace turn the corner with Patricia at his side before turning the key and walking inside.

What is done in love is done well. ~Vincent van Gogh

♛

Constance

Florence, May 1886

Constance received a letter from Henry in May announcing his intent to introduce her to his friend Francis Bootts. It came just in time, as she was looking for a place to live.

I have written to my friend Francis Bootts in Florence about your arrival. His daughter Lizzie has recently married at the age of forty. There is hope for us after all dear Fenimore, though don't bother buying me teacups anytime soon. Lizzie shall take you under her wing for she is a darling woman and I feel confident that you two will make quite a pair. I can't say much about her new American husband. He hasn't much to say about himself or anything else, but is a nice enough fellow. I shall come to visit as soon as you are settled. I recently spent a fortnight with Alice in Bournemouth. The warmer weather has done her good. While I was there I managed to see Robert Louis Stevenson.

Constance stifled a laugh. Managed to see? She'd heard he'd spent the majority of time with the famous *Treasure Island* author. When she wrote him back she let him know how good it was of him to care for his sister as his time was so valuable. His response said this:

It is lucky I haven't even a cow to feed. My spare existence is practically about all I can manage. I'm afraid if I had one it would wilt away to nothingness.

"You could always bring your cow to your many dinner

parties," she whispered to herself.

In September 1886 she wrote her sister, Clara, a letter about her new home.

I have moved into a large, ancient house of pale yellow, surrounded by an open court, and hidden by stone walls and a closed gate. There are five kitchens serving six families and everything runs like clockwork. It is an old building filled with ghosts. As I walked through the passages, the woman who lives above me, began to tell me about a ghost who is said to haunt my bedroom. I stopped her and said that, "I adore the ghost unexplained." She is full of superstition and quite a talker. I'd rather make up my own story of my ghost friend, than have it spoiled by another. I hope to meet this presence at least once while I live here.

Almost as an afterthought she added, *Henry James shall visit in the fall. He will be delighted to see that the Castellani is a setting perfect for a novel such as his* Portrait of a Lady. *Perhaps he will decide to settle nearby.*

"Constance. I have something I want to ask of you," Lizzie said one September afternoon as they sat in the rose garden just off the courtyard weaving cut flowers into wreaths.

"What is it dear Lizzie?" Mr. Bootts' daughter was as kind and good as Henry had said and Constance and Lizzie had become fast friends.

"I want you to be my child's godmother!" Lizzie's blue eyes shimmered with excitement. Her kindness was a comfort to Constance. But even though they were friends, Constance was set back with surprise. No one had ever offered such a thing.

"Me? But Lizzie, I'm an unmarried woman. Are you sure I'm the right person?"

"Of course you are. And if something really were to happen to me, my father would probably take the child to America."

"What about your husband?"

"He would go with him if he wished to be with the child. But this isn't about being a guardian. He or she will love you as an aunt. That's really all I am wishing from you."

"In that case, I am thrilled and flattered that you would ask me." She embraced Lizzie, kissing her lightly on the cheek, overwhelmed with gratitude.

Her happy disposition continued when her dear friend Doctor Baldwin came to visit one evening. She gave him a tour of the Castellani explaining how Henry had connected her to the Bootts and how she and Lizzie had become the dearest of soul mates.

The good doctor nodded. "It looks like a fitting backdrop for a story."

She flashed a smile, happy that he recognized its charms. "Indeed it is! One particular nugget is the watchtower connected to the Castellani by a secret passage. I look forward to evenings on the tower overlooking the magnificent landscape. Did you know the Villa was once occupied by Nathanial Hawthorne?"

"Is that so?" he seemed honestly surprised so she went on to explain the connection while they took a pass through the rose garden.

"He drafted *The Marble Faun* here. It is now occupied by a Mrs. Hobart and her dachshund named Pax."

"And how do you do with Pax?" He stifled a grin.

"Wonderfully well. Are you surprised? Sometime I should like to get a dog of my own. That is if I could settle down for longer than a month at a time. I'm always moving around which would be too difficult with a dog. But if I ever do, I shall name him Othello."

He chuckled. "I'll keep that in mind when I see stray mutts running rampant in the streets." They sat together on a bench, stretching out in the summer sun. "Have you heard or seen much of Henry?"

She frowned. "Not enough. I do hope he'll visit in the fall, but you never can plan such things."

"How is your hearing these days?" the doctor asked.

"Getting worse," she answered bluntly.

"There is a new procedure for hearing loss. It would

involve surgery. It's too soon to tell if it is effective, but you might want to think about it."

"It can't be much worse than what I already have, can it?"

He smiled and nodded. "I hear you haven't liked the horn Henry gifted you."

"I do believe he meant it for a joke, but it actually works, though I'd never use it in public. It's good for an old man in the corner chair. Not for a woman trying to make her way as a credible writer."

He laughed again, stood, replaced his hat on his head, and called out, "I must be on my way. I have to pick up a basket of bread for Mrs. Baldwin. Good day, Miss Woolson." And then he turned and walked to his carriage.

From Henry, news of his arrival finally came in the last few months of 1886.

December cannot come too soon. In advance, I have sent you a copy of The Princess Casamassima. *I hope it finds you before I do. Remember, I plan to keep this trip secret. My desire is to hide. I don't intend to see anyone but you and the Bootts. Will you kindly ask them to observe equal discretion?* Elle folded up the letter with much excitement and set it back in her drawer. Not only would she see Henry soon, but for the most part, she would have him all to herself. No silly unnerving dinner parties with swooning old women. Just Henry and Constance. Their patience had paid off, and finally, their time had come.

Because her lease at the Castellani would be up at the end of the year she went across the patio to inspect the two hundred-year-old Casa Brichieri-Colombi. It had a wonderful view and large rooms. She leased nine of its fourteen rooms for one year. Since it was just across the piazza from the Castellani, she planned to stay on there and give Henry the Casa Brichieri until he departed in January. Then she would move over to the Brichieri. It was all too perfect. It was as if the gods had aligned the stars.

While the trees morphed from green to the most vibrant reds and yellows, Constance busied herself decorating her new two-storied house, purchasing a writing desk, a table, and several rugs, always with Henry's tastes in mind. She also ordered a new dress from Milan, again hoping Henry would approve. She planned every detail, from the decorations to the meals to guarantee Henry would want for nothing.

Just two weeks from his expected arrival, there was a knock at the door. She opened it to find a very pregnant Lizzie, her swollen face and puffy eyes alarming to Constance as she ushered the poor woman inside and offered her a seat near the fire.

"I have some dreadful news, dear Connie." She removed her gloves and bonnet and set them on her lap.

"Is it the baby?"

Lizzie shook her head. "The baby is fine. But my father is concerned about our being so far from a doctor this late in the pregnancy. He has rented a home in town and insists we move until after the baby is born."

Constance let out a sigh of relief. "I was worried when I saw your face it was something serious." She could see Lizzie was still distraught. "But you seem upset. What is the problem?"

"Do you not see?" Lizzie's eyebrows raised in expectation. Constance stared blankly at her. She did not see a problem.

"Henry will be just steps away from you with no supervision. If the news got out it could be damaging, even detrimental to both of your careers. I am so sorry that we have put this predicament upon you both, but I don't know what else to do. My father insists on it, and my husband would never go against his father-in-law's wishes. We think that Henry should stay with us – in town." Constance's heart sank. No Henry? Not after all the work she'd done. She would have to calm Lizzie's worry. Make her see that there was no danger at all.

Constance sat on the small stool next to Lizzie and patted her hands.

"You poor dear, worrying about me and Henry when you should only be thinking of yourself and the baby." She calmly went on. "I have told no one of Henry's coming as I'm sure you have done. If he were to stay in town he would most likely be found out. I have promised him total anonymity and that is the beginning and the end of it. I am not worried in the least about our reputations. He will have my new place and I will stay here until he leaves. All will be well, and you will be close to a doctor when the baby comes."

"But how will he eat?"

"I've hired a maid, and a cook who will also serve as Henry's valet. I can promise you that his every need will be attended to."

"Dear Connie, such a burden for you."

She suppressed a smile. "It is no burden at all. Henry is a dear friend."

"But…" Lizzie, stopped and chewed on her lip as Constance helped her stand.

She didn't want to give Lizzie time to think of a new plan. "Let me know when the baby arrives. I must see this godchild of mine as soon as possible."

Constance walked Lizzie to the door and helped her with her gloves and bonnet.

"Oh my dear Constance. Such a head on your shoulders. If I were half the woman you are, I wouldn't be nearly as frightened about having this baby."

Constance tied the bonnet and stated simply, "If I were having the baby, dear Lizzie, I would be scared out of my wits!" She gave her a warm hug and offered a fond farewell before she sent her away in her carriage. Constance walked slowly back inside, shut the door and leaned against it, a smile spreading across her face as wide as the River Arno. Just Constance and Henry. The gods really were in her favor.

***

On the eighth of December Henry arrived at the Brichieri with two large bags, his hat, and a cane. Constance waved from the doorway, hoping to contain one hundredth of her excitement. He nodded, showing much less enthusiasm. He was much better at this 'secret' business than she was.

Though Henry had already been informed that the Bootts wouldn't be there, and that he might "suffer" for want in their absence, he feigned surprise when she explained they had moved into Florence in preparation for the birth of the baby.

"But do not fear, as I have probably forgotten something, if there is anything that you could wish for, Angelo, the cook, or your maid Assunta will be happy to get what you need."

"You have made every wish and fancy available." He looked over at the stack of wood next to the fireplace.

"Stacked it myself. No coal like England."

"Thank God."

"And there is plenty more in the back against the house. Ask Angelo and he will bring it."

"I won't have to lift a finger." He sat down in her drawing room and lit a pipe.

Constance couldn't contain her smile. This was the scene she had been imagining and hoping for, for months. Henry, sitting in her wing back, a pipe in his hand, reading about the latest stock market scandal. The sun lighting up the room like golden honey. She, in the chair beside him knitting, reading, whatever fit their fancy in the moment. One month would never be long enough. She wanted to pinch herself to see if it were a dream.

She called to the maid to bring them tea and biscuits and within minutes the dark woman with quick hands appeared at the door with tea, crackers, and cheese on a silver tray.

Constance watched Henry intently as he scooped up several squares of cheese and a handful of crackers.

"I heard Sargent has done your newest sketch justice." Constance said.

"Judge for yourself." He pulled one out of his bag and handed it to her.

Sargent was a famous painter and photographer who had an impeccable way of catching the soul of his subjects. "It captures your likeness just right. The strength in your profile. The thoughtful and assured look you give. When your beard was full I wouldn't have recognized it, but there it is.

"It makes you quite approachable."

He rubbed his face in his hands. "I hope not too approachable. After the past few months writing and being at my publisher's mercy, I want to hide for a while."

"Of course." She would remember that he wished to be alone.

"Not from you," he assured her.

He wished to be alone with her. Her cheeks warmed at the thought. "The Bootts are certain your entire trip will be a wreck with them gone."

"With Fenimore at my beck and call? Why, heaven itself will be made up of no less woman than you. In fact, you may be more than heaven." He reached for her hand. His thumb caressed her skin. If she could think of any way to describe her feelings it would be bliss. Pure bliss. She was tempted to take off his shoes and bring a stool for his tired feet. The idea of this made her blush. She moved her hand away and picked up her needlepoint and pretended to work on that instead.

That night they dined on sage hen and roasted potatoes, and after dinner, they moved back to the sitting room. While Angelo started a fire, Assunta brought them coffee in Constance's fancy Ginori teacups she brought from Venice and a platter of fruit.

"I think this room should be called the salon," Henry stated as he lit a cigar.

"What was that?" Her hearing was worse tonight. Or Henry was speaking too low.

"The salon," he said loudly. "Perfect for deep political discussion amongst all the dignitaries of the country."

Constance rolled her eyes at the thought. "I hope to never see it."

Henry could never forget that she disliked the constant social calendar that he seemed to love. "What have you against people? Without people you have no story."

"I can't hear what they are talking about anyway. No one likes to repeat themselves and too many people mumble. No.

Books are my people."

"Speaking of..." Henry clapped his hands together. "I bring gifts, my dear." He left the room and returned a few minutes later with several packages under his arms. She unwrapped the first: three volumes of his novel, *The Bostonians.* The inside cover read, "To my padrona Constance Fenimore Woolson, your faithful tenant and friend, Henry James."

"Padrona?" It could have two meanings. A mistress, a landlord, a woman boss. She wasn't sure which he meant.

"My landlord, of course," he answered.

She looked down at the books. Her heart sunk. Why would she expect anything else? "Thank you. I am anxious to begin." She flipped through the pages, the smell of freshly printed ink on thick crisp parchment prominent in the air as she set them down on a small side table.

"Now, I have a few things for you," she announced, removing two packages from a drawer in the large walnut Armoire and placing them in his lap.

He carefully removed the brown paper. "Whitman and Browning. Excellent." Henry's eyes sparkled like dark crystals. "You treat me better than I deserve." He took her hand and kissed it lightly. "Will you read something from them?"

"When you flatter me, how can I say no?"

"You can't." He handed her the book and she opened it up to one of her favorite poems.

"As Toilsome I wander'd Virginia's woods."

He smiled and rested his head on the back of the chair as she read about rustling leaves and soldiers and unmarked graves.

After she returned to the Castellani she lay in bed thinking of their perfect evening. Tomorrow she would only join him at dinner. That would give him the space that he needed. Besides, she had plenty to do in the meantime.

There are no boundaries or barriers if two people are destined to be together.~ Julia Roberts

Elle

The Grand

Even with her headache, Elle would have liked to see Jace play bass, and for a moment she was tempted to go back, even though she really didn't feel well. She sat on the bed and pulled off her shoes and reminisced about the evening, the food, the dancing, the company. It was as if she'd been Cinderella. *Cinderella with a headache*, she thought, rubbing her temples. She wondered if the bass player was even sick or if Patricia had made the whole thing up to keep him from spending any more time with her.

She fell back on the bed and stared up at the ceiling. In the corner of her eye she saw the scarab lying several feet away. She turned and stared back. Had it been a very vivid dream? Or something more?

She thought back to what she could remember. She had been Constance for a short moment. But how? How had it happened? Had Aunt Lois had this same experience? Felt like she had been someone else? Was that what had driven her mad? Was it really the scarab? She rolled her eyes. What was she talking about? Though when she looked at it, it seemed to stare back, coaxing her to come and see. Maybe she should tell Jace about the scarab.

First she needed something for her headache. She stood up, went to her medicine bag, and downed two aspirin with a glass of water. She swept the scarab back in the box with her shoe, grabbed her backpack, tucked the box under her arm, and walked out into the hall.

She stopped at the ballroom and peeked in. If she'd hoped they hadn't really needed him, that it had just been a ruse to get Jace away from her, she was sorely wrong because Jace was up on stage, looking very much at home in front of a crowd. There was no way she could or would ask him to leave. She would wait till he was finished. She turned to leave and bumped into a heavy woman in a fancy black gown.

"Elle, what a surprise."

Elle looked up. It was Nedra.

"Nedra, I didn't know you were here." She gripped the box tightly under her arm hoping the woman wouldn't notice.

"We've been upstairs at the bar. Marv isn't much for dancing. He likes to watch the boats go up and down the lake. You should join us. The view from the roof is breathtaking. Course, you missed the sunset, but the lights are still pretty." Nedra took notice of the box under her arm.

"My, what a beautiful little box. May I?" Nedra reached forward. Elle stiffened. She didn't want Nedra to touch it, let alone look inside, but Nedra was too quick. She took the box and admired it up close. "Oh my, this is old. Definitely not a door prize." She gave a short laugh.

Elle reached for it. "It was my aunt's."

Nedra held on tight. "Eighteen eighty-six. Is that right? My, my." She turned it over. Elle's heart pounded in her chest. She felt very protective of the box, and didn't want anyone especially Nedra, seeing inside or touching the scarab. What would happen if it fell out and Elle grabbed it? Would she faint again? In front of Nedra?

Nedra looked around. "Where's Jace? Did he go home?" She turned to look in the ballroom and quickly spotted Jace. "Looks like Patricia got him in the band again. And he left you all alone?"

"I was just going outside. I have a bit of a headache." It wasn't a lie. She really had a headache. A headache and a lot of questions. Questions that could better be answered at the house. Nedra looked from Jace to Elle and shook her head knowingly, like she understood that things had grown awkward between them and Jace ended the night early, which was the farthest thing from the truth. She really liked Jace and she thought he liked her too. But there was always Patricia lurking around.

Nedra lifted the lid. Elle began to panic. "So these things belonged to Lois?" Nedra asked. Elle's hand itched. The desire to take the scarab was overwhelming, like the need of a drug. She'd never done drugs or understood how that felt, but for one second she thought she might tackle Nedra if she didn't give her back the box. She knew that wouldn't sit well with hotel security or Jace, but she'd do what she had to do.

Without answering Elle grabbed the box from Nedra. "I really need to get back to my room. I have a terrible headache." She placed it in her backpack.

"I thought you were going outside."

"Yes. I am. And then I'm going back to my room." She walked away without saying goodbye.

Once she turned the corner she looked over her shoulder to make sure Nedra was not following and then walked out a back entrance. It was not meant for guests as it only led to the workers quarters. First she walked one way and then another, always blocked by a wall or a building or a tall hedge. Why hadn't she just gone out the front door? Finally she settled for the hedge separating the front yard from the back of the hotel. As she jumped the back of her dress snagged on a branch leaving her suspended in midair. A shoe dropped to the ground. She yanked at the dress, causing a loud tearing noise as she fell into the grass. Her shoulder throbbed as she got up, grabbed her ballet flat, and walked quickly to the far entrance where she called to the doorman to get her a taxi, looking every few minutes over her shoulder to make sure Nedra wasn't around.

The house was dark when they pulled up. "Are you sure you'll be okay?" he asked. "This house has been vacant for a while."

"It belonged to my aunt. She died and now it belongs to me," she said as she searched her backpack for her keys and phone. The driver shined a flashlight so she could see. She mumbled a quick "Thank you," as she located her things and jumped out of the carriage.

He nodded. "I'll stay until you get in safely."

"Thank you," she said, again feeling slightly nervous about going into the house alone at night again.

She got the door unlocked and then waved back at the carriage. The driver clicked his tongue at the horse and then turned around and click-clacked his way back down the lane.

She stood in the dark living room unable to decide where to begin. She scanned the room. There wasn't much to find in here. She moved to the second floor, to Lois' room where the light from her phone caught the edge of a small writing desk under the window. She scavenged the drawers and found several letters and photographs which she dumped onto the bed. She recognized her mother's handwriting on a few of the envelopes. She removed the letter dated May of 1976.

I am sorry I am so far away. You should tell the father and then go to a doctor right away. It's not right to keep it from him. Even if you don't love him. At any rate you can tell me. You know that. I can come visit as soon as I finish this last class. You could come live with me if you want. I'd be happy to help you, though heaven knows I wouldn't know the first thing about babies. But I must know, who is the father?

Elle picked up another.

Have you gone to a doctor yet? You should be in your tenth week. Have you told the father yet? Does he think you are crazy or have you told him about the experiences you've had? I can't make a judgment myself until I am with you. I will plan a trip for October. Hopefully the weather will hold out long enough for me to visit before this baby is born. Have you changed your mind about Florida? They have good hospitals here and there are no judgmental nosey neighbors.

She threw it down and picked up the next letter.

I'm so happy you finally told him. This cave of which you speak sounds interesting. What do you mean you remembered visiting it before, but then you didn't remember visiting it? Are you talking about having déjà vu? If so then yes. I have done that before. If that is what has you worried then worry no more. You are not hearing voices in your head. As far as marrying him, I have one simple question: Do you love him?

Elle sat the paper down and opened the next letter from Linda. It was short and to the point. The writing much less fluid.

Sometimes? Your answer is sometimes? And you're considering marrying him? If you need your head examined, it's because you don't marry someone because you love them, 'sometimes.'

Why haven't you told me who it is? I think I already know that answer. I want the truth. And I want to hear it from you. And how on earth can you answer that you love him sometimes! All this time you feigned disinterested. Your behavior has been so childish, sneaking around, finding your special cave, acting like this is all so romantic. The both of you make me want to laugh. You deserve each other. But just remember. When he grows tired of you he will cheat on you. Just like he cheated on me. How's that for best wishes? I'm done with you both. Hope one of those voices in your head helps you out with that baby.

Elle put the letter down. She felt sick to her stomach. Her premonitions were right about her mom and Lois. It had been about a man. And more importantly, had that man been Mr. Gordon?

Christmas waves a magic wand over this world, and behold, everything is softer and more beautiful.
~ Norman Vincent Peale

Constance
Christmas Day 1886

On Christmas day Henry and Constance dined in town with the Bootts as Lizzie's new baby boy was just a week old and they were not ready to travel in the cold weather. The table was lavishly decorated with a scrumptious feast of roasted turkey, turnips, beets, winter-squash, a cold boiled ham, boiled onions and dressed celery, white bread, and mashed potatoes. For dessert, there were mince pies and plum pudding.

After cigars, and after the baby had been sufficiently passed around and adorned with gifts: a silver spoon, a rattle, a baptism gown from Constance, a pair of crocheted booties with matching bonnet and a silver-plated comb and mirror set from Henry, the writers offered their well wishes and 'Merry Christmases,' and traveled by carriage up to the Castellani.

"You're very quiet tonight," Henry remarked after several minutes of silence.

"I'm tired, I suppose." The carriage was slow and bouncy from the snow.

"You're not tired. You're thinking. I know that face."

She gave a confessional grin. "I suppose you're right. I'm thinking and tired."

"What are you thinking? No wait. I can guess."

"Really?"

"You are thinking what a miracle it is that such a cute child has such a ridiculously dull father."

She laughed. "You were on the right track. Little Charlie is a treasure. So small and innocent. I've never been a godmother before. It's quite a kind gesture." She glanced out the window at the grey buildings, the yellow street lamps glowing in the windows. A light snow had just begun to fall.

"And a very good one you'll be. Were you thinking anything else?"

She shook her head. "Not really. Just contemplating mortality and the fact I will never be a mother."

"You have been a mother, several times over with your stories."

"Yes, thank you for recognizing that. They are like babies to me."

"Did you like the books I gave you?"

She brightened at the mention of his Christmas gifts. Books, books, and more books. Exactly what she'd requested. "Yes, quite. Thank you, again."

"I was waiting until after dinner to tell you I have one more gift for you. I hope you can keep your tired eyes open long enough to open it."

"Oh Henry! Really. How you spoil me."

"I figure it is the least I can do since you have taken me up these past weeks."

"I've loved every moment of it. Our walks, our poetry readings. Our dinners. It's been lovely."

They reached the piazza. Henry helped her from the carriage, their wet footsteps echoing against the building walls. Henry wrapped an arm around her and then took her other hand in his. The feel of his skin made her forget how cold it was outside as their intertwined fingers set her heart ablaze.

Since they had given the servants the day off, and had been visiting the Bootts, the chill of the storm seemed to follow them inside. Henry went out to gather wood from an enclosed shed. Constance kept her coat on as she split kindling to start a small fire in the cook stove. Once the fire was started she chose her favorite tea kettle from England, green with embossed flowers on the side, and set it on the iron stove top. The clink of the cups echoed in the otherwise silent room.

The door opened and in walked Henry with an armload of dry wood.

"It's going to be a cold one tonight." he said, the cold air circling around him as he shut the door with his boot.

She opened the pie cupboard and removed two biscuits for each of them which she placed in the oven for a few minutes to warm while Henry worked to start a roaring fire in the 'salon,' as Henry called it. By the time the tea was whistling and the biscuits were warm on the plates, the room was warm enough for them to remove their coats and sit beside the fire.

The tea cup clinked as Constance returned it to the plate. "I could do this every night." She admitted after a few minutes of comfortable silence. "Every night we would sit and talk business and politics and gossip about the neighbors." The idea was invigorating.

"And when the stories and the fire dimmed? What would we do then?" Henry asked, the firelight reflecting in his eyes.

"I don't know I suppose we'd go to bed." She quickly turned her face away from Henry so he wouldn't notice her blush. Perhaps there was value in always having a chaperone. The mind seemed to wander without one.

"And would we go together?" There was a sparkle in his eye. He was teasing her.

She decided to surprise him back.

"I would hope we would go to bed together." She did not blink or turn away. *Play to that Mr. James,* she thought to herself. But he did not play. Instead, he took a final drink of his tea and walked over to the large hutch and pulled open a drawer. The same drawer Constance had kept her presents for Henry when he first arrived in Italy. He pulled out a package decorated in bright green paper, tied with a red velvet bow.

He placed it in her hands and sat back down in his chair. "This is my gift to you for letting me stay here."

She took the package and admitted, "It's beautifully wrapped. I hate to open it."

"The present is better, I assure you. And you can't always say that, now can you?"

She looked up at him, still surprised how aware he was of people and human nature. He often spoke of things so true to her heart. Constance agreed, "My mother used to wrap our gifts in the most beautiful papers and ribbons, but the gifts were often more disappointing compared to the fancy ribbons she would use."

By now she had removed the paper. There in the middle sat a silver stamp box, intricately decorated on the outside with the date 1886 stamped across the top.

"Oh, Harry, I love it!" she gasped.

"You can keep whatever you like in there, stamps, pictures, letters. But they must have something to do with me, whatever the case."

"I shall keep your picture in it always. And maybe a few letters."

"Not letters. Letters go in the fireplace."

"Not right away. I like to read and then reread some of the better passages. When I am leaving for a while or moving, which I tend to do more than I'd like, I dispose of them." She examined the beautiful box and then set it aside. "Thank you. I shall treasure it forever."

"You're welcome." They sat in silence sipping tea and watching the flames dance in front of them. "Tell me about your favorite Christmas." Constance finally asked. It was his turn to tell a story.

He grunted. "Oh, heavens. I don't know if I ever had a favorite. My father and mother did Christmas grandly with candles and a small fir tree. I remember one year getting a sled as a boy."

"The tree was always a centerpiece, the candlelight, the

fruits, and treats tied to the tree. We used to sing Christmas songs, especially, We Three Kings, while we took turns getting a candy from the tree. And then we danced. Father with mother, sister with brother, then we would switch. Then, my father read the bible nativity story and we'd go off to bed dreaming of sugarplums and molasses candy. What about you? Any sweet memories on your charming island?"

"I have many as a girl on Mackinac Island, but my most memorable Christmas was just last year." Constance went on, feeling the earlier wine lending to her reminiscent spirit. "A lady had made a Christmas tree for the children of the workhouse, and she invited me to go with her and help distribute the toys. We drove at early dusk Christmas Eve. I had never been in an English workhouse before, and this one transported me, with the aid of memory, to the early pages of Oliver Twist.

"Then came a large herd of the saddest creatures indeed, and they filed up and received their little offerings, and then, lifting up their small, hoarse voices, directed a melancholy hymn toward their benefactress. The scene was a picture I shall not forget, with its curious mixture of poetry and sordid prose—the dying wintry light in the big bare room; the beautiful Lady Bountiful, standing in the twinkling glory of the Christmas tree; the little multitude of staring and wondering, yet perfectly expressionless, faces."

"Have I ever told you I love your story voice? Every night I wish to drift off to bed with your story in my ear."

"You'd have to stay here in Florence. We'd have to share a bed."

"Don't tempt me tonight."

"And be tied down, ball and chain?" She looked hopefully at him.

Henry glanced out the window at the large snowflakes and gasped. "We're having a right Northern storm."

Constance followed his gaze.

The snow flurries were hurtling across the path and burying the stones across the piazza that led to her door.

"We might as well be in Boston. I think you better stay here tonight," he advised. 'No sense starting two fires when there need be only one. There is an extra room."

"I, I'm not sure." The thought was unnerving. Hadn't they just spoke about sharing beds and stories?

"I won't bother you. Though I've heard I snore."

Constance wasn't sure if that was her concern, but she didn't argue. He continued to persuade her until eventually, the path was covered in two inches of snow and the dark sky was not relenting.

"Stay," he suggested again.

"I suppose it would make sense," she agreed. When the fire was down to red coals they rose and puttered around cleaning the tea set in the kitchen and making sure the stove was out.

Constance followed Henry down the hall to the spare bedroom knowing as well, if not better than Henry, that there was an extra blanket in the tall armoire in the spare bedroom. Henry brought a quilt from his bed as well and laid it on top of the bed.

"What will you use?" she asked.

"I have another. Besides, I'm like a small furnace. I sleep warm. You are a small delicate bird who will need extra covering." As if he had been thinking about it already he added, "You'll need a dressing gown. I have something you can borrow."

"Oh, I don't know."

"Would you rather sleep in that stiff dress?"

She glanced down at her crepe black dress. "Heavens, no."

"Then I'll be honored to have you wear it." He disappeared into his own room and returned a minute later with a white sleeping gown. They were silent in the exchange and for several seconds after that couldn't even look at one another.

Finally Constance said, "Thank you for the stamp box. It will be one of my greatest treasures."

Again an uncomfortable silence. "Shall we say goodnight then?" he asked. She stared at Henry, avoiding his lips, his tender eyes, his perfect jaw line, which was near to impossible as her heart beat rapidly.

She didn't want to say good night, but they were both talked out. She wanted to wrap her arms around him and take him into her room and pull the covers over them both. But that would never happen and somebody had to end the misery.

"Good night, Harry."

"Merry Christmas, Connie." He cleared his throat and offered a bow of his head. He retired to his room, though it wasn't really his room at all. It was her room, her bed. Her sheets. When he left it would be hers again and she would sleep where he now lay. She had thought about that many times over the last few weeks and the reality of it hit her strongly.

She closed her door and was thrust into blackness, quickly realizing she had forgotten to bring a candle. It was too late now. She fumbled through the dark, undressed and slipped the gown, Henry's gown, over her head. In the blackness she worked the pins from her hair, wishing she had some light and her hand brush. Wishing even more that she were with Henry right now.

A candle was imperative for middle of the night emergencies so she decided to venture to the kitchen for an extra one. She opened the door and found Henry standing there, two candles in his hands. He had taken off his vest and shoes and socks. The first few buttons of his white cotton shirt lay open. Seeing his feet exposed caused her to blush.

He waved it in the air. "In our haste we forgot to bring two."

"Yes, I realized that too late."

His smile grew wide.

"What are you grinning at?" She touched her gown nervously, feeling exposed.

"I apologize." He looked away bashfully. "I've never seen

a woman in my dressing robes before."

"I must look ridiculous."

"No," he said softly, his hand caressing her hair rolling in soft waves around her shoulders. "I don't think I've ever seen your hair down that way. It's very becoming on you." He met her gaze.

"Only in the dark when there are no candles about," she teased and then grew serious under his watchful eyes. His stare made her flush.

She took the candle from his hand. "I was about to get one myself and you've saved me a trip." Their fingers touched. Neither moved nor spoke. A thrill flitted through her veins like fairies pixie dust. Time seemed to still. The room began to ripple and then expand. Perhaps she had stopped breathing. She trembled as she grasped the candle. Why was she shaking? She wasn't a schoolgirl. She was a grown woman doing no more than one of her characters might do. And what would they do now? They'd say goodnight.

"Goodnight then and thank you," she said and began to turn away.

"Connie." He spun her around. They stood inches apart, their lips nearly touching. The heat of his candle warmed her cheek like a hot August sunset. Shadows danced across the dark walls taunting them with their ability to sway and dance this way and that, bound by nothing, but their own flicker of light.

Then he spoke. "If I could be your husband…" he stopped, as if afraid to even say the words.

"Harry." She wished he wouldn't speak and yet she held on to his every word.

"There are moments that I..." He lightly brushed her long hair off her shoulders. "I would wish it."

She closed her eyes and savored his touch. "I wish it, too." She opened them to find his eyes were a reflection of the candle. She caught her breath as he leaned in. His soft lips pressed against her own. They were sweet like brandy, still and deep and warm. She had only kissed one other man when she was seventeen. Her soldier. It had felt nothing like this. This was intimacy that reached deep inside and carried her to the moon and swept her away to the farthest seas, the warmest oceans, the brightest stars.

Her fingertips curled through his beard. It was coarse and soft and all Henry. The reality hit her like fireworks. Her Henry. Her darling Henry holding her, kissing her. Touching her. Wanting her as much as she wanted him. Knees grew weak, as their kisses grew daring, passionate. She pressed against Henry, the man she had loved silently for six years. To love Henry.

And then without warning a hot pain licked her fingers. She gasped and pulled back to see that it was only wax from the dripping candle. Henry stiffened and took a step back.

"Forgive me."

"It was just the candle. I'm fine." The pain was already a distant memory. She took a step forward, but he put up his hands to stop her.

"No. I shouldn't have. I took advantage of the situation. It won't happen again. I promise you."

"Henry!" she called, wanting to reassure him that she hadn't minded in the least and had enjoyed it just as much as he might have. Without another word he turned and disappeared into his room shutting the door tightly, leaving Constance alone, the spilt wax already hardening across her fingers.

All journeys have secret destinations of which the traveler is unaware. ~Martin Buber

Elle/Constance

Elle pushed the letters aside, unable to read anymore. It was getting late and she still hadn't tested the scarab. Maybe it had just been a fluke. What if it didn't happen? After several minutes her curiosity won over. She opened the box and picked up the stone. Her hand clamped around the scarab. Then the suction as she shot through darkness and light all at once. And in a flash of brilliant light everything went dark.

***

There was a knock at the door. She was lying in a bed. The room was cold, stark, with white plaster walls and planked floors. A frosty gray light seeped from a drawn curtain. The knock came again.

"Just a minute." She threw a hand to her mouth. Her voice sounded strange. Deeper, different, dense. It was the same voice as the one she'd heard at the fire. She climbed out of the bed. The wood planked floor was ice cold against her pale feet. She shivered. The room was an ice box. She'd never felt so cold in a building. It was like the heat was broken. Looking down she realized she was wearing a long cotton nightgown. A heavy robe hung on a post near the door. The knock came again.

"Coming."

She donned the robe and walked to the door, passing a mirror. She stopped and backtracked as she caught a glimpse of herself. Her hair was longer down her back and more wavy. Her face fuller, not as angular, but still it was her face. Or was it? She shook her head, wondering if her drink from the hotel had been spiked. She opened the door and peeked out. A woman with jet black, curly hair and deep lines on her face stood looking apologetic, but eager.

"I hate to wake you, but Mr. James has left a note for you."

"Mr. James?"

The woman nodded. "I knew you would want to read it, just in case he has asked for you to join him for lunch as you had discussed the other day. We are still planning to serve grouse." She held out the folded paper to Elle. Something in her serious demeanor kept Elle from asking stupid questions, like who she was and why was she serving grouse?

She took the note, managed a quick, "Thank you," and then closed her door. The crisp paper crinkled loudly as she unfolded it. The handwriting was strong, slanted, almost abrasive, and definitely old fashioned. She had seen it before.

Fenimore, it began. *I have gone out and won't be available for several hours. When I return I shall pack my things and move to the Hotel du Sud. Word of my being in Florence will also get out. Our time together has been sweet. You have been a consummate landlord. Shall we plan on that farewell lunch?*

Elle put the note down. Of course. She was having a dream about Constance and Henry again. And she was playing Constance. But just like before it didn't feel like a dream at all. She touched her cheeks. They felt warm. She held out her hands. Her fingers were short, callused, and stained black on the edges of her palm and middle finger. What could the black be from? She examined every soft line, every detail, even to the lace collar on her long cotton nightgown. All very period. She was impressed with her imagination. But no more fitting than the stark room which appeared to be in transition. A few paintings lay against the wall, they either needed to be hung or had just been taken down, as if she were moving.

At the base of the bed stood a large trunk exactly like the one in her attic. Of course it would be that trunk. It was something in her memory. She opened it and found several folded dresses. But not the ones she had found in the attic. She pulled off the robe and nightgown, and quickly slipped into a cold grey dress, shivering violently. She couldn't remember the last time she'd felt this cold. She might as well be outside.

She bent her arms and hands backwards to work the buttons but couldn't reach them. She'd have to get help. Was that expected? Would the woman who had delivered the note suspect something if she asked for help? What if she kept her hair down, would anyone notice the buttons? What was she worried about anyway? This was a dream. It didn't matter.

She took a brush from the dressing table and combed through her long, thick hair. This brush was Constance's favorite. She could tell by the way the silver handle fit perfectly in her hand and the way Constance seemed at ease.

When she was finished she opened and closed the dressing table drawers looking for makeup, but only found a loose can of facial powder that smelled like rancid roses. Something else smelled even worse. She sniffed her armpits and cringed. She needed a bath. She pulled the can of rose powder back out and used the puff to coat her arm pits that not only needed to be washed, but also needed shaved. How would she go out in public smelling like that? Certainly that awful smelling powder wouldn't mask the foul odor long. And when was the last time she had smelled so vividly in a dream?

She pinched her cheeks, opened the door, and walked down the hall, determined to play her part. At the bottom of the stairs she entered a large room with an old fashioned velvet sofa and coffee table facing a small fireplace and a fancy looking writing desk by a window. It was starkly decorated and cold. She shivered again.

"Miss Woolson." Elle spun around to find a dark haired

man around her age with an armful of firewood looking inquisitively at her. He spoke in a soft Italian accent. "I would have started a fire earlier if I'd known you would be up. After last night, I thought you would sleep late."

"Last night?"

"Yes. New Year's Eve. You were up very late with the Bootts and Mr. James."

She gave a fake smile. "Of course we were. The Bootts and Mr. James. And I had a lovely time." She was not very convincing, but she was amazed how her imagination was making all of this up. It felt so real, the cold plaster walls, the small fireplace, the way she was shivering uncontrollably. She'd never shivered in a dream before.

"I'll set out some meat and cheese for you madam."

"Meat and cheese?" She'd forgotten how Europeans breakfasted.

"Miss Woolson." The woman who'd brought the note stood in the doorway wiping her hands on her dingy apron. She stared at the grey dress. "Why didn't you ring? I would have helped you..." Her wide eyes moved to her hair. "...get ready."

"I think I'll wear it down today, thank you."

The woman opened and closed her mouth as if to speak. Elle added, "But if you could help me with the buttons." She lifted her hair to show the gap in the back.

The woman gasped at the sight of a half-buttoned up dress. She rushed over, her hands quickly buttoning as she exclaimed, "You haven't worn it for two winters. I didn't think it fit well."

It was the truth. It was too tight in the waist and the sleeves were short. Its ill fit was making her cranky.

The woman patted her shoulder. "Back to the bedroom to get you dressed properly. And to do your hair as well." She marched Elle back up the stairs to the corner of the bedroom and opened a bureau she hadn't noticed before. Several dresses hung on velvet hangers. The woman, whose name she didn't dare ask, as she was certain she should know it already, took a thin-striped, grey and yellow dress and laid it across the bed. It was much more formal than the simple one she was wearing with elaborate puffy long sleeves, a V-neck, a black lace trim front with pearl buttons, and an extended V-line waist.

"Is there a shower nearby? I really could use a bath."

"You bathed last week, Miss Woolson."

Elle cringed again at the thought of not bathing for a full week. The woman noticed and added, "But if you insist we could warm some water for a bath tonight."

"Thank you, I'd appreciate it." She put on the new dress which fit better than the previous grey one, but wasn't any more comfortable. And the layers! A petticoat, a white slip, and then the outer dress. She looked for stockings and found a pair of black, thick wool ones that were stiff and itchy. She sat on the bed and pulled them on thinking at least they would help warm her.

"Did you have a note for Mr. James?" The woman asked.

"Oh yeah. I should do that."

The woman stared at her.

"Um…would you mind getting me paper to write Mr. James a note?" She hoped that wasn't too presumptuous, but she had no idea where Constance kept her paper and pens.

"Would you like to sit at your desk or did you want me to bring paper to your room?"

The woman seemed perplexed by the way her forehead wrinkled. That usually didn't happen in her dreams. Her characters usually did as she asked. And she had never noticed anyone's wrinkles before.

"What do I normally do?"

"It depends on the day ma'am." The woman watched her carefully. She would know she was a fraud if she didn't start faking it better.

"I'll write at my desk, thanks." They stared at one another.

"Guess I better get on that," Elle stated looking around for a desk.

The woman scowled. 'Get on that' probably wasn't standard or even invented. This was too real. She was dressed head-to-toe in period clothing. The house was freezing. The food was authentic. The smells were strong. Whatever this was, it was not a dream.

"I mean, yes, I shall begin immediately." She suppressed a laugh. The woman nodded, seeing no humor in her stupidity, and led her back down the stairs to the large room.

The room was Tuscan style with red walls, iron sconces, tiled floors in the kitchen, and wood everywhere else. A small writing desk was set off a sunny window. A perfect place to pen stories. Again, she could feel a genuine appreciation for the space. Constance loved this spot. If she let her mind wander she could think of the story Constance had been working on. That was the key: stop trying so hard and let her thoughts create themselves.

Determined not to raise more suspicion, she attempted to walk more gracefully to the desk. She pulled out the chair and sat. "Yes. Well…" She scanned the area for paper, smiling reassuringly at the housekeeper who was still watching her. Did she need to dismiss her? She found some in the top drawer and pulled out a sheet. There were no pens or pencils in the drawer. No pens. What was she supposed to write with? On the desk set a fountain pen. Could she write with a real fountain pen? She gave the woman a reassuring smile and cleared her throat and set the pen down on the paper. Nothing happened. She dipped it into the ink jar and then slowly moved it across the paper. It smeared and then tore. Now she knew where the ink stains on her fingers were from. She tried again with a fluid motion. It left a squiggly line. She looked up. The woman's face could double over in irritation if she didn't relax. Elle had to get rid of her fast or they were going to have a problem.

"You may go. I shall be quite alright." She wadded up the paper and got a new piece. When she was in high school she took a class on calligraphy. She didn't do very well and had never tried it since, but maybe she could channel that memory. At any rate, it would be the shortest note in history.

Dear Mr. James.

Lunch would be great. Your place or mine?

"Your place or mine?" she muttered under her breath, wadding it up. "That was stupid."

Third time's a charm, she thought. She started again. It was covered in blobs and smeared in places, but she eventually got a note written saying she'd be happy to have lunch with him and planned on noon. She started to sign it Ell- crossed it out and wrote, Constance. She gave it to the woman, whose name was still unknown, and then ate some meat and cheese and some dry bread in what they called the breakfast room.

Henry arrived promptly at noon wearing a tan suit and vest and a bowler hat. He removed his hat and hung it on a hook while speaking. "I apologize if I kept you waiting." He moved into the room and finally looked at her.

Elle stood politely beside her desk, her hair up in a full bun, courtesy of the housekeeper, Mrs. Farve, from Manchester, England—so said the cook. At the sight of a 4-D version of the man, who by all means matched every photograph she had ever seen of Mr. Henry James, she was unable to speak. There was a thickness to him that made him seem statuesque and confident. He was much better looking than pictures portrayed, but one thing did prevail. A certain pride in men that she generally steered clear of.

"Are you unwell?" He seemed genuinely concerned.

"No. Not at all," she said as if she were a player on a stage.

"You seem more reserved than usual. You aren't upset with my leaving today? This was our agreement."

She had no idea what to say. How could she speak without giving herself away? She thought of all the Jane Austin movies she'd watched with her mom over the years. All she had to do was act like Elizabeth Bennett. Then suddenly the words came to her. She opened her mouth and let them pour out. "Yes. Though I was thinking if I were to take the top floor you could remain on the first and there'd be no need of moving out." They hadn't been her words at all. Why would she recommend he stay with her?

"That is very kind, but a break is needed and I have been asked to write an article on Miss Constance Woolson."

"And who is asking this of you?" Elle could hear Constance in her mind wonder if their month-long affair had only been a ruse for an article. *How very Henry James of him,* Constance thought.

But Henry had gone on talking and hadn't noticed Constance's grave eyes. "Besides, my little secret of being here has been discovered. Mrs. Anderson saw me this very morning. We both know she is one of the town's most reliable gossips."

"Lunch is served," Mrs. Farve interrupted. They moved on to a safer topic while they followed Mrs. Farve to the kitchen.

They lunched on roasted grouse, potatoes, squash, tomatoes, and slices of hard bread. Though it wasn't how Elle usually ate, it tasted wonderful.

Halfway through dinner, Elle asked the question she knew Constance was aching to know. "When will your piece be published?" She had no idea where the thought came from, but Henry didn't seem surprised by it. He wiped his mouth and hastily said, "February."

"And where?" Her voice was steady, the undercurrent of concern aroused.

"It shall be in Harper's Bazaar."

"I expect you'll be cruel." Again, she had not meant to say it. It was as if she had no control.

"I shall only speak what I know. If I am too admiring it will look like I favor you exclusively. That wouldn't do for either of us, would it?"

"Of course not." Though Elle really couldn't imagine why.

They finished their lunch and then Henry stood. "My bags have already been sent to the hotel." They moved to the door. He kissed her on the cheek, neither moving as memories of a candlelit hallway, an intimate moment, a shared passionate kiss came to her mind. Her forehead grew hot.

"Do come and visit," he remarked lightly. He set his bowler hat upon his head and walked out the door. When he was gone Elle wiped away his kiss, disturbed by the many mixed feelings Henry James provoked.

Deep into that darkness peering, long I stood there, wondering, fearing, doubting, dreaming dreams no mortal ever dared to dream before. ~*Edgar Allen Poe*

Elle/Constance

February 1887

Constance/Elle gripped the latest copy of the *Harper's Bazaar* and crossed the Carraia bridge headed to the Hotel du Sud where Henry was staying. It was February and rainy, but she felt none of its sharpness as she stomped through the puddles. Elle could feel rage coming from Constance so she remained quiet, allowing Constance to lead the way.

She crossed the street and entered the hotel knowing full well that Henry would state she was being emotional. That she should thank him for the good things he had written and not focus on the negative. That the article was clearly subjective. But first she would have her say. She burst through his door and slammed the paper down on the desk where he sat near the window. He jumped in surprise.

"How could you?" she cried. "And directly to my readers, like you want to single-handedly destroy my career!" She blinked angry tears away. Neither her long walk nor her deep breathing had done anything to calm her.

Henry peeled away a pair of spectacles and gave her a long look. "You'll find your readership will be no less than it was before."

Of course he would play it calm. Make her look ridiculous. But he would not get the upper hand today.

"You promised not to be cruel."

"I wasn't cruel."

She picked up the paper and began reading the sentence underlined in dark ink.

"'She likes the unmarried, but she likes the married even more. Her characters have a shipwrecked air as though on a desert island. Her work is worthy and pressed into service.'"

"I also said your work was worthy."

She went on reading "'Miss Woolson's dull walks draw her to a dismal swamp and brackish inlets.'" She set the paper down. "Not only do you say I am flawed by my feminine weakness for love, but that my characters are dull. This is nothing but a calculated betrayal to me. And all written while I fed and sheltered you in my own home."

He took the paper from her. "It also says I approved of your sacrificial wives in your recent works."

"But you said nothing of my heroine in *For the Major.* Where the woman finds freedom and independence in the loss of an overbearing husband."

"I only urged the author to reach further."

"And what is this that I cannot get along without a social atmosphere? And to say that I bristle to socialize with anyone with less than a generation of well-born descendants is preposterous!"

"I only stated that you do indeed like to mingle with a higher social class."

"Let me read what you said. 'She has a great liking for the well-born who have a pleasant sense of a few warm generations behind them, screening them in from vulgar draughts in the rear.' You make me sound a most dreadful spinster."

"You've said yourself you want to be separated from the riff raff.

"And since you have chosen to only see offense, I will

point out where I applauded you as a conservative lady of the utmost propriety."

"Which to you means only that I lack imagination and initiative. Henry, I've known you too long to miss the meaning behind your words. You are subtle, but you can be cruel. Not once did you mention that my last two books had been extremely successful. Perhaps even more than yours have been!" There, she had done it. He was not the only person who could be cruel.

Henry's eyes went dark. She bit her lip. His jealousy and self-loathing were a lethal combination and now she had spitefully cut him down.

He rubbed his eyes. He looked tired and beaten down. "Is there anything else you'd like to add?" He stared at her. She regretted everything she'd said. Why couldn't she just keep her mouth shut? Why did he make her so mad? Why did she feel so intensely sorry so quickly?

"I'm sorry. That was uncalled for."

"It is your true feelings."

"No, it's not, I'm just angry."

He put his eyeglasses on again. "Fenimore, I am sorry, but as you can see," he pointed to his papers on his desk. "I am very busy. Perhaps we can take the piece apart and debate its meaning another time."

Her face flooded with color. He'd always made her visits an exception to his work, even when he was writing, because she was careful to come only when necessary. Perhaps he felt he no longer owed her any favors.

"I am sorry that my article seemed hurtful. That was never my intention. Truly." He hunkered over his papers and began to write. With his back to her, he said, "I trust you can find your way out?" Her eyes filled with tears. She was tempted to grovel, but she was not a groveler. Not today. She spun on her heels and exited the room, her eyes blurry as she rushed down the hall, past the lobby, and into the dreary February day feeling worse than when she had entered minutes before.

***

Elle lay in her bed and stared at the ceiling. She wanted to sleep away her existence or at least wake up from this miserable dream. Sometimes she felt in control of her thoughts and other times it was as if she had no control over anything and was just along for the ride. And it had been so long. Months since she began this dream except she was almost certain this was no dream. A knock sounded at her door.

"Enter."

"How are you feeling today?" Mrs. Farve asked, going to the windows and pulling the drape back.

"Leave the drapes closed please." Her voice was not her own. Many of her thoughts were not her own. Between the foggy grey days and word that Henry had gone to Venice before she'd had a chance to properly apologize to him, Constance had grown depressed, and Elle, eager to end this charade. Where were the ruby slippers to take her back home?

Mrs. Farve released the drape and asked, "Can I bring you breakfast?"

"Just some toast, please."

"Will you be needing anything else? Another bath perhaps?"

Elle looked at her carefully. Was she being a smart alec? Perhaps she bathed more than Constance had, but it still wasn't enough. She'd bath more, but then she'd have to deal with how chilly she felt afterwards. She'd been cold for three months. The only time she felt warm was when she practically sat on top of the fireplace.

Perhaps to someone who didn't know better, the lifestyle could be tolerated. But she knew better. She had finally started to wear the thick black stockings, as she was warmer with them than without. But the other amenities: the bathrooms, the muddy streets. The smells. It was all becoming too much. And with Henry gone, she was bored to tears. And lonely.

Henry. She couldn't believe how angry she had gotten when he'd written about her—or rather Constance's writings.

She wasn't Constance, yet she had felt every angry, betrayed emotion as if she had been. And now she felt all the regret and loneliness that comes with shooting your mouth off in anger. What had happened? Days went by in a blur and others dragged on. And between them all, she thought of Henry.

She needed to make things right with him. She would begin with a proper apology.

"Could you bring me a paper and a pen, please?"

Mrs. Farve nodded and quietly exited the room. Elle sat up. She'd meant to send Henry a letter weeks ago, but every time she started, it ended up in a ball in the corner. Knowing that Henry was cursing her from Venice made her determined to do something right this minute or lay right down and die in this bed. It was time to ask for his forgiveness. If not for her own, at least for poor Constance's sake.

Mrs. Farve returned with pen and paper and a writing tray, and left Elle alone to grovel out a magnificent apology.

She heard back from him a week later while she sat at her writing desk revising her next story to please her demanding publishers. She dropped her pen and ripped his letter open.

Dear Fenimore,

I have not been well as of late, either. The weather is no better in Venice than it was in Florence, and the company is dismal. Browning likes it here, but I find it damp and gloomy. I may have jaundice, but not to fear, Dr. Baldwin is helping me. I am contemplating returning to Florence in April. Would I have a friend in Florence that I could share all my ailing woes? Lizzy has been sick, too. I suggest you check in on her as soon as you can. I too hope for a brighter future in spring. As for your apology, I forgive you as only an angel could. I wait for your post.

Poor Henry, as gloomy and miserable as she was! It made her want to dance knowing he was the same. Poor, darling Henry. Oh how she wished she were there now to put her arms around him and nurse him back to health. She wanted to jump up and dance and twirl around the room with the letter as her endearing partner. She immediately wrote a response.

Dear Henry,

I am very relieved that you have forgiven me. And yes, 'only an angel could' I am such a disagreeable old maid, I am lucky to have any friends.

There are three or four months of the year I wish to attach myself to a boat and explore the everglades where the flowering vines hang down from the treetops like a tapestry, and hear the rush of the birds and the slow ripple of a passing alligator. How I'd love to show you the channels and wild creatures that call that little corner of earth home. But alas, we must trudge through this murky season in Italy instead.

I agree that you should come back to Florence. In fact, I invite you to stay at the Brichieri as I have plenty of space for all of my "trinkets" (as you call them) on the third floor and could give you the whole of the first floor. If you remember, the rooms are vast and the ceilings vaulted. While my space is superior with its open rooms and light from the sun shining in on all sides, the first floor is still very lovely, and I think we could both benefit from each other's company.

Your ardent admirer,

Constance

Hard as it was to admit, she missed Henry. The memories that belonged to Constance now belonged to her and she'd found him to be the most interesting man she'd ever met. He forgave her for her outburst, which might have been more Elle than Constance for it was hard to know which thought was hers and which was Constance's anymore. She was becoming Henry's Fenimore. If she sat back and did nothing Constance would control the conversation and her actions. As time passed, Elle had become more comfortable as Constance, her own memories growing dimmer, overshadowed by Constance's experiences. Jace seemed like a distant memory, and her life in Florida dimmer still. But her thoughts revolving around Henry had only grown stronger, more complicated.

The cool, wet winter turned to spring and brought with it Henry to Florence in April. Seeing him there, his bags by his muddy traveling boots, his thick beard concealing a smirk across his lips, caused her great relief.

She had been so lonely during the winter, and so hurt by his stinging review, that she had shut out the world. But she couldn't hold onto a grudge any longer. Plus she believed that

Henry hadn't really meant to hurt her. That was all that mattered.

One evening as Henry and Constance were eating dinner by candlelight on the third floor of the Bellosguardo she asked about his new book.

"Nearly finished," he admitted between bites, a look of gratification in his eyes.

"Who is your main character and what is her name?"

"A widow named Mrs. Prest, a consummate American resident living in Venice."

"You didn't base her off me did you?"

He looked shocked, though she knew he was only mocking her. "Of course not. I based Miss Tina off you."

"Did you really?"

"No. Miss Tina is unintelligent, lean, dingy, naive. You are the exact opposite."

She lifted an eyebrow. "Any other characters based on real people?"

"Maybe one." He cut into his steak and plopped a piece in his mouth.

"Yes?" Constance could hardly wait to see who he had been spending so much time with these past few months.

"Guess."

"Henry, that's not fair. You've spent two months in Venice. She could be someone I don't even know."

"Oh, you know her. She is a great admirer of your work. Especially *Anne*." His smile said it all.

The distant memory of an American woman living in Venice came in her mind. "The widow in love with you? Mrs. Bronson?"

He shook his head. "Not in love with me. She just loves famous, accomplished people, though I do think she has a special place for Browning. I believe they were 'more than friends.'"

"She is quite the caretaker."

"And not just of the famous, accomplished people. She also takes it upon herself to care for the poor and needy."

"A worthy admirer," Constance said splitting her roll in half and slathering it with gooseberry jam, feeling somewhat relieved that it was Mrs. Bronson though still slightly jealous.

"One evening there were five or six gondoliers under her windows serenading her. She is the nursing mother to four-fifths of Venice. "

Constance laughed. "I certainly heard enough about your evening visits when I lived there. What did she used to say about you staying late into the evening on her balcony?" Her voice raised in mimicry as she quoted, "'The highlight of her evenings were spent with Henry James.'" She frowned and set her knife down. "I finally had to concede her advantage to get her to stop talking about it. If you will remember."

"She made a great study of a still-living widow recently freed from a hopeless marriage."

"That is the premise of your story?"

He nodded. "What about you? I know you are busy at work as well."

"Too soon to tell." His premise sounded a bit like her last work. The work he had failed to acknowledge in his paper a few months back. She wasn't ready to divulge in case he might want to copy. "Give me a few more weeks and I will have something more substantial to show."

She settled back in her seat and sighed. "I love this little house in the sky. It reminds me of the bulwarks of the Celestial City, in *Pilgrim's Progress*."

He studied the house for a moment and then agreed. "Indeed. I am in love with this irresistible, delicious, little Florence."

"I feel the same." She smiled at him. "The most beautiful view on earth hangs before me whenever I lift my head."

Just then Mrs. Farve entered the room. "Mr. James, a Mrs. Broughton is here to see you."

Henry frowned and wiped his mouth with his napkin. "Oh dear. Our perfect night ended in the breath of a name."

"Nonsense." Constance frowned at him and then smiled at Mrs. Farve. "Send her up," she offered graciously.

As Mrs. Farve exited the room Constance and Henry doused their dinner candle, and without speaking, moved to action.

Constance cleared their plates, while Henry grabbed his hat from the hook. They were players on a stage and each had learned their part and the reason for it.

Mrs. Broughton, a robust Englishwoman around Constance's age and a writer of romances, soon appeared at the top of the stairs wearing a grey dress and matching hat. Her cheeks were rosy and her breathing, labored. She noticed Constance soon after she saw Henry. Her eyebrows rose. Henry fiddled with his hat.

"Mrs. Broughton, I was just here to call on Miss Woolson. Shall we all sit or shall you and I return to the main floor?"

"We can stay, if you'd like." She gave Constance an eye of interest. Constance knew as a writer she was keen on body language. She would be careful to play her part well.

They sat together on the sofa, while Constance took the leather chair near the fireplace and began working her needlepoint. The two guests made small talk. Mrs. Broughton occasionally glanced up at Constance and gave a polite smile. It was obvious to Constance that she had not come to see her.

"I have recently spent time with your kinswoman, Mrs. Bronson, while I stayed in Venice." Henry said as he lit a pipe.

Mrs. Broughton's eyes widened in delight. "Did you now?"

They talked of their mutual connection and the days forthcoming with very little interruption from Constance. Eventually Henry took her by the arm and announced, "Fenimore, Mrs. Broughton and I have worn out our welcome and I shall walk her home." He tipped his hat. "Thank you for the hospitality. We bid you a good night." And the two walked arm in arm together down the stairs and out the door.

Mrs. Broughton appeared twice more in a two-week period, each time hunting Constance's scent, which, if she were really a dog, would have smelled it heavily in Henry's apartment. Though apart during the day to write, their evenings were spent on the first or the third floor of the Brichieri, and always together.

Near the middle of May, Henry announced his plans to return to Venice to finalize his impressions of the city in the water for his book, *The Aspern Papers.*

Constance frowned. They were walking across the bridge heading home up the hill in the most glorious of sunsets, but not even the beautiful view could keep her from feeling suddenly hopeless.

"But I intend to return to Florence in ten days. Then, if I have your permission, I shall stay on for four more weeks before I return to lovely old England." Henry, sensing her displeasure, grew soft in his response. "It is only ten days. Then we shall have a little more time."

"I have never been more at home and happy than I have been these past few months having you as a guest. I only wish we could make this last longer than a few weeks."

"But you know it isn't the writer's way to stay grounded to one spot."

"To marry and have a family, you mean," she interjected.

"Good Lord, especially not that." His eyes were filled with concern. "You yourself have said you have no desire to be Mrs. Bronson's kinswoman."

Constance rolled her eyes. "Of course not. Their idle chatter and gossip gives me hives. But not every wife has to be idle or a gossip."

They rounded the corner leading to the house and stopped in front of two tall pines that guarded the house entrance which blocked anyone from seeing them. Henry put his arm around Constance. His outward show of affection gave her the courage to say what was on her mind.

"How do you do it Harry? Leave so easily?" she asked, staring off into the glowing orange and purple fire sky that reflected off the River Arno.

"It isn't any more easy for me than it is for you."

She turned to him, her eyes moist and questioning. "How can you say that? In one moment, we are breathing in the air of near perfection, and in the next instance you calmly state that you are leaving me." She blinked her tears away and whispered, "Again."

"I never leave you." He pulled her eyes up to meet his. "Would you have me put away my writing to be by your side forever?"

"I wish you wanted it."

"No, you don't. Nor would I want you to stop writing for my sake. My dearest Connie. Two people such as ourselves are bound by our art. Love clears the path for one to spread their wings and fly."

"I only wish that we could have two lives. One with our writing careers and one privately together. Or that we lived in a world that allowed both."

You can! In my world you could have both! Elle said in Constance's mind. Constance, hearing the voice, rubbed her temples. Henry did not notice her sudden change in demeanor as he kissed her on the cheek.

It was the first time since that Christmas night nearly six months before that he had shown such affection. While it was only a memory for Elle, it was still very vivid in Constance's mind. Soon the foreign voice of Elle was soon forgotten.

"I promise to return to you. I always do."

Constance leaned up and kissed him back. "I know." She smiled. While it wasn't as often or as long as she liked, he did manage to find ways for them to be together more often than not. What else could she ask for?

As she climbed the stairs to the third floor, his kiss still warm against her skin, a sad sort of smile crossed her face. As she took the next step the walls around her began to turn. An explosion of color flashed behind her eyes. She reached for the railing to keep from falling as everything went white.

Let me embrace thee, sour adversity, for wise men say it is the wisest course. ~*William Shakespeare*

Elle

Mackinac Island

Elle opened her eyes. A slice of lemon sun streamed through the window. Not Constance's window, and not quite even hers, but Lois'. She sat up, but immediately fell down again. Her arms were useless. Her skin, ice. Every movement hurt. She blinked several times hoping it would jar her memory. Her head pounded, like she'd hit a brick wall going twenty-five miles per hour. She slowly opened her hand to examine the red outline of the scarab in her palm. It throbbed. Looking around the room things began to take shape. She remembered the ball, deciding to come to the house. Wearing the dress, saying goodbye to Jace.

She was still wearing the gown from the night before. And just as she was certain it wasn't a dream, she was certain it was. The most vivid dream of her life.

Just then there was a loud knock on the door downstairs followed by her phone buzzing simultaneously. She moaned as she rolled to her side. It felt like sharp little tacks were climbing up her legs. It took all her energy to answer it.

"Jace?" she asked, recognizing his number.

"Finally! I went to your room and knocked but you never answered. I checked the pool and you weren't there. I finally came to the house, but there was no answer there either. Where are you?"

"What time is it?"

"It's 5:34 a.m. I thought you said you were an early riser."

"5:30 isn't early enough for you?" She was surprised how snarky she could be at such an early hour. She'd never had a hangover before, but she was sure this could rival one.

"I'm here. I'll come down." She stood and looked down. Maybe she should change first, except she realized she had nothing to change into.

Jace's eyes went wide when she opened the door wearing her fancy ball gown from the night before. "You never changed?"

"I fell asleep."

"How did you get here?"

"I took a cab." She ushered him in, looking over his shoulder to see if anyone was watching before she shut the door.

"You scared me to death!" His face was partially relieved. Something was still bothering him. "Somebody broke into Mr. Gordon's last night. Trashed the place. I tried to call you, but when you didn't answer I went to the hotel. You said you were an early riser, but I couldn't imagine where you'd be."

"And you thought maybe I was involved?"

His brows furrowed. "I hoped you weren't hurt."

"Did you ask if they have any leads about Mr. Gordon?"

He shook his head. "My buddy Steve told me the place was wiped clean. No fingerprints besides Mr. Gordon's. And they can't be sure if anything was taken. But they are suspicious that his death was no accident now, though that is just between you and me."

He looked at her dress. "You came last night? I thought you said you had a headache."

She sighed loudly and rubbed her temples. There was so much to tell him. Where did she begin? She walked to the dusty couch and sat. "I don't know. I was reading letters and then something happened. I passed out."

"You passed out?" He came and sat down beside her.

She shook her head. "At first I thought it was a dream. I even played the part and didn't question anything, not the old fashioned houses, the fires in the fireplace, not even when I saw Henry."

"Wait. Henry?"

She gave him a 'just wait' look and continued on. "Henry James. He gave Constance the silver stamp box. And Constance, she's in love with him, but Henry just won't let it happen. He talks about keeping one's manhood to his side all the time."

Jace's small smile evaporated. "What are you saying? You were with Henry James?"

"Like I said, at first I didn't know what was happening. But then I came to the conclusion that I had traveled through time and was living as Constance, but then suddenly I woke up and I was back in the room and my hand was burned from the scarab." She held up her palm so he could see the red outline.

He took her hand and examined the red mark. "Wait. But, how?" His eyes went from her hand to her dress. Confusion mixed with concern stirred across his face.

She bit her lip. "You'll think I'm crazy."

He stared wide-eyed, but said nothing.

She sat on the couch and stared at her red hand. "I'd know it all in an instant, the sights, the smells—it was like nothing I've experienced. Sharp and woody and bitter and sweet. And sometimes just nasty."

"Could the book have influenced you? You have been reading it a lot."

She nodded. "Logic would say yes. But it was so real. This was the third time. It wasn't random. It wasn't a dream." Elle stopped talking when she heard a noise outside the house. She walked to the window to see a police buggy parked in the driveway.

"Why is there a police buggy here?"

"They probably want to talk to everybody that talked with

Mr. Gordon the last few days. I know they have zero leads about his death."

"I'm dressed in a fancy ball. It's going to look really strange not to mention suspicious."

"It's okay, we'll just tell them that you came here last night and fell asleep."

"Why would I do that? I don't even have you to verify the story."

"You have the cab driver."

"Right! Thank goodness." The officer knocked at the door. Jace answered it. It was the police chief, Doug.

"Hate to bother you both," he stated, staring at Elle and her fancy dress. She politely smiled, like this was what she always wore to breakfast.

"I guess you heard about Mr. Gordon's break-in last night."

"How did they know he'd been broken into?" Elle asked.

"Alarm went off. Probably happened sometime in the evening. Before ten. We think they tripped it on the way out. Not the way in. So I'm asking around to see if anybody saw anything unusual either yesterday or before Mr. Gordon died. Could you tell me what his mood was and if you saw or heard anything suspicious?"

Elle thought of Nedra and how hostile she had seemed and how Mr. Gordon had abruptly left when she showed up. But how did she say that with Jace in the room?

"I only talked with him briefly. He had to leave before our lunch was over. Do you think that someone killed Mr. Gordon?"

"Too early to say. But the break-in is so close to the death we're just making sure we turn over every stone. Can you both tell me where you were between those hours?"

"We were together." Jace said. The chief looked at her dress and over to Jace and asked in a straight face, "Over to the hotel?"

"Yeah," Elle admitted.

"And what time did ya get back over here?"

"Well, I came around midnight. Jace got here this morning."

The chief wrote a few notes down. "Okay. Let me know if you can think of anything else." He walked to the door, gave them both a nod, and then shut it behind him.

"That was uncomfortable," Elle admitted with a sigh. She dropped down on the old sofa springing dust into the air.

Remembering coming here last night reminded her of the letters and pictures. She told Jace about Lois and her letters to Linda.

"Could Mr. Gordon be the father?" Jace asked.

"I think so. And Linda felt so betrayed. But in her letters Lois says something peculiar. She says she sometimes feels like she is a different person. That she sometimes loves him. That's how it felt for me last night. I mean, one minute I am annoyed with Henry because I find him rather proud and a bit pompous and the next minute I'm blushing when he touches my hand. Like I'm two different people."

"Where's your book?" Jace asked looking around.

"It's back at the hotel. Speaking of the hotel, I was thinking about staying at the house."

He looked up at the dark lights. "If the power doesn't turn on you could always stay with us. In fact, you should come for dinner tonight. You've already met Nedra, but I'd like you to meet my dad."

She forced a smile. It wasn't like she disliked Nedra. The woman certainly had her charms, but she was so loud and pushy, but for Jace she could do anything. Even dinner with Nedra. "That would be great. In the meantime, would you give me a ride back to the hotel I am dying to shower."

Jace gave her a ride in his buggy back to the hotel where he asked if he could borrow the book about Constance. She was happy to lend it to him and then promised to check in after she'd showered.

Like it was some kind of modern miracle, Elle stood under the hot water for too long, allowing the steamy, clean water to warm her aching body. How she had missed the ability to take a hot shower in her other life. In her other life. Did it really happen? It was beginning to seem like just a dream. Maybe it hadn't been as real as she thought.

Feeling refreshed from her shower and the change clothes, Elle took a short nap, only waking when Jace knocked on her hotel door with the book in his hand and a bag of steaming tacos in his other. She let him in and offered him a chair. He sat down and opened the book up. "Tell me more about your experience. Like week by week," he said.

In between bites of soft tacos Elle told him about Henry and the article and how angry it had made her. "It's like he is afraid of my success," she said wiping her mouth with a napkin.

"Your success?"

She corrected herself, "I mean Constance. He is so jealous of Constance's success. He feels he is a superior writer, which he may be, but he downplays her success." She took another bite out of the taco and went on talking and chewing "It's infuriating. But then he apologized and I felt terrible for throwing such a fit." She threw the used napkin away.

"You said 'I' again."

"Did I? I mean Constance."

Jace took his first taco from the bag and slowly unwrapped it. "So what year was it supposed to be?"

"1887."

"Did you dress the part?"

"Oh yeah," She shoveled the rest of the taco in her mouth. Jace had yet to touch his. "I had to wear the dresses and the shoes—which were so uncomfortable—I'll have you know." She looked for her napkin and realized she'd thrown it away. Just as she went to wipe away spilled grease with her hand Jace handed her a fresh napkin.

"Thank you." She wiped her chin before going on. "It was so quiet all the time. No TV, no radio, no internet. Amazingly, eventually I got used to it." She was thinking of Henry and how she had enjoyed their long talks. She took a drink and avoided eye contact. Why was she thinking about Henry?

Jace didn't seem to notice her stumble. "How long do you think you were there?" He turned a page.

She thought for a moment. "I got there on New Year's Day. That was the day Henry announced he was moving to the hotel. I was there until May. Five months. And believe me, it felt like five months. My body feels it too." She moaned. "I haven't felt this stiff since the day after my first swim team practice."

"That's weird." He stared out the window.

"The swim team?" she asked confused.

"No. Just that you described exactly what happened to Constance and Henry in the winter and spring of 1887."

She stared at him.

"See for yourself." He set the book open on the table and pointed to the text. "New Year's Day, the hotel. The article about Constance in Harper's Weekly, his moving to Venice." He sat back in his chair. "You don't think you might have read it and then forgotten about it?"

"It wasn't just the fact that it happened. It's the fact that it wasn't a dream. It was more like a vision." She tried to take another drink, but it felt like her throat had sealed up and the food was now stuck in her airway.

Jace gave her a firm look. "How do you think it happened?"

"Actually, I have an idea. It only happened when I held the scarab.

"Where is it now?"

"It's in the stamp box in my backpack."

He went to the backpack and pulled out the box. "So if I touch it I'll travel back in time?"

"Not exactly. I touched it before and it didn't do anything. You did too, remember?"

He dumped the scarab into his hands. He seemed almost disappointed that it didn't do anything.

"It works and then it doesn't work." She took the scarab.

Nothing happened. She actually felt relieved. "See? Nothing now." She dropped it back into the box.

"I don't know why I keep getting distracted with Constance. I should be focusing more on Aunt Lois."

"Didn't you say she was going to have a child?"

"Yeah. That's right. My mom really went off on her in that letter. What happened to the child? Is she still alive? Does she know about Lois?"

"Lois didn't mention any other family besides your mom. There is no next of kin."

"Maybe she gave it up for adoption. If she's alive then she should get the estate. I should try to locate her."

Jace had finally finished his taco and was gathering up the wrappers when he mentioned someone who might know something. "You should ask Mr. Gordon's next door neighbor Ruby Gardner. She knew him as well as anybody. She knew your aunt too. In the meantime I'll go back to the office and see what I can find about an adoption."

"Good idea. And then I think I'll go to the house."

"I'll call you if I find something. And you let me know if you find something, too." Jace stood and walked to the door.

"Do you want the rest of these?" Elle held up the bag with two extra tacos.

He touched his stomach. "I'm good. You go ahead."

She breathed in the spicy aroma and sighed. "Wonderful, instant, greasy fast food, how I missed you!" Her smile lit up the room. "Thank you."

Jace touched her arm and gave it a squeeze. "If you find anything call me." They hugged, too quick to know if it meant anything, she thought as he waved goodbye and walked down the hall.

Whoso loves, believes the impossible.
~Elizabeth Barrett Browning

Elle

Ruby Gardner, an eighty-something year old widow was happy to have a visitor and seemed especially happy to meet with Linda's daughter. They set an appointment up for 3:30, and then Elle packed her bags and left them at the checkout desk to pick up later. Since it was a beautiful day and she still had a few minutes before Ruby expected her, she chose to walk the three blocks. She passed a quaint church with beautiful stained glass overlooking the vast green lawns of the majestic hotel and the lake below, and Elle wondered if Lois or her mom ever attended services there. An occasional carriage crawled by, the drivers always waving to her as they went by.

Ruby had lived in the same house for thirty years. Almost as long as Mr. Gordon. She was hunched over with brown hair that was obviously dyed to cover the gray, and wore pink lipstick and bright blue eye shadow that someone had probably told her accentuated her faded blue eyes years ago.

"Come in, come in," she said, ushering Elle into her small cottage that smelled like dust and stale soup.

"Thank you for letting me stop by on such short notice." Elle looked around and noticed the ticking clocks on her mantel. Some tall, some short, a reminder of the passage of time. Just like Mr. Gordon.

"I wasn't doing a thing. Just counting the dust bunnies on

my piano. And watching time pass me by." She pointed to the collection of clocks and winked. They sat together on a sofa right out of the Seventies in her small but tidy living room. Ruby poured iced tea and offered Elle a rhubarb muffin that crumbled all over her lap with every bite.

"Now what can I do for you?" Ruby asked politely.

Elle wiped her lip and set the muffin down on the glass coffee table in front of her. A small dusting of fallen muffin settled around it.

"I'm trying to find out about my Aunt Lois. I found a picture and a couple letters explaining she was going to have a child, and I'm wondering if you know what happened to the child and if you know who the father was." She handed Ruby the picture.

Ruby licked her top lip as she studied the picture and then returned it to Elle. She folded her long weathered arms across her belly and cleared her throat. "Well now, I don't know too much," she said, but Elle pried a little deeper.

"Lois is gone and I've been given her estate. If she had a child I'd really like to find her. And now that Mr. Gordon is gone. Well, I'd appreciate any information you might have."

"Can you believe it about Joe?" She shook her head and made a tsk sound. "He wasn't even that old. I knew his father years ago. He died too young. So did Lois. I knew Lois. It's true that she became…in the family way, if you know what I mean."

Elle suppressed a smile. "Yeah, I do."

"Lois kept it pretty quiet. About May I saw her pushing a baby in a carriage."

"Did you know my mom, Linda?"

She nodded. "There was a big falling out in the family. I believe Linda died years ago in a car accident."

"No, my dad did, but my mom died a few months ago of a stroke. Strangely enough my mom told me that Lois died years ago, too. Do you know why they told everybody that the other one had died?"

Ruby rubbed her lips together. "I really can't say."

Elle could tell in the way she rubbed her hands nervously that Ruby might know more. "But you think you know? You have a theory?"

"I don't know if now is the right time, what with everything going on."

"Mrs. Gardner, Lois and Linda and Mr. Gordon are gone, and if there was a child he or she should know."

"This is just my opinion, but I know Linda and Joe dated in high school. After school Joe got interested in Lois quite a bit. When she had the baby Linda became jealous mad. She even got Lois put into a mental hospital."

"Do you think Lois was crazy?" Elle asked.

"I don't think so. What did happen to the baby? When I try to remember what happened I really don't remember. Maybe she put it up for adoption. Everything in those days was very hush-hush about those kinds of things. But for Linda, I think it broke her heart that her sister had stolen her man."

"Did you know Linda's husband?"

Ruby squinted to remember. "I don't recall her ever getting married. Did she?"

"Yes. To my dad. R.J. Fielderson."

"Must not have been from these parts. Course, I also thought she died years ago."

"Can you think of anything else?"

Ruby sat and fiddled with her thumbs. "You know, I really can't recall. Her and Joe never got back together."

"Did you keep in touch with Lois?"

"No. She kept to herself. She was pleasant but she wasn't friends with anybody. Not even Joe hardly." They sat in silence for a minute.

When Elle realized Ruby had told her everything she knew she stood. "Thank you so much for taking the time to talk to me."

"Sorry I couldn't help you more. I wish I knew more."

Elle shook her hand. "Thanks for your time." She walked to the door and then turned around. "You say that Mr.

Gordon's first name was Joseph?"

"It sure was. But everybody called him Joe."

She let this sink in a moment before she thanked her again and turned to leave.

After returning to the hotel, she loaded up her luggage in a cab and headed to the east side of the island. To her new place.

She put her things in the guest room next to Lois, not ready to take ownership of the master bedroom, especially with Lois' things still there and removed the fancy dress from the bag so it wouldn't get any more damaged. The fabric was coarse and stiff between her fingers and reminded her of the dresses she had worn as Constance, which reminded her of Henry, which made her wonder what had happened to their story. The more she twisted the fabric between her fingers, the more she thought about Henry and Constance, and the more she longed to see them both again.

She had read that Constance had jumped out of a window in Italy and killed herself. But was it really true? Sure, she had some headaches and depression, but she had Henry to stave off the worst of times. She had Henry to tell her stories by the fire, help her make up a bed, and bring her his night dress, and give her books to read, and gifts, and little chocolates when he returned from a trip. It couldn't be true. It must have been a misunderstanding.

She looked down to see she'd swathed her fingers tightly in the fabric, like little cocooned caterpillars, making the tips of her fingers turn bright red. She loosened her grip, but didn't let go of the fabric. There was something about the dress that drew her to the past.

The dress. Could that be it? Every time she'd gone back in time she'd been wearing Constance's clothing. The dress could be the missing piece! She pulled her t-shirt over her head and stepped into the dress, not even bothering to button it up. Then, she unzipped her backpack, removed the box, and grabbed the scarab pin. And as quick as a thought, everything flashed white and she tumbled to the ground.

***

Elle found herself sitting across the desk of a man with dark hair, long sideburns, and a thick mustache. It was her doctor, Doctor Baldwin. They often talked of her depression and her headaches and the voices in her head. She had many memories with him, but few while Elle had been around, so Elle was quiet as she examined this new character.

"I haven't seen Henry around. Has he returned from Venice?" the good doctor asked.

"He was supposed to return after ten days. It's been two months." Constance was in a foul mood. And the fact that her head ached wasn't helping. "Apparently Venice has given him better treatment than Florence can afford."

"How is the writing?"

"I have worked nonstop to finish my latest work, but there is no joy in it. I find no joy in anything. I sound like a pessimist. I know how to solve it. If I could live twenty miles from everybody and on the line of the equator I could live as long as the Pharaohs." Elle could feel it. That dull hopeless ache in Constance's chest. It was a terrible burden.

"I don't think the equator or the sun can cure what ails you."

"You're right. So I trudge on as best I know how."

"When will I read your latest novel? Have you given it a name?"

She nodded, a slight upturn of the lip. "At the Chateau of Corinne."

"Sounds like something my wife will eat up."

"I hope so. I never know which book will be my last."

"You mustn't worry about that. Take one day at a time. Are you taking a walk every day?"

"I also have some pills to help stabilize things."

Was it really pills that she needed? Pills for what? The headaches? The depression? The fact that she missed Henry terribly? "Lately I haven't been able to muster the desire for even that. That was when I knew I needed to come see you."

"Well, I'm glad you did. I will check on you at the end of

the week to see how things are going. I know personally these pills helped me this past winter. I was in a dreadful state."

Constance frowned with embarrassment. "I wasn't aware." Leave it to her to be blind of others' plights. She wasn't the only one that suffered, yet it consumed her to the point she was unaware of anyone else.

He held up a hand in protest. "Nor would I want you to worry." He wrote a note down in her chart and asked without looking up, "Have you asked Henry to come back?"

She stared out the bright window covered in a film of hard water stains. Ask Henry? Was that even a choice? A possibility? Could she snap her fingers and make him understand?

She said softly, "Asking Henry to do anything other than his will is like asking the wind to stop blowing."

He chuckled. Constance picked at a thread in her dress. "Doctor. I'm not sure if I've mentioned it, but I have heard voices in the past. Not lately, but a few months ago."

This stopped the doctor. He scratched the inside of his ear and asked, "What kind of voices? Do they tell you to do terrible things to yourself or others?"

She shook her head. "Nothing like that. They are only thoughts. Like I have a second person in my head. And at times their language is terribly coarse."

Elle froze. Was she talking about her? What did she mean terribly coarse? She happened to think she could speak proper English with the best of the Jane Eyre crowd.

Even though she doubted that Constance could hear her thoughts she tried not to think of anything while Constance spoke to the doctor.

"Schizophrenia usually shows itself at a much younger age. How long has this been happening?"

"Eight months I guess."

He looked at the small bottle of white pills he was about to hand her. "Perhaps it has to do with the medicine. I may suggest not starting the medicine until your condition improves."

"Yes, I think that would be wise. Thank you, doctor, I appreciate your advice." She stood to leave.

He followed her to the door. "If you need anything else, don't hesitate to send a note. I'll stop by Saturday."

"Thank you, doctor." Constance stepped into a small waiting room lined with wooden chairs. A man sat against the wall, his arm in a sling. She crossed the room and exited the building as Dr. Baldwin called the man in.

The air was thick, her black skirt heavy as she hurried down the sidewalk. It was hot. End of summer hot. The swish of her skirt reminded her of a rhythm of a song, though she couldn't remember the tune. Elle felt anxious. Or rather, Constance did. Something pressed on her mind. She stopped trying to figure out what it was and listened to Constance's thoughts to understand. Her book would be out in two months and she was worried what Henry would think of it. He wouldn't like it. She had been far too obvious in her latest novel, not for the general public's sake, but for Henry's, and the man would take it personally. As he should. Just as she had taken his jabs personally. They were what they were.

But if she had worried, her worry was all for not, for she did not hear from Henry. Not even to congratulate her on her book's success. He was out of the country and busy finishing up his own novel. One day Lizzie Bootts pulled out her letter from Henry and read while Constance played with the now one-year-old baby Charles.

"'Fenimore appears to be really better of her dreary autumn illness and to be driving her pen for the public benefit as I judge—for she doesn't drive it for mine.'"

She set the letter in her lap and asked, "What can you make of that statement? Have you not written him these past few months?"

"I've written alright. And far too much. I think to myself I will not respond so quickly next time, that I shall think over my words like he does and wait until it is the perfect prose, but you can be sure I have a response sealed and waiting for the post within the same evening. I'm hopeless."

"Then why does he say this?"

"Because he thinks I have slandered him in my story. He takes it personally."

"Oh." Lizzie thought on this as Charlie wrapped his hand around Constance's fingers and attempted to crawl over her shoulders. "Little Charlie likes you."

"At least somebody does. Do you mind if I have that letter? I should like to ask Henry about it myself."

"Certainly. I could give you others that mention you as well if you like."

"They are yours. I wouldn't think to take them."

"Then I will bequeath them to you when I die." Lizzie teased.

"Fair enough," Constance agreed.

Charlie continued to cling to Constance. "I think he believes I am a climbing tree," she laughed. "Maybe he wants a cracker. Would you like a biscuit, little Charlie?" Charlie nodded and batted his adorable brown eyes.

"I think Charlie would also like a baby brother or sister," Constance teased, getting a cracker from a jar and handing it to him.

"Oh mercy, no! He never gives me a minute of peace. Thank heaven I have Margaret to help with him. I wouldn't know what I'd do with myself if I never had a break. I am constantly exhausted."

"Don't wait too long. I adored my sisters and brothers, though I scarcely knew three of them. Within three months I had lost all three to disease."

"Your mother must have suffered so."

"She went on as best she could. We all must."

"Death seems inevitable for us all," Lizzie said with a deep sadness.

"I actually look forward to it in a way. The work and difficulties will all be finished and I can rest," Constance admitted. "Though I do think that while we are alive we should do our very best and not waste a single minute."

"I don't wish for death to come any sooner than it has to.

Especially with little Charlie in my life. He is my joy."

"And you are his," Constance said, noting how Charlie was curled round his mother and offering her slobbery kisses. "I envy your motherhood. It is strange that my life has been put on to me. I, a person whose greatest desire was to be a wife and mother, am a nomad first, and wife and mother to none."

"You are Charlie's godmother. I hope you appreciate that."

"Oh I'm sorry, Lizzie! I drone on and on and become so ungrateful. I am the happiest of women as Charlie's godmother. I promise to make sure he is well cared for if anything were ever to befall you. But never mind that as you are the picture of health."

"Hardly so. I've grown so soft since Charlie's birth. I'm like a walking feather bed with a belt pinched around the middle." The mental picture sent them both into fits of laughter, and all talk of death and lost dreams were soon forgotten.

What is she writing? How fast her fingers move!
~Charlotte Bronte

Letters

Winter/summer 1888

Dear Constance,

I will make time to say congratulations on the success of your latest work. Have you read mine yet? I'm anxious to hear your critiques. I know you will have some. Don't hold back. You never have before.

Elle removed her pen from the jar and began writing. She was in charge today as Constance had fallen into a deep depression and had let Elle's mind take over. She had much to say about Henry James' novel and was thankful she had learned how to use a fountain pen.

Dear Henry,

I've given up on you and think I shall never see you again.

But as far as your writing goes. It is superb. My first argument may surprise you. You blame the seductive woman on distracting the man from doing his best art. I blame the man for keeping the woman from being successful in her own right.

Your female character reminds me very much of a certain cousin of yours. The one you have told me so much about. Minny, is it? I know how guilty you feel for not bringing her to Europe all those years ago. Her subsequent death was not your fault. You were young and busy, and perhaps worried what it would do to your career if she were around.

What would old Henry say to young Henry? Nothing, because rarely does one wish it done differently in the end. Even in our mistakes we find hidden sunrises and golden eggs that would have been lost if we had taken a different way.

Now this will certainly vex you. I cannot, for the life, of me understand how keeping all one's manhood is the only way to have great art. Unacted desire drains women of their creativity. Perhaps it is different for men, but for women, the power and mounting pressure of imaginative desire becomes all one can think on. We do not get out like men. We are in our homes and in solitude for much of the time, and our thoughts and our passions can nearly consume us. Do you understand me?

I would end with the hope of seeing you soon, but I will not hope it and I certainly will not say it.

Always yours,

Constance

Almost before she'd sent that letter tragedy struck her dear friend Lizzie. She sent news to Henry as soon as possible.

Have you heard the terrible news? It was only a few months ago that Lizzie sat in my living room while Charlie crawled around me like a little bear and we discussed the elusive subject of death. Apparently, it came on swift and hard. She was exhausted from caring for the baby, and hadn't the strength to fight it. I have cried all day and into the night. The funeral will be in a few days. Will you come? Please say you will. I can't bear this alone.

Constance

Fenimore,

News of Lizzie's death came by post from Francis only a few hours prior to hearing from you. I couldn't be more shocked. When I last saw Lizzie she was in perfect health. How strange that her Bohemian husband and conservative father are now joined together by this little boy who will never know his mother. Francis plans to return to Massachusetts as soon as possible. As you can see by the timing of this letter, I will not make it to the funeral. I have sent all the appropriate condolences to the Bootts family. Poor Fenimore. I know Lizzie was a dear friend to you.

Henry

Dear Henry, *March 15, 1888*

The funeral was beautiful. Winter lilies blanketed her casket and cut evergreens lined the pews. Her husband is in shock, as is her poor father, but they managed to get along. Charlie cried for his mother most of the service until I offered to take him out. Once outside and bundled in his little red coat and mittens, he was quickly distracted by a flock of pigeons milling about. He chased them around causing a great flutter of panic amongst the birds, which made him clap his hands and burst into laughter. For a moment, even I was able to forget all the sadness as I watched a child's innocent joy.

The flowers you sent were beautiful. Lizzie would have loved them. I tied the pink ribbon around her wrist before the casket was closed. I shall miss her dearly.

Constance

Fenimore, *July 1888*

I sit, impatient to work: full of ideas, capacity—as I believe—there is an immensity to be done. Having said that, there must also be some relief along the way. It has been too long and I will admit to you only that I work better with you under foot. But I would rather not return to Florence. I am working on another novel and want to go somewhere I won't be distracted by well-meaning visitors. I was thinking... Switzerland?

Remember the lake in Geneva? You on one side, I on the other? I should like to go again. First, I must throw the throngs of followers off my scent. Then I will call for you. Let me know if this will be possible.

Henry

***

Constance was humming at her desk when Mrs. Farve passed by with a load of wash in a wicker basket. "You are in fine spirits this morning," she noted.

Constance straightened up in her chair. "It's a beautiful morning."

Mrs. Farve nodded doubtfully and left the room. Constance looked outside. It was actually cloudy with a bit of rain. She gave a short laugh. Why *was* she so happy? Was it because of Henry's letter saying that he was all set to go to Geneva? She pulled it from inside her dress and read it again.

Fenimore, *September 25, 1888*

You will hear shortly that I shall be in Paris for a time, but this is only a distraction. I shall be with you in Geneva staying at the Hotel de I'Ecu. You can stay across the lake at a nice little hotel I can secure for you. Nothing will be easier than to come and go between these two points, especially by water. Discretion is of utmost importance. I wait to hear from you."

She returned the letter to her dress and slowly ate her porridge, thinking the proposition over. She hadn't felt happier in weeks and she knew it was because of his letter. His desire to see her made her incredibly happy.

She went looking for Mrs. Farve and found her hanging laundry in the small corner of the kitchen. "Mrs. Farve. I have decided I need a change of scenery. I am relieving myself of this house for a short season and packing for Geneva. I shall be confirming my passage and leaving within the week."

"Will you be retaining our services, ma'am?"

"Yes. But plan to take time off until I return."

"Yes, ma'am."

Within a week Constance was traveling by train through the Swiss Alps to the lovely Geneva where Henry was waiting at the train depot when she arrived. She smiled to herself when she caught his image through her window. Though they wrote every week, it had been over a year since they had seen each other. He was stout, his beard neatly trimmed, his hair receding, but his eyes sparkled, and the secret smile he wore on his lips said it all. She pulled on her new hat and straightened her vest and exited the train.

"How was your trip, Fenimore?" Henry asked. His demeanor appeared casual, but under his beard there was an upturn to his lips and a twinkle in his eye.

A man came off the train with her bags. Henry pointed to the line of carriages and instructed him to take them to the one in the front.

"They look as heavy as I'd expect. I assume you brought every trinket you own," he teased.

"They are full of rocks. When I leave I plan to stuff you in my bags and take you back to Florence with me."

His eyes laughed, but he maintained his high level of propriety in public. "Your carriage awaits, my dear," he said as he escorted her to the waiting car.

Once they were inside and on their way, Henry moved to her side and took her hand in his. "I am so happy to see you again." He kissed it gently and then set it down, but didn't let go. The movement surprised Constance. His sudden change reminded her of the night in the hall. Their one and only shared kiss. Since that day he had built a fortress around himself. His change came as a surprise.

"How do you do that?"

"Do what my dear?"

"Put on such airs in public as if you hardly know me and then bring them down just as quickly when we are in private. I sometimes wonder if I have gone mad or if you have."

"I must hold you up as a lady of decorum. Anything less would be scandalous as much as we are together."

"But which is the real Henry?"

"They both are, of course."

"I see," she said, though she didn't really.

He explained, "Ever since Lizzie's death, I have contemplated life and how short it can be. What if it had been you that had come down with pneumonia?"

"It would have been much better if it had been me."

"Don't say that. Don't ever say that." All humor was gone from his eyes.

She rested her hand on his and tapped it gently. "I only mean that I have no child to leave behind. I would have made that sacrifice for her if I could have."

He touched her cheek. "My dear Fenimore, a greater

success than ole' Henry James ever will be. It is good to see you."

She sat up, "Are you okay, Henry? Have you been drinking?"

He laughed and kissed her lightly on the forehead. "I think I will have a much more successful fall than I had summer."

"I will, too." She could hardly believe the change. Henry rarely opened up like this. Maybe things really would be different. She could barely wish it.

That night, after a dinner with Henry, consisting of pheasant, goat cheese, and vegetable medley, Constance returned to her room, undid her boots, removed her outer vest, and replayed their evening together. His eyes had glistened in the candlelight as he spoke of his travels. She had never seen him so excited. Then again, she had never been his "guest," as he was always her guest. She smiled to think how proud he was to show her to her room, pointing out the indoor lavatory, the extra blanket he had ordered for her when the night grew cold. The desk he had brought in.

"I had them put it by the window so you can write," he added. "And look at this lake. We shall take many long walks along there, I imagine." She finished undressing, pulled out her bun and brushed through her long hair, and then made her way into the high feather bed.

She wasn't used to being doted after, but she liked it very much, she admitted to herself, as she pulled the covers up over her shoulders and stretched her toes as far as they could go. She yawned, exhausted from the travel. After all these many years, perhaps the tide was turning. The dream of Henry and Constance seemed closer than ever.

***

"Tell me about what it was like going to school here," Constance asked as they walked along the path that held Mont Blanc in the background. The lake reflected an even bluer sky, with the most vibrant red, orange, and yellow leafed trees on every side.

"Personally, I hated it, though I wasn't nearly as vocal as my brother, William. I disliked the classes and the teachers, and disregarded the beauty, yet I did enjoy the time I spent with my brothers and sister and parents here. My aunt Kate was also here for a time. She was a big part of our family growing up. She had a short stint at marriage that didn't work out and then she was back with the family again. No, I didn't like it, but there are things we appreciate more later in life."

They passed a couple, arm in arm as themselves, nodded their hellos, and walked on. After they were out of earshot, Constance slipped her arm through his and said, "Tell me about what you are working on now."

"I've got a project running in January in the *Atlantic.* I will send off the first installment shortly, but I'd like you to read it first. I could bring it to dinner tonight if you'd like."

"I'd love that," she agreed, as several small birds flitted in front of them.

"I hope you brought your bird book," Henry said. "There looks to be a healthy new crop to mark off."

"Why do you think my bags were so heavy? But we won't have your dear lady friend's binoculars, I suppose we will have to settle for my opera glass."

"We will make do," he agreed with a grin. They fell back into a comfortable silence. After a while Henry said, "Did I tell you that I saw Sargant the other day?"

"The painter?" Constance asked.

"He had just done a painting of Ellen Terry. Do you know her?" She shook her head. "She is an actress. Rather beautiful in the face, but abominable as an actress. She has the voice of a screeching parrot."

"Henry!"

She laughed and clapped her hands in delight.

"It's true! She was dressed as Lady Macbeth, half Medusa, half Rosetti. It was absolutely magnificent, as well as frightening. It's so outrageous it will do him immense good in his career."

"I wish I had seen it. Who else have you seen?"

"I just finished a letter to Robert Louis Stephenson. He sent me a copy of his latest endeavor, *Master of Ballantrae.* It is wonderful and fine and perfect. He is a rare, delightful genius. I think I hate him."

"Behind you, of course. It is difficult to keep up with the demands of being Henry James. I do not envy your social calendar."

"You mock, but it is taxing. I wrote three letters today and I haven't even started on my manuscript. But enough about me, what is Fenimore writing? Another slandering story about Henry James?"

"I did no more or less than you did to me."

"I have no idea what you mean," he retorted. "So, dinner tonight?"

"Is that an invitation?" She smiled, glad he wasn't holding a grudge.

"Of course."

"Then, I'd be delighted."

"We shall feast on parsnips, and roasted duck, and *The Tragic Muse.*"

"Is that your new manuscript?"

He nodded.

"Then I can't wait."

For the next several evenings they followed this ritual, working all morning, joining for a walk in the afternoon, then separating for work, again followed by a late dinner, either on one side of the lake or on the other. They spent most evenings back at Henry's apartment. For it was more like an apartment than a hotel room, with a sitting room, a small kitchen, and a bedroom on both sides. While compact, it was very functional, and Constance could see how one could stay months in a hotel when it was like this.

Henry picked at her brain while she worked on a needlepoint project and he smoked on his pipe. "I find myself continually writing from the perspective of a woman and I worry that I am missing the mark every time."

"But Henry, that's the amazing thing. You don't miss the

mark at all. You really do delve into a woman's mind better than most women do."

"Then why do my stories fall flat? I have failed at nearly the success you've had these past several years."

She set her needlework down on her lap. "I read numerous books and I can promise you that your name will outlast that of all others in time. Trust me."

The small glass of brandy in his hand burned an auburn red from the reflection of the flames. He swished his glass while he spoke. "But if there is something that isn't resonating in your womanly heart, you would tell me? Some point I am missing that only the fairer sex would understand?"

"Haven't I always been honest if not somewhat abrupt with you in the past? Isn't that why you have made me your confidant?"

"I count you among my dearest and most intimate friends. And my greatest critic." He pulled his pipe from his mouth and held it loosely in his hand.

Constance felt it proper to state her feelings as well. "These past five days have been the best five days in over a year."

He finished his drink and set it on a small side table. "Remember Christmas at Bellosguardo? The surprise snowfall. The stories we told in front of the fire? I hope to have more of those this coming month. If only we could still have our fun with the Bootts. Poor Lizzy, may she rest in peace."

"Yes. Poor Lizzy." They stared into the fire. Constance had been thinking about the subject of death for quite some time and was anxious to hear Henry's opinion. "Can I ask you a question?" Constance asked.

Henry chewed on his pipe with a nod.

"Do you believe in the concept of reincarnation?"

He gave a short laugh. "Not in the slightest."

"But your soul? Do you believe you have one?"

"Of course."

"When my mother died I received her best china and

several of her dresses. Whenever I have used the china I have sensed her presence so much so that I find myself talking to her aloud. It is the same with her clothing. I couldn't bring myself to be rid of them. I could smell her and almost feel her hand resting on my shoulder when I would look at them."

Henry puffed on his pipe and then said, "When I die I'd ask you to be rid of all my things."

"But in our things we might continue to live," she explained.

"I don't want my soul hanging about like an uninvited guest. Would you want to continue to live?" Henry asked.

"Perhaps as another. To have the life I couldn't have here. Have a lover. Have a family."

He shook his head. "That is preposterous. You'll go straight to heaven. I'll get rid of all your things just to be sure."

"You'd wish me to never have happiness?"

"Aren't you happy, Fenimore?"

"I have a portion of happiness. But I know there is more."

"But to be a ghost walking about in your dresses? It's morbid."

"No more than thinking of your dear Minny day after day." She knew he was still haunted by his cousin Minny. He did not respond so she continued. "I shall remain with my things and whisper stories to another and I will tell all of Henry James' secrets."

"I haven't any secrets," he said, readjusting in his chair. "And if you die first I'll be sure to send your soul to heaven. There will be no sharing of secrets."

"And if you die first I shall hold on to all your things so you will be forced to linger with me forever," she declared only half teasing.

As Elle was driven back to her hotel in Henry's carriage she wondered if this game that Constance and Henry played was dangerous. In the end Constance ended her own life and Henry tried to get rid of her things, but right now they seemed quite content. Could it stay that way? Should she intervene? Risk exposing herself by talking truthfully? Get Constance taken to an insane asylum? How else could she bring them together for good?

As had been the case every time, there was no warning when the now familiar pull and white light flashed in front of her eyes and she was sent rushing through the air like a coiled spring to the present. No warning, no waiting. No stopping it. Gone, gone, gone.

Nothing in the world is single, All things by a law divine, In one spirit meet and mingle – Why not I with thine?
~Shelley

Elle

Mackinac Island

It took her a moment to regroup, to look around and realize she was back on Mackinac Island. There was no doubt that she had never fallen asleep, but had been carried like drifting smoke through space and time. She had been gone much longer. The pain, intense this time. It seemed that the longer she was away, the worse her body felt when she returned. It was as if her soul was returning to a body that believed it was dead.

She lay still as her body and soul readjusted to one another again. She longed to go back. But she didn't have the energy. All she could do was lay there. After ten minutes she was able to slither off the bed, painstakingly inch her way out of the dress, and slowly climb into shorts and a t-shirt.

The scarab remained on the bed. She picked it up. It was cold in her palms that now contained a distinct imprint of the beetle brooch. She'd have to rewrap her hand and tell people she'd burned it on an iron, she thought as she returned it to the box. She called Jace but he didn't answer. She wanted to tell him what happened. Maybe he was still at his office. She grabbed her backpack and phone and headed out the door.

In her haste she had forgotten that she had no transportation, but she didn't mind. A walk would do her good. She crossed the road to the beach trail that followed the shoreline into town. She stopped a few times on large boulders to rest, but as soon as she reached town she was feeling like her old self again. That was when she saw the police chief. Recognizing Elle, he left his comrades and sauntered over to her.

"Miss Curtis. Mind if I talk to you for a minute?"

Her hands began to shake. Did he know about the scarab? Of course not. Why would he? "I was just on my way to the library," she explained. Why did she say the library? She was going to Jace's office. She was a mess under pressure. She knew he was just doing his job, but his official uniform set her on high alert.

"I'll walk with you, if you don't mind."

She hesitated, tightened her grip on the backpack strap. "Sure."

"I thought you'd like to know that the coroner has changed Mr. Gordon's death from accidental to suspicious."

She relaxed her grip. Of course he didn't know about the scarab or Constance. Of course it would be about Mr. Gordon. What was wrong with her? A man has just died and all she can think about is Henry and Constance. She tried to remember what the reasoning would be behind the change. "Because of the break in?"

He shook his head. "It caused us to take a second look and we found what probably killed him was a hit to the back of his head. Now it's not impossible to fall backwards down a flight of stairs, but it's unusual."

"Like someone may have pushed him?"

He nodded.

"Who would do that? Does he have any enemies?" She couldn't imagine anyone disliking Mr. Gordon. Except maybe one. But maybe it hadn't been anything. Maybe she read too much into that one conversation. Maybe she should keep her mouth shut.

"Not a one that we know of. Joe was kind of an odd guy, but he didn't bother anybody. Kept to himself mostly." He paused, pulled out a cigarette and lit it, but kept walking with her. "When I asked you about your conversation with Mr. Gordon, I got the feeling you wanted to tell me something else, but you didn't dare.

"Was there anything you noticed that was unusual?"

It might be a betrayal to Jace, but she couldn't lie to an officer. Besides, Nedra wasn't his real mom. "Well, Jace's stepmom Nedra showed up at the bar we were at and she acted strange around Mr. Gordon. Kind of vindictive, I guess? And Mr. Gordon left soon after. Didn't even finish his lunch. It felt like they had a history, but what it was I couldn't tell you. Do you know much about Nedra?"

He shrugged. "Not much. Came here with Marv a few years ago. Hangs around that Patricia lady a lot. They seem an odd pair."

"Yeah, they do," she agreed.

"I heard you're Linda's daughter, is that correct?"

"Yes. I came to take care of Lois' estate. My mom died days after Lois so I'm all that's left, but recently I learned Lois may have had a daughter. I'd like to locate her if I can."

"Interesting that you should mention that because one of the men at the station said that Lois used to wander around the cemetery. Went there every day to a grave on the bluff. Called Anne's grave."

Elle stopped walking.

The chief continued talking. "So I went up there myself this afternoon. Sure enough, there is a headstone. Thought you'd be interested to know about it."

Elle nodded.

"The name says Elizabeth Curtis. Died in 1976. Strange that your aunt and mom both named their daughters Elizabeth. What year were you born?"

Elle was silent. The news was shocking. Too confusing. Finally she answered, "1975."

"Same as this one that died." He rubbed his jaw thoughtfully and stared out past the lighthouse. "Now this is just a theory mind you, but could it be a coincidence that there are two Elle Curtis'? Or, could the person buried in the plot on top of the hill be somebody else?"

"But who would be buried there?"

He pulled a toothpick from his pocket and jabbed it between his teeth. "It might help if you knew what happened to Lois' daughter."

"I'm trying to find her daughter so I can share the estate with her. If she's buried up at the cemetery then I guess it won't be necessary."

"Is Jace helping you with that?"

She nodded.

"He's a good man. I'd let him do that if I were you. Not bad lookin' either, so I hear from the women folk."

Elle couldn't help but smile. They stopped in front of the library. "Looks like I've got some work to do," she said.

The chief promised to keep in touch and then turned and walked back towards Market Street.

Elle went through the doors and over to an open computer where she punched in the name Elle Curtis and the date 1976 and the word 'obituary.' She found one reliable link on a gravesite index website, but nothing else. She decided the best thing to do would be to check out this grave for herself. But first she texted Jace. This time he responded. He was still at his office, but was happy to meet her there in twenty minutes.

The cemetery was old; the entry, an arch of stones opening to a simple dirt path that wound around headstones and looked as old as the island itself. Grass grew high between the juniper trees along the edges of the cemetery where the headstones appeared more modern looking. She waited a few minutes and then saw Jace coming from the opposite side. She waved and met him in the middle.

"Can you believe this place?" She couldn't help the wide grin. She'd always loved cemeteries.

"It dates back to the early eighteen hundreds."

Elle beamed. Jace was a walking encyclopedia on all things Mackinac.

"I could spend hours here," she admitted.

"On a dare I spent the night in here once until the cemetery groundskeeper found me asleep on one of those older stones in the morning. Got in a whole lot of trouble. But I was the bravest kid on the island for at least a year or two. Until somebody else got lost in a cave and had to spend the night there. When the school let out so we could look for him he earned the bravest kid award."

"You're a modern day Tom Sawyer aren't you?" she teased. She'd never flirted so much in her life, but it was too easy with him. And his smile was worth it every time.

"No. But Levi Holland was." They both laughed.

A bird cawed in the distance. Everything turned eerily quiet. "It seems haunted. Sometimes, this whole island seems haunted," Elle said. Jace took her hand. It surprised her, but she didn't mind. It felt comfortable, like they'd been doing it for years.

They wound around the stones until they found the one they were looking for. A small, simple slab, like a child's headstone would be, just barely off the ground. They stood in front of it and stared down at the headstone bearing her name.

"Is it weird to see your own name on one of these?" Jace asked.

"Would saying I don't like it feel like an understatement? Something isn't right. I'm missing something."

Though she didn't want to think about it, she had to ask the obvious.

"Why would they both have baby girls with the same name?"

"Maybe Linda named her baby after Lois' baby."

"It seems like a snub to me."

They were silent again. Then Elle remembered to ask about his mom and brother. "Are they buried here?" Jace nodded and led her to the other side where two headstones sat side by side. Seeing it hit Elle hard. Finally she understood that Nedra wasn't his mom. She was a lady his dad had married. Maybe she could be more honest about her. But first she asked Jace to tell more about Nedra.

"She's odd. She likes my dad a lot more than he likes her I think. But at the same time I don't know if she really likes him all that much, either, if that makes sense. I was glad to see her get into real estate. Keeps her busy and out of my business."

"She wasn't always in real estate?"

He shook his head. "She's actually a nurse. Spent a lot of years working in a hospital in St. Ignace."

"Do you know what the connection is between Nedra and Joe Gordon?"

"The bookstore, I guess. Maybe she didn't pay her bill or something. I don't think they knew each other that well. And besides, she has an alibi. She was with my dad at the roof bar at the hotel last night. She says she saw you, too. That you seemed nervous about something."

"Yeah, I was nervous. I had the silver box. I wanted to tell you about it, but you were busy playing bass. She seemed very interested in it. She was actually pretty snoopy."

She paused and then had a thought and asked Jace. "You don't think she knows about the brooch do you?"

"Naw. Besides, we don't know if it really works anyway. You really came and watched me play?"

"Yeah. You were good. Patricia looked happy too."

Elle grew quiet. She had to tell him what happened. But would he really believe her? What if he told Nedra about it? Why would he do that? Why was she worried about Nedra? She was dying to share it with someone, and who else might believe her or understand more than Jace?

As they walked through the cemetery she decided to tell him about her experience.

"It happened again. I saw Constance. Actually, I was Constance. It was real. I know that now."

His answer was hesitant, but thoughtful. "You're sure?"

She nodded and then explained. "As I touched the scarab I went flying through the sky faster than you can imagine, yet it seemed slow. Like how it feels in an airplane. But not in my body. My body stayed behind."

"When did this happen?"

"Last night. I'm thinking about trying it again. I want to find out what happens to Constance and Henry."

Jace pursed his lips. He seemed unsettled about something. "But what are you going to do about Mr. Gordon and Lois?

Her brows crinkled. "It looks like they had a daughter together. Then she died. It probably tore them apart. End of story."

"Really? You think that's it?"

"No. I don't think that's the end. There is still something missing. Some reason that Lois went crazy and that my mom stopped talking to her. Don't you think it's interesting that Mr. Gordon was so fascinated with Constance?" It was the one connection Elle kept coming back to. Mr. Gordon had been the one to introduce her to Constance. "If only we could go in his house."

"What do you suggest? We break-in? It's already been done and I'm sure police are watching it pretty close."

"Of course not. I would never 'break-in'. Don't you know someone who could let us in?"

"You don't think they'll be suspicious if we suddenly want to see inside his house?"

"The police chief is the one that told me about this daughter with my name. We have to find out if she was really his daughter and if she really died. No one seems to know anything about it. We have a perfect excuse. Find out who is patrolling and see if they'll let us in. Even for ten minutes."

"Elle, I don't know."

"Come on, Jace. Every time I go over the facts in my head everything seems to lead back to Mr. Gordon. Maybe there is some kind of letter or document that would clear all of this up."

"Do you think Mr. Gordon is connected to the scarab?"

They were at the entrance of the cemetery now. They sat on a bench while Elle thought about an answer. "I don't know, Jace. But we have to make sure no one else finds out about it."

"I have a feeling someone already knows."

"Why?"

"Just a hunch. I have no proof except all the people who knew about it are suddenly dead."

This thought frightened her. "Lois spent time in a mental institution. I keep thinking about the scarab. Telling people you've traveled in time would easily put you in the funny farm."

"Do you need help finding out where she was held?" Jace asked pulling out his phone.

"Would you mind making a few calls? I'll do some checking on my own as well. Meet me later?"

Jace agreed. "At the house, or your hotel?"

"I checked out of the hotel, so meet me at the house."

"I'll bring a propane lamp just in case," he added as they left the cemetery and walked down the hill together. They split up near Market Street.

As Elle walked along the shoreline path she heard someone call her name. It was Patricia, a bicycle by her side. "I'm surprised to see you here. I thought you were leaving town."

"Some things have come up."

"Oh right. Mr. Gordon?" Patricia continued to walk her bike next to Elle. "Nedra told me about the break-in this morning at yoga. So scary. She said you haven't decided whether to sell or not, but if I were you I would totally sell. That house is haunted." Patricia went on without noticing Elle's surprised face. "Yeah, I'd sell. The taxes are horrible. That's why I rent."

Why did Patricia say it was haunted? Did she know something?

"Patricia, do you know of any mental hospitals in the

area?"

Patricia's shoulders straightened. "There's one in St. Ignace. Why?"

"I'm just looking for information about my aunt. I believe she spent time there." Patricia told her the name of the hospital while Elle plugged it into her phone. Then she turned to Patricia and said with a smile, "It's nice to see you, but I've got some things to do so I better get going."

"Sure, sure. I'll see ya later," Patricia said with a weak wave.

Elle started walking in the opposite direction and dialed the number to the hospital. The woman who answered didn't recognize Lois Curtis as a patient in their system.

"It would have been years ago. 1976 I think." She then informed Elle that she'd have to go through the archives to check. Elle guessed as close to the date as she could and the woman promised to get back to her within a few days. When Elle hung up she had an idea of someone else she should talk to. She only wondered why she hadn't thought of it before.

Jace's parents' house was not far from the library. He'd pointed it out on one of their walks the day before. The yard was small. Two rocking chairs sat on the sides of the weather-beaten door. The front porch squeaked beneath her shoes. She knocked. No one answered. She knew it was a long shot that Nedra would be home, but she had some questions she wanted to ask her. She walked around the side of the porch. A bicycle sat chained up. Somebody should be home, she thought as she called out.

"Hello?" There was no answer, only a slight breeze tickling the chimes hanging above the back steps. She walked down the steps and around the back, only to find it empty as well. Maybe it was better they weren't home. Maybe she should confront Nedra when Jace was around. That was probably a better plan. She turned to leave and was stopped when she heard a voice call out.

It came from a patch of woods behind the house. She squinted past the sun to see who it was. A medium sized man walked into the clearing and carrying fishing tackle in his hand. Was this Jace's dad?

Her mouth had turned very dry. "Hi. I'm Elle Curtis. I was looking for Jace. Does he live here?"

The man walked toward her without speaking. Finally, he answered. "That's my son. What did you say your name was?" He was less friendly than she imagined him to be, but she could see the resemblance. His build, his jawline, his shiny eyes, his brown but graying hair, all like Jace. Yet there was a hardness behind his otherwise calm demeanor that evoked a sadness she felt sure had to do with his dead son and wife and the guilt he felt for it.

"I came to talk about selling my house," she lied. Why had she said that? It had just come out.

"You probably want to talk to Nedra."

"Yes. Nedra. Is she here?"

"Nope."

Elle was almost relieved to hear that. She was anxious to find out Nedra's connection to Mr. Gordon, but she was suddenly nervous about broaching the subject. "Catch anything?" she asked pointing to the basket.

"I got my fair share."

"Where do you fish? I noticed you came from the woods."

He stopped in front of her and gave her a long look. "What did you say your name was?"

"Elle Curtis. I was Lois Curtis's niece."

He stared at her for what felt like an eternity. Then he noticed her bandaged hand.

"Looks like you hurt yourself."

She held her palm up and smiled reassuringly. "Just a small iron burn."

"Looks like you burned the other hand too."

She balled her fingers into her other palm. "I'm fine." Her heart beat loudly in her ears. "So where did you go fishing? A secret spot?"

"On the lake. Just put the boat away." Then as an

afterthought he added, "Sorry to hear about Lois. I went to school with her."

"You did?" Her face brightened. Maybe coming here wasn't such a waste. "Did you by chance know Linda?"

"Yep."

"Did you keep in touch with her?"

"Linda was what we called an island snob. She came from the rich side. We were the poor kind. Lois was always nice though."

"Did you live here a long time?" She was doing some fishing of her own.

"Moved away after high school. Came back twenty-five years ago."

"Were you friends with Mr. Gordon, the bookstore owner?"

"Same class. Heard he died." He started towards the porch. Apparently, their discussion was coming to a close.

"Yeah, yesterday." But she wasn't ready for it to end. "Did you know much about him? If he had any close friends?"

He stopped on the first step and slowly turned around. "I don't know what happened to him."

She squinted in confusion. "No, I meant, did you know if he had close friends."

"I told you, I don't know anything." He walked up the steps to the side door and unlocked it. "Sorry." There was an awkward silence. Finally, he seemed to recognize his curtness. He looked down at his basket of fish and said, "Why don't you stop by later. I'm going to fillet these up."

"Are you sure?"

From his initial grumpiness, she was surprised at his change of demeanor."

"Then you can talk to Nedra and Jace about whatever." Before she could respond the door closed behind him.

Elle thought about the strange encounter the whole way home. He had been one of the most unfriendly people she'd ever met yet he didn't frighten her – only made her sad. He was a broken man. Poor Jace didn't have a chance to win his dad over. Maybe she should let Jace tell him about the scarab. Win his dad's affections back. Perhaps she was wrong to ask him to keep the scarab secret.

On the way home she stopped at a small grocery store and picked up a packaged salad to bring to dinner. She rummaged through Lois' kitchen looking for a bowl. Lois had nice things. There had been money at one time, but by the chipped stoneware and mismatched silverware, the money had long been gone. As she put the salad together she thought about Mr. Gordon and Lois. How did their child die? Was there an accident? Is that why Lois and Linda stopped talking? Did Linda have something to do with it? Or had Lois been guilty of some negligence?

She went to the bedroom to change for dinner. The fancy dress lay across the bed. The box beside it. If somebody was looking for the scarab they would come here next. She had to hide it. She looked around the room and opened the closet. Too obvious, she decided before hiding the box under the pillows on the bed.

"There, safe and sound. Well. Not really, but good enough."

Seeing the scarab made her think of Constance and Henry. She wondered what was happening back in Florence. Or had they moved on to England? She remembered how it felt to ride in a carriage, walk dusty roads, say hello to everyone that passed her by. The dinner parties, though dull at times, had also been exciting. And the food had always been generous. She missed them both.

Beyond the superficial things of that world, she also worried about Henry and Constance as a couple. Could she alter their outcome if she went back? She could be there for months, even a year, and it was only the length of one night in real life. Wasn't time the one thing that was relative? Hadn't they said that in her physics class? She'd only go for a little while this time, she promised herself as she returned to the room, pulled the dress over her clothes, and removed the box from its hiding place. She placed the scarab in her palm, prepared for the stinging effect, and allowed the white light to thrust her backwards through the portal of time.

There is only one day left, always starting over: it is given to us at dawn and taken away from us at dusk.
~Jean-Paul Sartre

Elle/Constance

Venice

She landed in the water, swimming. Was she in a lake? A canal? Her strokes were weak, the dark water refreshing on the hot day. But Constance was slow, only planning to float, and Elle wanted more than that. She wanted to fly through the water and feel the liquid stream through her fingers. After some time Elle manipulated her technique, channeling her skill with Constance's muscles to move swiftly through the still river.

Elle was an artist. Her stroke, her signature; her arms, the brush; her movement, the painting. "Beautiful," people said when they watched her slide gracefully across the pool. But Elle never noticed or did it for the praise. She was only aware of the rhythm, her breathing, and how many laps she had left. It felt good to be swimming again, even if she had to use Constance as her vessel.

She finally took a break to see she was surrounded by buildings. Gondolas bobbed up and down, tied to the pier. The smell of the river was ripe and the wind was hot. It was summer and had all the markings of Venice! What good timing. She lay on her back, her white underclothing floating to the surface. *How uncomfortable, not to mention less than effective, it was to swim in so much clothing,* she thought, but it didn't seem to bother Constance at all who was having her own thoughts.

"I float and float. I wish you were here to float, too." Of course, she was thinking of Henry.

She dried off with a thin towel and buttoned a muslin dress over her wet underclothing. Elle was grateful for the swim. At least she wouldn't stink as quickly. She was also grateful that she wasn't wearing black, for Constance wore far too much black. She replaced her wide brimmed hat and pointy white heels which echoed against the stone walls, and started down the walk. She was soon stopped by a handsome Italian. "Miss Woolson!" He had skin the color of rich leather, eyes of dark chocolate and was dressed in native gondolier attire. He smiled brightly and waved.

"Tito!" She returned the wave to Tito, her personal gondolier.

"We are still planning on tonight?" the white of his clothing made his brown skin even more rich looking.

"Of course, though I hope you are bringing help. We have a long way to go."

"I bring another very fine gondolier. Like me."

"A friend of yours?"

"A very good friend." He winked.

"You're sure it is safe?"

"With Tito you are always safe, no?" His white smile was hard to resist.

"I hear there will be a full moon. That will make for a perfect ride," Constance said.

"It will be a very fine night. Are you sure you will not bring a friend?"

"I haven't any."

Sadness washed over the man's face. "Mr. James is not here?"

Her face held no emotion. Something she had become skilled at. "Henry is in England." She held her chin up and forced a smile. "Is there anything of great interest on the island?"

"An old shrine. And a very beautiful night on the water. You will enjoy, no?"

"It will be a marvelous adventure," she said with a broad smile. While outwardly she professed to be happy, Elle sensed Constance was anything but satisfied. However, she quickly put it behind her and focused her efforts on the evening trip. They were going to St. George of the Seaweed, an island three hours away by gondola. She packed bread, cheese, and meat for the trio, and hot coffee in a canteen. She met the two gondoliers after dark, loaded her wares into the boat, and off they went, the full moon illuminating their way and reminding her of the many canoe trips on the marshes of Florida she used to take.

The ride was relaxing and the island, just as Tito had described, small with an old shrine neglected and covered with overgrowth. They sat on the cement floor and ate their late supper with the moon as their lantern. It was warm and peaceful and there were no pests because of the late hour.

It should have been a perfect night, one she would write a poem about, like the night she watched the far off ships sail where the ocean meets the sky in Florida, but she would have rather made the trip with Henry. Had Henry been there, there would be a rousing story or two, embellished, of course. And he would have made them laugh and she would have felt warm inside. And he would have treated her like a lady. She frowned. The thought irritated her. Why was everything better with Henry? She rode back in silence, staring up at the moon and wishing for that which never would be.

As Elle lived through Constance's eyes she could see that Constance was right that everything we owned and touched and lived in had residue of our souls. Elle could feel it everywhere she went. In the old houses, in the shrine, in the clothing.

This led Elle to a totally new thought. Could time travel move one forward as well? It was just a thought, but Elle kept it in the back of her mind as Constance packed up all her precious things, her favorite brush, her Italian tea set she served to Henry in Florence, and her dresses, especially the feathered one Elle was wearing right then in the future. She held the dress between her fingers. This dress made it all possible. But what about the scarab? She hadn't yet received it. She'd have to go to Egypt. But when that would be, she couldn't recall.

As Elle packed the silver stamp box containing a picture of Henry, she wondered when his picture would be replaced with hers instead. Maybe after she died Henry replaced them with Constance's things, removing any sign of a special relationship between the two writers.

Finally, after nine months of separation she saw Henry in London. He had lost a little weight in his face, and his beard was neatly trimmed. To see him again was like coming home again.

"You are looking very lovely, Fenimore," he said politely, taking her hand and kissing it gently.

Closer to her ear he whispered, "When shall I get you alone?"

His words sent a shiver of excitement up her spine. "Tonight. In my room, after the theater," she answered back. They were attending a play together and she was anxious to hear about his travels. After the play he drove her back to her place. He slipped a bag in the room next to hers. Outwardly, Constance didn't show great excitement that she would spend two days with him, but inside Elle could feel Constance's heart gallop whenever he smiled at her. Whatever happened in Geneva was nowhere near over. Maybe this was the night Elle would get them together and save Constance's life and her reputation for good.

Tea was served and a fire started and then Henry and Constance sat and talked the night away as they were prone to do after such a long absence.

"The good doctor enjoyed his time with you," Henry said.

"Doctor Baldwin?"

"Yes, Doctor Baldwin. If he weren't married he'd have taken you up by now. I hear all too much how thoughtless I am. I should think he would thank me for not marrying, as it gives him more time with you."

"If I didn't know better I would say you disapprove of my friendship with the good doctor."

"I rather wish he spent a little less time talking about your saving qualities."

"Have you thought he might be trying to convince you of them?"

"I know firsthand of your many redeeming points and would thank him to think less on them himself."

She laughed at him, "Dr. Baldwin is a dear friend, and I'm grateful for his acquaintance. Without him, I'd be alone, for you are often 'gallivanting across the continent,' as Alice would say. Does she still blame me for taking you away to Geneva?"

"Not at all. In fact, she asked about you. That is a good sign. "

"I have done my best to win your sister over, but she has not made it easy."

"Yesterday I came into the room and I said, 'I have to tell you something.' And she said, 'You're not going to be married!' I thought she would come after me with her book." He chuckled.

"Why is she so against it?"

"When William announced his engagement in seventy-eight, she collapsed with threats of suicide."

"I would let her live with us. Would that please her?"

"She wants someone unattached as she is, so as not to be needy. You know how it feels when everyone else is married."

"I do," she acknowledged, taking a sip of her tea as she changed the subject. "What are your plans?"

"I plan to stay in London. Then perhaps on to Florence for a time. What about you, Fenimore?"

She attempted to adjust her corset. It had been done up too tight and was cutting off her circulation. Elle found corsets to be impossible, but wear them she must. "I travel next to Paris, and then back to Florence to pack. I will then move permanently to England, and then perhaps a trip with my sister. Somewhere exotic," she added, telling him about her desire to see Egypt, "Particularly Cairo."

Yes, Elle thought, *Cairo*. That's when she would get the pin. She asked Henry if he would be willing to join her.

"I must finish my play. It is to be performed in Southport next winter. I must work sometimes, too, before I can gallivant with you across the continent."

Constance frowned. "I haven't seen you in nine months. I wouldn't say we have been gallivanting together anywhere."

Henry set his tea down. "Would you like me to go with you?"

"There is no one I'd rather be with, or travel with than you. You know that, Henry." Elle stood and paced the floor. Did he feel anything when they talked together, took walks together? Spent hours and hours rehashing this exact scene together? Did he want more as well?

"I don't know as much as you think I know." His answer quite surprised her. It seemed as if he were opening a door for discussion and Elle wasn't about to let the chance pass by.

"Do you know about us?" Up until tonight Elle had remained silent and allowed Constance to lead most conversations, but Elle knew if she didn't speak up nothing would change. Elle pushed an equally frustrated Constance aside in her mind and took over completely. "Who are we together?"

He settled back in his chair, took a puff of his cigar and stared into the yellowish flame before speaking. "Who are we to the public, or who are we in private?"

"Are they not the same?"

"No. At least for me. I can't speak for you."

"So who am I to you in truth?"

"You are somebody." His eyes beguiled her with their warmth.

She sighed, "Somebody? Would you care to expound?"

"Without putting myself in a precarious position?"

"Would that be so terrible?" She sat down and picked up her needlework, but then thought better of it. No.

This was not over.

She set it back down again. To let it end here was not an option. Everything was so restricted. The corset, the wool stockings, all the buttons to hook, the long sleeves, the tight collars around her neck, and then the shoes. She wanted to rip the combs from her hair and let it fall loose around her shoulders.

"I am so tired of these little black boots with the tiny heal. How they make my feet ache. And this corset! I want to tear off this suffocating contraption and put on a cotton t-shirt and a pair of sweats and then curl up by the fire." She was talking out loud and didn't realize it. "I wonder if I could make a pair of comfortable cotton sweats out of one of those awful dresses in the trunk." The thought was funny. She stifled a giggle.

"Constance? Are you well?"

She looked up to see Henry staring dumbfounded at her. "Did I just say all that out loud?"

His eyes were saucers as he nodded his head slowly.

"Well, good. Cause I've had it with prudence. Who is she anyway? An old hag if you ask me." Perhaps she had a fever. The room was growing warm, a trickle of sweat slid down her temple. And since she'd dismissed old prudence she figured this was as good a time as any to just be out with her feelings towards Mr. James.

She stood and walked. First to Henry, then to the fireplace. She leaned against the mantel. She let her hands fall to her side. She tossed a hand through her hair, forgetting how tightly it was up in a bun and caught her fingers in it. Her hands went to her sides again. Grace was not with her tonight.

"Do you care about me, Henry?"

"Would I be here otherwise?"

"But do you love me?"

Henry dropped his cigar into his lap. He jumped,

grabbing his cigar and swiping the hot ash from his crotch.

"Fenimore, what has gotten into you?" She quickly took a cloth from the table and dipped it in water and hesitated before she handed it to him. He returned to his seat and wiped the ash from his pants.

"I want to know if you love Constance, because it's pretty obvious to me that Constance is in love with you." She wiped at her glistening forehead. She was pretty sure she was getting a fever.

"What are you talking about? And why are you talking in third person?"

"What?" Had she really talked of Constance as someone else? Well, that's because she was someone else. Elle wasn't in love with Henry the same way Constance was even though she sometimes did feel Constance's strong emotions and think they were her own as well. Though they were two distinct people, it was getting harder and harder to discern her thoughts from Constance's.

She crossed to Henry. "Do you remember that night, in the hall. You kissed me."

"I shouldn't have, and I've said as much."

She stopped and leaned over to meet his stare. Then she said in a seductive voice, "But you did it." Her eyes danced in the light. He shuffled uncomfortably.

"Yes. And I am sorry."

"Sorry?" Her fingers walked up his arm. "You tell me how you must keep all your manhood about you so you can write better. But how can you possibly write about love and women if you've never loved one? Wouldn't being in love help you as a writer?"

He rose, walked over to the fire, and took a nervous puff of his cigar. "I never said I hadn't loved one."

"Who? Who have you loved Henry?" Elle followed him. "Do you love me?" She leaned forward. Their lips touched briefly. Elle let herself fall into him. She'd never seduced a man before, but she liked the way it felt. She kissed him harder, the fever making her delirious with want until finally,

Henry pulled away.

"You are ill. You are not in your right mind again Constance. I would not even know you or the way you look at me."

He took a step backwards. If she had checked, she would have known that she had a fever of 101 degrees.

"If not me, then who? Who have you loved Mr. James?" She came forward again, her eyes glassed over. "Was it Minny, your cousin? The girl you didn't bring to Europe because you couldn't be bothered?"

His eyes flashed. He pushed Elle away and smashed his cigar in the dish so it became a smoldering leaning tower of Pisa. "Do not attempt to talk about something you know nothing about."

She'd struck a nerve, which was probably what she wanted to do, but why? Why did she want to hurt him so much right now? That wasn't Constance's wish, it was Elle's. She grew dizzy and braced herself.

What was she doing? She was going to mess everything up. "I'm sorry Henry. I just don't understand what we are. We certainly can't be considered lovers."

"Heavens, Fenimore,"

She touched her forehead. "I don't think I am feeling well. And maybe my fever has freed my lips. We've known each other for ten years. Do we really need to play this game?"

Henry grew serious. For once it seemed he was aware the truth behind her words. "This game, as you call it, is what makes *this* work." He pointed to her and then back to himself.

He leaned forward and said in a serious deep tone, "If we stop playing, if we give into our carnal feelings, our game is over. I never plan to marry and you have told me the same. Do you really see the two of us as man and wife, 'til death do we part?"

"I don't know. I just know that I…"

"Connie," he whispered, taking her hand in his. "I understand your feelings, but we must gird ourselves."

Her bad ear was ringing. She held her hand up to it. "I think I have another earache. Can you repeat what you said?" She felt so foolish. The momentum seemed to dissipate with the tide.

He only stared at her and then with a shortness admitted, "Perhaps it is a blessing your hearing is so bad. Perhaps I should leave right now."

Her face flushed with embarrassment. She stood. "Fine leave! Give some other woman grief, make her crazy with your clever innuendo. Tell her to gird herself year after year with propriety while you go flaunting about all over the country. Men have no rules in this day. It disgusts me, the blanket of hypocrisy on which your great prudence lies."

She paced the floor. Whether it was Elle or Constance talking didn't matter. Their thoughts were in complete sync with the other and the words came as easily as a dagger sinks into belly flesh.

"Ignore and forget her except when it is convenient to you. Tell her how much you respect and admire her, say that she is the only woman you wish to be with, that you love her voice and cherish every minute you spend with her. Then turn and walk away like you do so easily for weeks—months at a time—and blame it on her. Her hearing loss, her inability to sit still. Her feminine weak mind, her many trinkets. Make it all her fault while she waits and stews and worries and wishes with all her heart to be by your side even for just a moment!"

The tears flowed from her eyes. She quickly wiped them away, not wanting him to have the pleasure of knowing how he broke her heart. She lowered her voice and continued. "Wishes to be your wife. Completely and fully your wife in every sense of the word. Oh how I wish it!" she cried, tears spilling over her lashes.

The room grew quiet. Henry rose and walked to Constance who stared into the fire, devoid of any more anger. Another tear escaped her eye.

He handed her his hanky and said in a low voice, "You're not well, Fenimore. You have a fever. You're unable to think clearly. Tomorrow you will feel differently."

She wiped her tear and handed it back to him while saying steely, "I can promise you that in the morning light, without any stain of fever on my brow, I will feel the same. And yes, I will feel dreadfully ashamed that I said any of this to you."

Then without warning he leaned in and kissed her gently on the mouth. His lips were soft, warm.

Suddenly the room flashed with a blinding light. The fire, the room tipped upside down.

"No!" She grabbed his arm to steady herself. "Henry, help!" But she couldn't hold on, like he was made of slick oil as she soared through a tunnel at record speed, wind whistling, the earth warping and then straightening out. Then, with a thud, she was back lying on the bed. The historical world of Constance and Henry gone.

The shadows of you gone still took the night. And I was left alone to face the painful light. ~Barry Tebb

Elle

Mackinac Island

Her body burned like hot water over frozen skin. A thawing process. It wasn't getting easier, if anything it was getting worse.

She opened her eyes to see Jace holding the scarab in his hand.

"Jace," she whispered.

He took her head in his hands. "Are you okay?"

"The pin. I need to help them." She attempted to take the scarab from him, but couldn't move her arms. "I need to go back. She loves him and I think he loves her, too."

"Shh…" He tried soothing her sweating brow with his hand. "Just relax. I was lucky your front door was open." He stared down at the scarab and then over to Elle.

"I just about had them together! I need to get back." She attempted to sit up, but Jace eased her back down.

"I think you're sick."

"Constance was sick, but I'm fine. I just hurt. Coming back is always difficult. Painfully difficult. But I need to go back, because then Constance will be happy and she won't kill herself and become obsolete."

"And you think that if you can get them together all of that will change?"

"I have to try."

"My dad said you stopped by today." He studied his hands. His face was unusually focused. Jace rolled the scarab between his fingers and said, "My dad would love this thing."

"Jace you can't tell him. You can't tell anybody."

"Why? You want to keep it for yourself? What's really going on? Why did you go back again?"

"I told you. I thought I'd just go back for a little while. I wasn't gone long. And I almost got them together."

"Do you really think you should be interfering in their lives?"

She managed to sit up. The room began to spin. She closed her eyes to steady herself and then began to speak. "Think about it. First, she won't commit suicide. And second, she can have the companionship she so desperately wants. She is so lonely."

Jace didn't seem to be listening anymore. "All my dad wants is to see his son again. To change the outcome of his accident."

"If what you are saying about this thing is true, it wouldn't hurt to let him try it."

"Nobody can know about this. It's too dangerous." Elle's fingers began to tingle back to life. She could feel the blood whooshing through her veins.

"My dad was a great guy once upon a time. He might even like me again."

"Jace. No! You can't imagine what might happen if this were to get in the wrong hands." She held her hand out to get the scarab. He was starting to scare her. He seemed to be in a trance.

"Whose hands are the wrong ones? Mine? Yours? My dad's? Look at your hands, they're red. Burnt." He tucked the scarab in his pocket. "He just wants to see his son again. Is that any less virtuous than why you keep going back?"

"I'm not saying your dad is bad. I just think this has to be very controlled."

He pulled a key from his opposite pocket and held it up to her.

She squinted in confusion. "What is it?"

"Mr. Gordon's place."

She'd forgotten all about Mr. Gordon. With her strength returning she was able to stand. "How did you get it?"

"I told my officer friend about you."

"What did you tell him?" There was panic in her voice.

He fiddled with the key. "I told the truth. That you might have a cousin that would be his daughter and you are trying to find her. Besides he owed me a favor."

"What favor?"

"I took his very needy sister out."

"Needy as in special needs?" She looked confused. He laughed.

"No, as in highly narcissistic needy. So he was happy to help out. He only asked that we not take anything." He dropped the key into the pocket opposite the one with the scarab. "But first we have to have dinner with Nedra and Dad."

"Jace." She pointed to the pocket with the scarab. "Look, I know this is important to you so I'll make you a deal. I'll agree to let your dad use it, but first I need to take care of Constance and Henry. Just one more time." She attempted to walk, but couldn't get her legs to move.

"I'll agree to it on one condition. You take me with you."

She couldn't hide her relief and surprise. "Really?"

"Yeah. I want to see this world you're talking about."

"You'll need some clothing the right time period.' She frowned. "But I didn't see any men's clothing in the attic."

Jace must have already considered this because his answer came quickly.

"The Fort has period clothing in its museum."

Elle looked doubtful. "Will they let you borrow them?"

"Probably not. But I think I know a way around that. Now I only have one question for you. Is that what you intend to wear to dinner, because it might require a lot of explaining."

She looked down at the dark dress and laughed. "No. Definitely not right for a fish fry. She slowly removed the dress, glad she had her other clothes on.

They ate in the backyard on a small deck surrounded by large poplars. His dad Marv, wasn't much for conversation, but the fried fish was as good as any fish she'd ever tasted. She told him as much.

"My son was the real chef," Marv said as he stared down at his half-eaten fish and side of baked baby potatoes. Elle glanced at Jace who refused to meet her eyes and figured he must have meant the dead son. The one he'd love to go back and save. What would happen if she told him about the scarab's powers? She looked back at Jace. She wished he had given her back the scarab. He had promised not to tell Marv yet, but how could she be sure he wouldn't?

Marv gave a small laugh. "He went to culinary school and had just started his own restaurant. Man that boy could cook." The table grew silent. Sensing tension or an uncomfortable vibe, Nedra brought up Aunt Lois' house.

"Is it yours now? You might want to have it inspected. Have you changed the locks?" Elle answered her many questions: yes, she'd change the locks; yes, she was staying through the weekend. The woman was like a hungry hippo. And when she brought up the taxes, she was mayor of doomsday.

"Do you know what the property taxes are on that house? You'd be lucky to last a year. The island punishes its landowners, doesn't it Marv?" she said with a nod.

Marv kept eating.

"I was intrigued by that silver box you had the other night. Was that something you found in the house?" Nedra piled more salad on her plate.

"It was my mom's." She didn't want to make polite conversation anymore. She could feel another headache coming on.

"This is a great salad," Jace said to Elle, but meant for it to be heard by everyone. Marv chomped on a leaf and nodded in agreement.

"Rob sure could make a good vinaigrette dressing. Best I've ever tasted." Marv said.

"The house is beautiful." Elle said, hoping to change the subject.

"Nedra put a lot of work into it." Marv pointed with his fork. At least he wasn't talking about Rob again.

Nedra nodded pleasantly as she passed the last of the salad back to Marv.

"So that silver box. Have you looked to see what it's worth?"

She seemed unwilling to let the subject go.

"It's a family heirloom so it's not really about money for me."

"Anything interesting inside?"

"Just sentimental things." She glanced at Jace for help.

"Nedra used to be a nurse." Jace offered giving Elle a look that asked if that was what she wanted.

Nedra stood and collected their plates. "Long time ago."

"South county," Marv said.

Nedra nodded and then disappeared into the house with a handful of dirty dishes.

Elle looked at Jace and Marv. "In St. Ignace?" Where Aunt Lois went? She asked herself.

Marv lit up a cigar and leaned back in his chair but didn't answer.

Jace gave a quizzical look. "I'm not sure," he answered.

Nedra returned and started to clear the table. She'd grown unusually quiet. Elle stood up to help and Jace followed. "Why don't I go grab us some jackets. It might get cold tonight." Jace said before disappearing into the house with a handful of plates.

"You worked at the mental hospital?" Elle asked as she loaded her arms with dirty trays.

"I did."

"I heard my aunt Lois spent time there. Did you ever know her?"

"Oh, well. I don't know. Lots of patients come and go." Nedra popped a piece of gum in her mouth. "You two have big plans?"

Elle shrugged. "Not too big. Jace is the one planning most of it."

Nedra made a "hmmm" sound in her throat as she opened the door and entered the kitchen. Elle followed Nedra into the house and set the plates down and began rinsing them in the sink while Nedra returned the leftover food to the fridge.

Elle set a plate in the dish dryer and asked, "How long did you work there?"

Nedra shut a drawer in the fridge. "Thirty years."

Elle continued to scrub plates, her heart racing. "And you don't remember my aunt?"

"I'd have to look at a picture."

"What about Mr. Gordon? He was a friend of my aunts. You seemed to have some history with him."

Nedra shut the fridge and turned to Elle. A controlled smile crept across her face. "No history. He just didn't like me much, is all."

"Why? Did something happen?"

"He was weird. I'm sure you already know, but Mr. Gordon was fascinated with dead people. Had a thing for an old writer. Constance Woolson. He couldn't help but notice the strong resemblance between you and her."

"How do you know that?"

"I saw him the other night sitting on a park bench staring out into space. He told me he just saw someone that could be the reincarnated Constance Fenimore Woolson. And yes, he was serious. He then proceeded to give me a literacy lesson on this old writer."

"Shame isn't it? Her committing suicide. And for what? What was it that she wanted that she couldn't have?" Elle was surprised that Nedra seemed to know so much about

Constance, but felt upset about what she was saying. Who was she to make a judgment call about someone she knew nothing about?

Nedra didn't wait for Elle to answer. "I think she wanted a child. Don't you? Do you think it's possible that she could have had one? That there could be an heir?"

The hairs on Elle's neck rose like tiny spikes. What was Nedra getting at? Did she think Constance might have been pregnant? Was that why she jumped? Or maybe she never really jumped. Maybe she was pushed? And why was Nedra asking?

Marv coughed outside the window. It startled Elle. "He'll kill himself with those cigars," Nedra said through clenched teeth. "But maybe that's what he wants to do. He'd love to be with his son again. If only he could see him again. But that isn't possible. Is it?" She stared at Elle with curious eyes.

"Ready to go?" Jace said from behind, causing both women to jump.

Elle laid the drying towel on the sink and grabbed one of the two hoodies in his arms. "Thanks for dinner, Nedra. We'll have to talk again soon." And then followed Jace out of the house and into the carriage.

In every conceivable manner, the family is the link to our past, bridge to our future. ~Alex Haley

Elle

"You didn't tell your parents about the scarab, did you?" Elle asked when they were safely down the road.

"Of course not. We have a deal, he reminded her.

She stared out at the last remaining beach dwellers huddled in blankets in the frame of the setting sun. "I think Nedra knows." She told him about Nedra asking about Constance and if she thought it was possible to time travel. "Like she expected me to know the answers."

"I've been thinking about Lois. I think she knew about the scarab and may have even used it. Telling people you've traveled in time could get you sent to the hospital. And don't you think Nedra might have met Lois?"

Jace pulled the carriage over. They were two houses down from Mr. Gordon's yellow beach house. "If that were true than Nedra would have said something more."

"She has seemed very interested in the house. And the other night when I saw her at the hotel she took the silver stamp box right out of my arms. I thought she might run out the door with it."

"And what about Mr. Gordon?"

She frowned. She really didn't have the answer to that. "That's what we hope to discover tonight. Right?"

He nodded, and together they climbed down from the

carriage. With the setting of the sun and the shadowy trees, the house looked menacing and dark. She shivered. Her feet lumbered up the walk. This great idea was suddenly looking less than smart. Despite Jace's borrowed jacket, she felt unusually chilled.

Jace slipped the key into the lock and held the door for Elle to quickly slip inside. Once in, they waited for their eyes to adjust to the darkness before moving around. A soft hum caused them to freeze in place.

"Do you hear that?" Elle whispered.

Jace turned on his phone light and flicked it around the living room. Clocks of every shape and size: grandfather clocks, table clocks, wall clocks, cuckoo clocks, small and big clocks, old and new clocks; and they all had one thing in common, a constant ticking that was slightly hypnotic.

She looked around and asked, "Should we keep the lights off?"

"Let's wait till we're upstairs. I don't want everyone to know we are here."

She nodded and asked, "Where do we begin?"

He lit up the stairs with his phone light. "Up," letting her lead the way up the steep, wooden risers.

Upstairs there was a small narrow hall with bedrooms on both sides. Jace flicked on the light. On one side was a cozy library lined with books. In the center sat an old desk.

Jace opened and closed the drawers. "Look for letters, photos, books. Anything to link him to Nedra or Constance."

They split up, rummaging through invoices from the store, a few utility bills, a couple wadded up receipts for Chinese takeout and piles everywhere. Piles on his desk, floor, and stacks and stacks of manila folders. It would take hours to go through them all. Hours that they did not have. Then Elle found something interesting. She held it up.

"Look." Jace walked over to see a visitors badge to St. Ignace Hospital. The date read September 24, 1976. The patient name was Lois.

"She was there." But why had he kept it all these years.

Judging by the dust on the bookshelves and all the stuff around them, it looked like he had a hard time throwing anything away. Especially if they seemed sentimental in any way. Elle found a whole collection of Constance's books on the bookshelf.

"Look at this. Some of them seem very old." Elle picked one up and flipped through the well-worn pages.

"I'd say he was slightly fixated on her." Jace held out a biography of Constance with notes and several timelines written on the side. She carried the book over to a row of photographs on a shelf. There was one of a young man graduating from high school, his short hair and bowtie a throwback from the early Sixties. The jowls were not there, and the eyes were sleepy in a handsome way. Mr. Gordon? Next to it was a picture in a small frame of a woman with medium brown hair. Her face, cautiously optimistic, her eyes friendly. She wore a long skirt and jacket and a wide brimmed hat. Lois?

"Elle, I found something," Jace called from next door. Elle had been so absorbed she hadn't even realized that he'd left the room. Without thinking she grabbed the photo of the woman and tucked it in her jacket before joining Jace in what was presumably Mr. Gordon's bedroom, given the large pair of pants hung over a small rocking chair in one corner. A bed was pushed up against one wall. There were no paintings or drapes. Only stacks of books rising like towers next to his bed, by the door, in the closet, everywhere.

Jace held up a large leather binder. "I found it under his mattress." He spread it open onto the bed. At first it looked like math equations with lines and graphs. Elle attempted to decipher what he'd written.

"Space line. No beginning and no end. Bending space-time." She looked at Jace. "I've heard of this. It's basically a theory for time travel." She turned the page. There was another drawing. This was more scientific, with rings and spheres connecting at different points. Mr. Gordon's bold handwritten explanation stared back at them. She read aloud.

"Wormhole is a hypothetical tunnel connecting two regions of space-time. The regions bridged could be two completely different universes or two parts of one universe. Matter can travel through either mouth of the wormhole to reach a destination on the other side."

"So a wormhole is the future and the past connecting," Jace said. "The ability to punch a hole in the fabric of space time would require a huge amount of energy. Like a star or a black hole."

"All he needed was the portal. He just didn't know where it was," she whispered, thinking how Linda had kept it hidden for all those years. Elle compared this to her experience. "I crossed two continents in the blink of an eye. I could hear the rush of wind, and see the earth below me, but didn't feel anything cold on my face. There was a vast white light. And then I was there. It was almost instant."

"But why? Why did he want to travel in time?" Jace asked.

Elle shrugged. "If he was enamored by her like Christopher Reeve's character in Somewhere in Time, maybe he fell in love with her picture."

Jace's face fell into deep reflection. "He really believed in it. Almost like he knew without a doubt it was possible."

Elle closed the book. "Do you think he told anyone else about the portal?"

"If he did he would have been mocked by the entire town."

"What if he did tell somebody and they wanted it for themselves." Elle's eyes lit up with another theory. "Or maybe he knew they planned to steal the scarab and he was going to expose them. That's just as dangerous as having something physically valuable."

"That would mean Gordon knew about Lois."

That stopped Elle in her tracks. Her stomach dropped.

"Jace."

"What."

"I think Nedra knew about Lois. I'm almost sure of it now that we know Lois was there in 1976. Don't you think it strange that the people that knew anything about the portal and the idea of time travel have all died?"

"Except Nedra," Jace said.

"Right. But we don't know for sure if she knew about it. We have to find out if she knew."

"You should have been a detective," Jace said admiringly.

"I wouldn't make a very good one cause I should have already figured that out." Elle looked around. "We better go."

He tucked the leather book inside his jacket.

"Are you sure we should take that?" she asked.

"No. But it's better with us than with somebody else. That reminds me." Jace picked up a picture of Constance the police chief had shown her earlier and handed it to Elle. "I don't know why, but I think you should have this." She slipped the picture next to the other photograph and followed Jace back down the stairs.

They drove a few blocks up the hill and parked behind a garbage container.

"What are we doing now?" Elle asked.

"We've got to get me some clothes so I can go with you." He pulled his hoodie over his head so no one could see his face. "I'm going in through the cellar. Stay here in case I trip the alarm. Can you drive a buggy?"

"You just say, ha, and whoa, right?"

He offered a less than confident smile and asked, "1890, right?"

She nodded, hoping this wasn't the worst decision she'd ever made.

"You might want to turn the buggy around so it will be easier to escape," Jace said.

"Escape? Jace! That sounds serious."

"Easier to leave. Is that better?" He pulled on a pair of black gloves.

"Am I going to find out you're a professional thief before the nights out?"

He turned and smiled. "The only thing I ever stole was a razor when I was six. I wanted to be just like my dad." Before she could respond he disappeared behind the building.

She waited several minutes in agonizing silence. "Okay. Nothing to be worried about here," she whispered. "Just because he even had gloves is no reason to be frightened. He's a perfectly good guy. I'm sure the police will believe that when they put us both in jail." She blew out air. The horse sensed her anxiety and took a step forward. "Whoa," she called. Her voice sounded anything but steady as she tugged on the reins. It had been years since she'd been on a horse, except in Constance's world, and then she'd always had a driver.

"You are in complete control," she manifested to calm her nerves. The horse settled down and Elle rested back in the seat hoping to blend into the darkness. While she waited her mind drifted back to Mr. Gordon and his book about time travel. Had he known how close he'd really been to the truth? But why did he wanted to see Constance so bad? Why wasn't he more concerned with his child? Or Lois? They lived on the same island for sixty years. They'd had a child together. Yet, his only interest seemed to be with Constance.

Though it had only been five minutes since Jace left, it felt like a hundred. The wind rustling the leaves sounded like a rainmaker stick as the air was starting to whirl and spin around her, like girlish ribbons on the loose. Thankfully, there was little moonlight and she was well hidden by the garbage container even if the smell was sour. It reminded her of London and life with Constance again. It really had become part of her very own history. She missed it.

Just then a black figure came running across the grass. A burst of fear shot through her until she recognized the person was carrying a bundle of clothes in his arms.

"Go!" he grunted, diving into the seat and dumping the clothes in the back.

"They had the clothes under a secured display. I had to break it to get them out."

"Did you set off an alarm?" she asked.

"Probably. Go!"

With a flick of the reins the horse took off. When they came to a T in the road she asked, "Which way?"

"Left," Jace called, scooting in and taking over.

She couldn't help but giggle. "What are we doing?" Her giggles a product of nerves.

He gave a crooked grin, "Becoming Bonnie and Clyde?"

She laughed again. "And we didn't even have to travel in time."

They clipped through the neighborhoods, taking side streets and back roads across the island to get to Elle's house, which they reached in record time. Jace tied the horse to a cement pole while Elle grabbed his bunch of clothes and rushed inside the dark house and went right to the kitchen, where she opened and closed the drawers looking for a roll of duct tape. Jace had caught up to her by then.

Finding what she was looking for she said, "Let's go upstairs."

"There are so many comebacks for that sentence," he teased which made Elle laugh.

"You can change in here," she said, pointing to the spare bedroom before closing her own door. While she didn't plan on changing entirely, she did want to get a better look at the photograph. it was Lois. But there was something different about it. She compared it to the photo of Constance. Yes, that was it. There was the similarity. The jaw, the lips. She'd have to study it better in the daylight. She pulled the dress over her clothes and opened the door. The other door was still closed. After a minute it opened and Jace, in an old fashioned suit, too short in the legs and too long in the sleeves, stood smiling in the doorway.

"Now what?" he asked, tugging and pulling and looking out of place in his garment.

"We hold the scarab in our hands."

Then she frowned. "Wait. If you go to the person who owned these clothes, you could be anywhere. And there aren't airplanes. I may not see you."

Jace rubbed his jaw. "How long did you say you were

gone before?"

"Nine months at least."

"Plenty of time for me to get to you." He checked his watch, "It's almost eleven now. We have at least eight hours How long does that give us?

She quickly did the math. "A year or more. We should be fine"

"Where's that book, the one about Constance?"

She found it on the nightstand and handed it to him.

"Let me see this so I know where you'll be." He stopped and scratched his head. "

"What's wrong?"

"How do we come back?"

"The pin, I think." It wasn't something she'd even thought of when she was Constance. "Remember a portal is open on either side."

Jace thumbed through the pages. "When did Constance get the pin?"

"She got it on a trip to Egypt around 1890." She knew it was going to be soon because she'd spoken to Henry about it during her last trip.

"Then you'll have the pin soon enough. Be careful how you hold it or it will send you back before you're ready."

"I did think of this." She took the roll of duct tape she'd found in the kitchen drawer and asked, "You have the pin right?" He patted his bulging pocket.

"Now what?" he asked.

"Let's lie down," she suggested.

They lay down. He broke out in a grin as they slid closer together, their bodies nearly touching.

"This is interesting," Jace said breaking the ice.

Elle ignored his smile and got down to business. "Now, I'll be in Italy or England, depending on when we show up. I wish I knew how to predict that. How will you find me?" Elle tried not to be affected by their close encounter, but she found herself wanting to touch him more than ever.

"I have no idea. But I'll come find you. Then we'll return

together."

She smiled and touched the end of his nose. "Perfect."

"You act like we're going on vacation," he observed, taking her hand in his.

She couldn't help it. She was looking forward to returning to the world of Constance and Henry. And she was excited to share it with Jace. She tried to think of any advice she could give him. "Try not to take over unless completely necessary. Let them do the talking. They become suspicious and think they have multiple personalities and then things like mental hospitals and stuff come up and you don't want to end up in there." Then she thought about Lois and Linda and the child. Her stomach was in knots. An undeniable theory was forcing its way out. She had to tell Jace.

"I've been thinking. I don't think there were two babies born. I think there was only one."

His eyebrows went up in surprise. He sat up. "Does that make you Lois' daughter?"

Elle stared up at the ceiling. "I know that they didn't both have a daughter named Elizabeth. The date of birth on the headstone isn't the same as me, but it's less than six months different."

"But that still doesn't explain why Mr. Gordon was obsessed with time travel. If he was in love with Lois, why would he want to go to Constance?" She frowned. That was where her theory fell apart. "That's what I'm hoping to find out." She pulled out a long strand of tape. "Place the pin in our hands and I'll tape them together."

"You think that's a good idea?"

"I don't know if any of this is a good idea," she mumbled as she ripped the tape with her teeth.

He pulled out the pin, his shirt between the pin and his skin.

"I'll miss you," she said.

Without another word he leaned down and kissed her gently on the lips.

When he pulled back he said, "I'll find you." And then

placed the scarab in his palm and pressed it against hers while she hurriedly wrapped their hands together. The last thing she remembered was the color of his blue eyes before the white light overcame her.

When it is obvious that the goals cannot be reached, don't adjust the goals, adjust the action steps. ~Confucius

♛

Elle/Constance

Cairo, Egypt—March 1890

Elle was at a writing desk in an unfamiliar room. A letter was neatly set out before her.

Dear Henry, it began.

Clara and I have had a time of it in Cairo. I had considered going to Florida this winter and, on occasion, when the rain chilled through our bones as we climbed the pyramids of Giza, I questioned my choice. Still, I have seen amazing things and even stole a piece of the pyramid rubble. Four thousand years ending up in my pocket. I should be arrested.

Elle looked at the other objects on the desk, a piece of pyramid rubble, and the silver stamp box. She opened it and stared wide mouthed at what she found inside. The green scarab pin! Perfect timing. She shut the lid quickly, as if she'd just discovered a wonderful secret, and returned to the letter.

Would you know that last week we met with an old friend of ours? Doctor Baldwin and his wife! What a coincidence. They, like many Londoners, have taken leave of the grey city and made their way to warmer climes. Too bad they chose Egypt. Florida is much warmer in January. The good doctor gave me a most extraordinary little scarab pin. I was told it has mystical, telepathic powers. It is a treasured artifact. The voice in my head has been silent of which I am grateful.

Dr. Baldwin's potion seems to have done the job as I was well enough today to see the good doctor and his wife off to their next destination: the Holy Land. Where are you off to?

Elle wondered how she got any writing done for all the letters Constance wrote. Outside her window the rain pitter-pattered like soft gumdrops. She wrapped a shawl around her shoulders, to ward off the draft, sealed the letter, and called out for an attendant. A Middle Eastern man appeared at the door.

"Please see this gets off as soon as possible." He took the letter, nodded and was off.

Less than two weeks later she received a response from Henry. She carried the letter over to the fireplace and opened it up.

Fenimore, *April 1890*

Coincidence indeed, the good doctor and his charming wife arrived in Cairo near the same time as you. I should sooner throw the fox to the hen house than believe that tall tale.

A scarab pin sounds dangerous. I have done research on them and they seem to have much power or so the ancients say. As far as the voice in your head, you shall have to consult the 'good doctor' about that one.

I am grateful he watches out for you. Just keep two steps ahead of him at all times.

I visited our beloved Bellosguardo in Florence, I think back often to that Christmas years ago with fondness, but lo and behold there is no Fenimore to be found. The totality of the change in our old place is upsetting. All our evening talks, your stories. The walks along the river Arno. I could almost see the ghosts of our past silhouetted in the park, visiting the great cathedrals, while you voiced your hatred for each facade and flying buttress.

Sister Alice is more and more ill. She says she is working away as hard as she can to get dead as soon as possible. But 'the trouble,' she says, 'is there isn't anything to die of.' She's near me on Argyll Road *at Holland Park.*

England misses you.

Henry

***

It wasn't until the next January that they met again in

Liverpool.

"The play was wonderful, Harry," Constance called to him when he joined her in the theater foyer.

"Was it?" It was raining outside, but that didn't stop Henry from feeling gleeful about finally getting his first play to the public. "I was too unnerved to notice."

She nodded excitedly..

The manager of the theater appeared with two ladies dressed in exquisitely fine clothes that showed off their curves and introduced them to Mr. James. The finely clad ladies gushed their approval pushing Constance further away from Henry.

She waited patiently as he was inundated with kissed cheeks, handshakes, and autograph books until it became too much for Constance and she slipped from the theater and made her way to her carriage. She waited in the dark until there was a knock at the door. She opened it to find a frosty breath'd Henry standing in his overcoat and top hat.

"You left me to fend off the mongrels on my own."

"I couldn't take the crowd. Are you coming?"

"I've got my bags," he admitted as he jumped in and called to the driver to go.

Back at Cheltenham, the teakettle had begun to whistle when Henry finally came down the stairs changed into dry comfortable clothes.

Tea?" Constance offered.

He shook his head. "I was hoping for something a little stronger."

"Brandy?"

"Please."

She took a decanter from the cupboard and poured a small amount into a snifter and set it in his hand. He sat in the chair – his chair, she liked to think of it – by the fireplace.

She knelt beside his feet and removed his rubber boots and set them a ways from the fire. "How is it to be a famous playwright along with being a famous writer?"

"Nerve wracking. Wonderful, if the crowd responds

favorably."

"Which it did. I'm sure you'll have more than a few new dinner invitations." She returned to her chair.

He sat back and sighed. "To see your story come alive with the characters. You can't believe it." He brightened with an idea. "We should write a play together."

She beamed. "Now that I truly would love." Hadn't she suggested it many times before? "Collaborating on anything with you would be such an honor." She poured herself some tea.

Henry looked around and realized they were alone. "Where is your housekeeper?"

"I sent her home."

"Did you forget I was coming to stay?"

"Mrs. Platt will be back early for breakfast."

"I'm on edge with energy. Will you tell me a story? Something soothing."

"I could tell you about what I'm writing now. About a girl named Dorothy, it is an elegy to Bellosguardo."

"Ah, our dear Bellosguardo. Do you remember Christmas Eve?"

She took a sip of her tea and nodded.

"I have always been ashamed of my taking advantage of you like I did that night."

She set her cup down and feeling bold said, "It was reciprocated."

He took a drink and set it on a small side table. The silence between them grew wider. Elle wondered if she had pushed Constance to say something so bold. She'd already broken her first rule.

"Tomorrow we shall go see the countryside and discuss this play on which we shall collaborate. I suggest it be about two writers who are deeply in love, but can't be together because of unforeseen circumstances."

"What are the unforeseen circumstances?" Her ears were more than perked.

Henry's eyes shined. "An ill sister who insists her brother

stay by her side."

Constance grinned. Henry sat back and sighed, resting his hands behind his head. "Oh my dear Fenimore. Thank you for being there tonight. How beautiful you looked in your fancy gown with the feathers." He stood in his black stocking feet in front of her and held out his hand. "I am afraid of what I shall do if I am alone with you for another minute." He took her hand and lifted her out of her seat.

"We should dance. Do you have music?"

"Henry!" she gasped in surprise, though thrilled at the idea. She hurried over to find her small box, worried he would fall out of the mood. "How is this?" She wound up the music box and lifted the lid. The sounds of "Nocturne" filled the room as they danced in a circle.

Henry spoke low in her ear. "When I saw you at the play tonight amongst all the jewels and sparkling dresses, your lovely dress and hair done up in that pin, looking out of your element for my sake…" He leaned in and kissed her. It stunned and thrilled her. "You were the jewel of England." He kissed her again. Longer. Effects of the brandy most likely because she had never seen him so free with his thoughts and feelings. They were no longer moving, but holding each other as if their lives depended on it.

"Henry, I fear you are the one suffering from a fever tonight."

"Am I?" A crooked smile on his lips. "Then so be it, my dear." He kissed her once on the forehead. She could hardly breathe. The music stopped. The ballerina stalled mid-air. They stood staring at one another. He stepped backwards and bowed.

"And that is why I am going to bed. Alone. But not before I do this." He tipped her chin back and kissed her gently on the mouth. He staggered to the stairs. Then he turned and saluted. "Goodnight, Mrs. Washington."

Constance's hands and knees shook. "Henry?" But he had already turned and exited the room.

The next day Constance knocked at his door to see if he

would like to have breakfast brought up to him. He hadn't come down and she worried he might be ill.

"Come in," he called from the other side of the closed door.

Henry sat by the window reading a paper, the contents of his bag spilled across the bed.

"Did you sleep well?" she asked. There were bags under his eyes, eyes that looked a million miles away.

"Not quite," he admitted. She looked down to see what he was reading. Beside the paper he held a photograph in his hand of a beautiful young girl. Her wrist up against her chin, her eyes defiant and expecting. "Is this Minny?" It was no secret to Constance that Henry had loved his cousin Minny. Though he'd never said it, there were times he'd get that far away look and she'd know he was thinking of her. He'd even based a main character on her once.

"I'm looking for inspiration for my next play."

"You mean the one we're going to write together?"

"What?" His eyes sharpened. "Ah, yes. Our play. Well, first I have to write the one I am already committed to. Then we'll write something together."

Constance tried to see whom the letter was from, but Henry had it quickly folded and put away in his inside jacket pocket before she could read a word of it.

Constance said nothing more of the letter or the photograph. "Can I bring you coffee or breakfast?"

"No need, my dear. I'll come join you in the kitchen." He smiled reassuringly as he took her by the arm. "Let's go."

***

Dearest Harry, *July 1891*

I have just heard the dreadful news that Alice has found a tumor in her liver. Though I am ready to quit England altogether, I shall visit Alice in your name as soon as possible.

I have started the Bellosguardo story and I wish for you to read it. Dr. Baldwin revived my nostalgia when he described the villa like 'a palace of pure gold, floating in the sunset sky.' There flashed a scene before my memory of the house waiting at the top of the hill like a bulwark of the Celestial City: I wish to have stayed there with you!

Instead, I have settled down in a five-hundred-year-old house on Oriel Street across from Corpus Christi College and you have run off to Ireland. I hope you will come visit when you return to England. I miss you desperately. Our time together last was something I will hold dear to my heart as long as the sun shall rise and set. I look forward to collaborating on a play very soon.

Dear Henry, you are like a stream of everlasting life to me. Come when you can!

Always yours,

Constance

Several weeks passed and there was no reply from Henry. She had just finished another epistle to Mr. James when Mrs. Rawlings, her new housekeeper, came to her room and announced she had a visitor. "A Mr. Stokes."

She sat with a puzzled look on her face. She didn't know anyone of that name. She held out the letter to her housekeeper and said, "Here's a note for the post. Tell Mr. Stokes I'll be there in a moment."

"Yes, Ma'am." Mrs. Rawlings took the note and exited her room. Constance checked her face in the mirror, put a little powder on her nose, smoothed her hair with the palm of her hand, and made her way to the front hall.

The man in the sitting room wore well-worn trousers, a stained, slept-in ivory shirt, and wore a hat covered in dust covering hair past his collar. A working man. Not anyone she had met before and she couldn't imagine what he wanted. His eyes lit up when he saw her.

"Elle?"

Why did his blue eyes seem so familiar?

"It's me, Jace." He removed his ragged hat and ran a hand through his tangled mess that needed a shampoo. "This is so cool. You really do look like Constance." he replaced his hat.

She waited for a cloud of dust to appear, but it stayed on the hat.

"I am Constance." She frowned. She did not appreciate his intimate tone. Constance was in complete control today.

A look of disappointment crossed his face. After a pause, he pulled up his shoulders and said, "So, have you finished what you came here for?"

"Finished with what?" She was ready to call Mrs. Rawlings back in to escort her unwelcome visitor out.

His smile faded. "Elle?" Upon hearing her name, Elle began to wake. She knew there was truth in what he said, that deep inside she was Elle, but it seemed like a far off dream. And then, as if watching a film in fast forward she remembered everything. Jace, Mackinac Island, Lois, Mr. Gordon. Yes. Of course. Could this stranger hold the soul of Jace?

"Where have you been?" she meekly asked.

"Tennessee. Worked in a flour mill, the rail yards, a coal mine and then had to work on a ship to get over here to England. And we're not talking a cruise line, we're talking wooden decks, under birth rooms that smelled of vomit and…" he held back the word. "I followed your trail from Paris, Italy, and then to England again. Do you ever sit still?"

Constance's cheeks had turned a bright red. Unaware of her discomfort he went on, "I'm ready to take a real shower, anyways." He took a breath and asked, "Did you ever get the pin?"

"Pin?"

"The scarab pin. Our ticket out."

"How did you know about the scarab pin?" Constance said even as Elle's memories slowly floated to the surface. She was Elle. And he was the lawyer. They'd met on Mackinac Island. How long had it been? A year? Longer? "Mackinac Island. I live on Mackinac Island. My childhood home."

"Am I talking to Elle or Constance? I'm kind of confused."

"And you're Jace, though you don't look anything like him. You're at least ten years younger than he is."

"Honey, you're about ten years older," he smarted back.

Her eyebrows knitted together. "That's a twenty-year span."

"Were you wondering where I was?"

"Yes, of course I wondered. I wondered every day at first. I guess I got busy here and sort of. Well, I've grown quite accustomed to this place."

"Did you do what you needed to do for Constance and Henry? Are you ready to go back?"

She didn't know how to answer that question. Had she? What had she come here for? Then she remembered Constance's bouts with depression. Her adoration for a man who was like a stone wall when it came to love, and her inability to break him down for longer than a few minutes at a time. She studied this stranger in front of her. He was thin, his face that of a young twenty-something, handsome man, though not resembling Jace physically except for his mannerisms and the way he spoke. He was so much younger than she was now. And he was too thin.

"You look like you haven't eaten in days."

"I haven't eaten much in months."

The motherly instincts kicked in. "Come with me." She took him to the kitchen, grabbed an apple from the bowl on the table, a roll from dinner the previous night from the bread box, and cut a chunk of current cake and placed it in front of him at the table.

He inhaled the bread and cake and then sat back and chewed on his apple like he'd never tasted anything so sweet.

"You seem to have complete control of your host," she observed.

"My host?"

"I can't think of a better word to describe the body you have inhabited."

In between bites he explained. "His name is Jonas. He was much stronger in the beginning, but I took over and have been making decisions for a long time."

He took another bite of his apple and said between crunches, "You never took over, did you?"

She shrugged. "It was so much easier not to. I didn't have to figure out how to do things like cook, chop firewood, speak the languages that she knows, recognize people, know what to say. So I let go. It's like I've been watching a movie."

"More like a virtual reality movie. You could make a lot of money doing this. Forget about changing the past, just live in it."

His statement struck her hard. It was as if he opened the door and let in a very bright light. "Jace, that's it!"

"That's what?" He looked utterly confused.

"Whoever broke into Mr. Gordon's place wants the scarab so they can do exactly that. Make money off other people who want to live in the past. Be someone famous for a day. Live in their shoes. People would be lining up to have a chance at that."

"For a hefty price," Jace said.

"Exactly. Maybe that is what Nedra is planning."

"Why do you think Nedra wants the scarab?"

Elle shrugged. "Call it a hunch."

"A hunch?" Jace didn't seem convinced. "Because she wants to sell the house?"

"She has been so interested in Lois and her things. And especially the silver box. Like she was looking for something. I wonder if she knew about it. Maybe from Lois."

"You think Lois knew? Do you think she traveled back here?" Jace asked.

"I see no sign of her whatsoever. As far as I can tell she didn't. I'm no closer to knowing the answers to that mystery. But can you imagine what people would do to travel back in time?"

"Do you think it works to go forward as well?"

She shook her head. "It's untested. But I still think it requires part of a soul. Touching the soul of a great-grandmother could get you passed on to a future great granddaughter, that sort of thing. But if you want better control you'd need something physical like clothing. That way you could pinpoint where you want to go.

"Do you have the pin?"

"Yeah," she said with no enthusiasm. A deep sadness

pressed against her chest.

"Good. Then we should head back right away." Jace seemed anxious to go. But Elle was anything but ready. There was still so much to do.

She displayed a fake smile and said, "I'll go look for it." She quickly turned away as she could feel herself getting emotional.

The scarab pin was in the small silver box that Henry had given her several Christmases ago, on the dressing table. She stood in her room and brushed her hand across the top, reading the inscription, wondering what would happen to Constance if she left now? What would happen to Henry?

She lifted the lid. The scarab pin stared up at her with a look of concern, as if it knew what was happening. If she were to leave now, she'd never see Harry again. She'd never hear his voice or his stories and he'd never look at her the way he did that made her feel warm all over. His attention, his story telling. His everything, gone in an instant if she went back. It would kill her. This wasn't Constance speaking anymore. This was Elle. Was she falling in love with him? Maybe, but one thing she was sure of. She couldn't leave. Not now. She had to say goodbye first.

She shut the box and looked for a place to hide it. The trunk at the edge of her bed filled with the dresses seemed like a good spot. She tucked it in the bottom and quietly locked the lid tight.

"I'm so sorry," she said when she returned to the sitting room. "I can't seem to find it. I'll keep looking. It can't be far."

Always the optimist, he offered a smile and said, "I'll help you. I've got nothing else to do."

She smiled politely at this young man who professed to be Jace. It was hard for her to grasp. He was so much younger than Henry. He seemed almost to be a child. "I'm sure I'll find it soon. In the meantime, have you seen London? I'd be happy to give you a personalized tour of this great city."

"Elle. It's time to go. Who knows what's happening to

our bodies. It's not safe to be here so long."

She stared at him, searching for the right words. He seemed to read her mind. "You can't stay here. This life. It's not yours."

His words scorched her heart. "But Constance is my life. Henry is my life."

He watched her carefully. "You've fallen in love with him haven't you?"

"No," she said too quickly. She walked over to the window and glanced out the draped window.

He sighed. "He doesn't know you, Elle, he knows Constance and from what I've read, I don't think he loves her, either."

She shot around. "Yes he does!"

"You know this?"

"I do." Her face blazed fire engine red.

"Then why doesn't he marry her?"

She walked over to Jace who was leaning against the wall whirling his weathered hat in his hands. She grew angry. "I don't care who I am or what you want to call me. He told me. He kissed me."

He stopped twirling the hat. "He kissed you?"

"Yes. Several times. Look, I can change things. I can save Constance. I can make him love her."

"Elle, nothing you do here is going to change what happened. But if you stay, your real body will wither and die. This life isn't your choice. You can't force your will on her."

Elle crossed her arms in defiance. How dare he accuse her of forcing her will on Constance! She hadn't ever forced it, but had helped her do and say what she already believed. She just gave her a nudge in the right direction.

Besides, Jace was being a total hypocrite. "What about you? Your Jonas doesn't even have a voice anymore." Suddenly she didn't feel so bad about not giving him the scarab pin.

Jace paced the room. "You're right, I'm not being fair. It's just, I had a professor once say that every decision we make opens up a new branch or path, like a stream of light. If you change the past you'll only open up an alternate future. When you go back to the life you already knew, your past will be as it ever was. You either take the new path and ride it out, or you stay on the one you're currently on. You can't jump ship."

Elle frowned. She didn't want that to be true. "That doesn't make sense."

"You can stay here and change things for Constance, but when you return to your life the past will still be the same. Constance will have died the same way. You'd have to stay in this world to have it change permanently. And if you do, you're going to miss some pretty great stuff in *your* reality. Your *real* reality. And I'm not just talking about me." He sat down on the sofa, his hat still in his hands.

She took a step forward towards Jace. "I can't just quit now. Not when I've come so far. And I still have so many questions about Lois and Constance and Mr. Gordon."

"I think we'll have better luck figuring that out from Mackinac Island." He leaned forward, resting his forearms on his knees. "Your feelings for Henry are Constance's feelings. Try to separate the two and you'll see I'm right."

He was wrong on that count. She loved Henry just as much as Constance did. But she didn't want to fight him on this. She needed a new approach. She sat beside him. "Jace, I don't want to leave." That was the truth.

"I know."

"So what do I do?"

"You have to find the scarab."

She felt a pinch of guilt, but remained silent.

He stood from his chair and walked to the door. "What if I give you a few weeks to tie up loose strings? Two weeks to say goodbye to Henry and Constance."

"Two weeks to save Constance," she whispered hopefully.

Jace nodded.

He replaced his hat. "But only if you let me stay here. I'm tired of looking for a place to sleep at night."

"Sure." She didn't know how she'd explain this new guest, but she'd think of something. She also knew two weeks would never be enough time, but if she kept the scarab hidden, she could push for more time later. For now she would go along with his plan. "But only if you promise to let me get you a new hat."

Jace smiled and removed his hat and held it out to her. Two weeks. She thought. She'd have to work fast. There was still so much to do. But it would be better to have Jace's help then have him as an enemy. She clasped the hat in her hands, their hands touching momentarily.

From my rotting body, flowers shall grow and I am in them and that is eternity. ~Edvard Munch

Elle

August 1891

Freshly aware that she was living in Constance's head, Elle spent more time thinking of her other life, the one on the island, her aunt's home, her job in Florida. Jace. She had to work fast to find the connection with Mr. Gordon and Lois and Constance, and save Constance and Henry's relationship.

Constance sat at her desk contemplating time travel. Elle took a piece of paper and wrote down the question, "Is time travel possible?" The thought had been as much Constance's as it was Elle's for lately she'd been thinking about reincarnation which had given Elle an idea. What if it wasn't about Aunt Lois traveling back in time? What if this was more about Constance? An opportunity for a different life. A glimpse at the future. Couldn't she travel forward as well as back? She only needed a portal and a piece of a soul. Could sharing Elle's soul bring her forward?

She began leaving little notes for Constance, writing questions about time travel, the scarab, and the idea of a portal. Copying what she could remember from Mr. Gordon's physics books, she drew the idea of space-time and wormholes while Constance, on her own, spent a great amount of time reading about time travel and telepathy.

Elle wrote down the names and addresses of Aunt Lois and Mr. Gordon. Hopefully, when she was gone, Constance would read it and ponder, and if it were possible, she could travel in time herself.

Jace didn't mention the scarab for three more weeks as they were too busy exploring London, the cathedrals, Big Ben, and traveling through the countryside enjoying some warm August weather. As they spent more time together, Elle remembered the tender feelings she had for Jace. Though this man didn't look like him, in all other aspects he was the same. He even bought her a necklace. A simple pearl on a gold strand. It looked vaguely familiar. She was just about ready to tell him about her theory when she had an unexpected visitor.

They'd returned from the museum and had just sat down for a quick bite of lunch. It was August twenty-sixth, this character Jonas's birthday. Through the window she could see a carriage pull up and Henry step out. What would happen with Henry and Jace in the same room? Would she be able to explain Jace away enough to please Henry? Would he ask about the necklace? She wished he hadn't shown up unannounced, and felt slightly vexed that he thought he could just appear at any time and she would always be waiting eagerly by the window for him.

Henry stood in the doorway, his eyes following Constance, noticing the necklace, and then moving to Jace.

"Henry! How nice to see you." She walked toward him with an outstretched hand.

"Fenimore," he said gruffly. "It appears you have a guest. I didn't mean to intrude."

"Nonsense. Please, join us for lunch." She looked back at Jace who was eyeing Henry in the same way Henry was eyeing him. Like two wild animals sizing each other up.

Jace walked over and held out his hand. "I'm Jonas Broadbent."

"Jonas, this is Henry James, I'm sure you've heard of him?" She hoped she wasn't acting too nervous. Henry would be suspicious. Especially since Jace forgot to let her introduce him first as was customary in that day.

They shook hands. "Yes. I've read a few of your books."

"Oh really?" Henry seemed less than convinced. "Which ones?"

"*Wings of a Dove*," Jace said quickly. Elle squeezed her eyes shut.

Henry gave him an odd look. "I don't have a book by that name."

"I suppose I have the wrong author." Jace said, stumbling over his mistake with a flushed face.

He turned to Elle. "Constance," he said carefully making sure he got the name right as he'd grown used to calling her Elle. "I'm going to attend to some business. I'll be back in a few hours."

"Thank you." She smiled politely and escorted him to the door. As he walked down the street she wondered where he would go and hoped it wouldn't rain, as he had failed to take a jacket or an umbrella or even a hat and there were menacing clouds ahead.

"He's a little young for you isn't he?" Henry said when he was out of sight. "I'd say he's half your age. And he certainly doesn't know his literature. What book was he referring to?"

She shook her head. "I haven't any idea. Though it's a good title. No, he's..." Yes. He was young. Still in his twenties, she could be his mother. "The son of a friend of mine, and he needed a place to stay."

"How long?"

"What?" she said, turning back to Henry not sure if she heard him right. He repeated himself.

She finally answered. "Several weeks. Henry, he's just a boy."

"He doesn't think so."

She gave a thin laugh. "Ridiculous."

"I see it in his eyes. That boy's in love with you."

"What?" She had no air to argue.

"Be careful, Fenimore. You don't need scandals to increase your book sales."

This caught her attention. He was worried that she be involved in a scandal? How generous of him to suddenly care so much. Her face grew warm with frustration. Her eyes narrowed. "If I didn't know better I'd say you were jealous."

"Just concerned."

Her head was beginning to ache. "Well, you needn't be. Jonas is a very nice young man."

"Nice enough to sleep in your house?"

She was surprised by his hypocritical behavior. "It's not like I couldn't go to wherever you might be staying and find you on the arm of a female acquaintance or two. Believe it or not, I do have a life beyond that of admirer of Henry James."

"I shall be going now." He reached for the doorknob.

She grabbed his arm to stop him. "You don't have to leave."

"I only wanted to come by and invite you to the opening of my play, *The American, in London.* I have set aside one ticket, but I can see you'll need two."

"Oh Henry! That is wonderful!" She threw her arms around his neck. He weakly hugged her back. "Opening in London. Now you really are a full-fledged playwright. When does it open?" She took his hand in hers.

"October."

Her smile froze. "Oh." October was weeks away. How would she convince Jace to stay several more weeks?

As they walked outside Henry's mood changed considerably. "You'll need a new dress. Something from Paris. I'll send for one."

"That's very kind of you."

When he reached his carriage he turned back, remembering. "Doctor Baldwin mentioned stopping by to see you in the next week. Shall I warn him that you have company?"

"Doctor Baldwin is always welcome here."

"Of course he is." His eyes grew dark. His behavior was as curious as it was alarming. He climbed into the carriage and with the flick of the reigns was off, leaving Constance on the walkway, unsure of which way to go.

When Jonas returned later that evening he mentioned the scarab for the first time over dinner.

"I haven't found it yet," she lied.

"You haven't looked for it."

"Yes, I have," she said, looking down at her half-eaten bowl of vegetable stew.

"Have you looked in that chest?"

"My chest?" She feigned shock, trying to distract him.

He didn't seem amused. "The trunk at the end of the bed. The one that has Constance's dresses. The one that ends up in the attic of your aunt's house."

"Of course I did." She stirred the soup nervously.

"And you didn't find it?"

She shook her head, unable to look at him.

"Then why did I find it?" He held up the scarab, careful to hold a cloth between his hand and the pin.

Her eyes grew dark. "How long have you had it?"

"Couple days. Seems funny you couldn't find it."

"Jace, I told you I don't want to go. I want to stay and help Constance."

"Looks like you helped her real well today. Now Henry thinks she's stepping out on him."

"Henry has no right to judge. He has dinner nearly every night at another woman's house and is constantly bombarded by female admirers of all ages that swoon and make love to him, and when I have one male friend with me on a day he arrives unannounced, he becomes angry and jealous."

"It wouldn't have happened if Constance were in total control of her life."

"You don't know that. He is a typical...why can't she have a male suitor? They haven't made any promises to each other." She pulled down two bowls from the cupboard. "His play opens in October. He has asked me to come."

"Fine. Constance will enjoy it."

"I want to go."

"Why? What do you hope will happen?"

"Nothing. I just want to see it."

"And then what? You'll want a few more months after that. It's time to go."

"His sister has cancer. She's dying. Once she's gone, I really think Henry will ask Constance to marry him. I'll make sure that happens."

"Cause you have the power to make him do that? I don't think so. He either will or he won't, and as history proved, he won't."

His disregard for her feelings was irritating. "But I can change all that! Constance was too reserved. She didn't fight for his attention.

"She just acted like she didn't care if he came or left, but I know differently. I have felt her heart beating when he enters a room and how coy Constance plays. He calls her a modern woman, but she's anything but modern when it comes to professing one's deepest desires. She's as romantic and shy as any woman ever has been."

His mouth grew set. "If I go alone, I'll take the scarab out of our hands and force you back."

Tears sprung to her eyes. She rushed to his side and knelt down. "Please, Jace. Just a few more months."

"This is bad, Elle."

She wiped her tears and stood up. "It's not. It'll be fine. Just a few more months." She gathered up the bowls.

"You've completely forgotten who you are."

She was all over the place emotionally. She had to get it together. "I haven't. I promise, I'll come with you. I don't have a choice anyway, I can see that, now that you have the scarab."

"That's right. I have it. And I have a life that isn't this one, but it's a pretty good one. And a job. And if we're gone too long my dad and Nedra will come looking. How will we explain it when they do? And if Nedra wants the scarab like you think she does, she'll take it from us."

She rubbed his arms hoping to soothe him. "They wouldn't come so soon. You're a grown man. I think they would respect your privacy. I mean, we'll be back in time for brunch." She leaned in and kissed him softly on the mouth. He resisted, but then consented, wrapping his own arms around her waist. His kiss was hard, less subtle than Henry's kisses. Jace was full of fire and she could sense his frustration. She wanted to soothe him, but was she doing it to stay with Henry longer? The thought frightened her.

Jace pulled away and walked to the door. "I gotta go."

"Where are you going?" she questioned.

"I don't know. Somewhere. I gotta let off some steam."

"You're not going to a brothel are you?"

His eyes widened. "What?" He shook his head and laughed. Seeing him smile was a welcomed relief. "Why would you ask that?"

"I don't know. That's where a lot of men go to 'let off steam.' The moral code is quite strict. If there is anything questionable, people's reputations are lost forever. But if they go to a brothel, no one questions it. It's like it's excused."

"Hmm. I'll have to keep that in mind."

"Jace!" This time she laughed. The earlier tension melted away.

He laughed. "I just need some air. But I'm taking this with me." He shoved the scarab into his trouser pocket and walked out the front door leaving her alone in the house.

There are no accidents. Everything we do and everyone we meet was put in our path for a reason. ~ Marla Gibbs

Elle/Constance

London

The day of the play arrived and Constance could barely contain her excitement. She wore the dress Henry had sent her, a fancy, striped, purple number with a bustle apron and buttons down the bodice. He'd also sent her a matching hat with gloves that Jace had twice caught her wearing while staring at herself in the mirror, a small smile on her face. Elle recognized the hat from her mother's collection. Finally she had an opportunity to wear it, even if it was a hundred and twenty years earlier.

Elle took a carriage to the theater and asked the manager where Henry might be. He pointed down a long hall where Henry kept a private office. She walked slowly, as the dress swooshed and the shoes clanked noisily against the marble floor. She wished to surprise him. The door was ajar. She pushed it with her white-gloved hand and peaked in. Henry was seated at a desk, the room thick with smoke as another man stood quite close, his hand on Henry's shoulder.

"You have nothing to be nervous about," the man said, rubbing Henry's shoulder.

She took a step back, causing the door to creak. They both turned abruptly towards the sound. Constance stared back at them. There was an awkward silence. She had no choice but to make her presence known. She opened the door further.

"Constance." Henry said, rising quickly from the chair. "I didn't expect you."

She smiled, though she felt extremely uncomfortable, like she'd just interrupted something private. "I wanted to surprise you. I thought you might like to see your gift?" She showed off her knew dress.

"It's very beautiful. Fenimore." He turned to the gentleman wearing black tales and a silky scarf and said, "This is my friend, Mr. Harris."

"It's nice to meet you," Constance said as the man took her hand and pretended to kiss it. It was the first time a man had pretended to kiss her hand. They were usually more than happy to do it for real. It felt odd and only left her feeling more uncomfortable.

"The pleasure is all mine I'm sure. That dress is stunning. Direct from Paris. You'll be the most beautiful creature here tonight," the man said. Nervously, he looked at Henry and then back to Constance.

"Thank you." She turned her attention back to Henry. "I just wanted to say good luck. I'll be watching in the booth."

"I was just telling Henry what a smash it will be," Mr. Harris said.

"I've seen it so I know it will be," she agreed, though it bothered her that someone else was giving him the encouragement that had always been her job. She waited for the man to leave, but he didn't. Three was definitely becoming a crowd. "I'll see you after the show?" she asked.

"Yes, of course." Henry said without looking at her.

And with that she exited the room and shut the door behind her.

Knowing this was her last day with Henry she had hoped to have a better farewell. Perhaps they would have another chance after the play. Maybe Jace would forget or give her another day or two. The thought of leaving sickened her. She wasn't ready. Still. And Henry's behavior with that man had left her feeling slightly unsettled. Maybe it was nothing, but she wanted to be sure. Who was this Mr. Harris? What was his business with Henry? She couldn't leave it alone so she waited down the corridor behind a tall plant and watched Henry's door.

While Constance may not have been familiar with homosexuals, Elle had known plenty in her day. If that man wasn't gay she would be very surprised. And if he was? The way he had rested his hand so comfortably on Henry's shoulder in private like that? What chance would Constance possibly have?

After a few minutes the man left Henry's office and walked away in the opposite direction. She quietly made her way back to Henry's office and walked in.

"Who was that man?" she asked, shutting the door behind her.

He feigned surprise and disinterest. "Did I not introduce you?"

"I want to know who that man is to you."

"A friend of course."

"As I am a friend? One you are partial to?"

He finally looked up, his face looked weathered and tired. "What is this, Fenimore? What is wrong? Are you now jealous of the time I spend with a man as well as other women?"

"I'm not jealous. I'm concerned."

"You needn't be. The old boy is harmless. You are still my closest confidant and as much of a companion as I shall ever have." He patted her hand that rested by her side. "Now are you happy?"

"I just want to understand you."

"I thought you already did. Have we not shared the most intimate feelings of our heart these past years?"

"Yes, of course, I just…" Her voice dropped off. Maybe she had read too much into it.

"Tonight is a night of triumph. My play is presenting to a near-sold out crowd. Will you not share a drink with me?"

He filled two glasses from his decanter and gave one to Constance and then held his up in the air. "To our shared success and friendship."

"To us," she said, clinking glasses with Henry and taking a drink of his favorite bourbon. Her eyes watered and her throat burned, but her head soon felt light and happy. He swallowed his whole and then stood from his chair and kissed her on the cheek.

"Now may I show you to your seat madam?" He winked and held the door open.

"Gratefully," she answered, a rosy red upon her cheeks from his kiss.

Once she was in her seat she was surprised to see Jace walk in and sit beside her.

"I thought you weren't coming?"

"And miss Mr. James' play? I wouldn't dream of it. Mr. James was good enough to give me his seat."

Elle kept from showing the disappointment she felt. While she was glad Jace was there, she was upset that Henry would not be. She pulled out her opera glasses and searched the box seats for any sign of Henry. Finally she spotted him sitting with Mr. Harris on the opposite side of the theater. Her heart burned with jealousy and disappointment.

She clenched her jaw and felt another headache coming on. She took the glass down, unwilling to spy on the two anymore. She put on her happy face to keep Jace from worrying. Besides, what was she upset about? Was she really jealous of his friendship with another man? Was it any more upsetting than his dozens of lady friends? Not exactly. It was more just plain disappointment.

This had been her last chance. This was her last night with Henry and instead of sitting beside him watching his play, laughing with him, whispering with each other, she was watching him from afar. After all these years and all she had tried, she was still forced to observe him from a distance.

This was all wrong.

She whipped out her fan and nervously cooled herself.

"You look beautiful in that dress," Jace whispered. She smiled politely, but couldn't be rid of her agitation about the whole situation. Her last night. Her irritation might as well been stamped across her forehead.

The play itself was a success and ended with thundering applause. Within a few minutes the drapes were pulled back and the patrons began to spill from the theater, smiles and animated faces proving the success of the performance. The dresses were ornate, the jewels flashy. Feathered hats and fur coats everywhere.

Elle looked for Henry, but the crowd was too thick. Finally she spotted him talking to a large circle of people. His back was turned to her so she could not see what he was saying. She took Jace by the arm. She was determined to get closer to Henry. "Would you like to congratulate the playwright himself?"

"And while I congratulate him you can say your goodbyes. We are leaving tonight."

She gritted her teeth. "And Constance and Jonas are suddenly thrust together? Who's going to help them?"

"They'll be fine. And Constance and Henry seem to be on very good terms, as well. As good a time as ever."

She took a step backwards. She couldn't fake her animosity any longer. Jace didn't grab her arm. "As soon as I get back, I'll take the scarab away. You know that."

"But the time that it will take you to remove the duct tape could give me six more months. And six more months could be everything."

"Elle! You are not Constance, dammit! Constance is dead. Or at least she will be shortly."

Anger flashed through her. She slapped him. The shock of it set him back. It set her back, too. She had no idea where the anger had come from. A tear flitted in her eye. He touched his cheek where a red mark matched the corner of her gloved hand. His hurt matched the fear in her heart. Tears welled as she begged for forgiveness. "I'm sorry, I just reacted."

His voice lowered. The friendliness was gone from his eyes. "Don't make me force you."

Any remorse she felt vanished. Elle's voice dropped to match his. "If you so much as touch me I will scream." Jace did not move.

"Fenimore?" Henry had made his way to them. "Is everything okay?"

Without thinking she pointed to Jace. "I want him taken from this theater at once!"

"Constable!" Henry called to the man standing near the entry. Then he turned to Elle and asked, "What is the problem, my dear?"

"He is a liar and a thief and I want him out of this theater."

"I thought he was your friend," Henry said.

"He took my scarab pin, the one I got from Egypt. I want it back. And then I want you to take him to jail."

"Is this true young man? Did you take her pin?" the constable demanded.

"Elle?" Jace called, his face looking confused. She was beyond feeling. He stared at her, the look of shock and hurt evident in his eyes. She turned away, unable to look at him.

Jace bolted, pushing the constable away and running through the lobby towards the row of exit doors. Henry was right behind him. He gripped Jace's shoulders, but Jace elbowed Henry in the gut. Henry grunted and bent over, cursing under his breath.

"Stop that man!" The constable cried. Two gentleman grabbed for Jace but missed him. The constable closed in, his stick high overhead.

"Jace!" Elle screamed just as the constable's stick came down hard on the top of his head, dropping Jace like a bundle of bricks.

"No!" She rushed over to Jace, and bent over him. She dug into his pocket and placed the scarab in his hands.

"Go. I'll join you soon," she whispered into his ear.

"I'm so sorry."

"Is he dead?" Henry asked, breathing hard and holding his side. A crowd gathered. Voices whispered behind the fallen body.

The constable leaned over him. "He's just got a little bump on the ole' head. That's what you get when you try and steal from a lady," he said in his thick accent. He looked over at Elle, whose face had turned white with regret. "What did he steal ma'am?"

"A pin," she whispered, her throat swollen with emotion.

"The scarab?" Henry asked.

She nodded, hoping the pin would work its magic before the constable found it in his hands.

"Check his pockets," she said.

The constable thoroughly checked all his trouser pockets. "Not in there. But he does have a good wad of cash."

The crowd closed in. Elle wished she could disappear. She'd never felt more terrible about anything in her life. Yet, as bad as she felt for tricking Jace, she was still unwilling to change her mind.

"Are you sure he took it?" Henry asked.

"Yes, he showed it to me."

"Why would he take the pin?" he asked.

"He believes it has magical powers. That it can transport you in time." Her voice was absent of emotion.

"Check his hands," she whispered without meeting Henry's eyes, too embarrassed to play the part of distraught victim anymore.

"Ay, here it is. The famous magical scarab pin." The constable took the pin and held it up for all to see. There was a sigh and a laugh from the crowd.

He handed it back to Elle who quickly dropped it in her purse, grateful she was still wearing gloves.

The man, no longer Jace, she hoped, began to stir.

"Let's take him to that small room over there, so as not to cause any more of a scene." Henry suggested, pointing to a sick room near the box office window. The constable pulled him up over his shoulders, head down, and hands swinging, to the small room with a cot against the wall and laid him down. Elle was grateful to get away from the gawking theatergoers. The constable slapped the man softly on the cheek a few times to help him wake up. The man blinked groggily. When he realized everyone was staring at him, he clambered backwards against the wall, trying to escape.

"What is going on? Who are you people?"

"Don't try to turn it." The constable was in his glory, interrogating the witness as he teetered back and forth on his large, black rubber boots. "You were intending to steal from this lady here and we caught you in the act, we did."

Jonas pointed at the constable. "Why is that guy talking like an Englishman?"

The constable rubbed his chin nervously. "I may have hit him harder than I thought."

She finally saw what Henry had been seeing all along. Gone were Jonah's mature eyes, and in his place sat a scared twenty year old. "I've never stolen a thing in my life." He looked too young for her to have kissed him. She felt slightly ill and hoped he wouldn't remember.

She spoke up. "It appears this young man has gotten a slight case of amnesia from that bump on the head. I don't think we are going to get many answers from him any time soon. I have my pin back so there is no harm done. I don't wish to press charges.

"But if he stole I'll have to press charges." The constable seemed disappointed.

"No you don't. This is Henry's big night and I don't wish for it to be dampened because of a small theft by a starving young man."

Henry seemed less than convinced. "I thought he was a friend of the family? Jace was it?"

"He is. And no. It's Jonas."

"I thought I heard you call him Jace?"

"It was a mistake. His name is Jonas." She left no room for further discussion.

"Heaven knows the newspapers have already heard of

this and are on their way with their cameras. We want them to talk about Henry's play, not the thief afterwards."

"True, that's true," Henry nodded. He wanted nothing to do with scandal.

"Can I have a moment alone with him, please?"

Elle looked from Henry to the constable. They both relented and walked from the room.

As soon as they were gone she opened her purse and pulled out all the money she had. "This has all been a terrible misunderstanding. My friend took you on a voyage to England where you have been for several months. You were hit in the head and now have a slight case of amnesia, but I want to make this up to you by paying for your fare back to America." She smiled at the scared young man who looked like a cat out on a ledge.

"Take this." She slipped fifty pounds in his hand. "Find a place to sleep and then meet me at the hotel Consuelo tomorrow at three. I will have a ticket for your return home." He stared at the money.

"Remember, three o'clock tomorrow. If you don't show up then you're on your own." She stood and walked to the door. "I'm truly sorry about this, Jonas." And then she walked out the door.

Forgiveness is a virtue of the brave. ~Indira Gandhi

Constance/Elle

The next few months would change Constance's luck forever. At least that was what Elle hoped. The first was a touching deathbed scene with Henry's sister Alice who had grown very ill with cancer. When Constance visited, Alice had grown pale and could barely speak.

"I'm glad you've come." She had begun. "I have been worried we would not have a chance to speak before it was too late." Alice's lips were dry and cracked. Constance helped her sit up and take a drink. Then Alice began again.

"I have been unfair to you. Henry was always gallivanting around the continent with you, pretending that he wasn't in love." She paused and then added, "I made him promise that he wouldn't marry you."

Constance had heard this rumor, but now it was solidified. She said nothing.

"I'm dying. I give you my blessing to care for Henry. Take my place, be a listening ear. I need to know that you will do this. Marry him if you'd like."

Constance's heart skipped a beat. The freedom to marry! It was almost too much to imagine.

Alice had coughed violently and Constance, in her caring way, found a cloth and wiped Alice's mouth.

"I will care for Henry as long as he'll allow it. I promise you that." Constance had promised before she left her side, never to see her again alive.

But if she believed Henry would be overjoyed at the news she was deeply disappointed by his reaction when she shared Alice's blessing of their union.

Henry paced the floor. "My caregiver? Why has she decided that it is up to her to find me someone? I am not an invalid."

Her soft smile faded. "She doesn't want to leave you alone. It kills her to think of it. Don't you see? After all these years I finally won her approval."

"Ridiculous." He scowled. "I have no plans to marry. Not now or after Alice dies. She has misrepresented me."

"What?" Constance couldn't be sure she had heard him right. Her hearing seemed to be getting worse. But Henry did not repeat himself for he had grown impatient. He was short with his answers, as if he couldn't be bothered.

For the next several weeks Constance walked around in a fog, trying to make sense of Henry's abrupt change in behavior. His temper, his distractedness, it all worried her. She had to find a way to win him back. Maybe if she could hear better he would love her more. So she consulted Dr. Baldwin one day about a new procedure available that might help. She agreed to the operation.

But the operation failed and she was soon hit with infection. Add to her infection, a constant headache, and a letter from Henry stating he was unable to visit. The pain and disappointment from the failed operation sent her into a deep depression. She grew feverish and delirious. Was she Constance or Elle? In the fit of a fever she rambled on to Dr. Baldwin about how she wished to leave London.

"I could divide the summer between the Mather's house on Mackinac Island, and perhaps even dear little Cooperstown. Then I'd go to Florida. I'd stay there in the winter and explore the marshes like I once did. How I miss my mom. I could go for some of that Mackinac Fudge ice cream on St. George Street. I miss St. Augustine. Such a lovely little place with its cobblestone streets and seagulls flying overhead, even with all the tourists. Tourists?" Constance and Elle 's thoughts were becoming mixed in a blender, one indistinguishable from the other.

"Maybe I should go to Venice. I could take my silver, linen, and all my books. Perhaps Harry will join me. Then we will write that play together." The pain was the worst she had ever experienced. "It's like a knife," she tried to explain to Baldwin. "Do you have any Tylenol? I'd take Motrin. I hear that's good for earaches."

"I've never heard of Tylenol. Is this from the apothecary?" Dr. Baldwin asked.

Constance and Elle were both fighting to heal the illness, neither doing a very good job of it. "Walgreens, any grocery store has it. You can get the generic kind if you want. It doesn't matter to me."

"I've never heard of any of these places. Constance, your fever is having a very ill effect on you. Are you hearing voices again?" Constance nodded. Elle made her shake her head. She didn't want Constance to end up in a mental institution. He gave her a morphine tablet and promised to return the next day.

After a few months Henry finally came to visit. They sat in her parlor as he stared absently into the fire, fighting his own depression. "Now Alice is gone, who will encourage me on?"

"I have always reminded you of your talent. How can you forget?"

"While your works are continually published, my editors keep back my tales as if they are ashamed of them. It is hard to press on when your work is not wanted."

"Your play has done well, and you will have even greater success with your next one. I read it, remember?"

"I go day by day putting out my best work only to be ignored by editors. Then a story by a woman who can write only romance or gossip, but nothing of the real things of life is called a success."

"Women can write of the things in life. They are not all silly creatures."

"I do not include you in this observation, but it is true on most counts. And see how you become hostile? I can't speak of these things to you. You'll never replace my Alice."

She knelt by his chair and grabbed his hands. "England's gray sky is getting you down. Let us leave England. We could go to Venice, have a pied-a'-terre. Write that play together."

"I'm sorry Fenimore. You can now see what poor Alice had to put up with. I probably sent her to her grave with all my self-doubt."

"I promised Alice I would care for you as best I could, and if listening to you is all I have to do, I would say it is a privilege to fill her spot."

"It's this writing business. No one can understand how we work. We work in the dark—we do what we can—we give what we have."

"You can only do so much, Henry. The rest you must leave up to God. Come to Venice with me."

"I must finish this story." He left no room for persuasion and left soon after with barely a nod. *He was suffering for the loss of his sister. He needs time and plenty of love*, Constance thought to herself.

But if he was suffering from grief, his demeanor towards Constance didn't improve as winter turned to spring and spring into summer. While he still visited occasionally he had less to say, and even less interest in what Constance was writing. She was losing him. She could sense it, like a light in the distance, growing dimmer and dimmer. Maybe if she left England he would begin to miss her and perhaps visit her. "I must go to Venice. He loves Venice. Perhaps in the summer we shall meet again," she said aloud to herself as she watched him disappear around the bend one day, his head down, his shoulders slumped.

She wrote to her nephew, Sam Mather of her intentions

to move.

I am giving up being near my kind friend Mr. James. But I do hope one day he will come to Italy and perhaps we will write that play after all.

Elle had given up all control of independent thought and existed only as an observer. On the twelfth of May 1893, Constance left Oxford for London, and then on to Venice via Paris. Henry promised to come soon, and though she held on to hope his promises were valid, his trip was postponed again and again.

She stayed in a modest house with two floors above the water-story while she searched for a more permanent dwelling. "You have not the lonely life that is my lot. You have a wife and a family. People who care about you," she complained to Doctor Baldwin.

Doctor Baldwin sat back on the sofa of her dwelling and sighed. "If Henry were a different man he would be your husband. Do not doubt that everyone has private struggles. We must take comfort in knowing we are not alone."

"Nothing but sheer courage from day to day keeps me going," Constance spoke, mostly to herself.

"Just keep going. And come see me when it gets too hard to continue on."

She looked up at the kind man and smiled. "Thank you for understanding."

Soon after her visit with the doctor, her neighbor, a Miss Norton, stopped by and gave her a book called, *The Law of Psychic Phenomena.* It was the idea about time travel. She found the papers and drawings about time travel and the scarab in the back of her desk drawer and began to study them more fully. She explained as much to her cousin, Ariana Curtis, as they looked for a more permanent dwelling for Constance.

"So you're saying that a ghost is an embodied thought of a person?" Ariana asked hoping to understand.

"Yes, in a way. The houses in which persons have lived, become, after a time, permeated with their thoughts. Ghosts always wear clothing, so you must believe that even clothing has a soul attached to it. They may not be seen, but they can certainly be felt. I believe with the right combination, a person much like myself in thinking and in dress, could hear my thoughts in their mind even long after I'm gone." She then told Ariana about the scarab.

"You believe it has powers?" Ariana's eyes were wide.

"I have been studying some physics. Time travel. It's a crazy ambition, but something I am intrigued with." Elle could have explained all of it, but she was watching it all play out like a movie.

"I don't understand." The subject was over Ariana's simple head.

"There is nothing to understand except that you must safeguard it until the right time."

"You aren't planning anything final, are you?"

"Of course not. After all, Henry is coming to see me soon. We are going to write a play together."

"About that," Ariana said with hesitation.

"What?" She studied Ariana's eyes. They appeared worried. "Have you heard from him?"

"Did you tell him I was going to beat him with a few stripes for not coming in the spring like he promised?"

"He said that you must have misconceived that he wanted a pied-e'-terre in Venice, and he wanted me to tell you to stop searching for a place for the two of you at once."

"He said this?"

Ariana nodded, her eyes full of concern.

Her face flooded with hot color. "Why did he not just write me?"

"I can't be sure."

"But he said he wanted to come. He said it multiple times. I was looking for a place with him in mind."

"He also said that he hasn't been toying with any affections and blamed his clumsiness of language for the misunderstanding."

Constance's embarrassment could not be hid. Henry was anything but clumsy.

"He is a master of the English language." Now he was

making her to look like a fool. "What else did he say?"

"He said that he would like to come to Italy in the winter, but has learned not to make hard and fast plans, something about tricks of fate and such and if Miss Woolson has a problem, it is merely a practical matter, nothing whatever to do with him and calls for no more than polite regrets."

Polite regrets? She stood stunned in the middle of the alleyway. Merchants attempted to pass by her, but she did not see or hear them. She had no words. Tears stung her eyes. The humiliation was as striking as a slap.

"Do you still want to look for a place?" Arianna asked timidly.

She turned away and blinked hard to keep the tears from falling down her cheeks. Henry had offered the final blow. He had no intentions of ever being with her. Could it have been because of the rumors that circulated between him and Mr. Harris, the man with him at the theater on the opening night of his play? Or was he tired of her company and had moved on to ladies with fresher ideas, sharper thinking, younger faces? Of course he was tired of her. After all, she was Miss Grief. Wasn't this what Clara had warned her about all along?

She sighed, lifted her head, and blinked her tears away. What was done was done. She would think no more of it. "I wish to take a different apartment. I seek something bright and high enough to reach the sunlight." She forced a smile. "But I think for today, I shall go home and rest, as I am not feeling well."

Back in her dim apartment, she looked around at the boxes and the trunks she had yet to unpack and felt the weight of disappointment wash over her. She'd move out of this apartment and find something more conducive to her needs. Henry James be damned.

She removed the pearl necklace and dropped it next to the scarab pin.

A sudden flash filled her eyes. The room began to spin. The paper fell to the floor.

There is nothing like returning to a place that remains unchanged to find the ways in which you yourself have altered. ~Nelson Mandela

Elle

Mackinac Island

"What do you want me to do with her once she comes to?" a male voice asked.

"Take her down to the lake. If she's like Jace she won't be any trouble. Poor boy can hardly move."

Hardly move wasn't the half of it. Elle couldn't open her eyes. Every piece of her body stung, like it was on fire. Death would be a welcomed escape. The voices were familiar, but she couldn't connect them with names, her head was too foggy, and she had never felt so much pain, not even after Constance's ear operation, so figuring out who was talking was a distant second in priority. She couldn't even cry. She was paralyzed. This was surely what purgatory felt like.

Strong arms picked her up and carried her down a set of stairs. She went to cry out in pain, but even her voice was paralyzed. Where was she? Her mind was a cloudy mess, like she was coming out of a thick dream. A door opened. Birds sang above her. It was hot. Venice? The smells were different, yet distinct, like pine, fir, and juniper. A soft breeze rustled the leaves overhead. In the distance, waves washed across a pebbled beach. This wasn't Venice, this was Mackinac Island. She was back. Whoever found her probably thought she was ill and was taking her to the hospital. The man grunted as he set her down on a wooden plank. Her head racked with pain from the less than soft landing. What was it? A box? A wagon?

A horse whinnied. The female voice called from a ways off. "I'll take this little pin. You take Jace. Get him home and comfortable until I get there." The wagon teetered as someone jumped to the ground. The motion caused her to flinch with pain. It was like when her foot fell asleep, only this time it was her entire body.

"I'll go with Jace," another female voice called. Elle finally connected the voices to the name. The new female voice belonged to Patricia. She assumed the man was Marv, Jace's dad. And the first woman was Nedra. They must have gotten worried when Jace never came home and went looking for him. Or had Jace gone to get help? But how could he if she said he was unable to move?

Her eyelids were like anvils, as she forced them open, blinking away painful tears from the bright light. Eventually she could make out trees against the blue sky. It was hot, like mid-day on the Island would be in late June. Where was Jace now? And how would he explain what happened? How long had they been gone? Her eyelids closed again, relieved at the darkness. She knew she should tell them she was going to be okay, but she couldn't get the words out. Someone placed a blanket over her. It was hot and stuffy and unnecessary. But there was nothing she could do about it.

Wagon wheels crushed against the gravel and horse feet clopped past and then faded away. Was Jace in the other wagon? She tried to say his name, but she could barely move her lips. She remembered how she had tricked him because she wanted to stay with Henry. He was probably so angry, especially now that his parents had to come help. Why had she done that? Just then the wagon jerked forward. She winced as needles pricked her every muscle. She wanted to tell Nedra she was going to be okay, that a hospital wouldn't do her any good, but she still couldn't speak. Last time it took a half hour to recover, but she had been gone much longer this time. It could take even longer to get mobility back. There was nothing to do but be still and let her body get stronger. They drove for ten minutes. A bicyclist or two passed by as did another carriage. Nedra didn't speak to anyone and they didn't speak to her, nor did they notice her covered, deep in the wagon.

The carriage finally came to a stop. Seagulls flew overhead and the waves rolled over the rocky shoreline nearby. Nedra hopped down from the carriage. Elle could hear her gravelly footsteps coming closer. The wagon shook as she pulled down the wagon hitch and tapped Elle's bare feet.

"Are you awake?" Nedra asked.

"Yes," Elle whispered, barely able to move her lips.

Nedra pulled the blanket off her face. They were parked under an alcove, protected from the sun by trees all around them. "Good. Can you sit up?"

"No," she said softly. Her voice was raw. It hurt to swallow. "I'm okay. I was just…" she couldn't think of a way to explain it other than the truth.

"You were just trying to win Henry James over? Hoarding your aunt's magical scarab pin?"

Elle was shocked. "How did you know?"

"How do you think?"

"You knew Lois."

"I was there when Joe came to tell her that their child died. I overheard them talking about some pin. He was much younger then. And better looking too. When I moved here two years ago I hardly recognized him. He'd become a big fan of Constance Woolson. Had a time travel club."

The blanket was pulled away, allowing a nice breeze to waft across her sweating body, but Elle was too nauseous to feel relief. "And Lois?"

"What about her? He wasn't in love with her. He was in love with Constance."

Nedra picked up Elle's foot and let it drop with a thud. Elle gasped but refused to scream. Even though the pain was intense, she needed to save her strength.

"Interesting that it leaves you so paralyzed afterwards. These are good things to know." Nedra was so calm about it. Like she was talking about yesterday's work meeting.

"Did you hurt him?"

"Hurt him? No. He had an unfortunate accident."

"You did."

"I didn't. He fell."

"He was such a kind man," Elle whimpered, feeling an intense sadness ripple through her.

"Kind?" Nedra's voice grew cold even in the heat of the sun. "No. He was selfish."

Elle's hands twitched. She kept them hidden from view.

"Why?"

"He didn't get it. Who needs video games when you can live an alternate reality? People will pay through the nose for a chance to be Napoleon, Julius Caesar, John Wayne. Even their dear son if that's what they want. They can live in their shoes for a while. For a price." She pulled a pair of scissors from a bag and cut a large square out of the skirt and shoved it in her pocket.

"You don't understand. It's dangerous." Elle warned her, her voice growing stronger.

"Of course it is. That's why you stayed away from it. Isn't it? How many times did you go back? Once, twice, three times? It's addictive, more than it's dangerous. At least to a paying customer."

Footsteps sounded behind the trees. "There he is. Marv can get his son back. And I'll finally have a husband who loves me."

"He wants his wife back as well."

Nedra's mouth twitched. Her eyes peered over her shoulder. "Don't worry about that."

"What about Jace?"

"He'll come around to my way of thinking. Especially

when his father thanks him for bringing his son back."

"And his mother," Elle chided.

Just then Marv appeared.

"You got Jace settled in?" Nedra asked.

"Patricia gave him something for the pain."

"Jace will know you did this."

Nedra turned, her eyes sharp like tiny arrows. "He'll know you were so distraught about losing Henry that you rowed yourself out into the middle of the lake still wearing that ridiculous dress and drowned yourself." She shoved the material into her pant pocket. "Just like Constance. Two women giving up their lives for Henry. A Romeo, Juliet, and Juliet story."

She wanted to argue that Jace wouldn't believe she would commit suicide, but after the way she had behaved, she realized she hadn't given him any reason not to.

Marv covered Elle back up with the blanket and shut the tailgate. They climbed aboard the wagon and called out to the horse, which started trotting down the hill and out of the trees like they were just going for a Sunday drive. Elle had seen enough movies to know how this would end. She tried rocking back and forth, but barely moved. She wasn't going anywhere on her own anytime soon.

The wagon stopped a few minutes later. The sound of the waves crashed in her ears. Nedra and Marv walked away. Over the rising wind she could hear Nedra bark orders.

"Bring it over there. Not so high," They huffed and puffed, dragging something heavy across the rocks. Soon the hatch came down again. They flipped the blanket back and the two of them took hold of her feet and dragged her half way out of the wagon. Wood slivers gouged her legs. She gritted her teeth. There was no choice but to relax and hope she didn't get dropped on her head.

Marv carried her across the pebbled shore to a rowboat. She hoped she could talk some sense into him once Nedra was out of earshot. He was Jace's father. Maybe there was still a soul inside him.

My very soul demands you: it will be satisfied, or it will take deadly vengeance on its frame.
~ Charlotte Brontë, Jane Eyre

Elle

Lake Huron

Elle examined her surroundings before Marv covered her with the blanket. The fresh air, the lake, the sky, the trees off the shore. The white rocks stacked in formations along the beach by visitors. It was such a normal day, yet there was nothing more surreal than this situation.

Her surroundings went dark, the blanket nearly suffocating her. She tried to relax, reminding herself that all she needed was another half hour and she'd have her strength back.

There was a push and a drag and then the rowboat skidded heavily across the rocks until finally it became buoyant upon the water. Marv jumped in. The boat wobbled back and forth. Another sound of scraping against the rocks. Possibly Nedra following behind. And then all was silent except for the occasional dip of the oar.

Elle maneuvered her fingertips around the blanket edge and slid it off her face. Marv's back was to her as he paddled, which was good.

The longer they thought she was unable to move the

more effective her surprise attack would be.

After a few minutes of rowing she finally asked, "What are you going to do with me?" Even though she already had a pretty good idea.

Marv kept rowing, humming a song like he'd never heard her. Maybe he wouldn't be as easy to convince as she thought. A sudden wind burst whipped the blanket into the air. Marv caught it and set it back down, the edges dripping with cold lake water. Thankfully he didn't put it back over her face. "There's no reason to do this."

He looked up at the cloudy sky. "Looks like the storm's early." His voice was calm, like the two of them were out on a fishing expedition.

"Storm?" She couldn't keep her voice from straining. A storm on the lake could be a disaster, especially as weak as she was. Rowing the boat would be difficult. Swimming, impossible. "Did you know she killed my aunt? That she killed Mr. Gordon? This isn't you, Marv, I know that. I think Nedra is forcing you to do this."

"All I want is my wife and son back. Mr. Gordon told me I could bring them back. He said he knew what it was like to lose a child."

"But he didn't lose her. I am that child." Though it felt strange to admit it out loud, Elle knew it was true. Whether this fact surprised him or not, he continued to paddle.

The darkening sky rumbled. She heard Nedra call to Marv, who slowly turned his boat toward hers.

She had to talk fast, before they got any closer to Nedra. "Marv, you still have a son. You have Jace."

"He could have told me about that little stone of yours. How's that for gratitude?"

"You've been listening to Nedra too much. He wanted to tell you about it. I wouldn't let him."

Nedra yelled out from her boat. "That storm is coming. I'll hold the side, you hop in. And don't forget the oars."

What were they going to do with her? Leave her? She could barely move her arms higher than a couple inches. She'd never be able to swim back to shore. The sky rumbled again, deeper, like it meant business. The boat rocked side to side in the waves. Marv stood and moved to the back.

"Now try not to get us flipped," Nedra insisted, grabbing the side of the boat and holding on. Marv was silent. He picked up the blanket and tossed it to Nedra. He made the move from one rowboat to the next with little movement. She shouldn't have been surprised, knowing how much he fished. A boat like this was probably a second skin for him.

"Sit before you get us killed!" Nedra yelled. The air cracked overhead. Elle's heart dropped. If Nedra had planned to tie her up or toss her overboard, she'd forgotten all about it with the storm brewing. That was one advantage for Elle. And also a disadvantage since she was still so weak.

Both oars slapped in sync against the water. They'd get back to shore in no time with two oars working. She, on the other hand, wasn't going anywhere very fast. At least not until she got her strength back. She practiced raising her arms. They went up three or four inches. Better than last time. She wiggled her toes and stretched her legs. A sharp pain knotted her muscles. She bit her lip to keep silent. A Charlie horse. She used to get them all the time when she first started swimming. She flexed and pointed her foot back and forth hoping to loosen the muscle until the pain eventually subsided. How would she swim when she didn't have the strength to even stretch? At least they hadn't thrown her over yet or tied her up. She was free to try and finagle the rowboat back to shore. There were only two problems: one, she could hardly move her arms, and two, she had no oars. She'd have to get creative.

Something cold and wet slithered up her back. She turned to see a black puddle gathering at the bottom of the boat. She was taking on water. Within a half hour she would be swamped. Sooner or later she'd have to swim.

She lay perfectly still taking deep breaths to fill her body with as much oxygen as possible while she imagined swimming in the water. How long could she go before she'd come up for air? How long would it take her to get to shore? How cold was the water? And what about those dark clouds? If she could wait out the storm she'd have a better chance of making it to shore. But something about the water filling in around her told her she may not have enough time.

She lifted her leg, then the other. It was easier now. The cold water was actually helping to stimulate her muscles and nerves. She tried her arms. They went up twelve inches before collapsing against the bottom of the boat, sending sharp pain through her hands and fingers. Within another minute she could raise her hands all the way over her head. Maybe that was the key. Wake her body up. She rolled onto her stomach and banged her leg against the seat. She winced, but kept at it.

Lightning and thunder struck simultaneously. Raindrops the size of quarters fell from the heavens. She looked down, realizing the dress would only weigh her down. She'd have to take it off somehow. She pushed up on her knees and attempted to pull the dress over her head, but halfway through her arms got stuck and she fell back down, face first in the water. The rain was loud as it hit the wood boat. Her puddle was growing deeper around her, up to her shoulders, covering her hands. Her heart pounded, her fingers struggled to grip the edge of the dress as she inched her way out of it. Once off, she lay the dress over her, in an attempt to shelter her from the drenching moisture. But there was a deep fear growing inside her. She'd never make it if she went into the water. She didn't have the energy.

Waves pitched the boat up and down and side to side as the rain pelted her with its stinging bullets. The boat sank deeper. She shivered uncontrollably. What could she do? She lifted her head up over the edge to see Marv rowing, Nedra, under the blanket. Marv's strokes slowed as he fought the waves. Thunder shook and the wind blew. A huge wave hit their boat and tossed it on it's side. Elle gasped. When it straightened out the blanket was still there, but there was no Marv.

She calculated the distance between them. Two hundred

yards? In good weather, and in top shape, she could have easily swam that distance, but everything, including the weather, seemed against her. She looked down at the bottom of the boat. It was two-thirds full and sinking like a bad cartoon. Could she turn it upside down and hold onto it? Wouldn't that be better than just letting it sink completely? But again, she knew she didn't have the strength to turn the wooden boat by herself.

If only she hadn't lost so much strength! She felt angry for getting so caught up in the world of Henry and Constance. A world that she didn't belong in. Jace had been right. This was her life. The Island, Florida. And Jace. She had to make it back. Jace had to know how she felt about him.

In the distance Marv was attempting to climb back into the boat. The lump under the blanket remained completely still.

"Why doesn't she help him?" she wondered aloud. What was she doing? Then the thought came to her that made her sick. Was Nedra under the power of the scarab? Had she traveled back in time? Now? On the boat in a storm? What was she thinking? The wind flipped the blanket into the air and slammed it into the water. Nedra lay still. Marv was holding onto the side of the boat. Elle examined her own boat. It would be only minutes before it sunk completely. As much as she hated to admit it, she had to jump. The dress gave her an idea. She gathered it up in her arms and rolled over into the water.

The lake was freezing. She sucked in air, as if hoping to warm her body up through her breathes. Swimming in ice cubes would have felt better than this. The coldness stung her exposed skin as she lobbed her feet up and down. More air!

"God, please help," she whispered as she took the dress and tried to tie the sleeves to the small hook on the back of the boat.

Her fingers were like brittle sticks that might snap if they bent. The waves were relentless. They buried her and then rolled her out and then buried her again.

Up once again, she struggled for air as she tugged on the dress hoping it would turn the boat over.

She was no match for the sinking contraption.

The boat pulled her under. She fought her way to the surface, gasping for air. Her frozen fingers fumbled as they unknotted the dress. She might lose the boat but she didn't want to also lose the dress. She needed another idea. A buoy. She bundled it up in her arms. It spilled beneath her like a turtle shell. She got a second wind, her legs kicking against the rain and wind and rolling waves that aimed to thwart her progress.

Thunder and lightning crashed and echoed like a great gong. She sunk, the dress dragging her down. Water filled her ears, muffling the sounds of the storm. It was almost comforting to have it muted. She came up, took a breath. The other boat was closer, but still too far. Marv hung on, his skinny arms hanging helplessly. Electricity sliced the sky in half about two hundred yards in front of her hitting Marv's boat and flipping it upside down. Elle gave a weak scream. No Marv or Nedra. What about the scarab? What happened to Nedra?

She pressed forward, her body cramping from the cold and fatigue. Her arms splashed weakly. Her feet twisted side to side. Rain blasted against her cheeks as she came up for air and then went under again. The dress was no longer helping her. She had to find another way. She attempted to tie the bottom into a simple knot. Her hands were blocks of ice. She couldn't make it work. The dress was too waterlogged. She wrapped her arms around it. She didn't want to lose the dress. Just kick, she thought, occasionally glancing up to make sure she was going in the right direction.

She rested her head against the dress now buried under the water. She had little strength in her arms, but her legs had gained some power. She was within thirty yards of the boat, but there was still no sign of Marv or Nedra. But she was less concerned about them. She needed to reach their boat or she would drown. Twenty yards. She rolled on her back, still clinging to the dress, weakening with each kick. Fifteen yards. Back to her front.

I float, I float, I float, Constance said in her head.

Ear splitting lightning cracked like a zipper across the sky. Someone screamed. It sounded like Nedra, but it might have been herself. Elle couldn't go on. She had to be honest. Not with the dress. It was like a thirty-five pound dead weight. She'd have to let it go. Henry had loved that dress. It had been her favorite, surviving for over a century. And now it would go to the bottom of the lake. Her fingers loosened their grip. She choked back tears as it drifted away. A wave swallowed it up, then spit it out. She panicked and reached out for it, but was too cold to go after it as it slowly sunk deeper and deeper until it was finally overcome by waves. Her life support and connection to Constance. Gone.

She let out a sob. Tears mixed with rain rolled down her cheeks as she sobbed for Mr. Gordon and Lois, her father and mother. She cried for Constance who had fallen to her death never to have Henry's heart or the joy she had longed for. And Elle sobbed because she knew that if she didn't do something, she would be next.

She gathered the pain and loss, and channeled it into power from an unknown place. She fell into a determined rhythm, long strokes, legs kicking, heart pounding, fighting to stay alive. Her arms sliced the waves with tiny, doable strokes as she remembered her reason to get to shore. Jace. His name became a poem. A rhythm. He was her great king, she, the shadow huntress. Each stroke was another kill to present to him at court. Perhaps she was growing delirious, but it kept her moving, She counted down as her arms pushed through the waves and her feeble legs flopped up and down for support. Ten yards, five yards. Almost there. God willing.

She grasped the overturned boat with the tips of her icy fingers and held on. A voice called from inside. Was it Marv? Holding her breath she swam underneath and then came up inside. She finally exhaled.

It was eerily silent, yet almost impossible to see anything.

"Marv?" The voice belonged to Nedra. Elle's fingers clung to the edge to keep herself up. Her legs hit something. A dark mass floating next to her.

"Marv?" Elle whispered.

"Is he okay?" Nedra cried.

She poked the mass. It didn't stir. "Help me turn the boat over," she called. Nedra didn't move.

"You have to let go so we can try to get it over. On the count of three we'll both lift this edge." Nedra finally let go. She swam next to Elle. Elle counted, "One, two, three." Grunting and heaving they thrust the boat over their heads sending it crashing to the side, a wave of water ricocheting back in their faces. A strange yellow light filled the raining sky. It was then they saw Marv face down in the water. His hair charred, his skin black. Nedra screamed and turned to Elle. "What happened? Did we get hit?"

"Where were you?"

"I…I don't know. I laid down and suddenly I was in Venice. I was Constance. I saw her…I was her." Her voice dropped off. "I didn't know it would work so easily." she gave off a small incredulous laugh. "This thing saved my life!" She lifted the scarab in her fist.

Elle wanted to grab the stone, but she didn't have the energy to swim. She could only hold on. She felt nothing but revulsion for Nedra. She looked around for the paddles. They were floating about 20 yards out. They looked charred as well.

Elle swore under her breath. No paddles. Still a hundred yards or more from shore. And she was stuck with Nedra.

"We've got to get back in the boat. That's the safest place." She knew she needed that woman's help to balance it.

As if it just hit her, Nedra asked. "How did you swim all the way over here? Were you pretending you couldn't move?"

Elle ignored her and said, "I'll help you back into the boat, but you have to give me the scarab pin first."

"I'm not letting go of this thing. It saved my life once. It will save it again."

"Your husband is dead because of it! You killed Mr.

Gordon and I'll bet you killed Lois all for that stupid scarab!"

"You can never prove it. But I will say that now there will be no going back for you, either. "

"Cause you're going to kill me."

"No. Because there is nobody to go back to. Poor Constance, fell from her window. Splat."

Elle lunged at Nedra. Arms flailing, water splashing, Nedra fought her off with one arm, pushing and clawing to keep her away while she held the scarab tight in her other fist. Elle overpowered her and forced her clenched wet fingers open, but Nedra's foot connected with her abdomen. A surging wave engulfed them, sinking them deep into the lake. Holding her breath, Arms lobbing side to side towards the surface, Elle searched through the murky water for an escape. Finally she emerged from the dark abyss sucking in cold wet air to extinguish her burning lungs.

Her relief was short lived as a hand caught her hair from behind and yanked her back under the thunderous waves. She gasped for air, but was pulled down before she could catch a breath. Her lungs felt like they would explode. She turned and met Nedra who still had a hold of her hair. Elle did the only thing she could thing of; she dug her fingers into Nedra's eyes. Another wave shoved them deeper into the water. Elle needed air. She gave up fighting Nedra and turned away, hoping to escape, but was stopped short as Nedra's meat hooks clenched around her throat from behind.

She kicked her legs and grabbed the hands around her throat, her eyes bulging, her lunges ready to explode as they sunk deeper and deeper into the water. With her very last ounce of energy she ripped Nedra's thick fingers away and shot to the surface, gasping for much needed air. Nedra popped up a few feet away and then screamed. Elle could see her hands were open in front of her. No scarab. They both turned side to side, swimming in circles, looking for the missing pin.

"You lost it!" Nedra yelled. "You're just like them! Constance, Joe. Marv. You want what you can't have." A strange look crossed her face. "There!" Finally Elle spotted it about ten feet in front of Nedra, floating in a small calm plot of water. The scarab. Nedra lunged forward. Elle attempted to follow after her, but she could no longer move. Her arms and legs were stiff, like plastic.

"Nedra, come back!" Nedra's strokes were going nowhere, but she didn't turn around or even acknowledge Elle. The waves became too much. Her whole body was shaking uncontrollably. She called out to Nedra, but could no longer see her through the rain. Two more strokes forward, or was it backward, or was it nowhere at all?

A wave buried her. Elle began to sink down, down, down, her body paralyzed from the cold. She was going to die. Here and now. All over a little pin. She thought of Jace. The future. She wasn't ready to go. Not yet, not over a scarab pin. There had been too much sadness. Too much heartbreak. Wasn't it up to her to break the Curtis women curse? Her lungs burned. Her impulse to breathe became overwhelming. She couldn't fight it anymore. Her body sunk deeper, deeper, deeper.

Just as she was about to give in to the natural instinct of taking a breath, a vision of angels floating over fields of poppies and forget-me-not flowers spread beneath her. She thought of Constance, of Henry, of their walks together, their wit, their love.

In the distance she saw a light and attempted to swim towards it. Her arms wouldn't move. Through the shadows a figure, light and graceful, floated over the poppy fields wearing a beautiful gown that soared wide like it had wings attached. White arms extended out as a smile, grey eyes, long brown hair floated all around her like points of a star. Her familiar eyes were assuring as she wrapped Elle in an embrace and pulled her up, up, up, soaring through the water like an angelfish. Bursting through the poppies and dissolving them into algae Elle broke through the glassy ceiling, her lungs forcing her to suck huge amounts of air mixed with lake water. She choked and coughed while inhaling more delectable golden air.

After her lungs were satisfied, she embraced the woman and went to thank her, but quickly discovered she was gone. Her arms held only the drenched limp dress. Her dress. Or rather, Constance's dress. The one she thought she'd never see again. It had saved her.

Then she remembered Nedra. She turned in all directions, but only caught sight of the rowboat sitting empty ten yards away. No Nedra.

The storm was letting up. The thunder and lightening pulsed off in the distance. A steady rain showered the lake.

The distant sound of a motor boat broke through the noise of the storm. She could see it off in the distance, cutting up the lake towards her. Were they looking for her? Perhaps they saw the rowboat. She tried lifting her arms to catch their attention. They continued towards her and soon sidled up beside her. She heard her name. The voice was quiet, but strong and filled her heart with peace.

"Jace?" she whispered, as she turned to a man standing on a ladder, wearing a wet suit. Not Jace. She felt an incredible sense of disappointment. His strong arms hooked under her shoulders and pulled her up and over the side like a fish caught in a net.

"Are you okay?" There it was again. That voice. She blinked, wondering if she'd gone blind. Finally, she saw him standing beside the rescue worker, a face full of concern. His hand was wrapped in a white bandage and he seemed weak as he slowly managed to place a towel around Elle. Another blanket on top of it, and then another. The boat caught up to the abandoned rowboat. She recognized Chief Doug tying it to the speedboat.

She turned back to Jace. "Your dad, he didn't make it."

Jace stared out into the water. His eyes glossing over. "I know."

Her lips quivered from the cold. "Nedra. She's…the scarab. She went after it. I don't know where she is."

His brows furrowed as he looked across the lake.

"We'll find her."

She touched his bandaged hand. "How did you know where I was?"

"Patricia told me everything."

"She was in on it?"

"Sort of. She met Nedra at the hospital where they both worked. When she moved to the island Nedra saw a future daughter-in-law and lured her into their business deal. She didn't know it was going to come to this."

Elle nodded her head. "That still makes her an accomplice."

Jace nodded. "Right. But I think she was unaware of how serious it was. I told her to leave the island and I wouldn't press charges. My dad was in on it too, but for a different reason."

"I should have let you give it to him."

"I don't think he would have loved me any more if I had given it to him. And who knows if he could have really saved my brother or my mom. Some things are just going to happen."

Then she remembered her behavior the last time they'd been together. "I'm sorry about London. I don't know what I was thinking."

He kissed her on the cheek. "Save your energy. There will be plenty of time to sort it all out." She obliged, closing her eyes and burying herself in the warmth of his love.

Where there is love there is life. ~Mahatma Gandhi

♛

Elle & Jace

One month later,
Mackinac Island

Elle patted the earth around the small watered plant next to Gordon's new resting place. It had once belonged to his daughter Elizabeth. Except that when Elle convinced the city to dig up the grave they were shocked to find it empty. Not even a small box was found. Digging into county records they'd found that Linda had paid for the plot and ordered a stone. But there was no record of a coroner or a funeral. There wasn't even a death certificate.

When she heard footsteps she looked up and smiled. It was Jace. He had someplace he wanted to take her and they had agreed to meet here. He came and sat beside her. "How come nobody questioned the baby's death?" Jace asked. Elle wrapped her arms around her knees and explained.

"Same reason I never questioned that my dad died in a car accident. I believed her. She convinced Lois that I had died of a strange fever while she was in the mental hospital. In the meantime, Linda ordered a plot and had a stone placed on top and then quickly moved to St. Augustine, a place she felt she could love almost as much as Mackinac Island.

"Because people already thought Lois was crazy they probably thought the child had been given up for adoption. Linda was a good mother.

"It's difficult to believe she could have been so cruel as a sister."

It was still hard to talk about, but today was not going to be a sad day. Today was a day to honor a father she never knew she had.

"Maybe she really did think Lois was crazy. Maybe it was jealousy. Mr. Gordon fell in love with Lois. The man she had loved and couldn't have. And then they'd had a child together. I just wish she had told me the truth. I could have really used a father. And Mr. Gordon would have been a good one." Jace stood and helped Elle up. Just as they went to leave, Elle remembered something and went back. She removed a heart shaped rock she'd found along the shore from her pocket and set it beside the newly planted forget-me-nots.

"They say it was his favorite flower."

Elle wiped her hands and removed the photograph she'd taken from Mr. Gordon's house from her pocket. "It was taken on the island that very summer."

She handed it to him. "It doesn't look like Lois as much as the others."

He examined it in the light. "It looks more like Constance."

"Her spirit really did take over. Look on the back."

He turned it over and read aloud. "Come back to me. Always yours, C."

"Constance?" Jace asked.

She shrugged. "Even though I didn't know him very long, he will always have a piece of my heart."

She gave him a smile that said she was ready to move on and then Jace led the way to the trailhead. After a few minutes he asked about her trip to Florida.

"It went better than I expected. The realtor says she's shown the house five times this week. She feels like I'll have an offer soon."

"Are you going to miss it?"

"Miss Florida's sandy beaches and blissful weather in January?

"Without a doubt. But I could always get a condo and visit."

"And miss snowmobiling across the lake to St. Ignace? Christmas parties, sleigh rides?"

"I'd never miss Christmas, but maybe January or February. Wouldn't you like to see the beach? Get a tan?"

"Does that mean I'm invited?"

Elle stopped and glanced into his deep blue eyes. Jace's uncertainty was sort of sweet and so different from his normal confidence. She took him by his arm. "Of course! I don't want to be away from you for even a day or two." She took his hand in hers as they walked up the rocky path.

"Did you finish Lois' journal?" Jace asked.

She nodded, her voice reflective as she spoke. "After Lois and Linda's parents died, Lois found the silver box and the scarab in the attic. Eventually Mr. Gordon figured out the voice in Lois's head was a long lost cousin named Constance. I did some tracking on a family history site and found that my grandmother's mother was a cousin to Constance."

Elle touched the single pearl necklace hanging around her neck. "Mr. Gordon never did believe the baby had died and spent years looking for Linda. A few years ago he and Lois became friends again and Mr. Gordon convinced her to search for her long lost sister. She eventually did find Linda in Florida, but Linda never mentioned me, even once. She also denied having the scarab pin."

"So Mr. Gordon? Did he love Lois or Linda or Constance?"

"I think he liked both sisters, but eventually realized it was the Constance side of Lois that he loved. When she disappeared, he lost interest in Lois just like Lois lost interest in him. She wrote in her journal that Mr. Gordon tried to stop Linda when she was leaving the island, but he fell down a ravine and broke his ankle. That's how he got his limp. It also stopped his progress of finding Linda, who probably had me with her and was desperate not to be caught."

They stopped and Jace pulled out his water bottle and

offered her a drink, which she took gratefully. She handed it back to Jace who took a swallow of his own and then stuffed it back in his bag.

"It's still hard to believe that my mother would do that."

Jace took her hand. "Maybe she really thought Lois had gone crazy and was not capable of raising the child."

"I still think she was a little jealous, though," Elle admitted.

Realizing she was doing all the talking she turned the conversation back to Jace. "How are you doing?"

"It's been rough." Elle could see the pain in his face. Losing his father had been harder than he had expected.

"Even though he had written me off, I still loved him. I would have brought back his son if that would have made him love me more. But the reality is I never would have brought him back. Or my mom. I don't think it works like that. We can have an experience in their world, but we can't change things permanently."

"I heard they found Nedra," she said, wiping sweat from her brow again. The Douglas fir and aspen trees were no match for the mid-July heat.

"Yeah. I need to tell you something about that, but first I want to show you this." Jace pushed aside a large branch of evergreen needles to expose the opening of a small cave.

Elle sighed in wonder.

"I wouldn't have found it without Mr. Gordon's detailed map," Jace admitted.

"You weren't supposed to take anything," she jaded him.

"Where did you get that photograph again?" He scratched his head and feigned concern. Elle laughed as she looked around.

"So this was their love cave. Nice."

It was cool and dry, a nice relief from the mid-day heat. She sat on a large rock and rested her head against the stony wall and listened to the birds serenade them with their sweet song just outside the entrance. A bee buzzed by. She closed her eyes, suddenly very tired. Then she remembered Jace hadn't finished his story. She forced her eyes open. "You were going to tell me something?"

Jace pulled an object from his pocket and held it up. She gasped when she recognized the scarab pin. "I thought it was lost!"

"When they found the body a few weeks later it was still clenched in her fist. They had to really work to remove it." Elle could tell he was trying to say it as delicately as possible.

She stared at it and said, "All this trouble for a little scarab pin."

"The only thing little about it is its size," Jace corrected her, putting it back in his pocket. "But one thing I don't understand. How did Constance come forward?"

"I gave her the suggestion. The scarab was right next to that necklace for all those years. Maybe it naturally sent her to Lois."

"So in a way, Lois was a surrogate mother for Constance," Jace said.

"I thought about that, too. Maybe there is a part of Constance in me. Some DNA that belonged to her."

"You are related," he reminded her. Elle got up and walked to the back of the cave. She stopped when she recognized some writing.

"Look at this." She read it aloud.

> *"I love thee as I love the swell, And hush, of some low strain, Which bringeth, by its gentle spell, The past to life again."*

"Was this for Joe?" she wondered.

"I think it's more for you than you might realize." He paused and then asked, "Have you thought about going back?"

She bit her lip. For the last month she had been wishing she could go back one more time. Talk to Henry. But she had promised herself she wouldn't. As much as she cared about Henry, she had to let him go. He didn't love Constance. Not the way Constance needed to be loved. And he did not love Elle. He didn't even know she existed. Her love for him was just a fantasy. Besides, Constance no longer needed Henry, for she'd found love on the island in 1976. And that love had produced a child. And she was that child. A curious circle of life.

Seeing the scarab reminded her to ask about Patricia.

He shook his head. "She got immunity in exchange for her testimony. Plus, with Nedra and Marv gone there really is nothing else to do but let it go. She got in too deep is all."

Jace held up the scarab. "So what do ya think? One more trip?"

Her heart leaped in her chest, but she already knew the answer. "I can't."

"Not even to see Henry again?"

"Not even for the chance to fly to the moon."

"Hey, that's actually not a bad idea."

"Don't you think its enough to live your own life without trying to live somebody else's?"

"That might be the most profound thing you've ever said," Jace admitted.

"No. The most profound thing I've ever said is this: the whole time I was in St. Augustine, all I could think about was you. And as much as I love it there, I just wanted to get back to the Island. Back to you." She leaned in, wrapping her arms around his neck. "I don't need Henry. I don't need a scarab. I only need you." She stared into his eyes, feeling suddenly emotional as she slowly kissed him gently on the lips.

"Are you sure?" Jace asked when they came up for air.

She stood up and looked around. She knew right where the scarab should stay. "Let's leave it here."

"The cave?"

She nodded. Elle would keep the silver stamp box on her dresser, but the scarab would stay where Constance and Joe spent their summer days together. They left it in the back on a high shelf, promising to come back later and bury it.

She took Jace by the arm. "Now I have a surprise for you," she said, leading him out of the cave and down a dirt path until they reached a set of stairs up to a long wooden platform where the view stretched beyond the treetops and past the lake. "Beautiful, isn't it?"

Jace stood behind her and wrapped his arms around her, slipping his fingers through her belt loops and said, "Magnificent." As he burrowed into her neck.

She pulled away, a mock look of concern dusting her brow. "I don't think you're talking about the view."

He kissed her neck. "The only view I'm interested in is right here."

Faking disapproval she pulled his chin forward and pointed. "Down on the beach." He gazed in the direction she was pointing. There was a large heart made out of white rocks on the beach. "I hoped we'd be able to see it from here. It looks smaller than it really is."

"You made that?"

She looked over the horizon and smiled. "It's my heart. I'm giving it to you, if you'll have it." His eyes twinkled. He gently took her face in his hands. His thumb caressed her cheek as he turned serious, looked her square in the eye, and said, "There's nothing I want more." He leaned in and kissed her, firmly, gently, their lips a perfect blend of harmony and desire.

Elle finally pulled away, blushing. She looked past the straits, the magnificent bridge in the distance leading to St. Ignace and further into the future. "It's like we're a million miles from anywhere," she said.

"Umm hmmm." he agreed, kissing her again. It was butterflies in sunlight, and fresh dew in the morning. "...sounds like the perfect place."

He kissed her ear, and then his favorite part, the tip of her shoulder.

"Yes, it does." She closed her eyes and smiled. "Since I am the proud owner of one crammed little bookstore I can't exactly leave. But I do have a trip I want to make."

This finally caught his attention. He put his hand to his chin in thought. "Let me guess. Florence? Maybe Rome to see another grave?"

She smiled and kissed him on the forehead. "You know me very well."

He wrapped his arms around her and kissed her again. "I'll have my assistant book the tickets. When do you want to go?"

"I've heard Italy is beautiful in September."

"You would know," he reminded her. "Now, if you're all done, there's this place I want to take you."

Her eyes widened, "Another cave?"

"It's called Friendship Rock. I believe it's got a great view." She laughed and wrapped her arms around him.

"I believe I have the very best view right here."

"Better than Florence, or London, or Venice?"

She kissed him on the tip of his forehead, down the bridge of his nose, sweeping her lips along his cheekbone, jawline and then on to the tip of his chin. "Better than all of them put together," she promised.

Epilogue

Henry

1900—Lamb's House, England

"I did so enjoy reading your letters," Henry stated to the young American woman sitting on the red velvet tufted chair beside him. Recently graduated from Radcliffe College, she'd been introduced to Henry through her cousin Morton Fullerton, an acquaintance of Henry James. She was just a little over twenty and very pretty.

She smiled pleasantly, exposing beautiful white teeth. "I'm so glad you enjoyed them. Morton thinks I hold great promise." Her large blue eyes batted sweetly at Henry.

He scratched his beard and shifted heavily in his seat. "Yes, well, you have an unmistakable New England voice," he admitted. "Your use of the pen is natural and delightful."

She gripped her teacup in her hand. "Thank you, Mr. James. That means so much coming from you. I have always thought of you as the 'Tourgenieff' of our common country. Truly, I find you to be one of the greatest authors that ever lived. Your characters are always so believable."

He took a drink and held the glass loosely over the chair arm. "The way to make truly believable characters is to take pieces of real people you might know." He leaned over and set his glass on a small side table

She sipped her tea, nervously perched on the edge of her chair. "I have heard that several of your characters were based off of real people. You don't have to tell me, but I always wondered who you based Isabel Archer's character on."

The cup clinked when she set it down on the table. "I hear Constance Woolson used you as a character in one of her books." She went on while Henry stared into the fire, no longer listening, but thinking of Fenimore. Hadn't she promised that he would go down in history as a great writer? What a laugh that would be now. If only Connie were here now beside him. How he longed for her companionship.

"Miss Woolson," he said under his breath. He didn't meet Ms. Fullerton's eye, but stared into the fire. His eyes wet, fluid flames. "She always denied it, but how she did badger me for my thoughts and opinions."

"I was sorry to hear of her tragic death," Ms. Fullerton said reverently.

"Miss Woolson was a bright and thoughtful woman who lost it all. She changed. Went mad, really. It was as if she was taken over by some demon and I didn't know her."

She sighed, "Indeed a shame."

"She always wanted to write a play. We never wrote the play," Henry mumbled to himself. "Perhaps if she had just helped me with the play instead of that God awful-."

"Perhaps…*we*…could write a play together," she stated bubbly. "I do think our styles mesh very well," Ms. Fullerton said, wide eyed. She took a nervous sip of her tea and then set it down with a clank.

Henry spoke as if he were in a trance. "She wrote to me and said she had found a way to have another life. A happier one. She would become a mother." He looked up at Ms. Fullerton, his eyes empty and sad, and then shook his head incredulously, mumbling to himself, "She was an unmarried woman, not to mention too old. I insisted it wasn't true. I told her I wouldn't hear another word. In the end, she had made it up. A mad fever, I suppose."

"Yes, well…" she cleared her throat, clearly

uncomfortable with Mr. James' ranting.

"I wanted to go to the funeral. I was ready to go to the train. But suicide? And right at the top of the paper. It's an awful thing in which to be attached. She was a lovely lady. Just gone mad."

"Mr. James?" Miss Fullerton's voice went soft.

He continued. "She threatened to return. Said her soul would live on through her things. But I stopped that. I got rid of most of them. Drown them in the river. Never to return."

She touched his knee with her hand. "Mr. James?"

His trance broke. He tapped her hand and offered an apologetic smile. "I'm sorry my dear, I don't think I'm feeling well." He pulled a cloth from his jacket and wiped his sweating forehead and then returned it to his inside pocket. "Forgive me. What were we talking about?"

"Our writing together." She smiled brightly hoping to bring him back to the subject at hand. "Have you noticed our styles seem to blend effortlessly? With your experience and my voice we could create a masterpiece together." She smiled. Her blond hair was pulled back in a loose bun. Her youth and vivacity was infectious.

Henry chuckled. "Yes," he agreed. "Your writings are so close to mine that I seem not only to have written them, but to have written them many times over."

She clasped her hands in excitement. Henry leaned forward. "Perhaps with some time set aside we could collaborate on something. Though not a play. Great Heaven, not a play." He rolled his eyes and then fell silent, remembering the disaster of *Guy Domville* in January of 1895, when the crowd actually booed him off the stage.

It made him think of Fenimore, how beautiful she had looked at his first play in London. How proud she had been of him. If only they could have written that play together. If only she hadn't…He imagined the scene of her death. The curtains flung open, her small white heap contrasted against the dark stones below.

He shook his head to rid himself of the thought. "I try to

be rid of her, but still she returns. She is always there. Around each corner."

"Is that from *Turn of a Screw*?" Again, Ms. Fullerton appeared flustered. "We could write a ghost story together. I get chills thinking of the fun it would be."

"Yes… a ghost story." He already had an idea. After Constance's death he had gone to live in her home at 15 Beaumont Street in Oxford. His best writing had been done in Constance's very rooms. Her very bed. He paused and looked around at his dwelling. Fenimore would have liked this particular little corner of England. Perhaps she would have found peace here, as he had. Lamb's House was mild, Lamb's House was sane. Lamb's House was right. For the first time he really looked at Ms. Fullerton. He felt the familiar pang of dread. The woman staring at him was too young. Too pretty, too full of life. And he was too old.

"My dear, I must be truthful. While I have enjoyed your letters, ever so gently I must help you out of the vehicle in which you are perched. You are pure. So pathetically pure, and I…I am well aware of the great white light that waits to engulf you, sweet, young thing. You mustn't be engulfed. You must float and splash and scramble and remount the current; become distinct and distinguished in your own rights with the jolly reminiscence of having been fished from the whirlpool."

Her delicate brows furrowed. "Mr. James, the honor would be all mine. You are a master of your craft. I would love to learn from you."

"This may ruffle your charming feathers, but I cannot collaborate with you or be a mentor to you. You are great and talented in your own right. I am old and weak and haven't a thought to share."

A tear filled her eye. He was rejecting her, it was clear. "Are you afraid of me?" she whispered through very tight lips.

"Not of you. *For* you. My advice is to steer clear of any close association with Henry James."

"But I…I was hoping…" Her face flooded with hot color.

He stood from his chair. "May I show you something?" She nodded and followed him to his bedroom where he removed a silver box hidden inside a drawer. He unlocked it and took out a photograph wrapped in wax paper of a young woman. He did not say her name, but touched it as if it were sacred. "I should like to keep it," he said. "For the day when thinking of her will be nothing but pure blessedness. One day you too will have things like this. Things that keep you breathing and alive, hoping for a better day." He returned the contents to the box and returned it to the drawer.

From the bedroom he ushered her to the door. Knowing their future was not to be, Ms. Fullerton thanked him for his time and soon left. Henry looked over his home. His things. His favorite painting, *The Garden of Hesperides,* that hung over his desk. He knew Clara hoped to have all of Constance's things: the silver stamp box, the scarab, the bird book, her photograph, all returned to America. Perhaps he would take a trip to her beloved Mackinac Island that she had loved so much. She had always wanted to go back. Maybe that's what he would do. Go back. If that was what she wanted. He would go to her beloved island. Return her things to their rightful place. So she could come back. Yes. That was what he would do. For Fenimore. His sweet kind Fenimore.

Perhaps.

THE END

AUTHOR'S NOTES

I first learned about Constance Fenimore Woolson while researching Mackinac Island for potential story material. Unfortunately, while I was on the island I was unaware of the monument dedicated to Constance and completely missed it. I am still kicking myself for that one! After reading her novel, *Anne,* I discovered this once famous writer had a close and also a complex relationship with Henry James. I read books, articles on the internet, and painstakingly took their relationship apart year by year. I went away with the same bothersome question that everyone has, which is, why did Henry James drown Constance's dresses?

The answer is: I don't know. But I hope I have painted a scenario that leaves you with a possible motive.

What is the truth? Constance did believe in telepathy. She did believe that parts of our soul remained with our things. She did have a scarab pin and believed it had magical powers that would enable her to return as a spirit and whisper her stories to other writers. Whether it was all tongue in cheek we may never know. Was this what motivated Henry to bury her things in the canal? To keep her from ever returning? It's hard to believe he would be so cruel. What I do know is that there were several eyewitnesses to this event as well as Henry's own testimony to a woman in his later years.

Most of the characters, including the Bootts and Mathers family, who created a monument in her honor, existed in real life. I took a lot of my timeline information, as well as snippets from letters from the wonderfully done book, *A Private Life of Henry James* by Lyndall Gordon. W W Norton & Co Inc (April 1999) An excellent account of Henry and Constance and their longtime friendship. I also found several public domain biographies online to draw from. A few of them being, *Society for the Study of American Women Writers*, and *The Heath Anthology of American Literature,* as well as Ancestory.com and Wikipedia.

Interestingly, there are only four existing letters between Henry and Constance, which, considering the day and the famous amount of corresponding they did in their lifetimes, might lead one to believe that their letters were carefully disposed of, quite possibly in the fire when Henry came to take care of Constance's estate in the drizzly spring of 1894. Thanks to many of the letters sent to Constance and Henry's friends and family, we are able to piece more of their life and their thinking together.

What about Henry? Was he gay? His letters to several of his male friends might have you believe he was. However, some of his letters to his female friends would have you believe he wasn't. While I don't know if Henry was gay for sure, we do know that after Constance's death he did spend a large amount of time on her estate, and eventually moved into a home that she had rented in England, and even slept in her bed, leaving one to think that perhaps he had cared for her too in a way that can't be fully explained. Maybe he loved her as a sister? Maybe he loved her, but not as a wife. I do believe Constance did love and care more about Henry because of a line she sends to Henry about women holding on to feelings and not being able to move on like men can. She would only understand this if she had felt it herself.

What about their meeting up so often? They crisscrossed Europe like nomads, always meeting up at convenient and inconvenient times, usually very discreetly, and occasionally in full denial of the other's presence. It tells me, that they did not want rumors spread about them, which would have squelched their friendship, which in my opinion means it was very important to them both.

They also depended on each other for support, conversation, and companionship. Their friendship and their writings were intertwined. One connected with the other. What could be more devastating than harsh or critical words from Henry. Loosing that support would be devastating. Did Henry have harsh words towards Constance's writing? Constance was no small-minded female writer who leapt to her death because Henry wouldn't marry her. It was probably deeper and more long suffered than that one thing. Losing his friendship would have been heartbreaking. Feeling that he did not respect her work, devastating. She did suffer from depression. She did want success just as much as Henry. She did love Henry. His shunning her might have been the final straw. Underneath it all, I believe that Constance, who spoke often of her desire to settle down and be a wife and mother, cared deeply for Henry. If only we had a few more of their letters. But since we don't, the world of fiction will attempt to fill in the blank spaces according to our whims.

If you are interested in knowing more about Constance, please go to constancefenimorewoolson.wordpress.com.

ABOUT THE AUTHOR

Rebecca started writing one summer day in 2008 to escape from the stresses of life, never imagining she would actually publish a book one day. Becoming Fenimore is her third novel. Her previous novels, *The Sand Bar, 2012 and Far From Perfect*, 2013 were runners up on Readers Favorites. In the category of women's fiction.

In a previous life Rebecca graduated from Brigham Young University-Idaho with a degree in Interior Design. When she is not writing or taking care of her five children, she can be found working in the theater, and has been known to do a commercial or two on the side. Rebecca resides in her home state of Idaho with her family and Buddy the dog. Sadly, Hammy the hamster didn't make it in the move. To learn more and to check out her other novels go to beckybryan1.wix.com/rebecca-bryan

www.ingramcontent.com/pod-product-compliance
Lightning Source LLC
Chambersburg PA
CBHW030019180626
46810CB00001B/123

* 9 7 8 0 6 9 2 5 8 1 3 5 3 *